ABOVE

ABOVE

Isla Morley

G

GALLERY BOOKS

New York   London   Toronto   Sydney   New Delhi

Gallery Books
A Division of Simon & Schuster, Inc.
1230 Avenue of the Americas
New York, NY 10020

First Gallery Books hardcover edition March 2014

GALLERY BOOKS and colophon are registered trademarks of Simon & Schuster, Inc.

For information about special discounts for bulk purchases, please contact
Simon & Schuster Special Sales at 1-866-506-1949 or business@simonandschuster.com.

The Simon & Schuster Speakers Bureau can bring authors to your live event.
For more information or to book an event contact the Simon & Schuster Speakers Bureau
at 1-866-248-3049 or visit our website at www.simonspeakers.com.

Interior design by Paul Dippolito

Manufactured in the United States of America

10   9   8   7   6   5   4   3   2   1

Library of Congress Cataloging-in-Publication Data is available.

ISBN 978-1-4767-3152-0
ISBN 978-1-4767-3564-1 (ebook)

To Bob and Emily

Part One

BELOW

DOBBS WINS THE fight easily. He shuts and locks the door. I feel a small sense of relief. With a hulking slab of metal separating us, I am finally able to breathe just a little. It is only when I hear another thump, another door closing someplace above me, that I understand: not only am I to be left alone; I am to be hidden.

I am a secret no one is able to tell.

Just like that, instead of wishing Dobbs gone, I am waiting for him to come back.

Surely, it won't take long.

When Dobbs returns, I'll take him off guard. I'll push past him, dash outside, and sprint across the field. I will steer clear of the road. I'll head for the line of sycamore trees along the creek. I'll make my way east, and he won't think to follow me there on account of its being trappers' territory. Even if I do get snared, it'll be better than this, because someone will find me. Nobody's going to find me here, whatever here is. A dungeon? I can't make any sense of it. A big round room with a massive pillar right through the middle of it. Contraptions, wires, pipes, spigots, dials. I keep my back turned to the space, keep my face pressed up against the door. It is made of steel and has a handle, although not like one I've ever seen. Something a bank might have on its vault.

What has he done? What's happened to me?

Surely, Dobbs should be getting back by now. He'll take me out of here. He'll explain it to me, not like before, which didn't make any sense. He won't be rough, either. Or cross. He'll be nice, like how he is in the library.

I look at Grandpa's pocket watch; only fifteen minutes have passed. Even though it is still ticking, I wind it tight. If only I were still at the Horse Thieves Picnic, our town's annual tradition that I look forward to all year. The gathering that attracts a couple thousand people has since moved from its original location among the walnut trees of Durr's Grove to Main Street, and its contests no longer include Largest Mustache for Boys Under 17 or Baby with the Worst Case of Colic, but there is still a parade and a carnival. Apart from the parade, the next most popular event is the concert at the bandstand, where Daddy, no doubt, is now line dancing. It takes no effort to imagine what my sister and brothers are doing. Suzie, with Lula Campbell, will be strutting around the midway looking for boys, and Gerhard, not actually bleeding to death from wrecking his pickup on I-70 like Dobbs had first said, will be off with his pals to scale the water tower. Having left the Horse Thieves Picnic early on account of Theo's fever, Mama's likely fallen asleep on her bed, the fan moving what the lazy July evening can't be bothered to blow through the window. No one has probably even noticed that I'm gone. How long will it take them before they do? And when they do, where will they imagine I am? What will they think the cause for my absence is? They won't be imagining anything bad, that's for sure. Bad things don't happen in Eudora, Kansas.

I look over my shoulder at the space behind me. The enormous concrete pillar and two partitions divide the round room into halves. Behind the partitions is where Dobbs said I could get myself something to drink. I can see a bit of the recliner, where I was I told to sit and wait.

I don't like the looks of anything behind me, so I keep my eyes on Grandpa's watch. The minute hand and I go for long walks around the numbers. And then the numbers, the watch face, and everything else disappear, just like the time lightning split the maple tree outside our living room and we all vanished in its blinding flash. It's like that, except in reverse. The darkness has swallowed me whole.

I can't see my hand, even when I hold it up to my face. Nothing seeps through the darkness. I keep waiting for my eyes to adjust. The outline of the partitions or the big concrete pillar should be visible. I start shivering.

I think I hear something. "Dobbs?"

The darkness snatches my voice and issues nothing in return.

"Hello?"

Don't panic. The electricity's gone out; give it a minute.

If this were home, Mama would be feeling her way to the pantry for the lantern and the matches she keeps on the top shelf. Gerhard would have the flashlight under his chin, his bottom teeth thrust outward and his eyes crossed and buggy, and Suzie would be getting all hysterical, as if he really were the bogeyman. And Daddy would be chiding Gerhard, but only halfheartedly, because there's nothing better than spooking girls.

But this is not home. This is not any kind of place you'd put a person. What kind of things do people put in a place like this? How far underground am I? There were a lot of stairs and a long passage that kept making sharp left and right turns. And too many doors to keep track of. Locks.

Just think of home. Just give it a minute. Just wait.

There is no way to tell what time is doing. Has it been five minutes or half an hour? Shouldn't the electricity have kicked back on by now?

There is a creak somewhere behind me, to the left. A shifting. My ears strain. I hold my breath so I can hear better. Is there something in here with me? Something doing the breathing for me? In. Out. Sounds like air through clenched teeth. Something with its lips drawn back. Oh Lord, what if it comes for me?

I mustn't move. Not a sound, or I will give myself away.

How could anything have entered? Is there a hole in the wall? Maybe the noise is nothing but a draft coming through a vent. But maybe it isn't. Maybe some inner door opened. Because this no longer feels like a confined space but a very large one, widening still.

There is something behind this door, too. Something that turns it freezing cold. I scoot back, exposed. On my hands and knees, I shuffle over to where the kitchen is supposed to be. I must hide. Hurrying as fast as I can, I ram straight into something. My head about cracks. I can't make any sense of what I've hit—something with knobs. I keep hurrying, this time with one hand outstretched.

My hand locates the leg of the table. I get under it, bring my knees up to my chin, and grip myself tightly. Maybe whatever is making the sound is one of those things that can see in the dark. Which means it can see me under the table with the chair legs pressed against me. It doesn't help to tell myself my imagination is playing tricks on me. Please. Oh, please.

Sit still. Don't move. Quiet. Ssh. Help me, someone, please, God.

THE SOUND OF scraping is so loud I think the entire floor is going to give way. I hold on to the table leg.

The light snaps on. The first things I see are Dobbs's shoes. Suede beige moccasins. The second thing I see is the gap behind that massive metal door after he's entered. Maybe he will think I've run off. Maybe he'll think me gone, head back upstairs, leave the door open.

"What are you doing under there? Silly girl. Come on out." The shoes approach.

I don't move.

"Come on. We've got work to do. I said I'd be back, didn't I?"

I crawl out. "I'd like to go home, please."

"We're not going home now. I've explained that. Ten times already. I need us to finish our task. Teamwork, remember? Me, you, a team?"

"Please, I need to get back home. I've got chores and there's my book report and my mother's not going to be happy if—"

He puts down a sheaf of paper on the table and then pulls out a chair for me.

"Is this about the library books?" Theo had scribbled in them. I'd offered to pay the fine, but Dobbs had said not to worry. Now he's changed his mind; he aims to punish me. Has to be it. It can't be anything else. Why else would he be so calm, like people are supposed to be when disciplining kids? I've never noticed before that his eyes are spaced too far apart and are too small for such a long face. Barely noticeable are the features that are supposed to give a face definition: his eye-brows are thin and, like his eyelashes, fair; and his lips are the same pale color as the rest of his face. His skin from hairline to lips to drawn-out chin is that of a chicken before it goes into the oven. If it wasn't for his thinning hair neatly combed over his ears, plucked is how he'd look.

His plaid shirt is tucked in. Clip-on tie perfectly straight.

"Sit."

I do as he says. "Can we hurry? Because my mom and dad are going to get worried pretty soon. And then they'll think—"

"They're going to think what we want them to think." Dobbs Hordin snaps the lid off the pen. The noise startles me. Only now do I realize there are no other sounds down here.

He pushes the pen in my hand, puts a crisp white sheet of paper in front of me, then takes from his top pocket a note, which he irons flat with his hand. "Copy this, word for word; no embellishing." Tidy words, like buttons in a row. They're for me to fasten up, fasten something that needs covering, putting away. The note I'm supposed to copy reads:

> Dear Mom and Dad,
>   I know this will come as a shock to you. I have taken the bus to a city far away. Please don't try to find me. I will write again when I am settled. Please don't worry.
>   From your daughter,
>   Blythe

They'll know from the very first line this didn't come from me. Won't they?

I scoot back. "You're taking me away?" Shouldn't there by a why in there someplace, too?

"Write." He taps a long nail on the blank page. "The sooner you write this, the sooner we can move on."

There are going to be a dozen ways to escape, none of them from here. I write the first word, but I'm seeing myself at the counter of some down-at-the-heel diner where the waitress has everything sized up before Dobbs is through ordering. Finish the letter and get going, I tell myself. The sooner you get to that diner, the better. And if not that, then out the window of a 7-Eleven restroom.

Dobbs leans over me and watches me copy each word. He's too close. I can feel his breath on my neck. He smells of mouthwash.

He puts his hand on the table next to mine. Underneath it is the poem I'd written while waiting for Arlo at the Horse Thieves Picnic tonight. He mutters and shakes his head.

"You had no problem writing this." I ask him to give me back the poem, but he tucks it into his shirt pocket and says, "You really feel this way? Over that boy?" As though there is something deficient about Arlo, as though the last thing a sixteen-year-old should be doing is giving Arlo Meier the light of day, much less her heart.

I feel the heat rise to my cheeks.

He bends toward the paper I am working on. He says, "I've always admired your handwriting," before taking it away and tearing it up.

The next two attempts go the same way, but I can't write the note without some little clue for my mother, something she can use to show the police officer, so she can say, "See, Blythe would never be so careless with her loops." Or "She never forgets to cross her *t*'s, but see here—three in a row." And if they don't believe her, she can fish out my diary and hold it up against the note. It won't take but a quick comparison by a handwriting expert to see what is going on. "Yes, she is being held against her will. Be on the lookout for a man with wispy hair and teeth so uniformly stubby they look filed or gnashed, like the Bible says. Five ten, hundred and seventy pounds, middle forties, queer habit of clearing his throat when agitated. Look for a silver Oldsmobile with a rosary draped over the rearview mirror."

"I'll take that," Dobbs says of my next attempt, and hands me a fresh page.

With him watching so closely, I try to be more careful. On every other line, I write a letter backward.

Dobbs slips the paper from under my hand, crumples it. "We can do this all night, if you want."

On the new page, my handwriting is impeccable. Every *i* dotted; every *t* crossed. He thinks I am complying. He doesn't seem to notice when I press down on a letter a little harder. If Mama turns the page over, those letters should stick out a little. If they do, even a blind man will see what's happening. All she has to do is run her fingers lightly over the letters, rearrange them in her head, and they are going to spell *d-o-b-b-s*. Nothing more need be said, because she'll be right back to that night two years ago when Dobbs Hordin turned up in our living room, rousing her suspicions like a stick in a nest of sleeping copperhead snakes.

Eudora's country roads, gravelly and rutted, are chancy at night. A car found this out the hard way. We heard the crash, and we followed Daddy out to see, even though we'd been told to stay put. And there was the Oldsmobile: high-centered, back wheels spinning, turn signal flashing as though it intended to wind up in Lester Pickett's cornfield. Daddy helped the driver from his car and ushered him up to our front porch, where I could see it was Mr. Dobbs Hordin from the school library. Apart from a tiny spot of blood on his forehead, he seemed fine. Mama served him a glass of warm sugar water, while Daddy went back to the car to wait for Sheriff Rumboldt.

"You have a wife we can call, Mr. Hordin?"

He sipped his water, clutching the quilt around his neck. "Please don't go to any trouble, ma'am. I'm mighty sorry for the inconvenience to you and your family."

"Some relative, perhaps?" Creasing Mama's brow was the same little frown she got when she read a recipe and came to an ingredient that seemed out of place. Dobbs Hordin wouldn't have known, as we kids did, how you could measure the length of Mama's frown and determine the amount of trouble you were in. "There must surely be *someone* I can call."

"You know my children?" she asked after learning he worked at the high school.

"There are three hundred and some youngsters at Eudora High, Mrs. Hallowell."

It wasn't exactly a denial, but it was an omission, and Mama says omissions qualify as lies. Dobbs Hordin had, in fact, recommended two books to me the previous week. He'd been especially nice about it, too. Asked my name, asked what it was about nineteenth-century poetry that caught my fancy so. And there he was in our living room, telling Mama in so many words he'd never seen the likes of me.

Later, when the car had been towed away and Sheriff Rumboldt had given Mr. Hordin a ride back home, I could hear Mama and Daddy talking in their bedroom.

"He wouldn't let me call anyone. Can you imagine that?"

"Shock can do funny things to a man."

"Seemed awful calm to me. There's something about that man that doesn't set right. Why would he be driving down our way when he lives clear across town, especially at this time of night?"

Mama, you're going to have to look especially close at this note if you want to know who's got me. Before signing my name to the note, I give him a hard look. "We were nice to you. We helped you."

He's got that same calm expression, just as he had when Mama quizzed him. Dobbs folds up my letter and tucks it in an envelope. When he licks it, his tongue is basting with spit, like his appetite's been whetted. "Now, let me show you around."

What he calls the kitchen is not much more than the table I hid beneath, three chairs, several metal bookshelves loaded with canned goods, and a counter with a gas stove and a kettle. There is a stand and a washbasin and a storage space with cubbies. Each plastic tub in it is clearly labeled: TUPPERWARE, FIRST AID, LAUNDRY SUPPLIES. Where are the windows is what I'd like to know. There must be one in the restroom.

"I need to use the facility," I announce, to see if I'm right.

He leads me around the partitions to a narrow door that opens to a stall the size of the broom closet. "Powder room," he announces.

There's a drum with a toilet lid on it. Next to it is a stack of boxes labeled WARNING: CHEMICALS, along with a mound of toilet paper rolls and written instructions taped to the wall about how to separate the toilet bowl from the waste reservoir beneath it, when to add disinfectant, and how to use something called an accordion valve to flush water from the top tank into the bowl. He taps the sheet. "A chem-john's a little different from what you're used to, so be sure to follow all the steps, please."

He closes the door. No window, only walls made from the kind of pressed board with holes in it. I can hear him shuffling about on the other side. Can he see me in here?

Mama! Help me. What do I do now?

How do I get up those stairs and back on the other side of that door? When he brought me here it was still light outside. We drove up to what looked like a concrete outhouse, except it was an entrance of some sort: a door, two narrow concrete walls on either side of it, and a little overhang, and that was all. You see a door like that, with nothing behind it but a big open field, and you think it's a joke. He says it leads to the safest place in the world, and because you've already had the bejesus scared out of you being told your brother's been in a car crash, you want to be somewhere safe. You step through it. You go down concrete steps so steep and so narrow that you have to hold on to the wall. Through more doors and into a circular room that looks like a giant drum. That's all it takes to be completely cut off from Eudora, Kansas, population 2,200, on the town's biggest night of the year. I'd still be at the Horse Thieves Picnic if I hadn't got fed up waiting for Arlo, if I hadn't decided to walk home without telling anyone. If I hadn't climbed into Dobbs Hordin's ugly car.

"You done in there?" he asks through the holes in the wall.

I step out. "I want to go home. Right now."

He scratches his head. "I don't know how else to explain it to you."

It's eerie, the silence down here. No cicadas screeching from the elm trees; no kettle on the boil. No lawnmowers; no tractor churning up a nearby field in the last light. If we were aboveground, I might be able to hear the distant strains of music at the carnival, or at least the faint roar of freeway traffic on K-10, maybe a crop duster headed for a barn. But underground, there is nothing but the sinusy breath of Dobbs Hordin and those briny eyes thinking of a way to explain something that makes no sense.

"Maybe if I show you. Come with me." He offers me his hand.

I shove mine under my armpits.

He makes a sweeping gesture as though by some miracle this is not the room in which I have just spent the last couple of hours but some new place that wants discovering. "I call this the Ark."

We move to the section that is meant to look like a living room. Between two brown recliners is a bronze floor lamp with a yellowed shade. On top of a rickety chest of drawers is an artificial potted plant. It is exotic-looking, leaves shaped like tongues. The shag carpet in mustard and orange colors matches the curtains, which don't frame a window but hang around a paint-by-numbers picture—a boy reclining next to a creek, his straw hat pulled over his eyes, a fishing pole at his side.

"My mother took up painting when my brother died. She said that's how she pictured my little brother, Elby, in heaven."

It's hideous, I want to shout.

On the other side of the Peg-Board partition is a supply closet and what he calls "sleeping quarters." The cot has a folded quilt at one end, a pillow at the other, and smack-dab in the middle a white teddy bear with a big red bow—something you might win at a stall on the midway. Hanging from the ceiling is a plastic curtain that Dobbs pulls till it makes a cubicle, like the one they have you change in at Dr. Hubacher's office. "For privacy," Dobbs says, as though that explains everything.

He points to the clothes rack. "These should all fit."

The dresses are from another era, with pleated sleeves, modest necklines, fitted bodices, and long A-line skirts. Beneath their hems is a tub marked INTIMATES. Next to it are two pairs of ballerina flats—one black, the other tan—and a pair of house slippers. "Blue—your favorite color, right?"

I stare at him. He looks so pleased with himself.

I start to shake. I tell myself this is not the time to be weak. This is the time to be strong. To fight him. "You tricked me." My voice quavers. I try again, loudly this time. "You lied!"

"Yes, I'm sorry about that."

Could it really have been little more than two hours ago when Dobbs had leaned out of his car window, stopping beside me on the street? I had my face set to smile even though the evening, having started with such promise, had been such a letdown, and even though I had the long walk home ahead of me. The poem I'd written on the bleachers was crumpled in my hand, the misery of waiting for and then giving up on Arlo too clichéd for iambic pentameter. "There's been an accident," Dobbs had said. "Your brother." That was all it took for me to leap into the passenger seat. He had to reach across me to close the door, had to belt me in. I had forgotten simple tasks. And then he was driving down Winchester Road, and I couldn't imagine why he was still going the speed limit. When he turned left on the county road instead of heading for Lawrence, I asked, "Aren't we going to the hospital?" "I'm sorry it has to happen this way," had been Dobbs's reply. I thought he meant my brother, twisted and bloodied, fighting for his twenty-year-old life, and my having to carry such a load at the age of sixteen. It hadn't made sense. Not so much the words as the tone of his voice—flat. The way he kept his eyes on the rearview mirror—flat, too. There was a bumpy dirt road and a gate and a sign: TRESPASSERS WILL BE SHOT. Dobbs had gotten out of the car. He'd unlatched the gate and pushed it into a thick patch of foxglove.

That's where everything might as well stop. Right there, with me sitting patient as you like, hands folded tightly in my lap, watching Dobbs wedge the gate in the weeds. Before the word *if* had a chance to cross my mind.

Now, it is fully formed.

If I had slipped into the driver's seat. *If* I had backed out of the driveway. *If* I hadn't sat there, so quietly, with all the alarm bells ringing in my head.

Whatever this is, I fear it is worse, much worse, than trickery or lying. "Take me home! I want to go home!"

"Like I said, you've got nothing to fear—"

"Don't come any closer!"

He holds up his hands. "I need you to be calm, that's all."

I glare at him.

"Stay calm and everything is going to be fine."

And that's when I open my mouth and scream.

I know what this is. This is what they warn every teenage girl about.

I keep yelling.

Dobbs doesn't move.

My scream ricochets off the concrete walls and swirls around us like a dust devil.

When I've run out of breath, he says calmly, "Getting all het up won't help."

I scream again. This time, the effort rips out half my throat. Something tears; Lord help me if it's my resistance.

"Nobody can hear you," he says in the next lull.

What is this place? I run to the door. I yank on the handle, screaming where the crack ought to be. I slam my fists against the door. "Help me! Somebody! Help!"

Behind me, Dobbs might as well be chiseled from marble.

"Let me out of here! I want to go home!"

He grabs my wrists, but I wrest them easily from his grip. He should be stronger. It is sickening just how weak he is. And then I realize he isn't weak at all; he's purposefully trying to keep from hurting me.

"This isn't like you, Blythe."

I deliver a kick that catches more air than shin. Don't fight like a girl, I think.

I roar at him, and he suffers rather than counters each blow. His hair bounces out of its neat side parting and falls over his eyes. I swing my hand and it catches him in his face. I feel his skin roll under my nails like the pale dough Mama uses for biscuits. Apart from red welts on his cheek, there is no response, no about-face.

It's clear now what his intentions are.

I don't want him to soil me without first leaving a bruise. I want his spoils damaged.

A thick vein sticks up out of his sinewy neck, and his eyes flicker like strobe lights. With my hands bound in his grip, I buck and kick.

He says, "I don't want to hurt you, Blythe."

"You *are* hurting me!"

And he just keeps saying those same stupid, useless words while I fight him, a not-quite-full bag of flour.

"I DON'T WANT you to struggle now because that will only make things worse. Think of something nice."

I look around. My head feels like it's about to split open. I try to protest, but my lips won't work. My tongue's swelled up. Last thing I remember, my arm was twisted behind my back. We were in the kitchen. A rag.

"You've only been out twelve minutes. I used just a drop."

Why is he wearing a plastic jumpsuit? I ask him for a glass of water.

"No, not now."

I lift my hand to insist, but it won't cooperate. I look down. Both my arms are tied to the chair. On the table in front of me is a pair of scissors. I start shaking worse as soon as he picks it up.

"Be still now."

I swing my head to see where he's going with them. From behind me, he tells me to settle down. I shake and buck and bounce the chair about.

"You want to get an ear snipped off or not?"

"No, please. What are you going to do? Please don't! I haven't done anything to you!"

Mama, why haven't you come? Daddy!

I hear the sharp blades slide open. He leans close to me. I feel his hot breath on my neck. He pushes my head forward.

"Mama!"

"Hush, now."

A warm spread happens between my legs.

He smells it, too. "That's okay; accidents happen. We'll get you cleaned up after I finish. Now, hold still."

I can't stop crying, but I keep my head very still as soon as those blades come toward it.

"Think of something nice, like I said."

Snip. I feel the weight give way. One auburn braid lands in my wet lap.

Think of something nice. Think of something nice.

Daddy hollering up the stairs this afternoon. "We're leaving in fifteen minutes. Don't make us all late for the picnic, you hear?" Suzie has long overshot her allotted ten minutes in the bathroom. Gerhard is pacing out his frustration in front of the door. And there I am, the youngest girl, with Theo giddyapping on my back, using my braids as reins. What will Theo use now?

Snip! There goes my other braid.

Think of something nice! Me trying to look nice for Arlo, winding my hair around a hot roller when Suzie barges into Mama's room. "What's this? Remedial hairdressing?" Suzie calls my hair a national embarrassment. She says braids are childish. "Are you wearing Mama's perfume?" Suzie sniffing my neck, declaring, "Blythe's got a boyfriend! Blythe's got a boyfriend!" Making wet kissing noises, knowing full well I'd never been kissed.

Snip.

I wanted to look like a grown-up, not a freckled, pudgy sixteen-year-old. Mama likes to say round cheeks are an indication of good health and that Gene Tierney had an overbite, too, and that didn't stop her from being considered one of the most beautiful movie stars back in her day. According to Mama, if I'd just show my green eyes instead of letting my bangs hang in them and if I'd accentuate what she insists are Grandma's bow lips, I'd be more grateful for what God gave me.

Dobbs is hacking at my bangs. The scissors are going to gouge my eyes out. I squeeze them shut.

My sister, watching me weave my hair quickly back into braids: "Who is he? The retard?" She means Arlo, who'd inexplicably changed from the friend I had known since first grade, the one with whom I used to play down by the creek on Sundays only after the others had left, to someone whose attention the girls in my class compete for. Suzie refuses to notice that Arlo has shed his baby fat, his bowl haircut and fidgety mannerisms, probably because he's never taken much notice of her, and these days, even less so. But she's right: Arlo is the one who I am fixing to meet at the Horse Thieves Picnic. Suzie pulls a face at me and mouths the word *freak*.

Snip, snip, snip.

Worse than freak now.

He starts cutting more quickly. Bits of hair fly about.

I can't think of something nice. Mama's face is all, but she'd be crying, seeing this.

It goes on for ages and when I think there can't surely be anything left to cut, he throws a thick wet towel over my head.

I struggle for breath. He's going to smother me. I wrestle and kick and the chair tips all the way backward and I land upside down. My skirt is up around my waist. The smell of my urine is shameful.

He rights the chair, then smooths my skirt back over my knees. "I do not want to give you chloroform again. Please, sit still now. This is the tricky part."

I try to be still, but I'm shaking too hard. He lathers my head with something that smells like tar. The package on the table reads, VAN'S CARBOLIC HOUSEHOLD SOAP.

"Please, no," I beg when he picks up the plastic razor.

It scrapes my scalp. The blade is too dull. It nicks and cuts. He daubs where blood runs down my temple. My head is stinging all over, but the sound is just as terrible. The sound of scraping; the sound of skin crawling; the sound of the razor tapping against the bowl.

I can't think of anything except the word *freak*.

When he's done shaving me, he comes back with a nail trimmer. I dig my fingers into my palms, but he pries each one loose and clips my nails down to the quick. He sweeps up my hair from the floor and the table, bags my nail trimmings, and stuffs it all in a tin can.

He undoes the straps. "Easy now."

I run my hand over my head. It's bristly in places, slick in others. I can't imagine how hideous I must look. I burst into tears.

He lets me have a drink. This time I really do need to use the facility.

There are locks on all the other doors in this place, some with the kind that uses buttons and some that need keys, but this toilet door barely latches. I pull down my wet underwear. I squat over the commode. What's to become of me? I can't bear to go with him being able to hear me.

When I leave the stall, he hands me a rag, an ugly polyester nightgown, and big white granny briefs. I go back into the toilet. I put on the underwear. I decide I will just sit here forever, or until someone comes, but he raps on the door, and I have to get up.

"One more thing." He gives me a queer look, like he's almost embarrassed to say.

It doesn't matter what that thing is; that there is more makes me drop to my knees. I bend my head till it reaches the floor in front of his shoes. Those ugly beige moccasins. It feels so terrible that my braids are not beside me, that my bangs are not there to offer some small relief from the cold concrete floor.

He pulls me up by the armpits. I am set down on the cot. He places the bar of carbolic soap, the rag, and a bucket of water beside me. Then he hands me a razor. "You are going to have to do down there."

"What?"

"I will be checking, so don't try to pretend."

He draws the doctor's office curtain around me. I look at the razor for a long time. I cannot understand what is happening.

"Are you done yet?"

I stand up and turn my back to the curtain. I pull down the underwear. I make a little lather in my hand. Raising my skirt, I shave myself without looking.

When I am done, I slide the bucket and razor under the curtain.

"Very good." He flings back the curtain. He hands me a wet napkin and asks me to wipe myself because he has to be sure. I aim to close the curtain again, but he stops me. He has to see me do as I'm told. I turn my back to him. I think I am going to be sick. I wipe myself and hand him back the napkin. He inspects it for stray hairs.

"Excellent!"

I was a girl with hair. Auburn hair. Now color has gone. Everything fades. Mama's flushed cheeks, the smutty palette of the evening sky, our yellow clapboard farmhouse. As goes color, so the senses. I try to conjure the scent of Theo's head, all sweaty from play; Gerhard's voice; the smell of Suzie's nail polish. Nothing. What does rain feel like? Only yesterday, I'd gotten drenched in an afternoon downpour. If I could just hear the sounds of the carnival, or visualize the colored lights strung along Main Street, if I could feel Arlo's fingers on the back of my hand. Instead, everything condenses into a small point of memory, like a knot in Grandma's needlepoint, and then—*snip!*—gone. In its place is absence, and the color of absence is gray. Gray walls, gray floors, gray ceiling. I can taste the gray, smell it. On my arms, the hairs have risen up to meet the stale, gray air. Gray pushes its way into my ears and up my nose. Down my throat, too thick for lungs. I start to gag. It settles in my stomach, and retching moves it not one inch.

Dobbs bends over me. "You okay? Here, use the bucket." On my back, his hand is heavy and damp. His forefinger rubs back and forth over my vertebrae.

"Don't!" I right myself and clutch the rumpled curtain so we have at least this between us.

"Blythe, don't be like this."

"Be like what? You don't be like this! Why are you doing this?"

He does nothing but stare at me.

"Please! Say something!" I scream.

"I'm sorry about your hair. They aren't going to suspect me, but if they do, they won't find any trace of you on my clothes. Hair fiber's the kind of mistake amateurs make."

I don't want to cry in front of him, but I can't stop myself.

"I'm going to have to leave you again. This time, it's going to be for a bit longer. The fluorescents are on a timer, seven a.m. to nine p.m., but if for any reason they fail to come on, or you need a light in the middle of the night, there are glow sticks under the basin." He points. "Crack one, and it'll give you ten hours. Try not to use them, though, because I can only get them on special order."

He moves toward the door. I do, too.

"I'll be back to give you the grand tour tomorrow."

I clutch his shirt.

"You've got to stay now."

I grab him around the waist.

"Be a good girl."

"Please. Please don't leave me here."

"I can't expect you to take this in all at once, and I don't expect you to feel the way I do. But you'll see—it will all make sense in a little while."

I try to get through the door when he unlocks it, but he pushes me back. Before I can recover lost ground, the lights go out. The door closes with a heavy thud.

"Dobbs?" I beat my hands against it. *"Dobbs!"*

THERE IT IS again, that terrible silence that comes when the lights go out. And the kind of chill that doesn't come from weather. I crawl on my hands and knees back to the cot for the sweater Grandma knit that Mama insisted I take to the picnic in case it turned cool, but I can't find my way. I tell myself crying won't help. I give myself the small task of finding the sweater, believing if I can do this, I will be able to do greater things when the time comes.

My knees are scraped raw by the time I find it. I clutch it instead of putting it on. I find Grandpa's watch, too. It doesn't matter that I can't tell what time it is.

I rub the inscription on Grandpa's watch.

> Thus let me live, unseen, unknown;
> Thus unlamented let me die;
> Steal from the world, and not a stone
> Tell where I lie.

I didn't think twice about pocketing it. I took it from Mama's jewelry box before heading out for the Horse Thieves Picnic because I didn't want to be late for meeting Arlo. I thought Grandpa's watch was going to help me. Now, the words make my blood run cold. Not a stone tell where I lie.

Any minute a great commotion is going to come for me. Any minute, my father's going to bust through that door and take me home, and Dobbs Hordin will be marched off to the county jail.

Any minute becomes just like every other minute.

I can't decide which I hate more: the quiet or the dark.

Wait. What had Dobbs said about glow sticks? Where did he say those were kept?

The blackout has done a number on my balance, so I get on my knees. I navigate my way over to the right, where I am hoping the kitchen still is. With hands patting dead air, I shuffle forward until I hit something. Feeling around its rounded edges doesn't help. I can't fathom what it is. Several steps to the left is the counter. I stand up. Everything on it is unfamiliar. Why hadn't I paid closer attention when the lights were on? Something clatters at my feet, and something else bangs down on the floor. A can, maybe. After a sweep of the counter, I find the burner. The space below is covered by a curtain. Behind it are pots and pans and a stack of plastic containers. I am in the ballpark. In one of them, I find the glow sticks. I have to use my teeth to tear through the plastic wrapper. I snap one. A sporing of neon green light. There are my hands; there are my elbows, my legs, my feet. Still in one piece. I snap another one. In the green glow just three feet away, and not the half mile I imagined, is the table. By the time I'm done, there are half a dozen sticks glowing throughout the room. It's like one of those toxic algae blooms down at the reservoir in the spring.

I look at Grandpa's watch. It's a little past midnight, which means six hours have passed since we first arrived at the picnic. Only six hours separate me from my life. Six hours ago, I was watching my town do what it does best. With the carnival set up between the old school and the fire station and crowds jamming the sidewalks, downtown was barely recognizable. Main Street was lined from K-10 to city hall with parade floats, tractors, hay wagons, and vintage cars gussied up with banners and apple-cheeked officials. If an outsider were to have driven by, he'd have likely mistaken Eudora for the land of milk and honey. It wasn't only the festival; nature helped put on a show, too. Summer's always when our town looks its best, like it is yay-close to living up to its potential. The creek runs full, the trees are so leafy it's a wonder we don't get light-headed walking beneath them, and the sun brightens colors like a washing detergent commercial. Fall's more honest. It shows our town as it truly is: worn-out. A ghost town except with the people still in it. Come October, it'll look like someone needs to take a great big broom to the place. Yards will be stacked with dead leaves; trash will have blown against the chain-link fences; flower beds in tractor tires will have dried up. The only signs of life will be old vans parked in cracked driveways and the occasional dog tethered to a stake in a yard. Nobody will be outside. Instead, waxy children with stringy hair will be playing silently indoors, trying not to get on their parents' last frayed nerve. But the weekend of the Horse Thieves Picnic in the middle of summer: well, it gets everyone's hopes up. Especially someone on her way to meet Arlo Meier.

I knew what Mama was going to ask, so before she had a chance to open her mouth, I told her I had to run. Having none of it, she thrust Theo at me and repositioned her bun.

"But I'm supposed to meet someone in a few minutes."

"Who?" Mama was ill-tempered on account of Theo's tantrum. He was insisting on riding his trike down the parade route, even with a sudden fever.

"Mercy," I fibbed.

"Well, surely she can wait while you walk your brother down the parade. It won't take but ten minutes." Mama, unlike a lot of people in this town, would never come right out and say it's better for people to hang around their own kind, but she lets her disapproval of my friendship with an albino girl be known in other ways—that she sees nothing wrong with keeping Mercy waiting, for example.

There's no arguing with Mama, so I did as I was told. The Girl Scout leader was trying to organize her troop into neat rows behind us; she might as well have been organizing geese. Faring even worse, the person tasked with lining up the kids' parade couldn't keep wayward cyclists from pedaling madly into the crowd. As Theo and I made our way to the back of the line, we passed the new statue of Chief Paschal Fish and his daughter. It commemorates the one hundred and fortieth anniversary of the town's beginning. Legend has it that back in 1857 when the chief traded 774 acres of his land to three German settlers for ten thousand dollars, he had one other deal in mind. If they named the town for his daughter, he'd promise no harm would come to the place. You'd think the statue would depict him assured of this vow. Instead, he and Eudora appear to be struggling at the front of a storm. Held in his left hand is an oar, as though a current is threatening to wash them away. Eudora is not skipping ahead of her father, as is the custom of carefree children. Rather, she has her father gripped around the waist, his shirt clenched in her fists. With furrows on her forehead, she seems to be looking something terrible in the face. If statues could talk, this one would have Eudora hollering, "Save me, Daddy!"

Daddy's going to come. He'll come. I know he'll come. He always does.

THE CLICKING WAKES me up. I expect to be in my bedroom, but something's not right. The light isn't filtering through the leaves of the elm tree, softening the morning. Instead, it comes abruptly, blindingly, from above. I open my eyes to a fluorescent bulb overhead.

I can't remember what I'm doing on a cement floor, or why there are no windows. The clicking stops and the handle of the door turns and Dobbs walks in with two impossible words: "Good morning."

I sit up. Every muscle in my body is stiff, as though I've been left too long in the spin cycle of a washing machine. I try standing. Rush him! Knock him down! Run!

The dizziness brings black spots to my eyes, and I sit down hard.

Something else is wrong. I remember: my hair. It's not there. I feel so ashamed, as if this is somehow all my doing.

He steps over my trap—fishing tackle tied between two kitchen chairs—and pulls a doughnut out of thin air. "You look like you need to eat something. Here."

I can't even look at it.

"You sleep okay?"

Dobbs isn't dressed for a road trip. Pressed short-sleeve shirt, clip-on tie, trousers an inch too short, lace-up shoes . . . these are church shoes. Sunday, then. Because Mama didn't get around to it yesterday on account of the picnic, she would be stripping the beds today. The house would be one big hum—washing machine, dishwasher, vacuum cleaner sucking up all but Suzie's sulk. Through the windows would come the sound of Daddy's bench saw, Gerhard's motorbike on a stand, revving and sputtering with his tinkering.

"They've found your letter," Dobbs says, and just like that Mama's house is deathly still. Dobbs drags the chairs back to the table and gestures for me to sit down. He unties the tackle and winds it back onto its spool. "It's all over town."

In a town of two thousand people, news travels the way it always has ever since those German settlers rushed home to tell how the great Shawnee chief who sold them the land was actually—gasp!—a white man. Word of mouth—it's trusted more than the *Eudora Bugle*, which has the annoying habit of printing only facts. For the real scoop, you either call Dolores Weathers or Mel Barker, and if their lines are busy, you show up at church on Sunday morning.

He starts unpacking groceries from an army duffel bag.

"Folks are saying how you and Arlo Meier looked awful cozy on the bleachers last night. Some are speculating you've run off with him."

Dobbs's mouth is bent crooked. It's not what I would call a smile. His eyes have chase in them. I cannot be the half-dead thing with no run in me.

"Take me home!"

"What if I told you that you have Arlo Meier to thank for all of this?"

Why does he keep bringing up Arlo? I remember the first time I met Arlo. Lined up outside the first-grade classroom, I was too shy to play with the other kids at the swings. Arlo walked up to me and pointed to the birthmark on my neck. "What's that?"

"It's a map of the world," I said, because that's what Mama always called it. He said he wished he had one, and I guess that was all it took to get me to be his friend. Arlo lived three blocks away, and I can't count the number of times we ended up roaming the creek bank together in the late afternoon, or practicing our birdcalls, or spying on the teenagers necking under the bridge. Arlo moved away two years ago without so much as a good-bye. When he came back a month ago, I pretended not to notice. Maybe it had something to do with the scandal that led to his family's moving; maybe it had something to do with the fact that he seemed different. I hadn't yet figured out what turned me shy around him when he snuck up behind me at the checkout line in the library and held his hands over my eyes. I knew it was him from the way he smelled—that same smell: a pile of leaves turned boggy and something new, aftershave.

"Hey, Rand McNally." He made to touch my birthmark, asking if he'd fallen off my map, but I swatted his hand away and turned my books over to Dobbs. That same afternoon, walking to the bus, I heard Arlo call to me as he pushed his way through a throng of kids. "So you guys have moved out to the country. Is this your bus?"

No, it's my very own personal limo that I just happen to share with twenty other kids, I'd wanted to say, to show him I was like other girls now, mouthy and sure of themselves. At the very least, I wanted him to know that if you up and leave a friend without so much as a good-bye, you couldn't expect to be welcomed back with open arms. I said nothing and hurried into my seat. Arlo slid down next to me, took my backpack on his lap as though it were a toddler we were going to raise together, and started talking. I spotted Mercy in the crowd outside. She was about to wave and then saw who was leaning in next to me. She stuck out her hip and wagged her finger instead.

I got out my notebook and turned to the poem I'd been working on all week.

"You still scribbling in those books of yours?"

On the page the words kept rearranging themselves. They got smaller and then bigger. When Arlo pressed his forearm snug against mine, they ran clear off the page.

I slammed the book shut. "What is it you want exactly?"

He grinned. I hoped it had nothing to do with my cheeks, which felt like seared and tender slabs of flesh. "I want to marry you and be the father of your children and live with you till they bury us side by side in Oaksview Cemetery."

"What?"

"Okay, I'll settle for a conversation. Like the old days."

Except it wasn't the old days.

"It's a stroke of fortune, Arlo's not turning up this morning," Dobbs says now.

There's not enough air left to manage the question out loud: What's he done to Arlo?

"Don't look at me like that. I didn't have anything to do with it. My guess is he's sleeping off a hangover at one of his girlfriends' houses."

No, he's lying! I am supposed to be Arlo's girl, or at least, on my way to being his girl.

Arlo got off the bus at my stop and walked me the quarter mile down the dusty road, past the rows of parched corn, until I told him my house was coming up and he best be on his way. I looked at him properly, then, to show him I meant business. Running from his sideburns to the bend in his square chin was a line of acne that hadn't been there before, but the same big wheat-colored curls fell across his blue eyes. He looked back at me, and it seemed he'd found something different about me, something worthy of his curiosity. "I didn't forget about you," he said. And just like that, there was no arguing with him. When he asked me to meet him at the Horse Thieves Picnic, I couldn't seem to insert any delay between his asking and my agreeing.

Dobbs clucks. "Arlo Meier. The apple doesn't fall far from the tree."

Dobbs starts whistling. He doesn't act like a crazy person, and our town certainly has its share. All of them are what Grandma calls "harmless crazies," like the man at the old-age home where Great-aunt Maeve lives. He likes to get out his whatsit and play with himself just as the lady chaplain comes by, but nobody pays him no mind. Mr. Lambert who shaves his head and calls his classroom the Temple of All Knowledge— he's crazy. As is Mrs. Littleton's son, who looks like he'd just as soon lop off your head as eat a cheese sandwich. But Dobbs Hordin is not like any of them. He has a kind of craziness you can't tell from the outside. Only the whistle gives him away. There's harm in that whistle, in that terrible tune.

Dobbs is putting cans on the shelf beside the kitchen counter.

I notice the door is ajar. I move to the other side of the table. I chance another look. Open, definitely open. By my estimate, fifteen feet separates me from it.

"I didn't care for how that boy's been sniffing around you since he's been back. Full of ideas about taking what has no business being his. Just like his daddy with my Evabelle Horne back in high school."

"Arlo's my friend."

"Friend. Right." You'd think something's got a hold of his funny bone. "Boys don't want to be"—he punctuates the air with quotation marks—"friends . . . with girls. Our young Mr. Meier was after one thing and one thing only." He tilts his nose as if he's caught a whiff of something starting to sour. "Looked to me like you were set to give it to him, too."

"You were spying on us?"

Arlo showed up at the picnic just as he said he would. He plunked himself next to me on the bleachers and talked about his new job working at Pyle's meatpacking plant and that the funniest thing had happened that day: Two guys who worked the rodeo found a deer in their backyard and got the bright idea to lasso it and take it to Pyle's for cash. Somehow, it got loose and took off down Main Street when Becky Willoby stepped out of her salon and defended the fleeing animal by stopping the men dead in their tracks with her hair dryer. While Arlo was telling the story, my hand had been resting on the wooden bench between us like a purse no one wanted to claim, but as soon as I laughed, he brought his hand down gently on it and wove his fingers through mine. There wasn't time for this monumental event to sink in because his head was suddenly tipping toward mine.

It was a proper kiss—the kind Suzie was always going on about. No longer were we ten-year-olds snickering from behind a tree at the embrace of young lovers; at sixteen, we were the young lovers. By kissing someone, I thought you exchanged some hidden knowledge. I couldn't have been more wrong. In place of everything I knew about my childhood friend was a widening, thrilling uncertainty. It made me want to stop and keep going both. And then someone was calling for Arlo over the PA system, and the matter was settled.

"Didn't even bother to come back, did he?"

Seeing Dobbs smirk like that makes me realize: Dobbs was the one who had Arlo called away. Just as he'd arranged to be driving down the road when I was walking home because Arlo didn't come back as he said he would. I should've just stayed glued to those bleachers instead of wanting to show Arlo a kiss didn't mean I'd wait on him forever. If I had, Dobbs's great big plan would've amounted to nothing. And I would not be here. A convict—except I can't figure out my crime.

"When are we going?" I ask Dobbs.

"Going?"

It's hard to answer him because the muscles in my face have fallen slack. "The letter said—"

He waves his hand at me. "No, no, no. We have to stay put for now. Way too risky to be getting in a car and driving off when everyone's looking for you."

"You said they weren't going to be looking for me. You said that's why I had to write the letter, so they wouldn't think I'd been—" I can't say the word. I mustn't say the word. As long as it is not spoken, it won't be true.

"Kidnapped? It'll be a while yet before someone gets the notion a crime's been committed. And even then, what with that new gung ho deputy and his wild-goose chases, they'll be dredging Clinton Lake and rummaging through the Hamm Landfill before they think to follow other leads. You might as well hear it now, Blythe: the trail's already cold."

Dear Jesus.

Dobbs starts clapping me on the back, like it's a bad piece of meat that's got the better of me.

I pivot out from under him. He goes back to rearranging items on the shelf. He's jabbering away about Arlo being a carbon copy of his father. I take three steps toward the door.

"Came real close to ruining everything, that boy did."

Three more steps. Halfway there.

Run!

I sprint as hard as I can. I try flinging the door wide, but it screeches and groans and barely moves an inch. It's like moving a tank. I get my arm out and then my leg, and I'm about to squeeze my body sideways through the crack, about to scalp myself when Dobbs grabs me.

He pulls me back into the room. He leans against the door till it closes, then locks it with a key from the bunch on his belt.

"You gone awful pale again. You sure you won't eat something? Let's heat up some water. Here, this is how you use these gas burners." He points to a valve on the propane tank, gives instructions. "Always remember to switch it back off once you're done. You don't want to gas yourself."

He fills a kettle with water from the barrel and sets it on the hot plate. "This water's purified and will last ten years before going stale. Even then, I've got some tablets that will dissolve in it and freshen it right up."

"Dobbs?"

He points out the nonperishables as though he is the owner of a grocery store and this is my first day on the job. "I can't promise you fresh produce very often. Besides, the canned stuff is better for you in the long run, what with the government doing those chem-sprays over all our farmlands. Airplane vapor trails, my foot." He fills a small bowl with canned peaches. "This is a special occasion. What we don't finish, we'll put in this cooler, and they'll last you a good week or so. Once I get that old icebox up and running, you'll be able to order T-bone steaks if you want."

"Why are you doing this, Dobbs?"

"When I come back, I'll bring you cold cuts, but just about everything you can think of is here in a tin or a packet or a box. MREs— know what they are? Meals ready to eat. You don't even need to cook if you don't want. Give you more time to work on your poems."

Poems? He expects sonnets in this hole?

"If there's something you want that's not here, put it on the list." He gestures to a bulletin board with a small piece of paper pinned to it. Then he stirs a packet of powder into an enamel cup filled with hot water and hands it to me. "Tastes good; try it."

I push the cup aside. "Why are you doing this?"

"I realize you have a lot of questions, and we are going to discuss them, in due course."

There are pauses between his words, whereas mine come out in a rush. "Whynotnow?"

"Because you're all wound up, and I need for you to be calm. We'll discuss everything when we can talk, one adult to another."

But I'm not an adult. I'm sixteen years old.

Taking a sip of the hot chocolate meant for me, he watches me over the rim of the mug. I do my best imitation of being calm, so he will talk to me like an adult and tell me what is going to happen next.

"You weren't like other girls," he says instead. "You had your head screwed on right. The first time I saw you in the reference section, I knew. The others: a dime a dozen. But when you came along, I said to myself, 'Now here's one who doesn't buy everything she hears. Here's one who isn't brainwashed.'" He talks, and I watch the silent movie projected above his head.

We're in the library. He's bringing me a book. Saying something nice. "I'm not a teacher, so you don't have to keep calling me Mr. Hordin. Why don't you call me Dobbs."

The next frame is Mercy, smacking her lips together, saying it's creepy for him always to be suggesting I read survivalist books. Mercy, my best friend—why hadn't I listened to her? Instead, I defended the man. "He's an Eagle Scout," I told her. "He thinks we'd all do better if we were properly prepared."

"He's probably one of those conspiracy theorists. Ask him who killed JFK; I bet he's got an answer."

Dobbs had, in fact, mentioned previously that the head of the World Bank was responsible for the assassination, but I wasn't about to tell Mercy that.

When Dobbs's tone starts changing, I look at him. His voice is scary, not at all conversational anymore. He shakes his head at me. "You started changing when that kid showed up again. I wasn't about to sit by and watch you turn out like the others, what with Arlo Meier zeroing in."

"Please, Dobbs. I don't know what I did wrong. I'll do whatever you want. I won't tell anyone about this. Please; please, just let me go."

He stops blowing steam from the top of his drink, drains it in one go. Slamming the mug on the table, he says, "I know what you need. You need to get up and walk."

And I'm already on my feet, thinking, Yes! Finally, this all comes to an end. He only wanted to set me straight about Arlo, and now it is over.

Something doesn't seem quite right, but he is taking the keys off his belt, and sure enough, he unlocks that door and swings it wide.

A narrow metal staircase rises from the small platform. Up that short flight is the first of the really big doors, which is now propped open. I can't recall if there were two or three more doors between me and the outside. However many, I can practically smell the outdoors. I've always grumbled about summer, about how it can beat the smell out of any living thing; now, I need to smell the open range more than ever.

Instead of going up, Dobbs gestures to the right. "I believe I promised you a tour."

Only now do I notice that we are in some sort of concrete shaft, that to the right of the platform is a staircase that goes down even further. It is this direction Dobbs intends for me to go.

No, not deeper!

As fast as I can, I belt up the stairs, my footsteps clanging loudly. I clear the first doorway and enter a small concrete corridor. At the other end is another one of those enormous gray-green doors with thick horizontal bars across it, top to bottom. I race through it, and make a sharp left turn. It's like passing through a maze. I can feel Dobbs behind me, closing in. "Get back here," he calls.

The concrete corridor takes another right-angled turn. I am about to make the next turn when he grabs me around the neck. He drags me down, whistling happily.

I BOB TO the surface. Where I'd been held under was a dreamless nothingness that suited me just fine. Now, I have to contend again with gravity and three dimensions and time. It's impossible to tell whether time has run out or whether there is a glut of time, more time than can be stomached.

"I'm sorry, but you were hysterical. I didn't mean to knock you out for so long. Chloroform's not an exact science."

I sit up, scratch my mouth where a rash has blistered. He explains that it is from the chloroform. I notice that I am now wearing a yellow dress.

Dobbs holds up his hands when I spring from the cot. Instantly, the room begins spinning.

"Take it easy. You've got to wait for the dizziness to pass."

Dizziness? I put my hands to my head to make sure there isn't a vise clamped around it.

"Just to be clear, nothing improper happened. I dressed you, is all. When it was called for, I averted my eyes."

We are in the large round room again, between the partitions where sleeping is supposed to be done. "I want my own clothes."

He looks at the cubbyhole at the foot of the bed where my clothes are washed and folded neatly. I grab them and storm into the bathroom.

By the time I come out, he has a cup of tea and a slice of toast waiting for me and insists it will help with the nausea. I refuse to eat, and he refuses to stop talking. I stand by the only door out of this room. On the other side of it is the staircase. I listen for the sounds of thundering footsteps. They're going to be calling for me soon. I need to be where I can yell back.

"I don't think you were paying too much attention earlier, but as I said, this is one of twelve silos in the state of Kansas. Nebraska, Oklahoma, and a few other states have theirs, and that's not counting all the A's, D's, and Titans. This here's the F——the last type of Atlas complex to be built. Where we are now, the upper level, used to be the crew's living quarters. The lower level is where all the controls were. And, of course, there's the silo." He goes over to the central pillar and points to the twelve-inch gap between it and the floor. "You can see the lower level from here."

He explains that the floor of this level and the identical one below are stacked on top of each other. Forty feet below the ground, both levels are mounted from the ceiling by pneumatic rams. He goes over to a gray cylinder with a gas pressure gauge and assorted steering wheels and spigots. "This is what suspends the floors. They designed it so that if a blast went off on the surface, the whole thing wouldn't come crashing down."

Somehow, we are back on the walking tour. Somehow, I am still holding tightly to the belief that if I go along with the lesson, this will all eventually come to an end. There is a chance I can nod my way out. He unlocks and opens the main door again. Briefly, I glance up the staircase, but he shoves me to the right. We go down the flight that makes a half-turn after six stairs. Another six steps and we are directly below the room above. The entrance to this room is not a steel door like the one upstairs. It is more like an office door.

"Welcome to the Launch Control Center." He unlocks the door and swings it open. We step into another spherical room. At its center is the thick concrete column. Peg-Board partitions divide the space into a series of slice-of-pie-shaped rooms. Against the circular outer wall are angled support beans, a mess of wires, and pipes bent like straws. Dobbs says something about having remodeled the space for "optimized self-sufficiency."

"All the old control panels are gone, but it doesn't take much to imagine the controllers strapped into their chairs and waiting for the order to launch."

"Launch what?"

"An ICBM. The A-bomb. You know—*kaboom*?" He makes an exploding gesture.

That's what people put in a place like this!

"No, no, don't worry. There isn't a missile in here anymore. These days, nobody cares that these places even exist, much less the reason they were built in the first place. Most of them were constructed in the early sixties, only to be decommissioned a few years later. Some you could snap up for as little as fifteen thousand dollars. Of course, those were the ones that were vandalized or flooded, and you needed a ton of money to get them halfway livable. Some jokers have spent thousands fitting them with wall-to-wall carpeting and simulated daylight. They bring down all kinds of fancy furniture and stereo equipment and satellite TVs. It's a disgrace, if you ask me. It's a mockery of what these structures represent."

I can't do anything but nod.

"Ten years ago was when I bought this beauty."

He raises those colorless eyebrows and presses his lips together so the corners of his mouth turn down. I am obviously supposed to be impressed.

There are three clocks on the wall, each with little plaques beneath them: DC, LONDON, MOSCOW. Somewhere on the other side of the world, people are sitting down for supper, saying grace.

"There was a time when this country took the safety of its citizens seriously. Folks were encouraged to prepare for the inevitable, to be self-sufficient. These days, you talk about fallout shelters, people think you're nuts. What do they think? The government's going to take care of them? Now, that's something to laugh at."

He opens a plywood door, and we pass into a cubicle he calls the Vault. It's about the size of my bedroom. In the middle of this space, stacked back-to-back, are gray cabinets like the ones at the school library where they keep all the index cards.

"You ever heard of the antediluvian period?"

I shake my head.

"You know who Noah is, right?"

He waits for me to nod.

"Well, between the Creation and the Great Flood was the antediluvian period. The Bible calls it a time of great wickedness. People lived too long, so there was overpopulation, and that's always the main problem right there. It was also a time giants called Gibborim ruled the earth. 'Men of renown,' if you read Genesis six. See where this is going?"

Again, I am required to nod.

"The entire world was run by just a few powerful men, and then, bam! Everyone and everything gets wiped out, except for Noah and his family and a few thousand species of animals. Come, I want to show you something."

Dobbs pulls out a drawer crammed with packets of seeds. "Here's where I keep the herb seeds." In another drawer are flower seed packets. "What's your favorite vegetable?"

I don't like it in here with him. It's too tight. He smells of disinfectant. We're too close.

"Come on. Green beans? Carrots? How about rhubarb? You like rhubarb pie, don't you?"

Because I can picture Mama cutting thick slices of tomato for sandwiches, I say, "Tomatoes."

"Fruit." He pulls open a different drawer. "Heirloom, Roma, plum, cherry—take your pick." He fans several packs like a hand of cards. "A bunch of scientists have been tampering for years with the genetic makeup of seeds. They've got patents on seeds that can't reproduce themselves. Can you believe that? You can't grow your own crops without having to go to a seed manufacturer. And who do you think the seed manufacturer works for?"

"The farmers?" I offer cautiously.

Dobbs returns the packets and slides the drawer shut. The sound echoes through the room like an exclamation mark. "The Gibborim, the handful of corporate CEOs who run this country. Once again, everything is controlled by the mighty few, right down to the lowly tomato. It's not just our food they're controlling. For years they've been hiring researchers to do experiments on weather control. Half the earthquakes, tornadoes, and tidal waves around the world are caused by man-generated electromagnetic waves. They've got Mother Nature on the run. They control the weather, the food, the politics, the money. But it's about to collapse. Every system in our society is at breaking point. In my view, we're already having a meltdown. Have you seen what's happening on Wall Street lately? Mark my words, by the end of the year, we'll have stepped off a cliff."

Dobbs opens a drawer of another filing cabinet. "Microfiche. In here are newspapers going back one hundred and twenty years. I've got photocopies of other documents. The Declaration of Independence, the Articles of Confederation, the Homestead Act, the Test Ban Treaty, you name it."

"That's nice." Now, if we can just get out of this room and go upstairs.

He has me turn around, and I reel backward. On a bookshelf are rows and rows of jars, each one stuffed with some sort of animal. "See why I call this place the Ark? DNA. That's our ticket to the future."

He raps on a steel cabinet with a padlock. "We'll leave insects for another time, but all told, I've got DNA samples of two thousand species."

An adjoining door opens into another wedge-shaped cubicle. He has me face a glass display case of old coins. "These ones are actual gold. Krugerrands. Used to be money had value. Now we're supposed to be happy with a piece of paper with a string of numbers on it, and sometimes not even that much. You ever been to a bank and asked to see your money?"

Could it be that he has forgotten I'm too young to have a bank account?

Another door, another room. This one he calls the Inner Sanctum. A desk, a chair, and a cot like the one upstairs. Except for the metal shelves full of old books, it looks like a prison cell. He taps on the spines. *A New Theory of the Earth* by William Whiston, *The Genesis Flood* by John C. Whitcomb and Henry M. Morris, *The Coming Race* by Edward Bulwer-Lytton. *Mein Kampf* is the one he pulls out.

"You won't hear anyone admit it, but there are people—people in our government—doing the same thing as Hitler did. You ever heard of eugenics? Back in the thirties, government scientists worked round the clock trying to come up with the human thoroughbred. Back then, you could go to any county fair and there would be half a dozen judges reviewing the genetic panels of entrants like they were blue-ribbon hogs. Fitter Family Contests, they called them. Next thing, the government started rounding up criminals, mental cases, cripples, people with incurable diseases, you name it, and stuck them in camps and started sterilizing them. They want you to believe that's all in the past, but you'd be surprised what they're doing behind the scenes. You have any idea what the welfare costs are for a cripple in this country? Back then, they estimated 1.2 million dollars. Quadruple that amount today. Economics is what it boils down to. Keeping people from draining the system, keeping people from sucking off their profits."

The last room has a steel wall and a steel door with a keypad. He punches a code, and a soft click releases the dead bolt. It is not much bigger than the walk-in closet Daddy built for Mama. As soon as I see the glass cabinet, I step back. "Nothing to be afraid of," Dobbs says, pushing me in. He closes the door, locks it, then uses a key to unlock the gun safe.

"This here's a .38 caliber revolver—the perfect weapon for one of the gentler persuasion. No safeties, easy to load, no magazine to lose, and it doesn't have the heavy muzzle blast you get with magnum cartridges." He offers it to me.

I clasp my hands together, shake my head.

"Never heard of a country girl afraid of guns." He puts it back and takes out another gun. "This is a must-have. The 9mm Glock model

17—it's my preference over the standard-issue Beretta." He handles it the way you would a small furry pet. "Bolt-action Winchester 69; that one used to be my grandfather's. It's fine for hunting small game, and the ammo is cheap. This is a Mosin-Nagant 91-30. It will stop a moose. And this is my father's 12-gauge Remington 870."

In a drawer at the bottom of the safe is ammunition, along with gas masks and a gadget that looks like a game console. He calls it a radiation detector. "The government has hoarding laws, if you can believe that. See if they stop me." Dobbs laughs, and it sounds exactly like something bound up in a garbage disposal.

"Can we go now?"

He locks the cabinets, then the steel door, and we make the circular route around the central pillar, passing from room to room until we are back on the landing of the lower level.

"Saved the best for last."

More?

He has to pull me down another six stairs to a tube of corrugated iron about fifty feet long with a diameter of about eight feet. It has a false floor that makes me think of a gangplank off a pirate ship. Running at eye level on each side is a slither of thick cables. The utility tunnel, he calls it. At the far end is the door. Even from fifty feet away, it looks ominous. Everything in me says, Don't take another step. Whatever he says, do not go in there.

I back up. Dobbs starts shoving again. I dig in my heels. He puts his shoulder into it and leans against me.

"Please, no farther."

He pushes me all the way to the end. Off to the side are two small rooms. One is not much bigger than the size of Mama's pantry. He says it's the battery room. The one next to it is the generator room. Huge contraptions take up the space. He points to big steel drums and tells me they're the fuel for making our own electricity when the time comes.

"I'm not saying the end's going to happen tomorrow. When it does, though, we'll have no time to react. There are some who think it'll be biological. Anthrax is easy enough to get your hands on, but it won't travel well. Smallpox, maybe, if they figure out a way to use it in aerosol form. Can't be too hard to hack into the grids and shut off the nation's electricity, but I think it's those bankers who are going to shut us down. I may be wrong, but whatever it's going to be, you have to prepare for it all."

We're up against the enormous door again. The handle has a thick chain around it with a padlock. I keep my face turned away because I can smell Dobbs sweating with excitement.

"You're about to see engineering on the level of the pyramids."

He turns the massive red steering wheel. "Now, we're already a good sixty feet below the surface, but this baby plummets to a depth of one hundred and seventy-four feet. That's like an eight-story skyscraper."

"Please. I don't want to. I'm afraid of heights."

For some reason, he finds this incredibly funny.

I can't imagine how he gets that door open all the way. It's three times the size of one of those filing cabinets. "Six thousand pounds, right there," he says.

Even before it has swung all the way open, the pitch dark comes at us like an avalanche. Dobbs's flashlight is no match for it.

"It can be a little spooky, so you might want to hold on to my arm."

No, I can't go in there! He can't lock me up in there!

"It's okay, I got you." Dobbs has a hold of my wrist. I twist, but he won't let go.

"No!"

"But this is the best part." His eyes are wide, as skittery as loose marbles.

He pulls me onto some kind of platform. It clangs when we step on it, and a gust of air rushes up through the holes. It's too deep down here. I don't even like swimming in deep water. I'm always afraid there are monsters that are going to see that churning water and come all the more quickly. Thrash all you want—the horror is going to reach its tentacles up and grab you by the ankles.

Something creaks. Something sounds like a chain rattling or the strain of a terrible weight that can no longer be borne. He intends to throw me to the darkness. The floor is giving way. We've stepped on something else that starts to sway. It's too much. I scream.

A draft takes my shriek and flings it against some far wall, where it ricochets and returns to us as a cackle.

Dobbs tells me to quit screaming. He tries to get me to step out farther onto the platform, which his flashlight means to assure me is solid, but I won't be budged.

"There's a railing."

"No!" My insides are about to drop out of me. I squeeze my legs together, hold myself down there. Then, my legs give out. Crying's no use. Pleading's no use. Nothing's no use.

"Okay. I guess we'll have to do this another time."

By the time he gets the door closed, it's too late. Whatever horrors he meant to lock back in place, some of them have escaped.

WHEN WE ARE back on the upper level, Dobbs looks at his watch. "Don't know about you, but I worked up an appetite."

He does not solicit my help. Instead, he insists I rest. I stand in the kitchen and watch him open a can of meat and spread it on bread along with something unidentifiable from a packet. He pours the contents of another can into a pot and puts it on the burner. He sets out two place mats, two cups of water, and a milk glass vase with fake daisies. By the time he is done, on the table are two bowls of mystery meat and a platter of sandwiches cut into triangles. He motions for me to sit like we're at some fancy restaurant.

I've listened to his stories and taken the tour and paid attention, all reasonably well. Because he is smiling at me, I take it he agrees.

"Can I go home now?"

He stops chewing, puts his sandwich down.

"I really need to go home."

He doesn't have to shake his head. I can see it in his eyes. My voice rises, as do his hands, like he means to pat everything back into place.

"Settle down, now."

"Please! Please just take me home! What have I ever done to you? I thought you were my friend! I trusted you!"

"Blythe—"

"No! I don't want to hear any more of your stories! I just want to go home. You're sick!"

It's the wrong thing to have said. I can tell by the way his mouth puckers, like an empty coin purse. Stupid of me. Who's to say he won't drag me to the silo? Kill me? Torture me?

He passes me a handkerchief. For a moment, I can't think why. "Don't cry. I hate to see you sad."

I understand now that it is better to know. "Are you going to—?" I can't say it. He must have the idea.

"Am I going to what?"

"Are you going to . . . Because . . ." I look at my hands. Sex can't be as terrible as dying or being locked up. And if we get it over with, he can let me go. "Because, I'll . . . let you."

He scoots his chair back and marches to the wall where an old calendar hangs. It's a picture of a red barn near a meadow full of longhorns. You'd think he was staring out a window. "You think I'd ever do anything to hurt you?"

I don't know what the right answer is anymore. What does it take to please this man?

"You think I'm a monster. I understand why. You will see things differently in time. Everything you need, I'm going to take care of. You'll see."

I ball my hands into fists. If I still had fingernails, they'd be slicing open my palms.

He juts out his chin, moistens his rubbery lips. After scanning the ceiling, he locks his eyes on mine. Here it comes—here comes the explanation.

"It's the hair, isn't it?"

"What?"

"Shaving you—that's what's got you so upset." He goes over to the cubby.

It's as though some invisible monster has come for me, some beastly slithery thing from the silo that a six-thousand-pound door can't keep caged. It's come up behind me, through the gap in the floor. I pivot around, but there is nothing there. Above me, then, because a tentacle dangles down and begins winding itself around my neck. I put my hands to my neck, but there is nothing to yank away. Impossible to take a deep breath.

"I'll get you a wig. Until then, I have just the thing." His lips are moving, but the words have trouble catching up. I can't hear because another tentacle has dropped down and stiffened into a knitting needle, and is poking itself into my ear. My head, skewered.

Dobbs is holding out a basket of scarves to me. "Pick whichever you like," I think he says.

Another tentacle straps itself around my chest. I start to feel numb. My fingers tingle. I am having a heart attack. "I think—a doctor . . ."

Dobbs is digging around for just the right one. He lifts out a gray scarf with tiny yellow dots. I shake my head and tug at my collar.

"Will you allow me?" He intends to fasten it beneath my chin.

I shake my head. Can't breathe. Black spots. Camera flashes.

"You're all right. Just take a few breaths; it'll pass."

His face has gone funny.

Have to keep standing. Can't sit. Can't listen to him telling me how he's bought it all for me.

There's an old gumball machine in Mr. Minta's store. You have to give it a good hard whack after you put in your quarter if you want a gumball to fall down the chute. It's like the gumball's just fallen down. I motion to the rack with the clothes on it.

"Yup, I bought those for you, too."

I glance at the shoe rack.

"Guilty, Your Honor," he says. He smiles. He is enjoying himself. "Take a look at the bookshelf."

Brontë, Austen, Harper Lee, Louisa May Alcott. Not only my favorites but also books that are on next year's reading list. I turn around. No longer is the room an arrangement of objects in a missile silo. It is some kind of a museum. Around me are relics from the part of my life I have yet to live.

I'm sure I am standing quite still; it's only the question that keeps revolving.

With the shallowest of breaths, I ask, "How long have you been planning this?"

This is when he's supposed to say, "Planned what? I haven't planned anything." This is when he's supposed to say, "Don't be crazy—I'm not going to *keep* you."

This is what he says: "The part regarding you, about two years, give or take. All the rest, eighteen years."

"How long . . . ?"

"Well, I just told you."

I shake my head. "How long are you going to keep me here?"

He shrugs, looks away.

It must be asked. "Forever?"

The monster sucks me all the way down to the bottom of the silo. It is a long way down, just as Dobbs said, but I still manage to hear every last word. "We are the Remnant, Blythe. After the End, you and I will rise up together. You and me—we will one day seed the new world."

YOU NEED TO quit thinking there's any escape. You'll only drive yourself mad," Dobbs says.

He's caught me staring up at the escape hatch again. I know the circular trapdoor in the ceiling goes nowhere. I've already pulled on that handle. Nothing but a forty-foot concrete plug. If this were 1960 and the silo still operational, a four-ton column of sand would be released, providing clear access to the surface.

"There's no way out of here. You should know that by now. It's been two months already."

"Two months, three weeks, and two days."

He looks at me like I've got maggots crawling out of my mouth. He rounds off weeks as though they don't matter. That I keep strict records bothers him. The only time to be concerned about is the End of the World, he tells me. I tell him the End of the World has happened.

"All I'm saying is the sooner you think of this as home, the better off you'll be."

He exits through the door, walking backward, as is his custom now. He will come back in a few hours or a few days and enter the room just as cautiously. He is used to stumbling over tripwires, or putting his foot in a pot of hot water, or finding a chair poised above his head. It's why he wears a helmet when he comes. Sometimes, he'll have on the thickly padded false sleeve like the kind they use to train police dogs. The bite marks took a long time to heal.

No matter how many times I've heard it, my skin always crawls when that door closes. Fingernails on a chalkboard.

Home. It makes me angry that such a word can come out of his mouth. But I'm glad for the anger, because it's the only way to fight time, which is trying so hard to make all this start to feel normal. This will never be home. I scream it, breathe it, protest it with every drop of sweat and every angry tear. He can keep me down here two lifetimes, and home's still going to be the yellow clapboard house on Fall Leaf Road. Thinking about it is what keeps me from going mad.

It was Daddy's idea to move us out of town. Before that, we'd lived in a rental behind Broken Arrow Park that looked like some fleshy thing had molted and scurried off leaving its crackled skin. "I just don't see the point of moving kit and caboodle to the back of beyond," was how Mama took to the idea, even though "back of beyond" was just three miles outside Eudora's city limits.

With the Crawford property up for sale, Daddy said he had a way to buy back land his family lost during the Great Depression. With Mama's bridled consent, he plunked down a deposit, bought himself a John Deere, and walked around from then on like he were a rich man. Moving day was a community effort, much like a rummage sale or a funeral. By eight o'clock in the morning, just about every pickup in Eudora was parked outside our house. Flasks of coffee and packs of cigarettes were passed around, and it seemed like every wife came by just to pat Mama on the shoulder. "Picked the hottest day of the year to move, didn't he?" they commiserated, as though Daddy hadn't yet shouldered enough blame.

The moment my bare feet hit those creaky oak floorboards, I was home. The windows were warped, and some had been painted shut, and Gerhard would eventually put his hand through one of them trying to get it to open, but, oh, the view. Land—acres and acres of it. For the couple dozen or so disheveled rows of corn Daddy planted, a modern sprinkler system would have been just fine, but he called our place a farm and said any farm worth its salt had to have a well. Not quite a month after moving in, while I was helping Mama hang up the wash,

Mr. Walt Wallis pulled up in his Ford pickup. He was wearing standard bib overalls without a shirt, which meant you had to look the other way unless you wanted an eyeful of graying body hair and jiggly flesh. Mama waved at him when he called out his howdy and pointed to the toolshed where Daddy was fixing the plow.

The two men stood talking in the shade a while, until Mr. Wallis went over to the willow tree and indicated the place where Daddy's hacksaw had to go to work. Mr. Wallis whittled the branch some with his pocketknife until it made the letter Y. Daddy flagged me over just as Mr. Wallis handed him his thick spectacles. The old man spat in each hand, rubbed his callused palms together, and then clapped them heartily. He looked at me. "You believe in magic, little lady?"

He took the ends of the fork in his hands and bent them till they looked like they were ready to snap. Mr. Wallis raised the branch to the level of his navel, so that the end of the Y stuck out in front of him like an arrow.

"All set!"

Set for what I couldn't say, not with him zigzagging around the yard through a menace of gopher mounds and old tree stumps. Just when Mr. Wallis looked set to collide with the bird feeder, he made an abrupt turn and clomped through the thistles, sending fluff flying. He was making a beeline for Mama's tomato plants. I could tell what Mama thought about this by the way she put down the clothespins, fastened her hands on her hips, and called Daddy by his first, middle, and last name.

At the last minute, Mr. Wallis made a sudden turn and went marching down the middle of the yard like he was leading Custer's men. When he cried, "Geronimo!" we rushed over to where he came to a standstill. "Found your water, Hank."

All I saw was a dry piece of dirt between two scuffed work boots, but Daddy might as well have been witnessing the parting of the Red Sea.

Mama scratched the back of her neck. "How can you be sure, Walt?"

"Haven't been wrong about an underground stream but once in the last fifty-seven years, Mrs. Hallowell. Can't say I know how these things work—wish I could. All's I can say is I guaran-darn-tee you, you're going to find water. You got to go deep on this one, I'll give you that."

While Daddy and Mama commenced their arguing, Mr. Wallis winked at me.

"Magic. What'd I tell you?" He beckoned me out of earshot. "Come on, have a go." He held out the green branch like it was a BB gun and I was at the shooting gallery on the midway. "It ain't going to hurt you none." Mr. Wallis wrapped my hands around the ends of that sweaty branch. "You got to keep it bent, like that. Keep the tension. You feel that?"

I nodded. All I felt was a useless piece of wood.

"Good. You just keep the end as level as you can. That's it. Now start walking. Just keep going till the magic grabs hold."

So as to get this silliness over as quick as possible, I double-timed it to the tractor tire. I did a quick loop, and when I turned to head back, the stick made a little jump. Of its own accord, the end of it started to tilt down. I tightened my grip on each handle and tried to rotate the tip back into its horizontal position. In response, it jerked itself downward with alarming force, as though an invisible hand had reached up out of the ground to snatch it from me. I fought to right the darn thing, but it wouldn't budge. I squeezed my hands and turned my wrists, and felt the ends of the stick twisting in my palms, shearing off some of my skin with it. The stick began turning further, looping through the space between my arms.

I hollered, "Daddy!"

"Hold on, sweetie!" They came trotting toward me. I could see Daddy was worried, like maybe I'd found another patch of poison ivy and he was going to be skinned by Mama.

Mr. Wallis took one look at that unruly branch and said, over and over, "Well, I'll be!"

"What do I do?"

"Keep walking, girl; keep walking!"

I took a few steps forward and the stick twisted a little more.

"Don't drop it. Keep hold of it."

I cut across the corner of the yard, all the while fighting that stick like it was a serpent. Just in case the end swiveled up and bit me, I kept my elbows far apart.

Mr. Wallis made a rough sketch on the back of his cigarette box and then told me I could quit. I handed him his branch and that's when we all saw how it was coated with blood. Daddy turned up my palms, raw where the reddened skin had bunched up.

Mr. Wallis passed me his kerchief. "Hank Hallowell, I do declare you've got yourself here a water witch."

Daddy had them sink a borehole right where I had stood bleeding that day. They didn't have to go but six feet for a geyser that gushed all afternoon.

Mr. Wallis said witching was a rare gift. He said it like it had singled me out, made me special. "You can divine water, ain't no telling what other secrets will give themselves up to you."

Besides me, there is another secret down here, and its name is Escape. If I can witch water from the dusty earth, I can witch my way out. If I can divine down, I can surely divine up. I can surely divine out.

And just like that, my head's picturing that Y-shaped branch, not the one Mr. Wallis handed me, but the one stuffed in Dobbs's steamer trunk. I rush over to his recliner and tip out the contents. Mr. I Think of Everything has overlooked something. I shuffle through spinning tops and die-cast tractors until I find it: a slingshot in perfect condition.

The only good thing about this place is the ample warning I get that Dobbs is about to make an entrance. The thud of the middle blast door and then the lock turning on this door gives me more than enough time to take my position.

"A Catholic, a Muslim, and a Jew show up at the Pearly Gates," I hear him start, before he's even got the door open all the way. Sometimes he brings food, sometimes he brings a book. Sometimes it's this: a dumb joke. According to him, it's because I always look so glum.

Dobbs stops when he sees me poised with the slingshot. He seems more confused than threatened.

"I want you to unclip the keys and slide them across the floor to me. Slowly."

"Put that thing down, Blythe."

"Do it!"

I've got the mothball lined up perfectly with his forehead.

He does as he's told. The keys slide all the way and bump against my foot.

"Get back!"

Dobbs, having taken a step forward, lifts his hands in the air. "You can't take aim at an unarmed man." He starts smiling.

"Don't move!"

He shrugs, then he folds his arms. "Go ahead. Pick them up."

I now see what he finds so amusing. I can't pick them up, not without losing my aim.

I hear him snort. Funny, is it? How about this? I pull back the sling till the tendon in my arm feels about ready to snap. And then I give my fingers the sweet relief they've been craving.

The ball catapults forward, whizzes through the air. Not laughing now, are you! It hits him in the throat. He doubles over, coughs.

I realize my mistake. I don't have time to reload.

He crosses the space in one bound. The slingshot goes flying from my hand. My arm is too late in trying to break my fall. My shoulder hits the concrete floor first, then my head. Still, I manage to grab the keys. The weight of them. If the earth could be condensed to the size of a tennis ball, this is how heavy it would be.

HE SLAPS A newspaper article on the table in front of me, along with a bar of chocolate. He thinks I'm that easy.

"They've taken Bix Littleton into custody." When Dobbs is pleased, he preens. He rakes his fingers through his hair, then digs the wax out of his ears.

I try to concentrate on the outside world neatly arranged in two-inch columns. The article tells about a girl in Lawrence claiming my piano teacher's son exposed himself to her in the grocery store parking lot. It says the police are questioning him in connection with my disappearance. It says I disappeared a few hours after my piano lesson, four months ago. Isn't there anyone except me keeping track? Four months, one week, six days.

"Certainly looks the type." Dobbs leaves a sticky mark where he taps Bix's mug shot.

Mama began sending me for piano lessons every Saturday afternoon at two o'clock not for my own enrichment, but to help Mrs. Littleton when her husband up and died. Other mothers in Eudora signed up their kids for music lessons, too, and off we were marched to the little blue cottage on Maple Street because Mrs. Littleton was not one to accept charity. For fifteen dollars, however, she was willing to instruct even the most tone-deaf child for an hour.

During lessons, Mrs. Littleton's son liked to park himself on an old stereo speaker in the far corner. He dressed like a soldier, in army fatigues and boots caked with mud. I was told to call him Junior, which seemed silly given he was a grown man, so I called him nothing at all.

"You're a quiet one," he would say, putting his hand on my head. I can still feel it, the weight of it. Like it could have pushed me straight through the piano bench, through the floor to the basement below. I'll never forget the last time he spoke to me. He stopped me in the hallway on my way out. "Girls like you don't stand a chance."

Maybe he's right. How much of a chance do I stand when accusing fingers go pointing in all the wrong directions? They gave up pointing at Arlo as soon as his grandma gave him an alibi, but then they did the rounds of equally unlikely candidates. Mr. Walt Wallis; Gerhard's friend Jimmy Perkins; the carnie who left his booth at the fair for several hours about the same time I disappeared. The fingers always swing back to Daddy, though. Dobbs says they always will. He feels not the least bit guilty about this. He holds the position that a more vigilant father wouldn't have let this happen in the first place. In Dobbs's opinion, everyone's guilty, one way or another, even the Mayor, the Governor, and the President, who is the Biggest Criminal of All.

Why doesn't Dobbs ever crop up on the list of suspects?

Dobbs has been quiet the whole time I've been reading. He can hold a silence as though it were a bag of water. I do to it what a pair of rusty scissors would.

"They're going to find out eventually. They're going to figure out you're the one who's kidnapped me. They'll find me, and you'll go to jail. You'll get locked up and then you can see how you like it."

He looks at me calmly. In the beginning I would never have dared talk to him like this, but fear and crushing loneliness make a person reckless. Like any second, you might just not give a damn.

He doesn't say, "No, they're not going to find you." He doesn't say, "I'm not going to jail." He says, "I didn't kidnap you."

To define the terms by which I am here, he uses words like *delivered* and *rescued* and *saved*. I've developed a physical reaction to those words. Nauseated is how I get. Which is a problem now because he's started to prepare a meal, which will lead to the same fight about me and my hunger strike. I cannot control but two things down here: when I go to the bathroom, and when I eat.

"You should be thankful you're not up there." He's round-shouldered, which makes him look like he's cowering at his own words. He cranks his chin at the ceiling. "It's only getting worse. Won't be long before there's a run on the banks. Washington's throwing money it doesn't have at the problem, and it's not going to make a dime's worth of difference. You wait. Wait till Europe goes belly-up. Wait till China goes belly-up. You'll have the president declaring martial law and mobilizing the National Guard, but it will be too late. It's the beginning of the end, no question. You'll be thanking me one of these days, Blythe. You'll be thanking your lucky stars you won't have to put up with the anarchy. We've got order down here."

What kind of evangelist proselytizes with a bunch of keys on his hip and a lock on the door?

"We're preserving a way of life, don't you see? *The* way of life. They'll look back a hundred years from now and call you a saint. Imagine that. Imagine one day some kid praying to you." He squirts some ketchup into a pot of runny swill.

"I chose this for you, granted, but I do believe, given enough time, you would have chosen it for yourself." He goes on. "I can't explain it, Blythe; you're going to have to experience the truth for yourself. I thought with the books and all, you'd have understood by now."

By books, Dobbs means the spiral-ring binders scribbled with his mumbo jumbo. He means the tracts he sets out for me to type up for him. *The Manifesto*, it's called—the blueprint for the New World Order that he and I, the Remnant, will establish.

"Anyone in his—or her—right mind would choose this. You ever hear of the Tribulation? What they are about to see up top will make that look like a garden party. Do you want to be preserved or do you want to be part of the destruction? That's the question. When it boils down to a simple choice like that, it's not really a choice at all, is it? Thing is, though, the people up there, they're insane. They just don't know it. You try talking some sense, and they look at you like you're the one who needs to be thrown in the booby hatch! That's how crazy it is. All you have to do is breathe one word about the end of the world and they think you're some whacko from a street corner with a sandwich board and a bullhorn.

"But the world *is* ending; it is blowing up in our faces right this very minute. And what are we doing about it? We're going out to Wal-Mart to buy stuff we don't need!"

As soon as the table is set, Dobbs bows his head in silent prayer before taking up his spoon.

I watch him. He is precise about everything except eating. Juice runs down his chin. Listening to him eat makes it easy for me to swear off food.

He cocks his eyebrow at my plate. As has become my custom, I push it away.

When he's finished his meal, he rinses his bowl and concludes his speech. "I chose you, Blythe. I *chose* you."

I laugh, softly at first, but quickly the sound gathers itself into one hysterical ball. *I chose you.* It runs away with me, this laughter.

He reddens.

I should shut myself up, but it's all just so funny. Being chosen. Like I'm Mary, the mother of God.

"You think this is a joke, do you?"

I nod.

"Starving yourself is a joke, too, I suppose? Your big plot to overthrow me?"

I quickly grow sober.

"How hard do you think it would be for me to replace you with someone else—your sister, say?"

He leaves the table, goes downstairs. I rush to the center column and try peeking through the gap between it and the floor, but I can't make out what he's up to.

When he returns, I quickly take my place at the table. He puts an old-fashioned doctor's case on it. When he pulls out a strange-looking pair of pliers with a long screw on the end, I start shaking all over.

Next, he lifts out of the bag a long rubber pipe. "Do you know what this is?"

I shake my head. It looks like what Gerhard uses to siphon the water from his fish tank.

"It's a feeding tube."

I scoot back from the table.

"Don't think I've overlooked anything."

That's all it takes for me to take a mouthful.

"Tastes good, doesn't it?"

I can't look at him. I only nod.

IF I THINK about Mama too long, I lose my way, so I try not to think of her, but she finds her way into my dreams, or in the snatches of a lullaby that runs through my head from time to time. I have to shut her up, and that's the plain and simple truth. Keys are what I have to think about. Mama's no use to me here, but those keys—they are everything. I have yet to figure out how to get them.

The time I've wasted. Waiting for them to come; waiting to see if Dobbs is going to skid out of control and do me in; waiting for Jesus. Add up all the hours spent waiting, and what do I have? Nothing! It might as well be ten thousand years that I've been down here. How am I going to put up with one more day?

I am so bored that I have measured out this space in inches. He says each level is six hundred square feet. In total, the space of an average-size house. Of course, I don't get to use the lower level. It doesn't matter. To me, the whole thing is a crate. It doesn't help to rearrange the furniture or set up a little writing nook where my poems are blank pages stacked neatly on top of each other. It doesn't help to hang my sketches on the outer wall or decorate with the plastic junk he brings from the Dollar Tree just as it wouldn't help to go putting up paper lanterns in hell.

I sit on my cot and wait for him to get done downstairs and come for supper. When we are done eating, I will come back to my cot and wait for him to leave, and then I will go to sleep sitting up. When the fluorescents kick on in the morning, I will straighten the quilt and then sit on the cot some more and wait for him to return or for somebody to come or for an idea about how to get the keys to drop into my head.

I've tried writing poems. Nothing comes of it. Sinking sand is how I've come to think of poetry. If I write about being in here or something about what I miss from out there, he'll read it. Still, there is something soothing about a pen. Sometimes, to feel its comfort, I will pick a certain word or phrase and write it over and over again in as many different ways. *Tabasco*, for example. Or *odometer* or *100 percent cotton*. I'll flip through the pages sometime later, and, for an instant, it will look as if many people wrote in my book. Sometimes, I'll write every name I can think of that begins with the letter *D* for the same reason. Because I can't do this all day long, I have agreed to type up his notes on the old Olivetti. The sound of clacking bars bolsters me. I like to watch the little bars punch the paper. They can be so fierce. Sometimes, they take their frustrations out on one another instead of the page, and I have to pry them apart. I have become a very accurate typist, but I like it when I make a mistake because then I have to pull the page out and put a new one in and start all over again. I never read the words. It's always just one letter at a time, *click-bang-punch*.

I get out Grandpa's watch to check if it is time to start cooking.

Dobbs hears my cry from the lower level. "What's wrong?" he calls up through the gap.

"Nothing." But it's not nothing. I keep winding it, and nothing happens. I have to sit down to bear it. I put the watch against my ear. Not a single tick. I swallow hard. Grandpa's watch has stopped at a quarter to ten.

All those hours spent on a tractor in the hot sun were bound to make anyone loopy, was how Grandma accounted for what Grandpa had engraved. Grandpa argued that, loopy or not, the immortal words of Mr. Alexander Pope were to serve as a reminder that the shady spot out by the oak tree was where he intended to be buried, and God help him—or her—who got the notion that some flowery carved tombstone beside the very people he couldn't stand in life was better. Grandma thought it low-bred to talk of such things, meaning, the Everley family plot was bought and paid for. When he gave the watch to Mama for safekeeping, he made sure she understood it was his last will and testament. The watch has worn out, but I cry as if it's Grandpa's ticker that's stopped.

I rush to the Olivetti and quickly feed in a fresh page. Grandpa, I type. *Grandpa, Grandpa, Grandpa.*

Dobbs comes up and pesters me to tell him why I am weeping, why I am typing the same word over and over again.

Because I can no longer carry the words inside me, I tell him. "There is nobody to protect me."

He gets down on his haunches beside me. He looks so caring. "Protect you? All this—this is to protect you."

To him, this structure is a fortress; to me, it is a monster. It's not protecting me, it's digesting me. The air is acid. All you have to do is look at my skin. Cracks everywhere. It flakes off.

"And I'm here to protect you. Nothing's ever going to harm you. Ever." He reaches out to pat my shoulder. It hurts, even before he touches me.

With his head resting on his folded arms, Dobbs looks as though he's weeping. Except he isn't. He's snoring. Dobbs has never fallen asleep down here, not once. I wonder if he sleeps as soundly in his own bed as he does at this Formica table. I am about to make a study of his sleep when something hits me upside the head: This is it!

Suddenly, my heart starts racing. I start shaking. My thoughts jumble around so that I go to the counter, then to my cot, then back to the counter. Whack him first, then pack? Pack first, then whack? What's to pack? Just hurry up, and whack!

With stealth, I move to where the dishes are drying. As quietly as I can, I lift the pot. I get a good grip on the handle with both hands. I tiptoe over to his side of the table. I stand and watch him, just to make sure he's not faking. I move behind him. I raise the pot. His sleep is even and undisturbed, as though he's found his patch of peace. Mustn't think about these things. Must steady my arms. I grip the handle even tighter. It has to be done in one blow. There won't be a second chance.

Unarmed, asleep, dreaming of angels, perhaps.

Do it!

Are they robbers when they sleep, or do they become again the innocent?

Whack him, for pity's sake!

Perhaps I should find another weapon. One of those scarves he expects me to wear. Maybe it would be easier if I just tied it around his neck real tight.

The pot. Smash it down on his head! How hard can it be?

I make my arms go tense. I take a big breath. I lift the pot as high as I can reach . . .

I can't.

I consider waking him. If I could just look him in the eye.

I put the pot down. This is what I tell myself: I don't have the physical strength to knock him out cold. I'd only hurt him, and what good would that do? He'd end up winning again. Better to get the keys. I tell myself this, and myself spits back, Weak!

The latch on his key ring looks simple enough. I've watched him use it a hundred times—one small click and a slight pull downward, and the ring will fall clean away from his belt. With a rag, I kneel beside his boots at an imaginary spill. Only five inches separate my face from the keys, then only four. I slow my breathing and lift my hand, expecting to have to steady it as I did with the pot. It trembles not even slightly now. The tip of my index finger locates the little stainless steel button, while my other hand cups just beneath the cluster of keys.

His breath snags.

Dear God, don't let him wake up.

He shifts in his seat but then settles. The rhythmic pattern of his breathing starts up again.

There's no click as the keys are released. There's no jingling as my waiting hand closes around them. The only sound is that of victory, and it pounds in my ears. Freedom is clutched between my fingers.

I draw away from his belt. Easy, easy. Moving onto my haunches, I only now realize how my knees could have cracked. But luck is on my side. There is a meadow waiting for me, a brook ready for a game of chase.

I've done it! I've outsmarted him.

I straighten up. One step backward.

There's a shift in the silence. His breathing—has it changed? What is that sound?

I hesitate, trying to figure it out. And then, it's all too clear. The clack of his eyes moving.

It is over. There is nothing to do but wait and listen to his eyes move.

His arm slides out from under his head and swings across the table. His hand is cupped, waiting.

His hand is patient.

I drop the keys in it.

It closes into a fist.

His breath comes real shallow, while mine forgets even to sigh.

THE LIZARD IS back. I never see him coming. One minute the place on the wall is only an empty place on the wall, the next, it is a reminder that I am still alive. One lizard eye looking at me is all it takes for me to know I am still here. It is both a great relief and an unbearable burden.

A ladybug caught a ride down here on Dobbs's shirt once. I kept it hidden in a tin. When Dobbs was gone, I would take it out to play with it. It would just sit there after a while, not moving. I didn't know what to feed it. I tried everything, but it still died. I cried for that ladybug like I still sometimes cry for Mama. Another time it was a trail of ants that came down the wall where Dobbs sat reading in his recliner. I wish they'd come in some other way. He sprayed the entire place, top to bottom, said he couldn't be having an infestation eating up his archives.

He hasn't seen the lizard, and it's been weeks.

The lizard keeps his head still, the glassy ball of his eye fixed. I've learned moving isn't the answer—how quickly companionship can become once again an empty place on the wall. Blinking he understands. We've established our own kind of Morse code of the eyelids. I send him a series of slow, long blinks. He responds with push-ups.

What is to become of me, I blink.

Down, up, down.

Is there a way out?

Up.

It's getting hard to remember what conversation sounds like. I cannot hear my family's voices in my head anymore. If I try real hard, I can feel them. Suzie's irritation a slap; Gerhard's alto a stiff indifference; Theo's baby gibberish a tickle. Mama's words are sometimes as warm as a heavy quilt, sometimes the abrasive side of a scouring pad. Just about anything Daddy says is a cool compress. Dobbs's words have their way, mostly. Even when he is not here, I feel the hook of what he has to say, some ragged barb dragging itself across my softest bits.

Two long blinks, one short: Am I ever going to get out of here? Am I ever going to be free?

The lizard doesn't reply. A hard question. Not a straight up-and-down question.

He scurries off as Dobbs enters the room.

In huge ways I've forgotten about the way things used to be, but in the small ways, too. Like round chocolate cakes. The one Dobbs plunks on the table has nuts all over it. In the middle is a white candle.

"What's this?"

He laughs. "What does it look like?"

A trick, I'm tempted to say. A bribe.

He fishes out a cigarette lighter from his jeans pocket. "February second ring a bell?"

I run over to the wall calendar, alarmed. I haven't turned the page. We're still in January. Two days have slipped by my attention.

"Blow," he says, when I come back.

I let the flame dance between us.

It's my fifth birthday. We're in the backyard, where Mama has set up the card table and covered it with her pretty lace tablecloth, the one she uses only when company comes to visit. On top of it is a tray of orange slices, a bowl of hard candy, and a chocolate cake with my name spelled out in goopy pink icing. Mama has to swat Gerhard's finger from making more telltale swirls on it. Everyone gathers around the table: grandparents, Uncle Vernon and his girlfriend with the gap between her teeth, the twin cousins from Idaho who only ever play with each other.

Mama leans over to me. "Got your wish ready?" but I can't answer her because I've just sucked in a great big breath. She lights the candles, and everyone sings. I begin to panic. I suddenly can't think what I want more than anything in the whole world, and it's coming to that part, and my lungs are bursting. Finally, a wish comes and hovers just in front of my nose. I am in the process of choreographing wish and breath, when a gust of wind whips through the crowd and across the table, and snuffs out my candles.

The grown-ups all laugh, but I start to cry. Someone laughs even louder.

"Oh, now, Blythe," Daddy says, but he's on their side, trying to keep himself from laughing, too. He relights the candles, and I take another deep breath, but it's not the same this time. It is hard to find my wish, even with the wind hushed and the faces bulging with smiles. "Hurry, Punkin."

I look at Suzie. She mouths the word *goofball* and makes her eyes go squint.

"Blow, quickly!" Grandma says.

Mama leans in, the grin on her face so hard you could file your nails on it. Through her teeth, she whispers, "This is not the time for one of your hissy fits."

I make a wish. It goes like this, "Go away, all of you. I wish you'd all go away!"

I got my wish, didn't I? I did this. It's my fault.

Dobbs is getting impatient. "You want me to blow it out for you?"

"Fine." Dobbs extinguishes the candle, takes it off the cake and sucks the icing at the bottom of it. "Sometimes, there's just no making you happy, is there?"

He dishes out cake on two paper plates. He sits down, tucks his napkin into his collar, and forks a huge piece into his mouth.

"How old am I?"

He stops chewing to stare at me.

What, have I sprouted hair?

"Seventeen," he says, as though it were an accusation.

He's mistaken. I am turning into an old hag. The skin on my hands is papery, like Grandma's. A tooth has started to rot, and the pages in books are already starting to blur. I'm getting a crooked back, and my legs are so used to being folded they complain when they're upright too long. I can't be seventeen and this old, not after six and a half months in this hole.

"No cake for me." I push the plate aside.

I know that look, so I explain. "I'm allergic to almonds."

Oh God. He doesn't believe me. Knowing full well he will employ the feeding tube if he has to, I take a small bite. It doesn't satisfy him, so I take another bite.

"I brought you a present."

In front of me is a gift. It's wrapped in pearl-white paper and has a bow on it. The paper is not easy to tear. It's the expensive kind, like the ones they sell in the school fund-raiser.

"You're like my mother," he says. "She always had to save the gift wrap."

Aren't we a happy family?

"Do you like it?"

It's a mirror, an oval one in a fake gold frame. It takes me a moment to realize who the stranger in it is.

"Well? Is that a yes?"

I look like a cancer patient. I touch my scalp. It is pocked with red bumps and tiny scabs. He permits me to shave my own head, but keeps forgetting to bring a sharp razor—either that, or he doesn't trust me with one. Running across my forehead are deep lines, and my jawbone looks as though it could slice through a T-bone steak. Follow the hollows and ridges, and there are two deep green wells where eyes used to be. No water down there. I frighten myself. This is me turned witch.

"Pretty as ever," Dobbs says.

I put the mirror down.

He goes to the bathroom to prop it up on the narrow shelf. "Every lady needs a mirror. I don't know why it didn't occur to me before. I hope you'll forgive me."

"Got you something else." From a paper sack he pulls a red wig. "It's not like the other one; this one's real hair." The jet-black wig Dobbs brought me months ago, which looks like it came from a Halloween store, is still in the brown paper sack under the sink. "Go on, try it out."

"I'm not feeling very well."

"Do you need some castor oil?" For Dobbs, there isn't an ailment that castor oil won't cure.

My throat starts to constrict. My lips start tingling.

"Here, it'll make you feel better." Before I can stop him, he puts the wig on my head. I feel like I'm wearing someone else's scalp.

"Goodness! What's going on with your face?"

I can feel it swelling. My lips about ready to burst. My tongue thickens. My gums start to itch. Then, everything starts to itch—the inside of my nose, my eyes, my skin. I start gasping.

"The nuts!" he yells, jumping up. He races over to the shelf with the cubbies and pulls out the first-aid box. I don't think I've ever seen Dobbs like this. He tosses everything on the floor and finally finds what he's looking for.

The EpiPen. He jabs it in my thigh. "I'm so sorry! I should've believed you."

The effect is immediate.

He watches me closely, repeating over and over again how sorry he is. As soon as I can, I say, "I'd like to be alone, if you don't mind."

"But . . ." He's taken aback.

"I want to be alone." I look over at my cot. It has never looked quite so inviting.

He scoots his chair closer, puts his hand on my knee. "I can't leave you like this."

I push his hand away. In all the time I've been here, Dobbs has been careful about where he puts his hands. When he takes me for a walk to the entrapment vestibule or to the utility tunnel, he might fold his palm into the small of my back. If he brings me a book, he might lay his hand casually on my shoulder when I sit down and open it. But never this, such a show of affection.

"I'm really tired."

There is a freshness to the silence, a clean margin around it.

Dobbs shrugs his giving-up. "Okay, then. You'll probably fall asleep now anyway. I'll drop by before I go to work tomorrow to see how you're doing."

He leaves. For the first time since I've been brought here, I've made him do something. A tiny piece of freedom. Now, that's a birthday gift!

Instead of lying down on the bed, I go to the bathroom and pick up the mirror. Cancer girl is gone. A redheaded stranger is in her place. She fluffs her bangs, pulls a tendril of hair across her cheek.

"Hello," I greet her.

"Hello," she replies. She smiles. "I hear it's your birthday."

I nod, and she nods, like she knows all about it.

"Do you think my family remembers?"

"Oh, sure."

I talk to the lady, even though the drugs have made me quite drowsy. I think my visitor just might keep the loneliness at bay.

"Will I ever see them again?" I eventually ask her.

She tucks her hair behind her ears. For some reason, she starts trying to braid it. I am about to tell her she's going to need both hands for that when the mirror slips. It crashes to the floor. Come back! I bend down. The lady with the pretty red hair is gone. But she has left me a gift: a shard of glass in the shape of a dagger.

THERE IS ONLY one way to get out.

Dobbs has been on the lower level ever since we finished dinner. Through the gap between the floor and the outer wall, I hear him ferreting about in his filing cabinets. I stand at just the right angle by the center column and catch a glimpse of him. "Dobbs, can I come down?"

Not a minute later, Dobbs unlocks the door and leads me to the control center. He is so pleased.

It's only the second time I've been here. Upstairs, the room is open-plan except for the toilet, the supply closet, bookshelves and those two partitions, but this space is cut up into triangular little offices. We go into the first office, the one with the cabinets and the specimen jars. I remember this room being neat, but it is now a mess. Stacks of paper are strewn about. Filing cabinet drawers are too full to close, and boxes are stacked on top of one another so high they almost touch the ceiling.

"I'm looking for some papers I edited a few years back. I need to update them."

"I can help."

He studies my face for a minute. I pretend to be that nice lady from the mirror. So that he will not be suspect anything, I'm wearing a belted dress and a cardigan rather than my going-home clothes. The dagger I've made with the mirror shard and duct tape fits snug against my back.

"I didn't think you cared about preparedness."

"It's better than sitting up there by myself."

Dobbs has me look for his *Famine and Survival* tract in files categorized under the John Birch Society. When that turns up nothing, he suggests it might have been misplaced with his father's documents. I go through the drawer and spot an old black-and-white photo: a woman in an apron cooking over a propane tank and a little boy in the background holding up a toy train.

"My dad took that picture of us."

"Where are you?"

"In our bunker." He has spoken very little of his family before, but now he tells me all about States Hordin and how he came back from the Korean War with a missing leg only to realize he had a war to fight on the home front, too. I hear about the fallout shelter he built with his own two hands and how he supervised his family's evacuation drills. Rather than taking camping trips, Dobbs says they'd spend vacations in their bunker preparing for a nuclear disaster.

"I was just like you, in the beginning." Dobbs stares at the photo. "I hated being underground. We'd be playing dominoes, and all of a sudden I'd start hyperventilating. Tomfoolery is what Pa called it. Said the only cure was for me to spend some time down there by myself. He left me there a whole week. And guess what? I survived. Next time, I spent the entire summer in the shelter."

"You didn't get lonely?"

"Nope. I had all the companionship I needed in the Bible. The people in there, why, they just come to life in the dark."

He digs out a photo album and shows me a picture of a towheaded boy with freckles and a missing front tooth, holding a jar. Dobbs explains how he'd sit for hours watching those tadpoles, hoping to catch the moment they'd change into frogs. "I kept all sorts of critters. Snapping turtles, cottontails, one time a catfish that got caught upstream when the crick dried up." And now me.

I must get him to turn his back to me, get him bent over his files, distracted—quit talking about the boy. "What else do you keep in these files? Do you have any of those government pamphlets from the old days?"

Dobbs does a double take and then grins. He opens a different drawer. I slip my hand around to my back and under the sweater. I grab the dagger.

He swings around. "Would you like to see the blueprints of this place?"

My hand stays behind me. "Sure."

He rolls them out on the floor and has me crouch down next to him. "This shows the crib suspension system. To launch the missile, the hydraulic system had to deliver three thousand pounds per square inch of pressure. These are the two silo doors. Each weighs one hundred and fifty thousand pounds. If it didn't take a boatload of money, I'd see about getting them operational again."

I make all the right noises so he will keep talking. "Knees," I say, so he won't find anything suspicious about me getting into a standing position. I keep my hand behind my back, my grip tight. No hesitating this time. Straight between the shoulder blades.

"This is where I spent all my money." He points to the level I live on, to a square with a long L-shape that goes straight up to the surface. "The ventilation system. One of these days, I'm going to have to get up in that pipe and change the filter. Miserable job."

Did he just say, get in that pipe? I bend over the diagram again while he goes on about having had both the intake and exhaust vents modified because the original duct had been clogged with debris.

You can fit a person in there?

"What do you have behind your back?"

Dobbs isn't looking at the blueprints any more. He's staring at me. "Nothing."

He rises. I fumble with the dagger, try to wedge it back in the belt.

"You want something, you don't have to steal it. You only need to ask."

I can't think of what to say. I wish I had stolen something from his precious collection.

He grabs my hand. It's empty.

He swings me around, lifts up the sweater. Slowly, he slides the dagger out from the belt. "This?" He holds the dagger. "This is what you've become?"

He puts on his coat and picks up the duffel bag, which has the dagger in it. I hand him the supply list, but he doesn't take it.

"I won't be back for a while." He means to punish me, to remind me he doesn't have to come here at all if he doesn't want to. A while doesn't scare me. I've got plans of my own.

I drag the kitchen table till it stands directly below the ventilation panel. I put a chair on top of it and then climb up. Still too short. The emptied supply cabinet and the kitchen chair do the job. The ventilation panel of the duct comes off easily. I stick my head and as much as my body inside, find a place to anchor my arms, and then spring up.

I'm in!

But there isn't an inch of free space. I wedge myself farther into the duct and bang into a chilly blast of air. I worm my way forward. Only a few yards into the duct, the darkness becomes an assault. In retaliation, I crack the fluorescent stick. I've also had the presence of mind to bring the serving spoon for digging and a backup instrument in the form of a fondue fork.

The shaft is unbearably narrow. The sound of my shuffle runs ahead of me while my breath turns tail and runs the other way. I am afraid to make a noise. Dobbs might hear. What if he's had a change of heart and is on his way back here to accept my apology? But there is something else that keeps me tight-lipped. The something with its wings folded around itself, hanging upside down from the I-beams, the something that slinks around in that tunnel. Sound is sure to rouse it. I keep my fear barred behind my ribs and my breathing behind sealed lips, and inch ahead.

It is a huge relief when I come to the vertical part of the shaft. I was beginning to think I'd gotten into the wrong tube. Reaching into the space, my hand locates a rusting pipe. It's damp. I draw my fingers away, put them to my lips. Tastes like Suzie's hair spray. The vent is twice as big as the duct. It is a space big enough for two people. The only snag is that it goes straight up. No grade, no ladder, no footholds. I yank on the pipe. Unsure whether it will hold my weight, I pull myself up anyway. Three feet into this exercise, my arms about pop out of their sockets. There is only one other thing to try.

Keeping my back wedged against one wall and my feet pushed against the opposite one, I work my body upward. I shimmy and grunt, using my elbows as levers, my feet as gears, and my rear end as a stopper. What was easy at first becomes increasingly difficult.

Several feet into the exercise, the bottom disappears. I may as well be suspended in space. I look up and half expect to see stars. What I do see is just as surprising. In the darkness is a spark, a fissure of light. Is this the devil up to his old tricks? I work myself a little farther up the shaft, and the light changes from a spark to a silver vein. There is no mistaking it now: daylight. I press on.

If Dobbs comes now, it will be my absence that greets him. Will he picture me without chains, clearing farm fences, and crossing pastures? Because that's how I am picturing me. I am giddy with the thought of running free. I start to giggle. It isn't all nerves. Part of it is imagining Dobbs all alone with his papers and dead animals. A cackle sends the silence rolling up like a cartoon tongue. I keep rushing upward, toward the light, toward that punch line.

Which is farther than I thought.

Just keep laughing.

I get up where the light pours in, thick as a running faucet. Thirsty for daylight, I turn my face and open my mouth.

I am close enough for the light to cast a shadow. My shadow! How I've missed you. I get so excited, the tension in my legs lets up. I slip a little.

I push against the side till my muscles in my legs are burning. My hands are so slippery with sweat, I have to keep drying them against my pants. I keep scuttling up. My back screams in pain. And finally, I've gone as far as there is to go. I've reached the light.

I press my fingers against it. It is protected by a grate. Rising above the grate is a small aluminum canopy, something that allows for fresh air but keeps rain and dirt from entering the shaft. I bang against the grate to dislodge it and slip a little. Should my leg muscles slacken, I will fall.

"Shut up!" I tell the voices. "This *is* going to work. It's just going to take a little patience."

Years of crud and moisture have sealed the edges of the grate. Getting myself into the most bracing position possible, I have a go at them with the end of the spoon. Bits of dirt fall in my eyes. I scrape all around the edges, scrape some more and then give another whack. The grate budges not an inch. I jam the handle in the crack and try wiggling it, but the spoon bends. As for the grate——nothing.

An angle. That's what's called for. I reposition myself and give the grate a decisive thump to make it give way. Nothing.

My back might as well have a white-hot poker rammed through it. Tremors run through my legs so hard it's only a matter of time before they get to my feet and dislodge them. There's not much holding me up other than sheer determination.

I put the fondue fork to work and hack at the light. It gets even by snapping off the tip. My grip keeps slipping. I cannot give up. Another bang, and the fork slips clear out of my hand. A mocking clink comes up at me from the depths.

"Damn you!" I yell at the stupid light. I pummel the grate. "I'm not giving in!" I slam my fist against the grate and hear rather than feel the gristle in my knuckles give way. The light is not the least bit moved. I thrash some more. There is stuff dripping from my hand. I will not give the light the satisfaction. So what if it's blood? I put my mouth against the wound. Defeat has a saltiness to it.

I scream up through the holes. "Help! Somebody! Help!" How far does the sound of a scream travel?

"Help!"

AS DANGEROUS AS it is, as futile as it is, I still scale the shaft periodically. Getting down, as I discovered the first time, is still the tricky part, and so far I have fallen only once. A twisted ankle, nothing serious enough to prevent me from going up there occasionally to yell for help. Mostly, though, I wedge myself against the grate just so I can be reminded that there is still a world up there. One of these days, I won't be able to do that. Muscles need exercise, otherwise this happens: pudding. Dobbs has hauled down a piece of equipment, something with a seat and cables that are supposed to give the impression of rowing upriver. Doesn't help. Nothing helps.

No one helps.

I've lost track of the days. May, he said a little while back. I'm not doing very well with the calendar now that it's on its second round, so there's no way to know if it's actually been ten months or if he's lying. Instead of day and night, there is Lights On and Lights Out. Instead of Monday, instead of month, hour, and minute, there is only Sleep and Awake. Two seasons, I'll say that much. Despair, a packed-down bitter cold, and Memory. Memory doesn't pester me to do my exercises or read a book the way Despair does. Instead, it draws me away to some forgotten thing—the field where Daddy and I sometimes used to go for walks, say. I'll be drifting among the big bluestem, listening to the wind moving across the prairie. Wading deeper into the field, I'll suddenly get the feeling that I'm drowning, like I need to tread water to keep my head from going under. That's how it is with Memory—a two-faced, double-crossing backstabber. The stalks will start to fold over me until I can't stand it anymore. I'll have to turn around and run as fast as I can. It'll be closing in on me, the invisible thing, and I'll clear the last line of bluestem just in time. And then I'll open my eyes and look around and see the circular walls have moved in another inch. A memory like that, and I'll have to get up in that ventilation shaft and climb up to the grate just so I can gulp air.

Can't say I have much control over my thoughts. If I did, they wouldn't be all about giving in. Just so they don't always get the better of me, I have my notes to remind me. They are taped everywhere. Every cupboard, chair, pipe, door reminds me. THEY ARE COMING. YOU ARE NOT FORGOTTEN. YOU ARE THE CHILD OF HANK AND IRENE HAL-LOWELL, NOT THE PUPPET OF DOBBS HORDIN. You'd think he'd mind, the things I write, but he doesn't. He's near impossible to provoke. He says it's a creative outlet. He says he likes to read them so he knows what's going on with me. HOMEWARD BOUND is the sticker I've taped to the seat of his chair.

But what if they aren't coming? What if they think I'm dead?

I tear out a strip of paper from my notebook. After writing on it, I tape it to my chair. I AM NOT CRAZY.

Because the lizard is gone, and the lady in the mirror, too, I rehash conversations from the past. Some I finish; some I embellish; some I invent. I talk to Mercy the most. Sometimes to Arlo. I can't bear to ask him if he has another girl, so I pretend I'm still his girl. Mostly, Arlo's too busy to talk because he's out looking for me. I talk to Theo, who must be a big boy by now; to Grandpa; to Mrs. Littleton, who says there is really no excuse for not practicing piano. Anyone will do when the silence starts to hurt. It's like having someone scream in your ear, then quit. That gap, when your eardrums are still vibrating from shock—that's what it sounds like. I have to talk, just for the sake of ears. I think I'll talk to Mama today—it's been a while.

But out of nowhere steps Bernice.

One spring afternoon, when thunderheads were barreling across the plains and dumping enough water to make the rivers go on rampages, Mama found in Daddy's trouser pocket a love letter. We all knew it was a love letter because Mama anchored it to the kitchen counter with the sugar bowl and seemed not to mind the little procession that passed by and read it.

The note said: *Call. Anytime. Bernice XOXO.* At the bottom was a phone number with a little heart around it.

The fight went on for days, even though what Mama said to Daddy lasted less than a TV commercial and what Daddy said to Mama was shorter than a knock-knock joke.

"It's nothing, Irene," was how he put it.

But it wasn't nothing, because Mama couldn't pass through the kitchen without making something clatter or crash, couldn't pass by a door without testing its hinges with a good slam, couldn't do the wash without a great deal of wringing and sheet slapping. Mama's anger was like a boil that just kept getting bigger and bigger. Instead of having the good sense to let it be, Daddy kept poking at it. With shaving cream on his face, he'd walk down the hallway to deliver another of his one-line speeches. "You sure are enjoying this, Irene," he'd say. *Bang, bang, slam,* would come her answer. Or with a wrench in his hand, he'd storm through the back door. "Irene, give it up, would you please?" *Smash,* would go another pitcher.

To offer Mama our support, we kids whipped ourselves into a flurry of domesticity. Suzie ironed Daddy's forsaken shirts, Gerhard cleaned his room without being asked, and I took Theo for long walks in his stroller down the rutted country road. Our family rearranged its habits so thoroughly we were barely recognizable to one another.

Just when we thought their fight would go on forever, Daddy came home one evening and asked Mama to take a walk with him. We watched them go down the road, Mama with her arms crossed, Daddy quick-stepping to keep pace with her. When they came back a couple of hours later, Mama's arms hung somewhat stiffly at her sides. Daddy, red-eyed, kept blowing his nose and talking about his allergies acting up. We all sat down and had dinner together that night. Daddy came home early every day after that. Instead of calling each other by their first names, our parents went back to using their pet names. Eventually, Mama started rolling her eyes at Daddy's jokes, and Daddy stopped asking her permission for everything. Gerhard went back to being a slob, and Suzie stopped trying to garner sympathy at school by telling everyone our parents were getting divorced. It was meant to look as if the fight hadn't happened. But it had, and I had the note to prove it.

Maybe it was curiosity, maybe it was spite, maybe it was because spring had used itself up in just two weeks and we were headed into a long summer and that was somehow her fault, too. Whatever the reason, I unfolded the note, picked up the phone and dialed the number.

It rang. Somehow, I'd not expected that. I promptly hung up.

Seconds later, our phone rang and I jumped as though a porcupine had readied its quills. I let it ring. But the answering machine was about to click on, and Daddy's voice was about to proclaim this the Hallowell household, and who knew what that woman was apt to say?

I snatched up the receiver. "Hello."

"Hi there. You just called."

"Yes."

"Who is this?"

Dreadful at lying, I sputtered. "Suzie." I thought it might be a good time to hang up. There had to be a thousand Suzies in Douglas County, any number of whom could have dialed the wrong number, but she said, "Hank know you're calling me, Suzie?"

"No."

"Well, then. What's on your mind?"

I should have given her what for. I should have explained how thin Mama had become, how cautious she'd grown in her moods, as though she couldn't quite trust herself with anything other than lukewarm emotion.

"Suzie, you still there, hon?"

I wanted to say, "We're all different now." I wanted to say, "Happy now?"

"Are you married?" I asked instead.

"That's awful personal."

I almost apologized but remembered I was Suzie now, not Blythe. "You might have thought of that before you took up with my daddy."

After a long pause, she said, "I was married once, a long time ago."

"Do you have any children?"

"I do. I have a boy."

"How old is he?"

"Come the twenty-second, he'll be three months."

I felt my legs go numb.

"Suzie, honey, he ain't your daddy's."

So strong was the relief that I started to cry.

"Oh, now, honey, it's all right."

I tried to stop, but it just kept coming. I cried for Mama and Daddy and all us kids, even Bernice's baby growing up without a father, for how he, too, would have to go through the wringer and come out the other side flat as a pancake and be expected to get up and take on living some more.

Eventually, I settled down. "What's your son's name?"

"Elijah."

"Like the prophet?"

"Like the prophet. I suppose you might say this boy's going to keep me on the straight and narrow."

Must be nice, I thought, having your own prophet to keep you headed in the right direction.

She said, "You aren't Hank's oldest girl, are you?"

"No, ma'am."

"Blythe, then."

"Yes."

"Well, Blythe, before I let you go, I want you to know you kids is all he ever talked about. And that's *all* we ever did. Talk." To my recollection, that's where the conversation ended.

Somehow, her voice finds its way underground, and the conversation picks up where we left off so long ago. Now, Bernice says to me, "You've got your head screwed on straight. You're a deep one, a thinker. It's going to serve you well one of these days."

"Has my dad forgotten about me?" I ask her.

My eardrums start vibrating again.

She takes her time in replying. "Sometimes it feels like the end of the world, what we go through. But it's not. I promise you that. I'm not saying there ain't going to be storms. I'm saying you got to look for the rainbows. If you don't find any, you got to make your own." And then, Bernice is gone.

I look around. There is so little color down here. Everything is muted. Even my skin is losing its pigment. I pinch myself to see if it can still muster a bruise. How am I supposed to make a rainbow?

I get an idea. I race around the room, pulling from all the food supplies and craft supplies and garments those items least faded. I arrange them in piles according to their colors. Purple balls of yarn beside red tins of spaghetti sauce, yellow rain ponchos still in their packaging beside the orange hazard cone, a dozen blue boxes of toothpaste beside green Excedrin bottles. Merging blue into violet into red is almost as reassuring as hearing another human voice. Across the floor, I blend tins, boxes, wigs, and scarves into a rainbow.

Dobbs is stumped by what's happening on the floor. Puzzlement quickly gives way to vexation—nothing rankles him more than disorder. "What's all this about?"

"You keep saying this place is the Ark. Well, every ark needs a rainbow."

"Put those things back where they belong. How do you expect to find something when you need it?"

"I like it like this." I like *me* like this, is what I really mean.

"Don't test me, young lady. I'm not in the mood for one of your episodes today." He hoists the duffel bag onto the counter. Instead of packing away the groceries, I add the cans to my rainbow on the floor.

Dobbs kneels down next to me. Sometimes the smell of disinfectant on him is so strong I can't help but gag. "You heard me, I said put this all back. Before one of us trips and breaks a neck."

Defiance finds itself in cahoots with the yellow box of cornstarch. What on earth am I supposed to do with cornstarch anyway? I tear open the lid and empty out its contents. The air turns powdery white.

Dobbs grabs the box from my hand. "What has gotten into you?"

What has gotten into me is Bernice. The next package—a blue one—is flour.

"No!"

But he's too late. I give the package a vigorous shake, then make a dash for the pancake mix.

Dobbs knocks the box out of my hand. "Stop it! Stop!" he shouts, as twenty-four servings of pancakes go flying.

I reach for sugar. No reason why trapped air shouldn't taste sweet.

This time, Dobbs throws his weight at my back and I hear the soft poof of air go out of my lungs when I land. Were it water and not concrete, this would be a belly flop worthy of cheers.

He turns me over. It feels good not to breathe. I watch the white dust coat his hair. In seconds, he ages twenty years. And I must surely be an old woman, too. Perhaps old-lady breath will never figure a way back into my lungs, and I will not be robbed of dying an old woman after all.

Color seems to seep out of the irises of Dobb's eyes, muddying up the whites. He looks bilious. "Oh geez!" he says. "Breathe!"

The last time I saw Daddy was when he was parking the truck at the Horse Thieves Picnic. Good-bye, Daddy, I might have thought to say, if I hadn't been in such a big hurry to meet Arlo. I might have paused to listen to what he had to tell me. I keep giving him words. "Hey, Punkin, we love you and we miss you, and wherever you are, we'll find you." Not this time. Now, I see a shadow across Daddy's face. I wait for him to tell me to be brave, to hang in there, but nothing comes out of his mouth. My father looks me square in the face and says nothing.

"Come on, breathe!" I hear Dobbs insisting from someplace far off. He's shaking my shoulders.

Daddy's not looking at me, I realize. He's looking through me. This is why Bernice didn't answer my question. It's too late. If they were going to come for me, they would have been here by now.

My flattened lungs expand, the air rushes in. To spite Dobbs's relief, I hold my breath. He grabs my forearms and shakes me some more. Being limp, my head bangs hard against the floor.

"Why are you doing this?" he cries.

As soon as Dobbs threatens mouth-to-mouth, I try to wrestle away from him. He pins me on my back, pegs my legs down by stretching himself on me. He holds my hands above my head.

"I don't know why you got to be this way." His voice is screechy and high. "I don't like hurting you."

He's damp, always damp. Because we are exactly the same height, we are face-to-face. Only he's about three times bigger than me. I can't stand him this close. The pores of his skin are open, giving off a coppery smell, like a wet match against a strike pad.

I don't like the way his weight has shifted. I glare at him to let him know I know what's happening.

His eyes roll, one eyelid droops. He knows what's happening, too, and this time he's not going to stop himself.

My tailbone feels as though it is about to shatter. "You're hurting me!"

His gaze moves up to an area with which I am well acquainted. If you close your eyes just so and peer through your lashes, the circular wall forms the horizon on the other end of Clinton Lake. Look long enough, and a boat just might go sailing by. You can hear the voices of children, smell the sunblock on their faces. There's the other smell, too, the stench of stagnant water at the inlet. That part of the shoreline you've not explored before. You turn toward the sound coming from the underbrush. A deer, perhaps. You walk tenderly, hoping you won't startle it, because just once you want to see something rare. Instead, you pick out human sounds and you think what everyone thinks when they hear human sounds coming from a clearing in the thicket. But it is not a lovers' embrace you come upon. It is a man bending over a large flat rock, gutting a fish. The severed head is positioned in such a way that it has to watch its own slaughter.

The lake retreats, and the voices fade, and everything compresses into that one gray edge and becomes again the edge of the ceiling.

"I said, get off me!"

Dobbs lowers himself. He grinds his pelvis against mine. He starts to rock. I squeeze my legs tightly together. He knees them easily apart. He rubs himself against me. The thin polyester nightgown is no match.

"No! You've got no right!"

A cold hand shoves its way down, rips my underwear to one side.

Dobbs uses his head to push up against my chin, forcing me to look at that horizon. I feel his spit land on my chest, run down the side of my neck.

He is at the shore of the lake, and I am out deep where his hook's got caught in my resistance. I pull away. The harder I pull, the harder he yanks. I'm all thrashing. He wades into the shallows, drawing up his rod. Reeling, reeling, reeling. Everything in him is one taut line. Something gives way. He is out of breath. It takes one more mighty pull to rip me free from the current. He sputters and pants. I am his flapping, gasping catch.

Measure it, weigh it, take a picture of it for your scrapbook. Just don't throw me back so you can return tomorrow and cast your line again.

He won't look at me when he stands up. Anyone would think he's the wronged party the way he covers himself, hunches forward, hurries from the room.

I get up. I can feel color, awful color running down my legs, spreading in places I don't want to look. The floor is covered with powder except for one speck of bright red. Some rainbow.

I GET OUT the cereal and stir up some milk. I wolf it all down, then re-fill my bowl. This time, I add a dollop of strawberry jam and a dash of salt. Funny to have an appetite again, and an upside-down-and-back-to-front one, at that.

All my faiths have forsaken me, save one. Faith in my body. The fixed set of functions just goes on and on and on. Heart continues to beat; lungs expand; stomach growls; kidneys flush. And now, a new function. It took me a long time to cotton on. It wasn't the lack of a period that gave it away, it was this appetite, and even then, it took me a good many meals, not to mention a few pounds.

There are several of us Blythes down here. There's the girl from that day at the Horse Thieves Picnic, thinking she was in love. There's the one who wears herself out throwing things and overturning furniture and pounding her head against the wall. There's one who doesn't come out till it's dark. I have no clear picture of her except she snivels and whimpers a lot. And then there's this one. Fatty. All she does is eat, but not with any real enjoyment. I mark the changes. Swelled-up belly, swelled-up ankles, veins pumped up with all that blood. She's like a tick.

To keep from jumping off the top of the bookshelf belly first, this is how Fatty's convinced the rest of us to think of it: our way out.

Dobbs is still attributing my weight gain to eating too much, and he bellyaches about the cost of keeping the shelves stocked. It'll save him a lot of money, my going home. And I am going home. Because this is not part of his plan. He's showed me his plan. Procreate is in Section IX, right after Outliving Radiation Fallout. Heck, we haven't even come to Apocalypse yet.

I wash the dishes and make last-minute preparations. Instead of the bulky sweater, I find a dress that won't leave anything to the imagination.

"I said, I'm pregnant."

For a moment, I think he's going to do something creepy, like hug me, but he sits down heavily instead. "Are you sure?"

I smooth down the dress. He can see for himself that the weight gain is confined only to the waistline.

"How far along?"

"Four months, maybe five. It's started moving."

"And you didn't think to tell me before now that you're going to have a baby?"

I shrug.

"It's a baby, for crying out loud!"

I nod even though I don't think of it that way. Secret weapon is what it is.

His nose starts to run. He goes to the bathroom and shuts the door. I hear him blowing his nose. When he comes out, he picks up the duffel bag. "You tricked me."

"No, I didn't."

"You planned this."

If it would do any good to remind him of the facts, I would. After that first time, I thought he'd come back for more, but he hasn't. Only once has he even spoken of it, to make me understand that he wasn't "that kind of man." The way he put it, anyone would think it was my fault, virtually throwing myself at him. Some apology.

"Babies come early sometimes, you know. It can go bad when they do. My aunt almost died that way."

Dobbs begins pacing around the room. He keeps running his hand through his hair.

"Everything I've worked for."

I know, I know, is how I nod.

"You think this was all for me? It was for you, too." The pitch of his voice is right up there where dogs cover their ears.

When he turns to me, I rub my hand over my belly, which incenses him.

"It was all for nothing!"

Hear it? Past tense. *Was, was, was.* The word for things coming to end.

"You should have told me sooner!" When we could've done something about it, he means.

"It won't work like this," he mutters to himself. And then a few minutes later, "You've ruined everything!"

I turn slightly, giving him the side profile.

"Everything!" he screeches.

I have. I've ruined everything. I've brought him down. The tremors rock the silo. The bomb's gone off. The pipes are falling; the beams are collapsing; the plaster crumbling. It's all coming down.

TIME GOES QUICKER if you keep busy. By keeping busy, you can tackle boredom, fend off infirmities, stonewall sorrows. Keeping busy is the antidote for indecision, chaos, even insanity. To prove it, I've amassed crocheted scarves long enough to hang myself ten times over. I've filled enough notebooks with nouns to build a wall, drawn enough pictures to paper this dungeon top to bottom. Today, though, I rearrange the furniture to how I remember it being when he brought me here. I take down all my notes and pictures. I turn the wall calendar to July, the month I first came here. No matter how hard I've tried, each system for keeping track of time fails. The hash marks on the wall helped until the plaster started peeling off, and the pinto beans in the jar representing days was good until Dobbs cooked them up and ate them. It's either seventeen or eighteen months that I've been here, but it may as well be decades. It hardly matters. All that matters is today. Today will come to an end, and when it does, I will be free of this place.

I try several different outfits. I have to look my best. Imagine how Mama would feel with a beggar on her doorstep. Settling for the cornflower-blue empire-line, I rummage through the stacks for the sweater Grandma knitted so it can hide the part where the zipper won't close. I stand in front of the plastic mirror. He's let me grow my hair again. It doesn't quite touch my shoulders, and it isn't auburn anymore—more dirt-colored, except for the white streak sprung from my widow's peak. I trim my bangs as best I can with the nail clippers. I polish my teeth, then polish them some more. My face has lost its roundness, but at least I have green eyes again, not dark wells.

I set about packing. I've got to take the letters I wrote to Mama, though I doubt I'll give them to her. My notebook. The blank pages where my poems are going to be. I take the portrait of Dobbs to show the police. On second thought, I put it back. He's not going to let me leave with an Identi-Kit.

The voice says, "You think he's worried about some stupid picture?"

"Oh hush up!"

Dobbs is going to run, that's what he's going to do. He's always talking about some remote location in Mexico. He'll tie me up someplace and leave himself enough time to get across the border.

"And all this stuff?"

He'll come back for it when the fuss dies down. Or he won't. Nothing to stop him building a shelter and piling up more junk somewhere else.

"Or from finding another girl."

That's all it takes for Fatty to throw up her breakfast.

Hearing the latch, I meet Dobbs at the door, paper sack in my hand. "Hi!"

"Well, aren't you perky today?"

It's true. I am all smiles.

I follow him to the table, where he puts down the duffel bag. He looks at me flitting about him on ballerina toes.

"I think you know today's a special day."

I nod in agreement, smooth my hair. I am ready.

He gives the room a once-over. The only difference between this scene and the one from a year and a half ago is me. Me multiplied four different ways should make me a quarter of what I was, but I know it's worse than that. In percentages, I'd say I'm down to single digits.

"You've made the best of this situation, as I knew you would."

If anything, I think I've been impertinent, packing away all the little gifts he brought me.

"It hasn't always been easy on you, especially lately." He glances at my belly fleetingly. It must disgust him the way it does me. "But you've shown me what you're made of."

I am about to suggest we save the speeches for the car when I see him slip one hand behind his back. I am to be given something. I can't think of what I need when I am about to be set free. Unless. The key.

"I admit I was beginning to give up hope." He scratches the parting of his hair with a long fingernail and pulls it close to his face to examine it. "I didn't think you were ever going to see things my way. Until your—announcement—I wasn't entirely sure you felt the same way I do."

Suddenly, I don't want what is behind his back.

Dobbs drops to one knee. He holds out a small velvet box. The room starts to spin. He mouths something. I clamp my hands over my ears. I squeeze my eyes shut, but it's too late—I've read his lips—Will you marry me?

The engineers who built this monstrous steel drum and suspended it in a concrete cylinder had it all wrong. It cannot withstand impact. The entire rattletrap shakes and sways, and it is hard to believe rivets aren't exploding from the beams and flying about like bullets. Dobbs tries to help me to my feet, and all I can think is, Duck and cover!

"I don't want you to think of this as a shotgun wedding," he says, dragging me out from under the kitchen table. "I was planning to marry you in a couple months, on your eighteenth birthday, but this way we can think of it as an early Christmas present."

Birthday? Christmas? He thinks I care about these things?

"Go on, open it." He means the box, not the door.

His smile slips when I begin shaking my head. This is worse than being violated.

He takes my wrist, twists it face-up and puts the box in my palm. "Anyone would think it was going to bite."

I cannot open the box. I cannot even look at it. A squall forming up across the way, one of those late snowfalls that freezes all the daffodils barely up from their bulbs—that's what's got my attention.

He snaps open the lid and removes a ring. Something glinty catches my eye. There's nothing to do but look down. On a band of gold is a tiny winter stone, about the size of my heart. Dobbs takes out a piece of paper from his coat pocket—only now do I realize he is wearing a suit! He unfolds it, telling me he has spent hours laboring over our vows. He squeezes my hand as he reads the script.

I snatch my hand from his, and cover my ears again. His promises will have to find someplace else to land.

He offers me the piece of paper when he's done and tells me it's my turn.

I grab my little sack of belongings. "You're taking me out of here!"

He says not to worry, he will read my part for me. He does this while following me to the door.

"I can't have a baby in here! I'll die!" It's the other Blythe who has the floor now. The one who screams and kicks and throws things.

"Well, that's certainly not the reaction I was expecting," he says, once he's done with all the obey-this's and obey-that's.

She starts busting her foot on that door. I can hear toe bones cracking. He stops her from going at it with the other foot.

He unfurls her ring finger. He slides the ring on it. "There. I now pronounce us husband and wife. Mrs. Blythe Hordin, will you do me the honors?" Dobbs purses his lips, juts out that long chin, and leans toward me.

With every ounce of weight, with the power both of the forgotten and the unborn, I shove him away.

"Oh," he says, falling backward.

When I drop my hand to my side, the ring slips off my finger and bounces across the floor. He crawls to retrieve it, while I slump down, feet too broken for standing.

AFTER DOBBS SCRAPES the cold food from my plate into the trash, after he does the dishes and packs everything away, he makes up each cot with clean sheets and then pushes them together. Then he kneels at my feet and removes the dressing. My toes have set in all sorts of directions.

"Any day now."

I don't answer.

He gets up and brings me a book. "This tells you what to do to get ready for the birth. There's a big section on home delivery."

It's never going to come out. It's too big. Even if it does I shudder to think what it would look like. Two heads? It can't be anything except some twisted thing, something that belongs in one of his jars. I've asked him to put me out with the chloroform and just cut it out and sew me back up, but he says this is just the worry talking. It's not worry; it's terror.

I leaf through the pages and even the diagrams horrify me. A picture falls from the book. Dobbs hands it to me, making sure to brush his fingers against my arm. They leave a damp spot. I shiver in disgust.

"That's her, isn't it? Your friend."

It's a snapshot of Mercy with the aunt who raised her, and a little girl, maybe a year old, on Mercy's hip. They are walking out of the post office. Mercy's gained weight since I last saw her, gained a hunch around her shoulders, too.

"Who took this photo?"

"I got it for you." He watches me run my fingers over her image, and says, "Black folks look peculiar white, don't they?"

"She's not peculiar!"

Eighth grade was well into its second quarter when Mr. Landon came to the door with a new student. Sally Ludnow didn't even try to stifle her gasp, and Buddy Morris coughed in his fist, but everyone heard what he said. Freak. I thought Mercy was the most beautiful girl I'd ever seen. Rare, like an ancient map, lightened from the sun. Before sitting down at the vacant desk in front of me, Mercy gave me a searching look. Or maybe it was a testy look. Whatever it was, for the first time in a great long while, someone looked me in the eye and acknowledged my existence. Right then and there, I knew I wanted to be her friend.

The resemblance between Mercy and her child is unmistakable. "Lucky her kid didn't get it."

"I don't want you to talk about Mercy. Just leave her alone."

"I'm just saying if someone like her can do it, you've got nothing to worry about."

I remember our last conversation. She wanted to know if God ever spoke to me. Mercy went with her family twice a week to the Church of Christ Our Precious Redeemer, where folks were prone to hearing the Lord speak. I came from a long line of old-school Protestants. God didn't have heart-to-hearts with us.

I immediately suspected Mercy's question had something to do with her cousin with the green eyes, the one who couldn't keep his hands to himself. "Is this about Rowland?"

"Reverend Washington says God has a plan for each of our lives. He says we got to pray to make that plan a reality."

"Tell me you did not let that boy get into your pants."

She got real quiet, which obviously meant she had.

I start to cry. I miss her so much. And here she is, going on with her life, baby and all.

"You've got no right to take pictures of her. She doesn't belong to you. Not everyone in this world belongs to you. I don't belong to you."

Dobbs snatches back the picture and puts it in his jacket. "All you have to do is deliver it. I'll take care of the rest."

"You're going to dump your baby on someone's doorstep?"

"You just do what the book says when it comes time, and pay the rest no never mind." He sucks in his lower lip. "You ready for Married Time?"

All the many months before, and he barely touched me. I never thought of it as restraint, like with priests. I mistook it for him not being like other men, not being quite right down there. But it's wicked, what he now has. The pregnancy has brought it out in him. It's obvious the minute he walks in the door. He has his way, and five minutes later, he wants it again. Sometimes, he has me do him with my hand when he sees I can't take it anymore.

"I'm not your bride, Dobbs—I'm your prisoner."

He pretends he hasn't heard. "A wife has a duty to her husband." To make his point, he unbuckles his belt.

In the same situation, Mercy would have found a way to kill this man by now. By now, Mercy would have burrowed a tunnel straight up to the sunlight with her fingernails, and if not that, she would have dug her way to the red core of the earth and joined its fiery river.

Mercy is no coward.

Dobbs pulls me to the cot and forces me to lie on my side. When he spreads himself over me, I pretend it is a shroud covering me. I pretend Mercy is wrapping me up in her white love and laying me down. Where God's purpose for me ought to be is a blank space. To fill it, I tell myself I am Mercy's friend. I am Mercy Coleman's friend.

"I love you," Dobbs cries, quaking.

"Mercy," I whisper.

Thinking it's leniency I want, Dobbs thrusts quickly. "Hold still, it'll be over soon."

I tell Dobbs the cramps are starting up when he reaches for me again. Reluctantly, he lets me go for a walk. "I'll be reading till you get back."

Even though it's still painful to put too much weight on my buckled foot for too long, it feels good to get away from him. He's given me the run of the place now, except for the silo and the Inner Sanctum. His trust keeps coming, like an oil slick. I hobble downstairs to the tunnel connecting the control center to the silo. Dobbs has cleared out the loose electrical wiring and secured the larger tubes and conduits to the side so there is no risk of me tripping. He's put down a rubber runner, hooked up electricity to the old light fixtures, and installed a handrail.

I manage half a dozen laps back and forth till pain flares up in my foot. I don't want to go back to my cot, so I head for the stairwell, where I can sit and be quiet. Just as I am about to take a seat, I pee my pants. I watch a puddle form at my feet. Nothing much about my body surprises me these days, but wetting myself is surely a step too far. And then it dawns on me.

It's too soon. I'm not ready. Not now.

I try heading upstairs but only get as far as the first cubicle of the lower level. In the cabinet is where he keeps the medical kit. Something for the pain. I tip out everything on the floor—bandages, antiseptic ointment, iodine, dental tools, and some magical pack that's supposed to turn to ice when you bend it, as if a sports injury down here is likely. If that's not ridiculous enough, there's a neck brace, too. Finally, I find it—the prescription bottle with two codeine pills. For an emergency, Dobbs said. My belly about to rip asunder—I'd call that an emergency. I down them both with an almighty slug of cough syrup.

I'm not ready for this. I haven't even had a chance to read the book. I don't want to do this!

I double over. I feel as though I've been caught in a stampede. I'm being trampled to death.

"Dobbs!"

I get on my hands and knees and crawl to the pillar. I look up and scream for him again.

"What is it?" he yells back.

"It's coming."

Dobbs brings a bowl. Between contractions, he heats water, lays blankets and a clean sheet on the floor for me, stacks towels. I'm too scared to send him away. I watch him boil the only knife he lets me keep down here, one so dull it can't slice butter. I ask him what it's for and he says cutting the umbilical cord.

I don't want to think of Mama, because I hate what she'd have to say about this, but I can't push her from my mind. When a contraction passes, I picture her bedroom. As with almost every memory, a window is front and center. In this case, it's tall and veiled with blinds that twang when you peek through them. Buttercream light falls on Mama, who is lying in her high bed, just home from the hospital. Suzie, Gerhard, and I are huddled at the door, not too sure about this latecomer to the family. Everything about Mama is different—her hair tied in a ponytail with a bright yellow scarf instead of scraped into a bun, the airy way she waves us to her bedside, the sound of happy in her voice. Not that Mama was sad before. Folding laundry, fixing dinner, buttoning our coats—she'd do all of these things yet still leave the impression she was off someplace else. But here in bed, with a pea-pod baby tucked in her arm, it seems as though Mama's body has finally caught up with her daydreams.

Another blow. I take my position on the middle of the sheet. How the woman was illustrated in the book is how I lie. With the onslaught of pain, I am on my hands and knees, then on my haunches. To heck with the picture! By the time the contraction ends, the sheet is mussed up into a ball, the tower of towels knocked over, and the bowl of water spilled. I can't possibly go through another one of these.

"Why don't you help me?" I shout at Dobbs for the tenth time. All he does is show me how to huff and puff. How's that supposed to help?

"My mother used to say—"

"I don't want to hear what your mother had to say! Take it out!"

"Here, hold my hand. When it starts to hurt again, you give it a good ol' squeeze. Hard as you like."

"It *is* hurting!"

I get on all fours and do the rock-and-crawl thing as the next siege hits. When the pain backs off a little, I lie down and do the counting breaths. Dobbs has the book open on his lap. He says I have to wait till I count to sixty. When I reach sixty, I must be about the pushing.

I should have chosen a name for it, at the very least. It is about to be born, and I don't want the silence to have the final say again. I've got to find something symbolic—a birthmark of a name. I can only think of one thing: Freedom.

Dobbs counts for me. It's no use. The futility of everything—what's the number for that? Because I've reached it. The band tightens around my womb harder still. I get up on my haunches. Time to push!

"Freedom," I growl through clenched teeth.

It becomes a chant, "Free-dom, free-dom." Something starts to give way, something else rips.

Dobbs moves between my legs.

"Freedom, goddammit!"

And then it comes. My fingers reach down and run across the landscape more beautiful than the fields of home.

Dobbs puts the baby on the towel next to me, bends back down between my legs.

I gather that little creature.

I put her on my chest. The instant Mama placed Theo in my arms he was no longer a stranger. All the many months I'd spent wondering what my baby brother would be like, and there he was, the element we didn't realize that had kept us from being whole. At the same moment I felt both a longing and the fulfillment of that longing. Looking at this child is no different. All anyone has to do is peer into those dark, glistening eyes to feel a part of something big, of something with no edges. She lifts me clear off my feet and sets me up where the stars dazzle. Every faraway dream has taken root in this little one. And that's when I realize I don't want to be robbed again. I want to keep her, this perfect little baby.

She's so quiet. Not at all like the squalling babies on TV.

I whisper to her, "Hello, little one. Hello, Freedom." She is very pale and very still.

Dobbs is beside me, trying to start some sort of conversation. "Blythe—" he keeps repeating, until I just bark at him to hush.

"She's trying to go to sleep."

I caress her tiny head. So soft, like chamois leather.

"She's not sleeping, Blythe."

All at once, she doesn't feel right. It's as though my rib cage is about to crack open. "Shouldn't she be crying? Dobbs, you were supposed to make her cry!" And her eyes don't look right now, either, and I spread my hands over her to keep her from growing cold.

In a panic, I hand her to Dobbs and tell him to swat her bottom like he was supposed to in the first place. But instead of doing that, he cradles her and covers her with a blanket, and I think, I could do that! He's supposed to be making her breathe. He is the most impossible man!

"Give her to me!" I will do it myself. I sit up and a pain shoots up through my stomach.

Dobbs is saying something, but he's speaking too softly; I can't hear what he says. He's pulled the blanket all the way over her head. He starts walking to the door.

"Where are you going with her? Come back here!" I am on my knees, gripping the chair leg to help right myself. Why can't he just fix it?

"She's gone, Blythe."

"Bring her back here. I said, bring her back to me!"

"Freedom," I whisper when the door closes. Because she has found it. And I am robbed once again.

I FEEL AROUND for her, my fingers eager for those little folds. Emerging from sleep, I open my eyes and cast around, desperate for the sight of her. I remember she has been taken away. I lay my head back down. If there is a God, he will let me go to sleep and dream her back.

"What did you do with her?"

"I took care of everything. Don't worry. Here." He offers me a mug of lukewarm broth. "You have to get your strength up."

I put the mug aside. "You buried her someplace nice?"

With his back to me, he says, "I'm sorry it happened the way it did."

"No, you're not." She would have loved me. I saw it in her eyes. I've never felt so cut off by love, anyone's love, than I do now.

"Look, the sooner you put this behind you, the better off we'll be."

"You'll be, you mean."

Dobbs, the Taker Away of Things. Waste products, sunlight, the shape of a child.

What he brings I don't want. Today it is a cassette tape and a record player with batteries. I am violently ill when he pushes PLAY and a guitar starts strumming. I hurl it against the wall. Dobbs gathers up the parts and tries to put it back together again. He holds up the castor oil. I can barely be bothered to shake my head at him.

"You've got to snap out of this. It's been five weeks."

"Why don't you stop coming? That'll make me feel better."

He puts his hands on his hips, sighs. "I wish you wouldn't talk like that."

"I could follow her to the grave. What'll it take? A couple of weeks? A month?"

"You want another baby? Is that what you want?" He touches his belt.

Someone other than him is what I want. Anybody. Doesn't have to be my mother. Bring me any mother, a wife, anyone. Bring me Bernice, with her talk of rainbows. We could pretend for each other, and it wouldn't be so bad. We could make up new names for each other, new personalities. Ruth and Naomi. "Whither thou goest, I will go," I could tell her. She could say to me, "Your people shall be my people." She, too, will mourn for the loss of Freedom. She will cleave to my side and pledge her loyalty and cry the tears I cannot cry.

Dobbs finds the soiled sanitary pad. He acts like it's my doing, summoning a menses at will. He can't understand why, if I mope about a baby so much, I am not knocked up again. Especially given how he's gone about his business with a nose-to-the-grindstone thoroughness.

"I don't work right anymore. I keep telling you. Might as well find another girl to help you seed the New World." I get up, go to my cot, and show him the bent coat hanger I keep hidden under it. "I fixed it so I can't have another baby."

That gets his attention.

I run my finger across the tip. "So, no need to keep trying."

It's a lie, but he swallows it hook, line, and sinker.

"What good is it if you've got a woman who can't produce? Not going to be much of a New World, is it?"

He turns around. "I have to go away for a while."

So I've finally convinced him. He's going to do it this time, I can tell by the look on his face. I haven't seen him this determined since the day he brought me down here. He won't be coming back till I'm done for.

When he leaves, I pull out from under my pillow the slim volume. It is the Book of Common Prayer. I turn to the section of prayers in Latin. I begin with one of those. It is easiest to pray when I don't know what the words mean.

I've come to believe that if I can control one thing, I can be free, even if that freedom is the size of a matchstick head. I didn't have any control over my coming into the world, but I do have control of when I leave it. That is the one thing. It's almost two years since he brought me here. Long enough.

I gather every flammable thing I can find—all those hideous clothes, my notebooks, the knitting patterns, the classics off the shelf, a year's worth of paper goods, the bedding, the wig. It forms a great big pile right beneath the escape hatch that isn't an escape hatch.

Before I light the match, I present myself to the plastic mirror. My hair's long enough to braid now. It's brittle, though, and breaks easily. The same color eyes, the same small mouth, but there is nothing left of that girl. It's just a skinny cripple person looking back at me.

You don't ever think, this is the last time I'm going to kiss my mother good-bye, make it a good one. You don't think to turn back where she is standing at the Dutch door for one last look at her face. Just as you don't think to look in the mirror one last time, and say, Good-bye, dimple; good-bye, cowlick; good-bye, funny birthmark. You get in the back of your father's pickup and go for a ride and don't pay much attention to anything—not the bullfrogs croaking, or the pealing church bells announcing the official start to the Horse Thieves Picnic. It's a crying shame you don't even look up at the evening sky and wonder why night never falls in Kansas, why it comes slowly, reluctantly, dragging its tail feathers. Giant cotton spools sit in the middle of shaved pastures.

Good-bye, land, I wish I'd said. Good-bye, sunflowers. Good-bye, green; good-bye, yellow; good-bye, blushing pink clouds.

This time, I say it. "Good-bye, dimple; good-bye, cowlick; good-bye, funny birthmark."

I ask the cripple for her permission.

She is so glad someone finally does. Yes, she says.

I light the match and toss it into the pile.

III

I'S HARD TO say what it would be like if I had burned it all down, myself included, if Dobbs hadn't come back for his duffel bag. Turns out there's no escape through death, either. Still, I have been to hell and back. There's not much to show for the trip anymore, other than a bit of cellophane skin puckered in untidy heaps. Because of the shots he gives me, there's barely any pain, which is a pity; pain can be such an attentive companion.

The sooty walls are scrubbed clean, the supplies restocked; I've even been given new old clothes. There's been plenty of talk of me "learning my lesson," as if injury is a lesson. He thinks he rescued me, when the truth of the matter is that the fire rescued me from him, from needing him.

I don't need you anymore.

It's only when he spins around that I realize I am speaking aloud again. More and more the stuff inside my head and the stuff outside my head swap places. Thoughts are more real to me than concrete walls.

Dobbs is unpacking more than the usual provisions. A dozen boxes of mac and cheese, beef jerky, enough canned beans to last a year. "I'm going away again."

"Where do you keep going?"

"This is the last long trip. Before you know it, I'll be back." He turns from me. Dobbs is a hundred evil things all rolled up together, but one thing he cannot do is lie to my face.

I get up and confront him. "What's going on, Dobbs?"

"I told you." He starts chewing on the corner of his recently grown mustache. It looks ridiculous. All he needs is a pair of black plastic glasses to look like a man in a cheap disguise. "Nothing's going on. I'm taking a business trip."

"You're lying."

He gives me a tube of ointment that's supposed to help with the burn scars. "Use it twice a day."

"Are you going on vacation?"

"No."

"Then what?"

Dobbs finishes his task and then looks like he's going to embrace me. I step back.

"Good-bye, Blythe."

The second he leaves, I realize what it is. I rush up to the door as he's locking it. "Are you going to prepare another place for us?" I yell.

I turn around and hug myself. He is. He's going to take me above. I don't care where he takes me. Sunlight. Wind. Air. Faces.

For the first time, a dream with no pictures, just sounds. Only one sound, actually—the sound of a very small child crying.

I try reaching for him. He keeps crying, and my eyes keep staring into the dumb darkness. I want the crying to go on, because it is at least a voice, one that isn't mine.

Then, another voice, the one I know only too well. "Shut up, already."

The light snaps on. I am still in the same cell. The same captor has returned only to take up the bulk of the space with his bloated enthusiasm. Wedged between us, impossibly, is a curly-haired boy. Has he climbed out of my dream, out of my head, into this room? Snot is running into his mouth. He's been crying for a long time.

"Mama." He wails at the ceiling.

"Hey, little guy." My voice only makes him cry louder.

It makes no sense. If it weren't for the fact that Dobbs clearly sees and hears the child, I'd chalk this up to another hallucination. All manner of specters have appeared to me lately.

"What's going on?" I ask Dobbs, and am given that you-got-eyes face.

"Little boy?" The child rolls into a ball the moment I make a move toward him. Pill-bug boy.

I glare at Dobbs, who pats his hair back in place. He smiles, frowns, then shrugs, running through an inventory of expressions. But what is the right one for this, whatever this is?

"Who is he? A relative?" Dobbs doesn't have siblings.

"He's a kid, what's it look like?"

"What's he doing here?"

"Don't you start now," he says. "Bad enough having to put up with his bawling for two hours." Dobbs peels off his wet jacket.

The boy is soaked, too. For a moment, I am distracted by the presence of rain.

"See if you can get him to stop blubbering."

As soon as I move toward the child, his shivers turn to full-scale quakes. It occurs to me how frightening I must look to him.

"He's not going to listen to me. He wants his mama."

"Let's get some water on the boil." When Dobbs comes back downstairs, it's with a gas tank. He connects it to the burners. Apparently, I'm to be trusted with a flame again.

"What have you gone and done, Dobbs?"

"It's always the grand inquisition with you, isn't it? How about, 'Nice to see you after such a long time, Dobbs. How was your trip?'"

I rub my eyes. I am quite certain now that I am awake.

"Are you going to make him something to drink or not?"

I crawl closer to the boy to see if I can get him to unfurl a little. "Hello?"

"I want my mama."

"Well, your mama's not here!"

"Don't yell at him!" My hand pets the air above the boy's head. "It's okay, it's okay." Even without being touched, he cringes.

I start heaving. With my hands on my knees, I tell myself to slow down, breathe. We're going to figure this out. Something dry first. "He needs to get out of these wet clothes."

Dobbs tosses me a red backpack. It has a picture of a cartoon car on the front of it. "I've got the other stuff in the car. I'll get it in a minute."

In the backpack is a brown sweater, a pair of Pull-Ups, and Goofy. I hand the boy the stuffed toy. "Here's your friend. Why don't you hang on to him, while I help you get on this nice warm sweater."

A tiny hand snatches the toy and it disappears into the folds of a toddler. The crying dies down, but not the tremors. He lets me pull off his jacket but refuses the sweater. I drape a quilt over his shoulders.

I storm Dobbs. "Who is he?"

"You should probably make him something to eat. Maybe all that yowling is 'cause he's hungry."

"He's not going to eat, look at him. He's upset. Why have you brought him here? His family is going to get worried."

Dobbs starts pacing. "How hard is it to make the kid a sandwich, for chrissake?"

"Why won't you tell me what he's doing here?"

"Fine. I'll fix it myself." Dobbs finds a box of crackers, tears open a package. He scrapes the last of the peanut butter from the jar.

I snatch the spoon out of his hand. "Where is this child's mother, Dobbs?"

"You're his mama now! You want an explanation, there it is!"

Oh. But no.

"You didn't—You—? You couldn't have. Please, please—oh, please, tell me you did not take this boy."

Dobbs comes to a stop, and I know the answer by the way he stands: legs shoulder-width apart, arms crossed on his chest, like he's standing over a deer he's just shot, like he's thinking how nice its head is going to look mounted on the den wall.

"You take him back where he belongs! Right this minute, you take him back where you got him from!"

The boy has settled into a soft whimpering.

"I brought him for you. I'm not taking him nowhere."

"Yes, you are. Because this is wrong. This is evil."

He steps over the boy, throws his index finger in my face. "Don't you use that word around me again, you hear? I'm tired of it! You think I didn't do my homework? You think I just took a drive to Kansas City this morning and pulled up at the first preschool I came across and snatched the first kid I saw? Is that the kind of dumb-ass you take me for?"

Oh God, if he didn't do that, then it is worse than I can possibly imagine.

He points at the crumpled heap scampering to the corner, backpack clutched to his chest. The child is rail-thin, like he's not had a decent meal in months. "He's crying for his mama now, but do you know what he's got waiting at his home? A woman with a hypodermic needle in her arm and some cokehead banging away on top of her. That's what this little prince has waiting for him at home."

At this the boy starts crying all over again.

The child cowers when Dobbs walks over to him.

"No!" I rush up to Dobbs. "Don't you lay a hand on him!"

Dobbs gets down on his haunches and gestures with his thumb over his shoulder to where I stand. "You got to listen to your new mama now, like we already discussed. She's going to take care of you—real good care. But you got to do your part, be a good boy and all. You understand?"

The boy continues to stare at the floor in front of him. Thunderstorm tears plop down on his knees.

"No, Dobbs," I insist. "I won't be part of this. I won't do it. You take him back where he belongs. He's a child. He's innocent. He's done nothing to you."

The boy looks at me. He has beautiful hazel eyes and long black lashes curling up into his eyebrows. A dimple creases one cheek. He reminds me so much of Theo.

"Have you forgotten how you were moping over the other one, as though you'd never see the likes again? You've been starving yourself to death over it, telling me to lock you up and throw away the key. Made out as if your life was over, tried to kill yourself. Well, here's your second chance. You wanted a baby, you got a baby. Go to town."

I've had a baby, but that doesn't make me a mother. Mothers make the world a better place. How could I possibly make this a better place for this child?

When Dobbs comes back a few minutes later, he has a box. It's filled with clothes, a coloring book, a box of crayons, and a bottle of medicine. "That's supposed to make them go to sleep. Get some down his gullet, and he'll feel much better when he wakes up." Dobbs walks to the door. I grab hold of his shirt. When he turns around, I do what I have not done for myself in a long time: I beg.

"Get off your knees, for pity's sake! You're making a fool of yourself."

"Please, Dobbs. Please. Let this boy go. I'll never mention the baby again. Ever. I'll eat. I'll do whatever you want. Whatever you say, I'll do it. Please, please, please just take him back to where you found him."

He frees himself from my grip. "I'm this kid's last hope. He was a goner in that pigsty. Even if the state stepped in, it would have only made matters worse for him. I know people who'd sooner die than get dragged through the foster system. And what do you think his chances are when the End comes? Who is going to look out for a runt nobody wants in the first place?"

I care not one bit for his use of that word, but when I look again at the child, there is no mistaking just how sickly he appears. He's got the look of those boys they use in commercials for relief funds. Just thinking of myself as an aid worker has me shaking my head. "He needs his family," I insist.

"You're not hearing me. The End is not some far-off date; it's right around the corner. He's receiving a double blessing, and you'd just as soon turn him out to fend for himself?"

I mention again his mother, but Dobbs cuts me off. "He's young. Not long from now, he won't remember any of this. He'll only know you as his mama."

Among the scramble of lies are words he cannot possibly believe, but I offer them anyway. "I only want you, Dobbs. That's all I want. Me and you. Like you said, remember? The last couple on earth? Please."

With his head half-cocked, he looks as if he's measuring this, to see if it will hold water.

I have to get the level just right. "I made you do this. I see that now. This is my fault. And I'm so sorry I forced you to do this. I should be punished. You take him home and come back here and punish me."

Too much.

Dobbs sneers at me, gathers his jacket, and heads for the door.

"What are you doing? Where are you going?"

"I'll see you tomorrow."

"You can't leave him here!"

Dobbs slams the door on my protests. The lock clicks over. A few seconds later there is a sound the boy probably can't hear, yet—the second door. There will be a third, and its sound is left only to the ear of the imagination.

The child will not return my look. He fiddles with the zipper of his backpack. Sniffling, he seems a little calmer now that Dobbs is gone.

I sit on the floor across from him, a few yards away. It doesn't take nearly as long as I would have guessed for his gaze to wander over to me. For a few deep breaths, he keeps his gaze at my lap, and then, in one quick leap, it bounds up to my face.

I can't believe what I see. Boy.

"YOU AREN'T GOING to be here long. Okay? He'll come back in a little while and I'm going to talk to him some more, and he'll take you back to your mommy. Okay?"

It's been so long since I've talked to anybody other than Dobbs that my mouth can't seem to stay shut. The boy may or may not be listening. All manner of promises tumble out of me from who knows where, like I'm one of those underground springs, gurgling nonstop.

I ask him what his name is, but he won't tell me.

"How old are you?"

He holds up three fingers, looks at them, and then sticks up another one.

"You're a big boy. Are you hungry? I'm sure you must be starving by now. I know I am." Who knew a bag of bones could be this ravenous? I go to the kitchen and start holding up items. "How about some crackers? They're good for settling your stomach." I take a mouthful of them. "You want some cookies? These aren't too stale. No? That's okay. How about some macaroni and cheese? Do you like beans? These are kidney beans. I prefer pinto, but he always gets the two mixed up and brings me the wrong ones."

To every box and can of food I hold up, the boy shakes his head. I take this is as progress.

"Something to drink, then? Let me mix up some Kool-Aid. It's strawberry-cherry flavor. No? Well, I've never really liked that flavor, either. Let's see. You ever tried powdered milk? Look, it's magic. See here: You put a little of these granules in some water and give it a stir. . . . Bingo! I've got a little bit of Nesquik left over. You like chocolate milk shakes?"

The glass I hand him might as well be filled with dirty dishwater.

The boy takes it and puts it on the floor next to him, mouths his thank-you. Polite little kid.

I rummage through some of the boxes I haven't bothered to open in ages. Perhaps if I keep this up, he will be distracted from the fact that there are no windows. In one of the old cereal boxes is a puzzle. It is of a tractor in a wheat field, with big round hay bales in the foreground.

"I know! Let's make a puzzle."

He looks over at the picture on the back of the box, and his eyes, just for a moment, flash interest.

"You like tractors? I like tractors. My grandfather has one, except his is green. He taught me how to drive one. Have you ever been on a tractor?"

The boy shakes his head.

"Well, don't worry, there's plenty of time for that. When you go home, you have your mama take you to the county fair in the summer. They have tractor rides. You can also go feed the hogs, and usually there are baby piglets they'll let you hold. They're my favorite."

I sprinkle puzzle pieces on the table, then sit cross-legged across from him on the floor.

"If you and I are going to build a tractor together, we have to get better acquainted, don't you think? My name's Blythe. And this is where I live, and you don't need to be afraid because you're as safe as can be."

The boy's face is streaked with dirt, but there are no fresh tears.

"Now, can you tell me your name?"

He nods but says nothing.

"Okay, when you're ready, then. You want to see about that tractor?"

He nods.

I go to the table, gesturing for him to follow me. Years go by before he comes over to the seat. He still keeps a tight hold on his backpack. I scoot his chair up to the table. It barely comes to his nose. I stack two pillows under him. Every act makes me think of Theo. It's about all I can do not to take him in my arms and smother him with kisses.

"There, now. The only thing we need is our milk shakes." I slide his glass over to him and take a big glug from mine to show him how it's done. He takes a sip of his, and after thinking it over, finishes the rest all in one go.

"Well, all right then."

We turn all the pieces faceup. "Want that cookie now?"

He nods.

I bring over the bag and open it. "It's a big tractor; we're going to need plenty of energy if we're going to get the job done today."

He nibbles the first one hesitantly, but the next five go down the hatch without touching sides.

"How about I look for all the edge pieces and you hunt for the ones with red in them."

Before long, he puts his backpack on the floor at his feet.

"Oh, good eye—you found the steering wheel. That one's always the hardest to find."

He looks at me, smiles.

"I had no idea I was on a team with a champion puzzle builder. You neglected to tell me that."

The corners of his mouth fall, like he's made a mistake.

Quickly, I reassure him. "Ah, but I didn't tell you something, either. When it comes to puzzles, I have magical powers."

His smile returns, this time head-on. It's like looking into head-lamps. "No, you don't," he says.

Oh, what a sound. Even with a voice crackled from crying, this must surely be what God heard when the clay throat first spoke.

"Sure I do."

He leans on one elbow, like I am now supposed to pull a coin from his ear.

"My powers only work when no one is looking."

He laughs, and a meadow springs up around us. "You can't do magic."

"You just wait, young man. Come on, let's see about this tractor of yours."

After he has grouped a dozen red pieces together, he cannot keep his eyes from closing. Where his forehead meets the table, sleep draws over. For a long time, I watch him, listen to him sleep, listen to the air being shared among us. What miracle is this before me? What magic have I conjured? What awful terror?

Carrying the weight of the world, that's what I feel like I'm doing when I lift the boy up in my arms. I lay him on my cot and cover him with the quilt, and then force myself back to the kitchen seat so I won't be tempted to pick him up and hold him some more.

HE'S ASLEEP, AND then he's awake. There's no in-between. His eyes pop open and in them are several shades of expectation. He sits up, looks about the room, sees me, and a fog rolls in.

I snap with purpose. "Rise and shine, young man, and see what magic I did while you were sleeping."

Reluctantly, he comes to the table. "That's not magic." He runs his hands over the puzzle. The fingers come to rest in the gap I have left for him.

"It's not?" I pretend to be disappointed.

"No."

"Well, what is magic, then?"

"It's when you make something come out of the air."

Like you, I do not say. You, my magical little friend.

"Oh." I tap my finger against my cheek. "You mean, like this?" I tweak his ear and the missing puzzle piece is tucked between my fingers.

That does it. "Again!" He claps. Theo loved this trick, too.

"Go ahead, finish the puzzle so we can see what it looks like."

He is very pleased with himself. For a while we admire the finished product. Before the idea of wide-open fields occurs to him, I say, "Right. Breakfast."

"Is it morning?" He looks around for a window.

"Sure is. How about some cereal? Cheerios?"

"Okay."

I fish out a couple of plastic bowls and start mixing up some milk.

"Miss Blythe?"

"Yes?"

"Am I going home after breakfast?"

It is too early for such a question, and my answer too late in coming. "We'll see."

He looks down at his lap, while I stir and stir.

It's almost like being home, Mama leaving the job of tending Theo to me. After breakfast, I have him help me fill a basin of water. "First, we'll wash ourselves, and then we'll let the dishes have a turn." I give him a demonstration, wiping my face with the cloth. "Under the armpits, too." I thread the face cloth through the top of my shirt and hold up one arm, then the other. I rinse the cloth, wring it out, and hand it to him.

He takes it and hesitates.

"How about you just give the old mug a wipe for now, and we'll call it good."

He is still reluctant to move, so I offer to do it for him. He lets me.

"Oh, yes. Much better."

"What about teeth?"

"Teeth. Of course. Can't forget about them." I fish around in the supply basket for an extra toothbrush but come up empty. I take the tube of toothpaste. "You ever been camping?"

He shakes his head.

I give him a brief description involving tents, fishing poles, and campfires. "You've got to think of this as a campout. Okay? And when you go camping and you forget your toothbrush, you know what you use?"

Again, he shakes his head.

"Voilà." I hold up an index finger and promptly stick a dollop of paste on it. "Come on, show me your toothbrush."

He holds up his finger. Clearly, he is concerned about the state of my mental health.

I pretend to inspect it. "Not bad." On goes a bead of toothpaste.

He completes his task earnestly.

For a while, I show him how to tie different knots with his shoelaces. After each try, he ends up with a ball of chaos, which I praise mightily. And then I think of all the games Theo used to love playing whenever we took a car trip: I Spy, Guess What I Am, the Silent Game, which is a mistake because the child wins hands down and has to be coaxed into speaking again.

We spend a lot of time discussing the Hundred Acre Wood. He tells me Eeyore is his favorite character.

"But he's always so sad."

"That's because the others don't play with him. Everyone's always forgetting him."

I can't help but wonder if he's talking about himself. "Mine's Owl."

"Because he can fly?"

"Yes."

"My daddy was going to take me flying in his airplane, but he can't anymore because he died in the war and he's in heaven now."

"I'm so sorry."

"Mama says we're all headed for heaven, some are lucky and get there first."

Some headed for hell, too, if I get in any deeper with this kid. "You must miss him very much."

"I miss home."

Me, too.

"Here. It's not Winnie the Pooh, but I think you'll like it." I move to the shelves and select Kipling. After three chapters of *The Jungle Book*, he is asleep once again. We've made it through the day. When I get up, my knees creak and his eyes flutter open.

"Miss Blythe?"

"Ssh, go to sleep."

"I miss my mommy."

"I know. You're going to see her soon, real soon."

"Miss Blythe?"

"The Sleepy Man's not going to come as long as you keep talking."

"My name is Charlie."

"Well, howdy-do, Charlie. Glad to make your acquaintance."

He falls asleep during our handshake.

Stuck by myself like a chicken bone in Father Time's throat is better than this, having the boy in here with me. This is worse because I am starting to think of him as *my* boy, like he did just tumble out of my dreams. It is worse because I am going to love him. If I'm not careful, I am about to sin something terrible, loving someone else's child. I can picture Reverend Caldwell at the beechnut-wood pulpit, sweating up his favorite gray suit. One hand has a firm grip on the Bible, the other churns the air like the paddle on Mama's cake mixer. From the way his body bucks, you can't help thinking it would like to break free of its restraints and go galloping off. "It starts with coveting, brothers and sisters. It starts with desiring what you don't have, eyeing what belongs to your neighbor. The tempter snares you the minute you desire what is not rightfully yours. Desiring leads to acquiring, and acquiring leads to pride, and pride, dearly beloved, is a long and deep well the devil aims to push you down."

Often on the way home from church, Daddy would tell us not to take Reverend Caldwell's words to heart. "You have to remember the man's up to his waist in muck, day in and day out," he'd say, as though saving souls were akin to slopping hogs. Daddy would remind us: "There's goodness in the world, too. You remember that."

I look at this boy, goodness all right. I cannot go sullying it with my loving. Sullying it with sin, because he is not mine to love. It is only fooling myself to think he is mine. Madness to think I conjured him. Even though he can't get farther than a dozen yards from me, rightfully, I can claim not one inch of him.

———

Each time the boy wakes up, he seems a little less startled. It is a terrible thing, how hell is already becoming so familiar to him.

We have established a routine. Once Charlie is awake, we eat breakfast—or rather, I eat breakfast and he pushes his food around his plate. Then he helps me with the chores—making beds, washing clothes, compacting the trash. After that, we color pictures and make up stories to go with them. To keep myself from sitting and watching him when he sleeps, I think up more activities for the next time he wakes. I try to think, too, of ways to get him to eat. Dobbs says I shouldn't go making a melodrama out of every mealtime. When I tried to reason with him about how malnourished Charlie looks, he thanked me for proving his point. He expects Charlie to shake his hand one day and thank him for his kindness. For all his convincing, I still see Charlie headed downhill.

I am afraid to go to sleep. Ever since Charlie arrived, the sounds in the night have come back. I'll wake up in the dark to panting. Even if I turn on the flashlight, I can hear it: sometimes it gasps; sometimes it chokes. It doesn't help to tell myself this is just me being a crazy person. Insanity is no match for how frightened I am for this child. Until I have found a way to set this boy free, my mind will not let me rest, especially now that it has figured out how to climb out of my body. It will just sit and pant beside me, waiting for me to do something. It's easier not to go to sleep than to wake up and have it beg-beg beside me.

I can't imagine how we can keep this up much longer. Clearly, Charlie is sick. Now, maybe Dobbs is right in saying the cause of Charlie's ailments are to do with malnourishment and having an addict for a mother, but instead of getting better down here, he is getting worse. As am I. My symptoms, though, are quite the opposite of his. I cannot sleep, I cannot sit still, I am about to scream from the constant ringing in my ears. Alarm bells, is what they are. I tell Dobbs as much the moment he walks in.

"You have to take him back with you. He can't stay here anymore. Something bad's going to happen!"

Along with groceries, Dobbs has brought more clothes for the boy. "It's just a matter of adjusting, is all. He'll come around, soon as he quits being so picky about food."

"It's not that, Dobbs. You have to get him out of here."

It amazes me that Charlie sleeps through this.

"Don't be stupid. The whole county's looking for him. What do you think? I can just walk him up to the nearest police station and say, 'Here we go, Officer, I believe you're looking for this.'"

"You could take him now, while he's still sleeping. You could drop him off someplace where nobody will see. The Baptist church or the school or in the park—it wouldn't be long before someone found him."

He shakes his head at me. "And they are going to ask him, 'Son, who took you and where did he hide you?' What do you suppose the kid's answer's going to be? 'Santa Claus took me to the North Pole to meet his elves'?"

"He's four, Dobbs. He's not going to draw an Identi-Kit of you. He's not going to draw them a street map. Besides, we could fool him, we could tell him stuff to get his facts all mixed up. I've given this a lot of thought and I—"

Dobbs walks over to where the boy lies and then returns to the table where he sits down. "You say all this stuff, but I can tell you want him. It's written all over your face."

Of course I want him. Partly because I want him so much is why he must go. "He's not some pet, some hobby to occupy my time."

"You're right. He's not a pet. Which means there's a no-return policy."

We go over the issue and cover the same territory once again, until Dobbs slams his hand on the table. The boy startles but doesn't wake up.

"Look. He's here to stay. Deal with it."

Dobbs gets out his notes and doodles for a while before putting them aside and opening up his newspaper. He spends less time than usual working on *The Manifesto*. He complains he can't concentrate with me staring at him. He suggests I work on my embroidery. Knit the boy some mittens, he suggests, as though we might all go sledding in the morning. Eventually, he gives up reading and announces it's Married Time. Because my cot has Charlie in it, Dobbs orders me to sit on his lap. He tells me to quit looking at him like that. When he still can't get his equipment to cooperate, he shoves me aside and zips up his pants.

Before Dobbs leaves, he fishes from the bag several boxes of toys.

He walks toward the door. I stop him.

"I'm not well," I tell him.

He tries shaking off my grip. "Get some sleep. Want me to set the timer so the lights come on later?"

"I'm trying to tell you something. My head—it's not working right. I've started hearing those voices again."

"You're fine," he says. "You've never looked happier."

He doesn't give me a chance to say it's an act; it's magic. It's not real.

The boy wakes up to a remote control car. He looks over at me without touching it. "Can I go home now?"

The toys don't help. You can't call what Charlie and I do with them play. We treat them delicately. We watch them. We watch them like they might hatch.

When Charlie is awake, I smile constantly. Pop-Tart smiles, fresh and ready in seconds. When he sleeps, I make sure to cry softly. I wonder if this is what motherhood is. My mother cried only one time that I can remember. When her best friend, Livvy, was killed by a drunk driver. It was the most disturbing thing I'd ever witnessed. In place of my mother—my calm, reasonable mother—was some sort of wild animal. It didn't help to stand in front of her saying, "Mama? Ma?" I was too afraid to touch her. Afraid she might suddenly whip around and bite me, like Daddy rescuing that German shepherd and getting a bloodied hand for his troubles.

Fall had come early that year. Beginning in the trees, the season had a way of bronzing everything. The forest resembled a rusty junkyard, and the sun, too weak to climb the sky, set long shadows on the ground like oil stains. Not long into our walk, Daddy and I came upon the stray. It kept yanking its back leg, which was mangled in steel jaws. Worrying at the chain had made its gums bloody. We got close enough to see how it had about chewed off its leg, but it still had the cheek to give us a big show of teeth.

After Daddy used a stick to release the trap, he reached out to pick up the dog and got bit awful bad. Still, he wrapped the dog in his windbreaker and carried it home and explained that trapped animals couldn't be blamed for the hurt they caused.

Doc Caul came by to look at it on his way home. He said the dog had been on the road a long time before it got itself snared. He inspected the leg and said the dog had to be put down.

"Can't you amputate?" Daddy asked.

"We can try that. Odds aren't in its favor, though. What say you we put this guy out of his misery?"

Daddy was quiet for a long time. Under my breath, I prayed the words over to him. Daddy was going to say, "Appreciate your advice, Doc, but if it's all the same, I think we'll go ahead and see about those odds."

In the end, Daddy didn't say anything.

It seemed cruel to have gotten that poor dog's hopes up only to have them dashed once and for all. I was the one to beg the vet to spare the dog. He patted my arm. "Sometimes you got to be cruel to be kind."

I can't get his words out of my head. I can't help but look at this darling boy and see him bound up in a trap. Cruel to be kind. Cruel to be kind. You have to be cruel to be kind.

———

Each time Dobbs comes and goes and does not take the boy, boulders roll down my gut a little farther. Soon, my intestines will have enough rocks to build a dam. Maybe it won't be such a bad thing. Maybe it'll stop the sick from coming up all the time, stop all these bad memories and tangled thoughts from floating up to the surface. Heaven only knows how it is possible that when I speak to the boy out of my mouth comes light and hope. Catch the drift and fly up beyond the ceiling past the earthworms is my tone of voice. Hot air.

It's lack of sleep or too little food or too much worry that's causing everything to get muddled in my head. If only there were a way to take off my head and put it on the shelf, I'd do better. I'd do better without eyes, eyes that mark a child wasting away before me. I'd do better if I didn't have a pitchfork smile goading him all the time. If my mouth were up where the books are kept, it wouldn't keep putting two sentences together that make absolutely no sense. My ears, next to the coffee mugs, wouldn't keep eavesdropping on his thoughts about how afraid he has become of me. We could sit across from each other, headless me and vanishing boy, and draw pictures of bunnies and trucks and things from the lost world.

Everything about him used to remind me of the good things about home, but now I only remember the bad things: a dead dog, a missing kitten.

When No-Good Cat was getting ready to deliver her kittens in Grandpa's barn, Daddy drove me over to see them being born. Grandpa and I sat with her as she labored. One tiny pink pellet came out, and then another, and between births the cat licked and cleaned her babies. By suppertime, she'd delivered six. After dinner, I ran back to the barn with a flashlight. This time, I counted only five. I looked behind the cat and under her tail, and still came up one short. I ran in to tell the grown-ups. Grandpa came out to look. He said, "Yup, there's five all right." And then he told me the most hideous thing.

"That mama cat has gone and ate it."

I was appalled. She'd always seemed like a good cat.

"It's nature's way. A mama knows if any of her youngins ain't right. She spared it a life of suffering."

Spared it a life of suffering. Cruel to be kind.

I have to help the boy. Have to quit him, too. I just have to figure out how. If there were a way to get him out of here and back into my head. He came from my head, didn't he? I dreamed him up. All of this is my doing. Undoing is what I must now be about. It isn't cruel to undo him. It's kind.

Whereas before Charlie made some attempt at eating, he now refuses everything. Already the bones are poking out of his sheet-white skin. He won't talk about anything anymore, not even the good things. Not his favorite TV shows, not about Eeyore or even his grandma, who always has a penny for him to toss in her fountain, even though it doesn't have any water in it. No longer does he mention his preschool teacher and her puppet, Gloria, with the yellow yarn hair. He has never talked about his mama, and there are times when I think she doesn't really exist. I have to remind myself that I don't tell him about my own mama. The things most precious we keep to ourselves.

Everything about the boy seems rolled up in a great big ache, an ache so bad he can't complain about it. He's given up asking when he can go home, and I no longer have to find different ways of saying, Soon. What little trust he had in me has eroded over the past few weeks. He knows I mean to say, Never. If I can tell a lie that big, why bother listening to all the other little lies?

"He's fading away," I tell Dobbs, hoping Charlie isn't just pretending to be asleep.

"He's doing fine. Not crying like he used to, that's for sure."

"Look at him. Does that look to you like a child who is doing fine?" Even buried under a quilt, you can smell death coming off him.

"You sure you're feeding him enough? Kids need to eat every couple of hours."

"Strap him down and shove it down his throat, you mean?"

"I've never seen you like this. You're being hysterical."

The boy wakes up when Dobbs, cussing a blue streak, struggles to free my hands from around his throat.

"Miss Blythe?"

"It's okay, sweet boy, everything's fine. Go back to sleep." But I keep my fingers knotted around the man's gullet, a rotten core if ever there was one.

"Are you hurting Mister?"

I drop my hands only when Charlie comes over.

Dobbs rubs his throat, gives a stage cough, and dusts the front of his shirt. "What in God's name is the *matter* with you!"

"Why were you hurting Mister?"

"I wasn't, sweetie. We're just playing a game, is all." I usher Charlie back to bed, tuck the quilt around him. I sincerely hope my face is doing what it's supposed to and not giving off that mad look again. "The Sleepy Man will be here soon."

He shakes his head. "The Sleepy Man doesn't want to come here anymore."

"Yes, he does." There it is again, that weather-vane voice. What kind of crazy storm is going on that it can't pick a direction and stick with it?

When I return to the kitchen table, Dobbs lifts his palms, as if to say, See, what did I tell you? He's fine.

Each time Charlie wakes up in here, it's with more agony inside him. Used to be I couldn't tear my eyes away from him; now, I can't stand to see him suffering through the waking hours. I do such a remarkable job staring at the spot on the kitchen table, and Charlie does such a remarkable job of keeping still that he does disappear. For great big chunks of time. In my head, he is strong, like before he came here. He runs in figure-eight formations, airplane arms catching the updraft and lips making propeller noises.

The only time Charlie smiles is in his sleep. He's free only when he dreams. Fact is, he's not even free when he's in my head. He shouldn't have to be in this place one more day. He shouldn't have to go through what I go through. Any mother worth her salt can see what has to be done. Has to be done. Cruel to be kind, is what Doc Caul said. Spared a life of suffering, Grandpa said.

I get the pillow slip. I've washed it by hand many times over the last few days. It smells of hand soap. I stuff my pillow in it and press it against my face. So soft.

It would be fitting to say a prayer. If only I knew how.

"Sleep, little one. I will keep watch and chase the demons away. You go on ahead and dream your big dreams and throw your pennies into the wishing well and see how they are all going to come true. No more waiting. They are all about to come true."

I hold the pillow above Charlie's face and take one last look at heaven.

IV

DOBBS IS THE one who keeps the calendar these days. He claims his timekeeping methods are accurate. I'm not so sure. Going by his records, it's been almost three and a half years since I last saw Charlie. I look at the dates and entries in this ledger, and very rarely do they make sense. I don't know what a year feels like. I know what a long time feels like, and a short time. I know they sometimes trade places regarding the exact same event, like Charlie. Charlie was sometimes a long time ago, and sometimes he was right around the corner. I wonder what it seems like for him. Dobbs says he's probably forgotten he was ever down here. I hope that's true, and I hope it's not. I don't want him to remember me—I wasn't right in my head back then—but I do want him to miss me. Perhaps at night, before he goes to sleep, he could have a yearning for a particular kind of voice, a certain hand stroking his forehead. Or perhaps he could get up in the morning and go tell his mama about a wonderful lady who visited him in his dreams.

Dobbs and I don't talk about Charlie anymore, which is just as well. He'll only remind me how it was him who spared the boy, him who'd whisked Charlie out of here, and in so doing, spared me a lifetime of guilt. Him, the hero. I like to think I wouldn't have gone through with it. I'd already been standing there half the night when Dobbs came in. But I don't know. I'll never know. Because of that, I can't quite trust myself. There are still parts of me that haven't quite made up their mind.

I flip the calendar pages back and forth. It would make no difference to me if we undid the binding and rearranged the pages and put the book back together again. July 22, the day I was taken, is six years ago. That is so long ago it almost feels like Never. May 12, three years ago, is the entry for when Dobbs moved down here. That might as well be Always. But just a few months before that, February 4, is my favorite date. Adam was born. That feels like Blink.

I didn't keep the pregnancy a secret from Dobbs as I had with the first one. Soon as I was sure, I told him. As it turned out, Adam was conceived when Charlie was with us. "I am going to have a baby, Dobbs," I told the man. And because he had missed it the first go-around, I spelled it out real clear and slow. "*I* am going to have a baby. I. Me." There was to be no "we," I told him. Adam was born, and Dobbs had to be reminded all over again when he had the ridiculous notion I name the child after him. I'd remembered Mama deciding Theodore would be a good name for my little brother, saying if you couldn't pick your child's destiny, putting your faith in him by naming him after a great president wasn't a bad bet. I'd remembered Daddy's lady-friend, Bernice, and the baby she named Elijah, hoping her boy would lead her to great things. "His name will be Adam," I told Dobbs. He gave his approval, saying it was a fitting name, given that he had been formed in the earth, so I had to set him straight on that, too. It was breath that was to define my son, not soil. And I am right. The boy carries within him a breeze, the breath of God. His first breath knocked down concrete walls and let in wide-open spaces. Turns out that breath has also knocked down the barriers I put up, barriers to keep an emotional distance between him and Dobbs. Adam now understands that Dobbs is his father, not merely the Person Who Brings Food, but he still calls him what he was first taught: Mister.

"What are you doing, Mommy?"

My little boy has cat paws. "Oh, Adam! You scared me!"

He giggles. He always finds it funny when I get a fright, so sneaking up on me is his favorite thing to do.

I close the book and put it up high on the shelf. "Why are you down here? You're supposed to be asleep." Adam sleeps upstairs, in a space next to my bed that Dobbs has defined using shower curtains. Adam knows he is not allowed to use the stairs without someone helping him, even though he is three and insists that he is a big boy now.

He holds up his fingers. Between them is a brown tooth. He grins and then sticks his tongue in the bloody gap in his gum.

"Sweetheart! That's great!" Too early for teeth to be coming out. This one I have been trying to save with much brushing, but to no avail.

"I talk funny now: Thimon thayth touch your toeth."

"Come on, let's go wrap it up and put it under your pillow." I lead him out of the Vault. Dobbs doesn't like him coming in here, not since he went through the drawers and found the seed packets. Half of Dobbs's stock got spread out all over the floor. If that garden ever gets planted, we're going to have cucumbers come up with petunias. I don't like Adam to come down, either. Stairs scare the heck out of me. We've tried a gate, but the child always figures out how to dismantle the lock.

Adam insists I let go of his hand when we come to the stairs. He walks like a puppet with strings that aren't always coordinated. He makes it to the upper level without my help and grins again. Another milestone.

I tuck him in and kiss him good night for a second time.

"How much money will the Tooth Fairy bring?" He slides his hand under his pillow, making sure the tooth is situated just right.

Bottle caps are what we use for coins, but for Adam they're as valuable as Dobbs's cache of Krugerrands. "We'll have to see. Now, sleep, or she won't come at all."

"One story. Please?"

I sigh. "The turtle?" The old standby.

He nods.

I tell him the world has been taken for a ride into a cave on the back of a giant turtle. Everyone has gone into hibernation, which means to live indoors and get stronger. One day the sun will come out, and all the children will run into the garden of plenty. The end.

"Good night now." I slip the sleeping mask over his eyes and give him a peck on the cheek.

I tell Adam stories, and the fourteen-foot ceiling rises up, heaven lowers itself a hundred feet underground, the stars are coaxed from their impossible heights to dust his head. I speak, and the walls fold back so he can roam the prairie. It doesn't take but a few words for my son to be lying on a raft in the middle of an enormous silver ocean. Facts can't do that. The gospel truth isn't going to fuel his sense of wonder. Ever since he first opened his eyes, he finds everything wonderful—shoelaces, spit bubbles, toilet rolls, keyholes. At what point am I supposed to set him straight with words like *prison*? If I point to his father and say, "Warden," what good will this do? Before he was born, I spent sleepless nights worrying about what I would teach him about why we were here. I considered a plague, an emperor king calling for the slaughter of infant boys, an alien invasion, another ice age, war, anything that would make our circumstances down here be about choice, not captivity. Dobbs moving below three years ago and subjecting us to long-winded survivalist sermons convinced me that his clichéd nuclear disaster scenario was as good as any. Adam is being brought up to believe he is a treasure guarded by a mother of mulish good cheer and a charitable, if testy, provider. Someday, he will know the truth, but for now my job is to elaborate on the myth, to find a way to fight gum disease and to keep the Tooth Fairy from getting flush on my boy's teeth.

I fish out some old bottle caps and trade them for Adam's tooth.

Dobbs is out of breath when he comes back from his latest foray above. In a state, actually. He is gesturing and jabbering and doesn't make a lick of sense. Adam is having a nap on his pallet, so I tell Dobbs to hush. I think he's gone to his study to calm down, but he dashes back upstairs, this time with his shotgun. He grabs my hand and leads me through the door, up eight stairs, past the first blast door, which he now keeps open so we can have access to the corridor for exercise, and to the second blast door. He tucks his long, greasy hair behind his ears and shoves his ear against the door. I am beckoned to do the same.

"You hear anything?"

There's a yard of solid steel between us, beyond that the L-shaped corridor and a fifty-foot stairwell. What's there to hear? "Not a thing."

He is beside himself, so much so that he punches the combination to the keypad right in front of me. It used to be that a key opened this door, but a few years ago he rigged this and the outer door with magnetic locks. Only the inner doors to the upper and lower levels need keys now. He also installed a security camera up above, which is almost always on the blink, but he will still spend ages watching the fuzzy black-and-white picture. I wish he'd unplug the darn thing because Adam's now taken up the habit, and I constantly have to pull him away for fear that he will ruin his eyes.

Four numbers. I make out the first three: five, one, zero. I hear the lock release. Dobbs leans against the door. It swings wide. He yanks me by the wrist. I don't have any idea what he intends to do. "But Adam's—"

"Come on!"

We race around corners and then up the steep flight of stairs, Dobbs taking them two at a time. You'd think a man who spent so much time underground would let himself go. Not Dobbs. He spends hours "training." He says unless the hunter wants to become the hunted, one has to stay in shape. He tries to use the same argument to get me to "bulk up," and says I'll never be fit for life aboveground if I carry on at this rate. And he's right, because the stairs have done me in.

I notice the walls are green. I'd forgotten that. I haven't been up this far since he brought me here. He has to drag me the rest of the way. Again, I am told to stick my ear against the door. Just on the other side is Kansas. Birds, tractors, cars, crop dusters—all manner of noisy things. What I hear is concrete.

"They're out there! They made it look like their van had broken down, but it was parked! It's a reconnaissance unit."

My heart starts to race. He's been pursued? They've come for me? I press my ear against the door and strain so hard I think I'm going to burst a blood vessel.

"I told you they'd try this!"

I can't hear anything. "Who's out there, Dobbs?" I then wonder what the heck is wrong with me, and start to bang against the door. *"Hello, hello, help!"*

Dobbs yanks me away from the door. "Are you crazy? Are you out of your mind?" He all but throws me down the stairs. I try scrambling up them again, and he twists my arm so hard I think it's going to break. "Those are Scalpers out there. You have any idea what they'd do if they got in here? What they'd do to you? To Adam?"

On our way back to the living room, he locks all the inner doors. He goes on and on about the End of the World. I'm surprised Adam doesn't wake up. There's probably a fancy term for the way Dobbs has turned out. *Crazy*'s my word for it, and I consider myself an expert. Moody, jumpy, afraid to go sleep. Half the time he won't eat what I prepare because he's afraid I'll poison him, even though he's confiscated anything that could be used to that effect. We don't even have bleach down here anymore, which goes to show how far he's slipped. Ever since Adam was born he's been like this. If he's not running around with his gas mask on or doing bench presses and sit-ups, he's holed up with his seed catalogs and his preparedness tracts. Adam and I can go for ages without seeing him. Even when he does come out of his study and joins us for a meal, he'll be off someplace else. He'll look up with a mouthful of food, totally startled to see us sitting in front of him. He'll start talking that gibberish again about the Last Days being in effect and how we're about to be the last known survivors, and that's usually when I put my foot down and tell him enough's enough.

When Dobbs is this upset, it can take ages for him to wear himself out. There's only one thing that will shut him up. So that Adam will not wake up to a raving lunatic, I fetch *The Manifesto*. I've typed it and retyped it so many times I could recite it front to back. I settle Dobbs in his recliner with hot cider, take my seat across from him, and start to read to him.

By now, I realize the police are not going to break down the door. If they were not figments of his imagination, the Scalpers must have been teenagers wanting to vandalize private property. Still, Dobbs is agitated by the event. He has me come down to the lower level. Before I do, I check on Adam. He is napping again. He sleeps a lot lately. I hope he is not getting sick. Dobbs says this is another good reason why we're still here. People are Carriers of the Plague.

Everything on the lower level is much the same, only more cluttered. Instead of going into the Vault, we go the other way around, to the Weapons Room. He unlocks the door, opens up the gun safe, and gets out the .38 revolver and a fistful of ammunition.

"It's time you learned a thing or two about self-defense."

We tromp down to the utility tunnel, where he has pushed an old mattress up against the blast door of the silo. With masking tape, he has made an outline of a person.

"Head shots," he says. "You never want to think you can scare them off by injuring them."

The gun is cold and heavy, and it makes my hand shake.

Dobbs insists this is no time for being weak. He orders me to raise the gun at the target.

"Just think about how you are trying to protect your home."

I don't say, "This is not my home," because with a three-year-old boy, I have been trying so hard to make it home. If I can make it home, my son will not grow up a refugee.

I raise the gun. I steady my arm for the recoil, like he says.

And then I fire.

A deafening bang. My ears ring. I open my eyes.

"Bull's-eye!" shouts Dobbs.

Sure enough, there's a hole where a nose ought to be.

"Do it again!"

As commanded, I fire. Bits of yellow stuffing explode from a bullet hole. I try again. I notice that the trick is to fire between heartbeats. I shoot and shoot, and the mattress gets torn up.

Dobbs reloads. I tell him I've had enough, but he won't have it. All of a sudden he is repositioning the mattress, and I am holding the gun.

The blood drains from his face when he turns to me. We both hear the bullet drop into the chamber.

Every muscle in my body contracts into a supportive position around my forefinger. It is steady with purpose. It is being goaded by a single nerve sending a single message, Fire.

Shoot the bastard.

I hear a cry behind me.

"Mommy." The racket has woken up Adam.

I don't turn around. I know he's at the top of the stairs. I know that with or without my permission, he's going to use those wobbly legs to come down. "Stay where you are, sweetheart."

Dobbs's expression has changed. "Head shots only, like I said." Smug, is what it is. He doesn't need to say it; I know. If I shoot him and he dies, Adam and I die down here with him.

I'M STILL NOT sleepy, so I decide to change the landscape again for when Adam wakes up. I rummage around in the supply closet. Tarps, egg cartons, cardboard boxes—fine for craft activities for little boys, but if I want to engage a five-year-old in make-believe, I'm going to need something a little more dramatic. Down in the tunnel is much more stuff. Even if our door wasn't locked, I still wouldn't go down there. I hate that place, ever since the day with the gun. Sometimes, I wish I had shot Dobbs, shot him at the very least in the kneecap, made it so that his every waking moment would be a struggle. Adam would see the damage, might understand later when I tell him about the damage inside the man. Instead, I pretend. I pretend Dobbs is keeping us from all evil, and I pretend this isn't hell.

Behind the camping gear are the rolls of tinfoil that Dobbs is one day going to use to build solar panels. Perfect. I haul them to the kitchen. I turn the table upside down and cover the bottom with sheets of tinfoil. I wind string between the legs. An overturned kitchen chair serves as the helm. One crazy idea leads to another, and soon I have everything covered—the counters, the washstand, the sugar bowl and the coffeepot, the cutting board, which makes the most excellent shield. And still there are thirty rolls of tinfoil left.

I paper over the bookshelves and food shelves, and tape great long sheets across the floor and the walls. For the first time ever, there is no door. For the first time, there is no past on the other side of it, and no future, either. There is only the shiny now, in all its crinkliness. I shape a ship's wheel, a parrot, and a helmet. I leave the last roll for Adam.

The room looks like a pop-up book. Stories, what would we do without them?

When the lights come on, the room is a silver wonderland. It isn't snow on Christmas morning, it isn't looking out the window and seeing four-foot icicles dangling like wind chimes from the eaves, but it is pretty darn close to spectacular. I can tell by the way Adam gasps that he thinks so, too. The conniption fit Dobbs is going to throw when he gets back from his mission and finds his precious commodity squandered is nothing compared to the sound of Adam's surprise.

Adam can be such an old man, but today he acts exactly as a five-year-old on a snowy day is supposed to act. He twirls slowly. The wrinkled walls reflect his amazement. Without being told, he steps into his boat, picks up the wheel, and tacks into the wind.

I hand Adam the last of the homemade jerky and tell him that's what pirates eat for breakfast.

When he tires of sailing, I give him the roll of tinfoil.

"Let's have a snowball fight." I scrunch up a few balls to show him how it's done.

We take up opposite sides of the room, me behind my upturned cot, him in his boat. He raises his shield. Adam has never needed to be taught how to play.

Nor does he have to be shown just how quickly play turns to combat. One minute we are lobbing tinfoil balls at each other, the next they might as well be grenades. The more I cry for mercy, the more savage he becomes. This gentle boy has turned into a tyrant. When I hold my hands up in surrender, he is fueled for war. I see him casting around for something heavier to throw and yell at him to stop. He can't hear me. It's as though his mouth has become unstitched; his grin unravels.

I stand up to shout at him because this has gone far enough, but the projectile has already left his hand. Suddenly, he isn't grinning, and I am not quite standing upright anymore, and what has clipped the side of my head has come crashing to the floor.

It's surprise more than pain that makes me cry out, but gauging from Adam's look of alarm, I might as well have been leveled with a wrecking ball.

"What did you do that for?!"

He is sorry. I can tell by the way he avoids looking at me. He stares at the floor, his shoulders bunched up around his ears.

I right my cot and sit down.

"I didn't mean to hurt you."

Yes, you did, I keep from saying. I want to tell him it's in all of us to harm someone else, even those we love. We deceive them or betray them or we throw things at them. How else are we to know they bruise or bleed? How else are we to know the relief of being forgiven?

"Come here," I say.

It takes some convincing before he comes over. I pull him into my lap and bury my nose in his white-blond hair. After I delivered him, I lay him on my chest and searched him for a resemblance between us. Rather than finding it in the shape of his forehead or in the setting of his nose, I found it in his smell. We smelled the same, him and me. At times, it has been only his smell that has kept me from doubting my own existence.

"You're warm." I take off his sweater, and his hair stands straight up with static. I start laughing.

He musses my hair. "You look funny, too."

I tickle him, and the game is afoot once again.

"Anybody home?" Dobbs calls when he opens the door.

Adam jumps up. He rushes up to greet him. If Dobbs was spiteful and mean to Adam, I might be more inclined to put aside fable for fact, but as it is, Dobbs is mostly patient. With me, he sometimes still goes on his end-of-the-world tangents, although less than he used to, but with Adam, he could almost pass for regular. If turning my boy against him might lead to anything other than disaster, I would start and end each story with a wolf dressed up in Dobbs's clothing.

Dobbs has another treat for Adam. This one is too big for Adam to carry. Dobbs puts a vacuum cleaner on the floor, right in the middle of our stage. He hands me the duffel bag and a dead rabbit, which will later end up curing in the stairwell. The pneumatic ram with all the spigots serves as a rack for his coat.

He bends beside Adam, who is running his hands across the canister and the hose.

"What's it do?"

"Well, it used to suck up dirt, but it doesn't work anymore. I thought we could take it apart, see if you can put it back together again." Dobbs is clearheaded today. This is not always the case when he comes back from a "mission." He can be foul-tempered about how the world's gone to pot, or landmine-quiet. Only once in a while do we see anything of the deranged person he was a couple of years ago, although we still have to listen to his theory of people being Scalpers.

Adam is most pleased with his gift. I wonder why it can never just be a toy car.

"Hey, what's this?" Dobbs points at Adam's getup—my best attempt at chaps and a rather lopsided fringed vest.

"It's my costume. I'm Henry Pate."

Dobbs, giving me a once-over, notices the black pants, the button-up shirt, a poor imitation of a bow tie. I've scraped my hair into a ponytail and tucked it into the back of my collar. Adam's assured me I look like a gentleman. "And who might you be?"

"She's the narrator, silly. We're doing *The History of Eudora*."

Slapping the heel of his hand against his forehead, Dobbs says, "Ah, yes. Your mother's masterpiece."

I am determined that Adam know where his people come from, that he have an ancestral home tucked at the confluence of the Kaw and Wa-karusa Rivers, and that he feel part of some greater arc of history. To that end, I have my play. Each year, I add to it a little more. We are now up to the start of the Civil War. Being five and sharp as a tack, Adam gets more lines and more parts.

"Do you want to see it?" Instead of waiting for an answer, Adam steers Dobbs to a chair. "You need a ticket." He races to the kitchen table to the stack of tickets he made from old cereal boxes. He slips Dobbs one, then stands ceremoniously with his hand out to collect it. With big solemn eyes, a broad mouth quick to smile, and stick-straight-up blond hair, he's a good-looking little guy, nothing at all like his father. Except for the splatter of freckles on his nose, he's nothing of me, either.

"Maybe we should do this another time, Adam." I can read Dobbs better than a script. Dobbs doesn't like me teaching Adam American history. He says America is a Fallen Empire. He says what matters is the future.

"Mommy, please." He runs behind the partition, then gives me the signal to begin. I look at him, and he gives me puppy eyes.

I pick up the script, clear my throat, and begin reading, but he stops me.

"Use your narrator voice."

In a deep voice, I take us back to the time when seven hundred acres of Shawnee land is sold to three German settlers by Chief Paschal Fish. Adam comes out from behind his partition so the one-member audience can get a load of his homemade feather headdress. "If you name the town after my daughter, Eudora," Adam recites, "no misfortune will come to you." His somber expression splits into a grin, so proud to have delivered the line perfectly.

In Adam's mind, Chief Paschal Fish is right up there with God. I've told him that Eudora, smack-dab in the middle of Tornado Alley where great swaths of land are ripped through to the bone and entire towns tossed into the air, has been spared calamity, and in his mind, this is the chief's doing. One of the things you cannot teach someone with extremely limited experience is coincidence. Especially not when you're always going on about Destiny.

I narrate the part where Quantrill and his murderous ruffians raid the city of Lawrence, trying not to pay any mind to Dobbs's chuffing. Saddled on his broom, Adam gallops around the concrete pillar as the avenging party. He chases the marauding guerrillas into the Sni Hills, in reality a place of high bluffs and deep ravines, but down here the place behind the shower curtain with paper trees pinned to it. We are about to come to the part in the Battle of Black Jack, where John Brown defeats Henry Pate in retaliation for burning down Lawrence, when Dobbs stands up. It sounds like applause, but it looks like a man smacking two old gloves together to rid them of dirt.

"But we're not done yet."

He rubs Adam's head. "That's enough for today, Sport."

Adam is about to make another protest, but Dobbs cuts him off. "If you spent half as much time reading what I give you as you do making up these silly plays, you'd know a lot more about the world." Adam's smile slips. No matter how amiable Dobbs is with Adam, he has a knack for making Adam feel like he just doesn't measure up. Reading is one of those ways. Even though I've explained a hundred times that not all children are quick to pick up on letters, Dobbs is worried that Adam is slow. Nothing could be further from the truth. Give the child a pile of junk, and he'll build you the most wonderful machine. At the moment, Adam is constructing himself a companion with an alarm-clock head, limbs made from coils, and hands with spoon fingers. Tell me that's not genius. Adam can also recite any story I've ever read to him almost word for word.

To get into Dobbs's good graces again, Adam asks Dobbs to help him take apart the vacuum cleaner. While they are busy, Adam prods for information about Dobbs's venture Above. Dobbs is quick to tell him about bad guys and vicious animals and terrible storms. He knows full well too much disaster nonsense will give Adam bad dreams, but it doesn't stop him. If I tell Dobbs I don't like his filling Adam's head with stories—those kinds of stories, at any rate—he'll only say, what makes me think my stories are better than his. Instead of putting a stop to it, I go about opening cans, making as much of a protest as I can with a spoon and a tin plate.

What Adam believes about the outside world, the land we call Above, is something right out of a science-fiction novel. The death of masses of people is how the story starts, followed by the prolonged and agonizing death of the planet as a result of radiation. Severe climate change and barbarism sum up Dobbs's contribution. So Adam will not feel like the last kid on earth, my contribution to the oral history has been to include survivors his own age hidden in caves and sewers throughout the land, and to reiterate that the Disaster will soon have run its course. On one point Dobbs and I are in perfect agreement—that the ending be happy. Adam, in other words, will one day run free.

"Want to take this downstairs and work on it in my office?" Dobbs asks Adam.

"Yes!" Adam's out the door in a flash. He loves being invited into the Inner Sanctum. He's fascinated most by the animals in the specimen jars, even though what Dobbs will want to show him are the reams of preparedness tracts. Dobbs acts more like a recruiter than a father.

When I draw the covers over Adam, he is so tired he can barely keep his eyes open. Nevertheless, he wants a story. I offer to read, but he shakes his head.

"How about *The Hobbit*?"

"That's way too long, Adam."

"Just tell the part about the treasure."

It's such a relief that after Dobbs's gloom and doom Adam wants magic. "The Arkenstone is known as the Heart of the Mountain," I begin. I tell him about its luminescence, how it has a thousand crystal surfaces sharp enough to slice off a finger. It has its own light, and everywhere it shines, things are made new and beautiful. "And it's way down deep in the mountain where nobody can see to it."

"Like me," he says.

"Yes, like you."

Doomsday is no match for such purity, such radiance.

"WHEN CAN I go Above?"

Adam is almost seven. This is not the first time he's asked the question; it's the first time he's asked it with the calendar in his hand. He hands me a pen.

"It's not something we can schedule, Adam. Mister will tell us when it's safe." I pretend to keep reading.

"Can't he just open the door and let me see a little of it?"

I set the book aside. "You know what? I think you are old enough now to become a Boy Scout." I describe what I remember from Theo's Cub Scout days.

Adam interrupts. "You've told me that before. It's where you learn how to tie knots and fix a broken leg with a stick."

"Yes, that's right, and a lot more than that. Do you know why?"

"So they can get badges."

I laugh. "They do earn badges, but they learn this stuff so they can take care of themselves in the outdoors, by themselves if they have to. Be prepared, is the motto of a Boy Scout."

He sees where this is going. "If I can take care of myself, will Mister let me go outside?"

"There are a lot of badges you'll have to earn."

"Can I start now?" He starts bouncing on the balls of his feet.

I get up from my chair and walk to the kitchen. "Well, shall we start with teaching you how to cook?"

"I already know how to cook. I can make toast."

"I was thinking about something more substantial. When you live Above, you'll need food to give you plenty of energy, for building a camp, say."

Sometimes I wish I never went along with the end-of-the-world story so I could describe what it is really like outside at this time of year. Spring is when the trees are leafing out and the fields are turning purple with larkspur. It's that time of year when the mercury barely rises and children go rushing outside in short sleeves. You can hear their mothers calling about how they are going to catch their deaths, mothers who have forgotten how breaking the hard ground of winter is done in the hearts of children first. I can't tell Adam about spring without telling him about children, so I tell him instead about rivers.

There are rivers that run faster than ocean waves and some that run granddaddy-slow. "Some of them are so wide, you can't swim across them, especially after the rains, but my favorite are the ones that have stepping-stones across them. Spending a day at the river is like being lost in time."

"I don't want to be lost."

Sometimes, this is how it goes when I describe the outside world. It starts off sounding magical and ends up sounding scary.

I lift his chin. "You'll never be lost. When we go Above, I'll be right by your side. Now, how about we get back to cooking?"

I get out a box of kitchen gadgets I seldom use—the egg poacher, though we haven't had an egg in months and even then, it was something a pigeon might have laid; a cheese grater; a nesting set of measuring cups. I tell him he can take anything from the shelves he wishes, and I part the blue gingham curtain to show him the pots and bowls. "Doesn't matter what you fix. Get creative, use your imagination."

My son takes it all in with a seriousness that crushes my heart.

"When you have cooked three meals for us, you will earn your first badge."

He doesn't say anything, and for a horrible moment I think this is the stupidest idea I've ever come up with. As if fake Boy Scout badges are going to make him stop asking to be let outside.

But he asks, "Do we still have any of those chocolate sprinkles?"

I almost choke on my relief. "Well, now, you're the chef. You dig through that stuff and see what you find."

I retreat to the living room and rummage around for fabric scraps to start making badges, while Adam unpacks everything in the kitchen. By the time I have finished making the first badge, an embroidered circle of T-shirt material with a pot drawn on it, Adam's project seems to have stalled. "You done?"

"It doesn't look right." His face is streaked with flour and his fingers are gummed together with some sort of paste.

Beside the mixing bowl are jars and cans and packets and every conceivable mixing utensil. In the bowl is thick sticky dough the color of red dirt. It is lumpy with raisins and the last of the peanuts and other unidentifiable fragments.

"I'm not going to earn my badge, am I?" He is on the brink of tears.

"Oh, I wouldn't give up that easily if I were you." I scoop some of the mixture on my finger and pop it into my mouth. Way too much Cup-a-Soup, but not entirely inedible. "How about we add some sugar to it and see if these don't turn out to be cowboy cookies."

Anything with the word *cowboy* commands Adam's attention.

Encouraged, he dumps spoonfuls of sugar into the bowl. I find a cookie cutter, and he tips out the batch onto the table, flattens it, and presses out star shapes. After we've browned them on the skillet, we sit down. Neither of us speaks. The mealtime has the feel of a high-stakes card game. Adam studies my face. I chew poker-faced. Too much praise too soon and he'll know right away I'm bluffing.

He takes a bite, makes his own assessment—several quick blinks, a frown, and a hasty swallow.

When I take another bite, he shows his surprise. "You like it, Mommy?"

If it kills me, I'll eat every last one of these cookies. "Like it? I think you're going to put me out of a job soon."

He grins, then comes around to give me a hug. "Maybe I can earn all my badges before my birthday."

And just like that, I know scouting isn't going to be any help to me at all.

"They won't hurt him one bit." Dobbs is suggesting a blue pill because something has set Adam off on one of his marathon crying jags. "It'll just put him to sleep, is all." This from the man who used to rant about drug companies.

"It's from being cooped up in this room," I whisper fiercely. Ever since the incident with the so-called Intruders, Dobbs limits our access to just the upper level when he leaves on his missions. Only when he's around to supervise can Adam have the run of the place. I push the bottle of pills back across the table. "No."

"They're not poison, for pity's sake. Here." Nothing makes Dobbs happier than when he can prove me wrong, especially when it comes to Adam.

He slugs down a pill. "Watch. In a few minutes I'm going to have a really decent nap. You two want to have a party, be my guest. Raise the roof, if you want."

Sure enough, Dobbs is snoring before I finish doing the dishes.

Adam stops crying and goes over to look at Dobbs. He doesn't get to see such a spectacle because Dobbs does his sleeping in his study with the door locked. Adam decides to conduct a test. He lets off a piercing shriek three inches from the man's ear.

I find this amusing until I wake up from a deep sleep. I grab Adam's arm and tell him to hush, to let Dobbs be. I run out of the room and up the short staircase, past the first blast door to the second one. The keypad.

"What are you doing, Mommy?"

I remember the first three numbers of the code. Five, one, zero. One more. One, I try. Nothing.

"You mustn't do that, Mommy!"

"Go get your sweater, and grab Teddy." I pound five, one, zero, and then two. Nothing.

Adam yanks on my arm to make me stop. "No, Mommy! Don't!"

"Adam! This is important. Let go of me." Five, one, zero . . . three.

"You're going to set off the bomb!"

"Be quiet." And then I turned to him. I've never seen him so afraid. "What?"

Adam starts to rock back and forth on his heels. He shakes his head wildly.

I take him by the shoulders to explain. "Adam, there is no bomb down here."

He glares at me. "Uh-huh. The Atlas bomb. It's for Russia, but you tried to open the door, and now it's going to go off in here!" He twists out of my reach and runs along the passage and back down the stairs.

Five, one, zero, four. I hear the sliding sound. The door is unlocked! I push it open and run through the corridors and up the steep, narrow stairs.

One door! One!

I start punching combinations. My heart is pounding. It could be hours before that pill wears off! I stop and think. Five-one-zero-four . . . Five one zero four. A date but referring to what? I have no idea. The second combination has to be a date, too. What? His birth date. I try those numbers. Nothing. Adam's birth date . . . nothing. Mine doesn't work, either. I keep trying different combinations: the date I was abducted, the date baby Freedom was born. Then I realize these numbers are important to me, not to Dobbs. What dates would he care about? The End of the World! Let's see . . . how many have there been? Dobbs has spoken of several. There was the one called Collapse of the European Union, and there was one called Wall Street Meltdown. I don't remember when exactly these were—sometime in the early years. The one he called Diablo was a few months after Adam was born—something about a nuclear power plant in California. That was six years ago, early May, as I recall.

I start punching numbers. And then I hear an almighty scream. I race down to see.

Adam is under the kitchen table, beside Dobbs's legs. He has his arms folded over his head. He is rocking so vigorously, plates and cups clatter and smash to the floor. Rockets may as well have blasted off for the way he is hollering. "We're going to die! We're going to die! We're going to die!"

"Adam, we're going outside, like you wanted."

I try to crawl under the table, too, try to pull him out so he will quit shrieking, but he shrinks from my touch as though he's been scorched. I know not to touch him when he's like this, but we are so close to getting out. I try telling him that, and he screams back that he doesn't want to go out. I've killed him, he cries.

And then, *wham!* He kicks. Blood spurts from my nose. I stumble backward, and something else crashes to the floor. Adam has grabbed hold of Dobbs's knees. He's waiting to be blown to smithereens like it's 1950.

I press a wet towel against my nose and sit across from him, saying, "Sweetie, we're safe. You're okay. It's okay."

He keeps yelling and rocking until, eventually, Dobbs wakes up. The bucking thing inside Adam is stronger than both of us put together. Dobbs hands me the bottle of pills. Between Dobbs and me is a truce the shape of Adam. I take out a pill. Somehow, we manage to pry Adam's jaw apart and force the pill into his mouth. The tremors begin to lessen, and the flares in his eyes die out.

As I lay him down on his pallet and stroke his forehead, Dobbs says, "You feel that?" He cocks his head.

"What?"

He looks toward the door, then back at me, eyebrow cocked.

"A draft."

He goes to investigate and comes back with a very odd expression. "Both doors were open."

ADAM WAKES UP yellow.

I scream through the gap in the floor for Dobbs. I tell him to bring the book with him. The book has seen us through Adam's rickets, his broken arm from when he fell down the stairs, a tooth extraction, and several urinary infections. It has to have the answer for this.

Adam answers all of Dobbs's questions. Yes, his tummy hurts; yes, his head hurts; yes, he feels sleepy. Yes, to everything.

I hold his hand. His palm is yellow, too.

"It could be a dozen different things," Dobbs explains. "Liver problems, gallbladder. I don't know, Blythe. I just don't know." I'm not used to seeing Dobbs at a loss. It scares me almost as much as his cold-blooded control.

I put a cool compress on Adam's head. "Give him one of your pills."

Dobbs brings back a little foil package. "These are the last of the antibiotics." He breaks one in half.

Adam refuses it. The days of bribing him with bottle caps are over. Dobbs promises him three Krugerrands. Sick as he is, Adam only swallows the pill after Dobbs fetches the coins and puts them in his hand.

Apart from rickets and being a little small for an eight-year-old, Adam is a healthy kid. He's never been sick like this before.

Dobbs and I sit and watch him, waiting for the color to fade.

———

"I think his color is better. Don't you?"

Dobbs says, "I don't know." I hate the sound of this. After another long silence, he goes downstairs and comes back with one of the pistols. He packs it in the duffel bag. He tells me he'll be back as quick as he can.

"You're not going to leave with him being like this."

"I'm going to get him medicine."

Dobbs has taken two children out of here already, children I will never see again. I can't believe my own ears when I say, "Take him with you."

It doesn't help to plead or to cry or even to accuse him of being the cause for Adam's sickness. Dobbs tells me to get a grip, panicking isn't helping the situation.

"He's my son. You must take him!"

Dobbs gets in my face and lowers his voice. "He is my son, too."

I almost feel sorry for Dobbs until he adds, "You still don't get it, do you? He's our future. If anything happens to him, what would all this have been for?"

The Plan—it always comes first.

Dobbs is taking too long to return. Something must have gone wrong. To keep from torturing myself with all the what-ifs, I keep busy. It's silly trying to fashion a product out of worry, but I crochet anyway. As soon as I come to the end of a pattern, I pull the whole lot loose and start on something else. I read *The Hobbit* to Adam, even when he's asleep. Knowing full well he'll refuse to eat, I nevertheless cook him a meal from scratch. Hand-cut noodles from a lumpy mix of stale flour and chemically treated water. Tuna mixed with the last of the crackers. The result is something a dog would turn its nose up at. I scrape it into the trash can. Housework, then. I mop and polish and dust, even though dust doesn't make it this far down. I organize the already orderly cupboards. I clean where stains and spots should be. And still, Adam is sick. Still, Dobbs is not back.

I am up before the door opens all the way. Dobbs looks haggard. Heavy bags hang beneath his eyes, making them look even smaller. He hasn't shaved for several years, but now his beard is dirty and he reeks of sweat. He hands me the medicine, says to get two pills down Adam, even if it means more Krugerrands. He brings the hourglass and tells me we have to turn it four times before we can give him another dose. "It's likely hepatitis, the kind you get from eating contaminated food. We have to be careful not to catch it, if it is."

"And if it isn't?"

We sit and watch Adam, and then we watch the sand, and then we watch Adam again. Dobbs never answers the question, and I am too scared to ask it again.

"Did you bring me a treat?"

Dobbs and I both snap awake. Adam is sitting up on his pallet, his skin translucent and his cheeks slightly flushed. No yellow.

I rush to him. I hold him and cry.

Dobbs kneels beside us and pats him on the shoulder.

"Why's everyone being so nice to me? Is it my birthday or something?"

Dobbs and I exchange glances. What a brilliant idea!

"Yes, it is!"

"How old am I?"

"How old do you want to be?"

He thinks for a minute. "Fifteen."

I hate how he always chooses to be older. He ages so quickly as it is, but this is a favorite game and rules are rules. "Fifteen, right. You go into the supply closet and make a list of all the things you're old enough to do when you're fifteen, and we'll get ready."

Dobbs heads downstairs. I follow him to get the box of decorations.

Soon, the living room is decked in streamers and paper banners. Dobbs has wrapped a great big present in old newspaper comics, and I've dug up a bottle of maraschino cherries and a liter of Coke. I have a couple of presents for him, too. A knitted cap and Grandpa's old watch.

When Adam steps out of the closet, we throw confetti on him and cheer, and he acts like he's never been so surprised in all his life. We put on pointy hats. Dobbs starts whistling, and for the first time, the sound does not turn my insides around. Adam sings "Happy Birthday" to himself and pulls us into a conga line. We do a loop around the concrete pillar until he sees his presents.

Dobbs's gift is an encyclopedia that looks brand-new even though it was published in 1958. Adam thanks him politely, which means he wishes he'd received anything other than a book.

He tries on the cap that I made him and admires himself in the mirror. "Thanks, Mom." And then he unwraps the last present. Grandpa's watch. He looks at me hesitantly.

"You have to take good care of it. That was your great-grandfather's."

"I know." He rubs the inscription. He doesn't know how to tell time, which is just as well, because one of the hands is missing. "Are you sure I can have it?"

"It's yours."

Dobbs is suddenly not having a good time. He withdraws from the circle. Adam doesn't notice.

"Is it real gold?"

"Yup."

He clutches it to his chest and then he bounds into my lap to give me a hug. "I love being fifteen!"

MOTHERS AND TIME are not allies when it comes to the raising of children. We pull in opposite directions. I talk a good game about the virtues of Adam growing into a young man, but I'd just as soon he stayed my little boy. Time, on the other hand, has Adam by the scruff of his neck and is racing him full speed ahead. Adam is fifteen for real now, a number that makes about as much sense to me as binary code. For him, it's all about forthcoming attractions. No regard for the present, let alone the past.

Because the time for coming headlong at him has passed, I have to monitor the changes in him with the sideways glance—another growth spurt, a broadening around his shoulders, hair growing in thicker above his lip. There's less roundness to his face, more pointiness. Grandma would call it the stubborn set of the chin of all Everley men, but to me he looks more like a pixie than a man. So pale is his face that you can see the webbing of blue veins around his cheeks, and his eyes appear even larger and darker. Not that those eyes offer any clues about the changes going on inside him. His turning away from me is, I suppose, what most marks the change from boy to man.

About the only thing Adam will discuss with me is the future. Then, he is full of ideas. All the things he wants to do when he gets out. It scares me half to death the way he talks. If Dobbs catches wind of it, he'll say I'm contaminating Adam. Plotting, he'll call it. And it will set us back another few years. Sometime back, when Dobbs was spending every waking moment indoctrinating Adam about the End of the World and his destiny to spawn a new tribe, I had the notion to use Adam to get to Dobbs. Because Dobbs seemed so eager to give Adam whatever he wanted, I suggested to Adam that he ask to go on a field trip, to insist putting into practice some of those skills Dobbs was so intent on teaching him. It backfired. Dobbs dug in his heels. Adam quickly became sulky when he didn't get his way, and Dobbs interpreted this as my turning the child against him. I've had to play it the other way ever since Dobbs turned the tables and issued the decree that we'll leave this hole only when Adam is "ready." I think "ready" means when Adam puts away all talk of leaving. Dobbs increasingly makes mention of moving—resettling, as he puts it—but insists it all hinges on Adam. Who he says is becoming a loose cannon, just like his mother used to be. Never has their relationship been that of a father and son—at best, it has been something of a mentorship program—but of late, the tension between them has ratcheted up. So no harm will come to Adam, so Dobbs might actually keep his word and take us out of here, I find myself on more than one occasion doing Dobbs's dirty work for him. Talking Adam off his high horse, for example.

The cough comes on suddenly, and as always, it is worse during Lights Off. I hope Adam, now rooming in what used to be the battery room next to the silo entrance, will sleep through it. The cough is Death's promise to me. Ours was a courtship I protested at first, and then one I longed for like a spinster bride. Ever since Adam was born, though, I am the one who stalls, who bargains: wait for him to get a little older. I don't know how much longer I can put it off.

It hasn't helped to broach the subject of dying with Dobbs. He'll have none it.

"You're still young," he has said. "My God, you're thirty-four."

In earth years, maybe so. But down here, a person can age ten years in a matter of minutes.

I try to remember what it was like to be a girl, to be Adam's age, but my memories of the past are not as substantial as they used to be. They are now more like mobiles, casting intricate patterns of light and shadow on the walls of my mind. Suspended from gossamer threads will be a bright scene, a scene from Way Before. If I am patient enough to wait for it to stop spinning, I might see the four of us kids around the breakfast table, say. Gerhard's hair catches the dirty beam of light; Suzie pretends to eat; Theo, propped high on his chair by two telephone books, uses his finger to stir cereal formations in his milk. And there, a teenage girl with her head in a book. Try as I might, there is no telling what she is like. Dreamy, perhaps. Eager to get the awkwardness of adolescence over with and become an adult.

You'd think I'd have shared everything about my childhood with Adam by now, but to look back is to walk around an abandoned house. It pains me to search the lonely rooms for some overlooked toy, some snippet of conversation, and to realize even the old ghosts have given up haunting it. It must be in Mama's memory that the girl with the braids now resides, and in Adam's imagination, since he insists she is like him, prone to keeping secrets and wishing the grown-ups would meddle less.

Coughing makes my heart start racing. This time it also sets off a tingling that starts in my fingers and works its way up my arm. "This is it, Blythe. Go wake up your son," the voice says. I don't move. Am I to tiptoe down the stairs to Adam's bedside and wake him up for this? So he can worry, too? So I can say good-bye? What are a mother's last words supposed to be when all along they've been designed to keep him from realizing he's trapped in his own grave?

Like the wake of a boat comes the glow. I hope it's Dobbs getting ready for another mission. Dobbs leaves for days sometimes. Sometimes I worry he might go off wandering into the woods and never come back. When the foamy green light reaches my bed, I see it is Adam. Worry lines his face like freshly plowed furrows. I make a show of beating my chest as if all it needs is a good scolding.

"Silly old chest."

Adam blinks hard against welling concern. "Want some water?"

I shake my head, even though he is already pouring me a cup.

"Dusty down here."

After a few sips, the cough runs muddy like the Wakarusa River. I draw my handkerchief away. Fortunately, there is no blood this time.

We go through the ritual. Adam waits for me to finish drinking, finish playing Pollyanna, finish fussing with the bed covers.

"That did the trick. Thank you, son."

He takes my cup and peers into the bottom of it.

"You can go back to bed, it's passed now. I'm sorry I woke you."

Adam sits on the ground beside me, draws his knees up to his chin, and circles his arms around his shins. He's way too big to get in the cot with me, but I lift the covers anyway. "Want to climb in?"

He shakes his head. "What if you die?"

I have to remind myself that this is not the carefree boy of yesteryear. This is someone leaving his boyhood. Even in here, one world has to make way for another. And yielding, too, must be his mother, whose fairy tales are not wanted anymore.

"I'm not going to die, silly. It's a cough, is all."

"But what if you do?"

His lips harden, and his eyes are frozen into treacherous ponds.

"You saying I'm an old lady, is that it?" In some ways, the thirties are a relief, even if I am now terrified of dying. It is a special kind of hell to be twenty-three and clinging to the hope that the youth from which you were robbed is still waiting for you. So Adam will not wake up each day to a skinny old woman, and so Death might be fooled into thinking that I am owed at least some of my prime, I have taken to wearing braids again and have managed to gain enough weight to fill out those old dresses.

I try not to sigh for fear it may dislodge another coughing spell. "Mister will take care of you."

Adam shakes his head. "I won't live with him down here, you know."

This resentment of Dobbs is not a new thing. It's just now a moving thing, something that keeps gathering speed. I look at this kid, his legs bowed and his back growing more crooked every day, and see him pitting himself against his father in a war he won't win. If Dobbs lets us out, it will be on his terms, not Adam's.

"Hush now."

"When's it going to be safe for us to go outside?"

"Why all the questions tonight?"

"He spends most of his time out there. Why won't he let me go out, even on one mission?"

"I think I will take more of that water, if you don't mind."

The task is not enough to redirect Adam. "It could be safe to go Above right now, and we wouldn't know it."

"Adam, please. You're getting worked up for nothing. Go back to bed."

"There could be people out there who could help you, make you well. It could be like before." Before the Disaster, he means. "Anything's better than just waiting," he insists. "Waiting, waiting, waiting. It's all we ever do!"

"My boy."

"I'm not a boy! Stop treating me like one!"

I get up and go to the kitchen to make us something hot to drink.

"What if people have started living outside again? What if there are doctors again, or hospitals?"

I debate whether to tell him what I vowed I wouldn't until I knew for certain. Waiting for Dobbs to keep his promise and move us out of here is like going for a ride on a giant Ferris wheel. There's Main Street, ribbed with pickups. Cecil's Grill has been tarted up with neon beer signs and a wagon-wheel fence. The houses are pegged in place by blooming crabapple trees. We go a little higher, and the old fertilizer plant looks more like a carnival attraction than a rust heap. Down Indian Road is where I pick out the spot where we might live, and the next thing, we are up where the air is too thin to talk. The Ferris wheel gets stuck, and all I can do is look at the scene from an impossible distance.

"Mister is looking for a place for us Above. We're going to be moving out of here soon."

On his face is exactly what I have come to expect: suspicion. "When?"

If only we could go back to the time when I started all my stories with "long, long ago." He doesn't want "once upon a time" anymore. He wants stories that begin with "when." When will the doors open? When can we go free? When can we get a dog?

"Soon," I say. "Let's just leave it at that for now."

We hear the blast door open. Adam doesn't even look at Dobbs when he pokes his head into the room. He always does this, like he expects to see it empty. We hear him tromp downstairs. He goes to the weapons room and locks away his pistol. His study is directly beneath my cot. I hear him take off his keys. He puts them and the code to the magnetic locks in the safe. Ever since I got the doors open, he uses long combinations of numbers that he changes frequently enough never to be able to memorize them.

"It's like a morgue around here," he says when he comes back upstairs. Dobbs hands Adam a hardbound copy of *Ivanhoe* and tells him there's more where that came from if he plays his cards right.

The years have not been kind to the man. Long, wispy strands of hair do a poor job of disguising the bald spots. His face has a sagging look to it, not aided by the collection of skin around his chin. With his scraggly beard and untrimmed mustache, it is hard to believe that this is the same man who was once so particular about grooming and hygiene. There is a puttylike growth that now covers most of his left ear; it's a wonder he can still hear out of it. He's shrunken, a good foot shorter than he used to be, and he is a far cry from the warrior he once fancied himself as being. What we have to listen to most days is a rundown of ailments—constipation, bloating, arthritic knee, jaw pain, dry mouth. It's no use hoping he'll drop dead, because Dobbs Hordin has the heart of an ox.

"Seems to me some people have been a little testy lately, so I'm thinking what we need is an outing."

Adam and I exchange glances. Is "Soon" now?

Dobbs dumps the duffel bag on the table. He pulls out a dress, something a little girl might wear to a costume party. Clearly, the an-

swer is no. "You're going to want to dress up for a night at the movies."
He hands Adam an old movie reel.

Adam snorts.

"What? I thought everyone liked movie night."

Dobbs got his hands on an old movie projector and a box of reel-to-reel black-and-white films some time ago, which means once in a while we "go out." In other words, we go down to the lower level, where three chairs are set up in front of a sheet hung from a support beam. Popcorn is passed around, and scenes of battleships and bombers light up the screen. This beats game night, when Dobbs brings out a pack of cards and shuffles in such a way that his hand always ends up with all the jokers.

I get up to boil water. I set out three mugs, three small plates for sandwiches. We don't have the variety or quantity of groceries we used to have, and this latest foray outside amounts to only a dozen cans, none of them labeled.

Dobbs sits and picks at one of the many black scabs on his arm. All his shirts are stained from when they rupture and bleed. The twitch in his cheek fires repeatedly. He's been up to something. It's written all over him.

He flicks his head at Adam, who is drawing plans for some new machine in his notebook.

"What you working on, Sport?"

He gets no reply.

"Oh, I see, we're playing the Silent Game." As soon as he finishes his sandwich, he leans over and takes my bowl of slop. "You aren't going to eat that? Guess it's easy to turn up your nose at food when you don't have to earn it."

Adam monitors my reaction. When I do nothing, he tucks his notepad under his arm and stalks off.

"I'm going to have to start coming down harder on that boy." He says this, but the truth is that disciplining is left to me. Dobbs prefers to play good cop.

Dobbs launches into one of his lectures, blaming me for Adam's attitude. He says Adam is impressionable and I shouldn't fill his head with notions. On and on it goes. I tune out and watch his hands. Flaccid palms, tapering fingers. He still keeps his nails too long, but unlike before, there's often dirt underneath them. His hands have age spots now. These same hands used to crawl over my body, claiming even the unforgiving parts. And these same hands have crawled over someone else's body. I can smell it on him; the smell of another woman. He's itching for a fight because he thinks it'll distract me from that fact.

"You went to see her again."

A flicker of surprise.

"I'm not going to dignify that with a response." He gives me the wounded look. How can I accuse him of being unfaithful, a man who takes his vows to heart? Once in a while, he'll tell me he loves me. It's not love. It's what he feels for *The Manifesto*, for the seed catalogs and the silo. Ownership is what it is.

I can't imagine anyone wanting to be Dobbs's girlfriend. If he weren't so miserly, I'd say he was paying for it, especially since he never helps himself to me anymore. "You don't have to pretend for my sake. I don't care. Heck, why don't you invite her around for movie night?"

He lifts his hand for me to stop. "It's not like that—"

Oh my, after all these years, is this a confession? It's my turn to cut him off. "I told Adam you were finding us a place."

"I thought we agreed to hold off on that."

"What else am I supposed to say? He keeps asking me how long we're going to be down here, and I've run out of stories."

"Why don't you just tell him the truth?"

You'd think the man would have grown weary with the end-of-civilization plotline by now. Instead, it evolves. We're long past the Apocalypse. Now, I'm supposed to tell Adam there are thugs running about, bandits who snatch up women and children and use them for their own purposes.

"He's not going to put up with this arrangement much longer."

Dobbs arranges his facial muscles just so, draws in a deep breath. A picture of long-suffering.

It only makes me more insistent. "You can't keep telling him—"

"You were the one to mention going on a mission, not me." This is how it is with us now—completing each other's sentences, reading each other's minds, remembering a shared history as though it were a rerun of a favorite TV show. Lord help me for the times we behave like this, an old married couple.

"I'm trying to give him something to look forward to! If you cared for him at all . . ."

Dobbs sighs. "I'm working on it. Give me a few more weeks."

I raise my eyes to the ceiling.

"I promise, Blythe. I give you my word."

AS SOON AS Dobbs goes to his study, Adam comes back upstairs.

"You want your dinner now?" He doesn't answer but heads straight for the bookshelf.

"Where are my notebooks?"

"He confiscated them."

"Why?"

"Can't you show him a little respect?"

"Why should I respect him? You don't."

He's right. I haven't done a good job of hiding my feelings. Rather, I bake my loathing into Dobbs's favorite meals, spoiling them with too much salt. I stitch it in the shirts he gives me to mend, sewing cuffs closed.

"Am I going to get them back?"

I am still deciding how to answer this when he says, "Can't you just say yes or no? Why does there always have to be a story?"

Why does there always have to be a story?

Stories keep the fire burning inside us, stories keep us from dashing our heads against the wall. Without stories we'd be lost, dead, forgotten. I am a story, I should tell him. There used to be a girl who lived in a town where nothing bad ever happened. You are a story. Play your cards right, and you might live in a town one day, too. How about that for a story?

"Please just try and be nicer to him, that's all I'm asking."

Adam grabs a load of books from next to Dobbs's recliner and leaves the room in a huff.

After enough time has passed for Adam to cool off, I go down with a sandwich and a cup of hot cocoa. His private barracks is next to the generator room. He doesn't seem to mind the cramped space, the fuel smell from next door, or the engine noise when the generators kick on.

He's hunched over his desk. I put the plate next to him, keep my hand from landing on his head and smoothing the static out of his white-blond hair, and notice he's scribbling in one of Dobbs's prized books.

I seize *The Coming Race* from him. "What do you think you're doing?"

Frantically, I leaf through the others. Scribbled over the text of *The Survivor's Primer* are silly riddles. In *The Alpha Strategy*, Adam has drawn cartoons.

"Adam! How could you!"

He grins. "What else am I supposed to use?"

"You aren't going to be able to hide this from him, you know. He's going to find out."

"So let him."

"Adam, this behavior of yours—it has to stop." Every time I get a clear picture of that weathered farmhouse on the edge of town, where Adam is outside breaking sticks across his knee like a regular kid, there is this. Whatever the name for this is.

"He's the one who took my stuff. Why don't you yell at him? Why do you always take his side?"

"I don't always take his side."

"Yes, you do. It's always got to be his way, keeping him happy, like he's God or something."

"You're not being fair."

He shakes his head. "Is it fair that he gets to come and go as he pleases and we have to stay here all the time?"

"We will stay here forever if you do not get your act together!"

Because there is no taking the words back, I spin around and march out of the room, Dobbs's books packed tightly in my arms.

Nobody says a word when Dobbs comes upstairs. He's bathed and changed his shirt, and his hands are pink from all the scrubbing, as though to get rid of any trace of her. "Movie's ready."

All he has to do is take one look at Adam's face to know something's amiss. He catches me looking at the bookshelf. He walks over to it. The second book he pulls out, and the game is up.

I go to him, explaining we're living with an adolescent now, that we have to adjust.

He storms downstairs. Adam and I chase after him. Dobbs loads every single one of Adam's notebooks into a cardboard box, and uses the dolly to wheel them along the utility tunnel. Adam yells at him to stop. I stand in front of the silo door, but Dobbs pushes me aside. He unlocks the padlock and opens the door. The place reeks. He rolls the cargo onto the platform and up to the railing. As Adam screams his protest, he empties the load over into the darkness.

"You let me know if you want anything else disposed of," Dobbs tells Adam on his way out.

Adam might be small for his age and very pale, and you'd be hard-pressed to find a straight bone in his body, but he is not one to cower at a challenge. This is going to end badly.

I wake to find my son sitting at the table eating cereal.

"Good morning," I call to him.

"'Morning."

I put on my robe and amble to the table. He is smiling that sunrise smile I used to take for granted. He is not going to retaliate, and Dobbs is not going to hold a grudge, and we are going to live in that farmhouse after all. And then I see why Adam's smile is so buttery. He's covered himself in small print. On his arms, on his neck, all over his hands are words and diagrams and maps. It's not ink poisoning I'm worried about; it is the poisoning that comes from thinking you can win.

"My boy?"

I read him while he sleeps. With the pocket flashlight, I look at what Adam has refused to scrub clean. It is like being in Tutankhamen's tomb, reading the history of the ancient Egyptians. I discover my son has learned to swear. FUCKING SHIT, is wrapped around his heel. More alarming are all the pictures of weapons—daggers and cannonballs careening across his arm, a missile, a gun. If someone else were to read this, they'd get entirely the wrong idea about my son. Adam is still the sensitive, soft-natured boy he always was. He is just fed up with being kept down here. And with the ones who keep him down here. The caricature of me is unflattering, if not downright unkind. The one of Dobbs is vulgar. From what I can tell, the rest is a story of a young hero on a quest to slay a dragon and return a magical stone to its rightful heir.

Adam wakes up, startled. I didn't realize I had touched him.

There is a wall of darkness between us when I quickly switch off the flashlight.

He leans toward me, following my breath. With his face all but superimposed on mine, he says, "What are you doing, Mom?"

I find his cheek, stroke it. I have learned to distinguish color in the darkness. Gauging from the heat at my fingertips, I'd say he's steamed.

He bats my hand away.

"I'm sure he'll get your notebooks back for you." I lay my hand on his thigh, give it a little pat. It is as stiff as an ironing board. "You can't let him get to you, though. It'll only make things worse."

Again, no response.

"You're going through a lot of changes at the moment—physically, emotionally—"

"Mom, please!"

"You're fifteen, Adam. You're becoming a man. It's natural that the two of you are going to have these . . ." I can't bring myself to say, "tiffs."

"Can you just drop it?"

"I don't know how to talk to you anymore without you getting upset. We used to be able to talk about anything. And now you are keeping things from me, and I don't like it."

He sits up now. "Turn on the flashlight. Let's talk."

Instead of being joined by the dark, we are now separated by a measly column of light. I barely recognize the person on the other side of it. His blond hair stands up like brush bristles, and his eyes are still the same midnight blue, but it's in the way he holds himself that's new, like an arrow readied on a bow. I can't look at him without thinking, Hurt; someone's going to get hurt.

"We have to get out of this place," he says.

I shush him. The generators are off, which will make it easier for Dobbs to eavesdrop. "We can talk about this when he's on a mission," I whisper.

Adam tags behind me, following the thin beam all the way back to my cot. "You always do this! You say you want us to talk, but you mean *you* want to talk. You never want to listen to what I've got to say."

"You're right, honey. You should talk and I should listen. Just not right now. He's going Above tomorrow; we can talk then."

He shakes my arm. "We've got to get out of here or we're going to rot!"

All you have to do is take a look at my teeth to know he's telling the truth straight-up. "Don't say things like that. Nobody's rotting."

He can't keep his voice from rising. "He'll listen to you. If you tell him to take us Above, he will. You just have to insist."

Sometimes I think putting up with Dobbs and playing by his rules is being strong, but sometimes, like now, I wonder if I didn't misplace my backbone somewhere. "Is it getting cold in here or is it just me?" I pick up my blanket and hand it to him.

Adam throws it on the floor. "If he won't take us up even for a short time, like at night or something—"

"Keep your voice down!"

"—then we'll know."

"Know what?"

"We'll know he's lying to us."

All the care we've taken—I've taken—in remodeling the universe, every apostrophe and comma and parenthesis, and still he is on to us. How can it be, when I did such a painstaking job of re-creation? Sure, God spoke the world into being—a grand speech that went on for six days. Big deal. What the Almighty authored, I had to edit. It has taken fifteen years to boil it all down to something that has allowed my son go about his days in these fixed dimensions and not make mad dashes for the outside. I've even broken down man's greatest achievements into itty-bitty piles. Cities, I've told Adam, weren't all they were cracked up to be. I've chopped off the tops of skyscrapers, made them no higher than the cottonwoods growing along the flood plains. I've shortened freeways, lowered bridges, given parking lots back to the cows. It wasn't a big, wide world to begin with, I've told him; don't believe everything you read in books. Despite all this paraphrasing of the world, my boy is still spoiling for a fight to experience it.

"There are others who have had it a lot worse." When Dobbs takes us out of here, I will happily take the blame for the lies, but until then, I have to keep my end of the bargain, or Dobbs might keep us here forever.

He scoffs. "Here we go again."

"Adam, I want what's best for you, don't you know that?"

"I don't want to live like this for the rest of my life!"

The particles that make up darkness are much denser than those that make up light because they amplify sound. Either that, or my boy is shouting at me.

"Lower your voice."

"You know what? I am not going to die down here. I'd rather go Above and get rounded up by the vigilantes. I'd rather have my head shot off or get skin cancer or whatever the big threat is exactly, than—"

"That is quite enough!"

"—than live like you!"

We are both taken aback by a new sound. Like a sheet being torn through the middle, the crack of thunder.

A slap.

It is the first time I have ever hit my child.

After an initial gasp, he utters not another sound.

My God, I've killed my son. "Adam?" I reach for him, but he draws himself out of my reach.

On my palm is Adam's cameo, a stinging silhouette. I now understand the punishment of chopping off a hand for the crime of stealing. It should also apply to mothers who strike their children. What have I just stolen from Adam?

I say, "Go to your room. Right now." But he is already gone.

I'M TIRED, OLD. Thirty-four. I am my parents' age now, but I have my grandmother's hands. It is her graying hair I have to braid each day. My body is craggy, and there are places where the skin falls into deep pleats, like I'm a folded fan waiting to be spread out. Perhaps that's what death will be like—an unfurling of what never came to pass. Perhaps I will find myself to be a magnificent landscape, like the mural Adam has painted in his room, one across which colorful, wild animals migrate. Among bison and monarch butterflies and humpback whales will be a parade of trees, with hills swelling up behind them. A pied-piper breeze will egg on jolly hollyhocks, lift stray leaves and music notes into spinning pirouettes.

"Get that light out of my face!" I hear Dobbs shout from below.

I leap out of bed, run downstairs. Dobbs is standing in front of his study door. Adam is interrogating him with a flashlight. "Adam! What's going on?"

"Who was here before me?"

The flashlight makes Dobbs look very pale. Either that, or he is. "I don't know what you're talking about. Listen to your mother, and go back to bed."

"I'm going to ask you one more time. Who was here before me?"

This doesn't have the ring of a question but the tone of accusation. Adam is so upset, he's trembling. Before tempers flare any further, I say, very calmly, "Military personnel. The ones who worked here long ago, before we came. The Cold War, remember—we read about that."

"Children don't man missiles, Mother."

"You mean, someone your age? No, honey, children weren't in the armed forces, you're right about that." And don't shove me away with that word—*Mother*.

"Then, who's Charlie?"

"What?"

"Look, I don't know what nonsense your mother's been filling your head with this time, but I'm not about to put up with this."

Adam tries following Dobbs into his room, but he slams the door and triggers the latch. We hear him unlock the safe and gather his keys. A minute later, he barges out. He unlocks the fuse box and flips the switch. The generators groan in response, and a second later the fluorescents snap on. The light makes Adam look sick and Dobbs as guilty as sin. Lord knows what it is doing for me.

Dobbs glares at me with pure loathing. I know what this means: he's going on a mission and it might be days, a week perhaps, before he'll be back.

Adam intersects him at the stairs up to the entrapment vestibule. "I am coming with you."

"I haven't got time for your games!"

"This is not a game. I'm coming with you."

Dobbs glowers at me.

"Adam . . ." I respond weakly. I can't think straight, much less speak. How does Adam know the name Charlie?

Dobbs slings the duffel bag over his shoulder, giving me the I-told-you-this-would-happen face.

I scamper after Adam, who follows Dobbs through the right-angled turns of the entrapment vestibule.

"Running off to your girlfriend?"

Dobbs's rounded shoulders always make him look as if he's caved in, but never more so than when he turns to face Adam. "You don't have any idea what you're talking about."

"There wasn't any apocalypse."

Because someone has to put an end to this, I grab his arm. "Adam, could you stop this nonsense, please? If you have questions, then come and sit with me, and we'll talk about them." I have my own questions: What's this about Charlie?

He shakes free of my grip, all but snarls at Dobbs. "If it's such a disaster out there, why haven't you gotten sick and died?"

Dobbs scowls at me. This is my fault, his look says. Fix it.

"Come on, Adam, let him go." I am trying very hard to keep that picture of the farmhouse from going fuzzy.

Adam won't be budged. "I am not staying down here anymore. And neither is she. We're both going Above, right now. Open the door!"

Instead of taking out his notepad and punching in the code, Dobbs puts his hand against Adam's chest and drives him all the way back to the stairs. For a second, I think he's going to push my boy down them. "You're fifteen and you think you know everything, right?"

Dobbs demands he stay put, then hurries to the middle blast door.

I try to coax Adam down the stairs, but instead, he pursues Dobbs with something behind his back. He yells for Dobbs to turn around. When Dobbs does, the something from behind Adam's back gets pressed against his throat.

"Don't be a fool, boy!"

"You!" Adam charges.

Yes, but for what crime?

"My boy, please! Put the knife down. Before someone gets hurt."

The knife stays put. "There are people up there who are well. The only people who are sick are the ones down here!"

"My boy, please."

Dobbs blinks but will not answer.

"She needs to see a doctor."

"Your mother's fine," Mister replies. "It's you that brings her trouble."

"No more lies. We're going up. Open that door!"

"Baby, please—"

"Touch me, Mom, and I'll slit his throat!" A tiny bead of blood proves his point. "I said, open the door!"

"You're right! There was no apocalypse!" I yell.

Adam pushes the knife even harder.

"Put the knife down, Adam! I'll tell you everything!"

My son turns to me, wavering. There's no taking back the words now. He looks like I feel: shattered.

Dobbs strikes Adam's arm, knocking the knife from his hand. It skids across the floor. Adam, startled, tries to regain his position, but the war is lost. Dobbs twists Adam's arm behind his back and pushes him against the concrete wall. "Don't you ever threaten me again! You hear me? You leave this place when I say you can leave! Pull a stunt like this again and you'll be sorry you were ever born!"

"Dobbs! Let go of him!"

"Shut up, the pair of you! I don't want to hear another word!" Dobbs shoves Adam so hard, he sprawls at my feet. Adam doesn't lift his head.

"You put him up to this!" Dobbs accuses me.

I keep shaking my head, even though it is surely true. Every book I read Adam, every lie I ever uttered, every truth I ever hid. Yes, I put him up to this.

"I come down here again and find you've not taken care of this, I'm taking matters into my own hands!"

I am so busy nodding that I don't notice Adam rising from the floor. Suddenly, he launches at Dobbs. For just a second, the blade glints in the light. And then it is buried in the struggle. The two fall together, a ball of rags and coats and shoes.

A terrible moan. I cannot make out whose.

"Adam!"

From the pile, it is Dobbs who rises. "I didn't mean to . . . I was only trying to . . ."

Oh Jesus.

"Get the first-aid kit, Blythe."

"Adam!"

THE WOUND, DOBBS contends, is not deep but does need stitches. He tells me to fetch more towels and to sterilize one of my sewing needles in boiling water.

"You can't do this; you're not a doctor."

"Get the cough mixture. He's going to need several slugs of that. All right, buddy? A few small stitches, and you'll be as good as new."

"What if it hit an organ? How do you know it's not bleeding worse inside? You have to take him, Dobbs."

"Would you shut up and do as I say!"

I bring the cough mixture, then hurry to fill the kettle. It takes forever to boil the water.

"I'd take him if I could. If there was someplace to go. You know that, right?"

I put the bowl next to Dobbs. I kneel beside Adam and smooth his hair, tell him everything's going to be okay. He keeps trying to say something, and I keep putting my finger to my lips.

"Even if I did, there's no telling how long before I could bring him back. *If* I could even bring him back." Dobbs opens the bottle of hydrogen peroxide. There's only a drop left. This panics me almost as much as the sight of all that blood. "A thousand things that could go wrong up there. You don't know who to trust. I take him up there, I put his life at risk. Is that what you want?"

Blood soaks another tea towel.

"You've got to take him to a doctor." All the same, I'm handing Dobbs my sewing kit, letting him pick the color of thread.

He bends toward Adam, says real loud like the boy's gone deaf, "I need you to be tough now, Sport. This is going to hurt, but it's got to be done. All right?"

Adam struggles fiercely.

"You're going to have to hold him harder than that, for godsake!"

Adam wrestles against my weight, and his blood soaks through my clothes, too.

Dobbs unclips his keys from his belt, hands me the one for the medicine cabinet.

"No," I answer.

"Hurry up, or do you want him to bleed to death?"

I bring Dobbs the bottle of chloroform. Instead of taking it, he gives me his handkerchief. "You do it. Just a couple of drops, now."

When I hold the wet cloth over my son's face, when he bucks and twists under Dobbs's full weight, I can't help but think of little Charlie.

I come unglued the moment Adam passes out. I hold myself around my waist and start to cry. Dobbs tells me to shut up so he can concentrate, but I can't stop. I watch Adam twitch and jerk.

After stitching him up, Dobbs scrubs his hands, and says, "It'll get better. Just have to give it time to run its course." He is a great believer in things running their course.

"I didn't tell him about Charlie."

He doesn't believe me. "You've been trying to turn this kid against me for years. You think I haven't noticed? You think I don't know what you're up to? You should be ashamed of yourself! You did this!"

While Dobbs is cleaning up the mess, I tell him I'm going downstairs to fetch Adam a clean shirt. I hurry down to Adam's room to see if I might find a clue.

Adam doesn't like me to go snooping among his things, though this won't be the first time I do. I search his workspace. From aluminum cans, he has fashioned all manner of blades. He's in the process of making a handle for one of them with my hairbrush. Dobbs would have a fit if he saw these. I hide them among Adam's old toys. There is a new kinetics sculpture, but nothing out of the ordinary. I move to his cot. I rifle through the stuff piled on it. Nothing under the bed, either, or on the shelf next to it.

I glance around the room one last time. Some of the stories we've shared are reflected on his wall, and some are less stories than they are yearnings. In all, his mural is a thing of beauty, with migrating bison and shooting rockets and creatures with propellers. In Adam's panorama, the sky is shoring up the earth, and where clouds ought to be are machines. In the middle are a knight and a frumpy, toothless hag whose facial features bear a frightening resemblance to mine. The hooded figure with the sack over his shoulder is Dobbs. Winding itself like a road through the surreal landscape are fighting words, values I've tried to explain, values that the people Above would die defending: *freedom, justice, truth.* The latest addition is a girl—or rather I think it is. Adam's attempt at someone from the opposite gender has mostly to do with long hair.

I grab a clean shirt and head out, and that's when I see it. Sticking out from behind the door is a strap. Even soiled, there is no mistaking it. The red canvas bag is Charlie's backpack.

Immediately, I am back to that moment: Dobbs's shout; Charlie's eyes snapping open, taking a moment to figure out it was not a cloud above his face but a pillow; my tongue flapping some ungodly words; Dobbs casting me aside, taking Charlie up in his arms and rushing out. There must be an error in my memory, because I distinctly remember handing the backpack to Dobbs before he took Charlie away.

If someone wants to know what it is like to hold a ghost on your lap, let him come and ask me. I will tell how the blood fizzes through hardened veins, how a perfectly clear head turns icebox-cold, how a spine turns to rubber.

I unzip the bag.

Charlie's lunchbox. What was inside is now a tarry black scar. A green folder contains three faded crayon drawings and a typed note from the preschool director.

Dear Parents,

There has been a case of conjunctivitis reported in the four-year-old class. The symptoms of pinkeye include redness around the eye, swelling, mucus in the eyes, and itchiness. Should your child experience any symptoms, contact his/her health-care provider.

On a happier note, we are all looking forward to next week's pageant, especially the children, who have been preparing for weeks. Arriving early means being assured a good seat. Overflow parking will be available at Shepherd's Field. We look forward to seeing you there.

I look in the backpack again. Goofy is still there. I pull him out and hug him. At the bottom of the backpack is one of Adam's socks. Adam has put something inside it which rattles—marbles, perhaps, or coins. I turn it over and empty the contents on my lap. The room turns cold. A collection of white pebbles.

But they are not pebbles. They are not anything my brain wishes them to be.

Swiftly, I arrange them from largest to smallest, as the tectonic plates grind apart. The land is surely plunging into the sea, caves must be opening their mouths and swallowing mountains whole. The world is being rent in two as a tiny hand holds up five skeletal fingers and waves from an upturned grave.

THE SIGNS OF Dobbs's agitation are apparent: shirttails hanging out; neck reddened by heat rash; forehead blistered in sweat. He is scanning one of his pamphlets.

"What did you do to Charlie?"

"Adam," he emphasizes, "should never have had a knife in the first place. You play with weapons, you're going to get hurt."

He thinks I have my boys mixed up. "I'm not talking about Adam. I'm talking about Charlie."

He groans. "Not you, now."

"You never returned Charlie." Even I don't recognize my voice.

"I don't have any idea what you're talking about. Listen, you should get some rest; you're going to need it when he wakes up."

I open my palms so he can see Charlie's hand in mine.

The only thing that moves is the pamphlet, falling from his fingers. His face goes stiff and pale. I can count on one hand the number of times Dobbs has been at a loss for words. "Oh no." Having found two words, he repeats them again and again.

All these years I've believed Charlie was the found child I never was, the one written about in the papers, the one whose homecoming made an entire nation rejoice. He became the symbol of hope for every missing child. Whenever I pictured him, he was taking up the life that was meant for me. He was supposed to have traded secrets with the same friend since grade school, shamed the bullies, surprised his teachers, and carried his family name proudly. When I thought of Charlie, I thought of having bequeathed my life to him.

"You told me you dropped Charlie off at a park down the street from his house. You told me you made a call to the police from a telephone booth. You said it was on television, him and his family getting back together."

"I wanted to spare you the truth. I thought it would be better to tell you what you wanted to hear."

I cover my mouth with my hand.

Dobbs reaches for me, but I sidestep him. "I thought I'd tell you when you got stronger, but then you had a little one on the way, and I kept thinking about what happened with the first baby, and well—there just never seemed like a good time to bring up the subject after Adam was born."

Tell me what, exactly?

There's a tremor so large going on inside him that he cannot keep it from traveling to his arm. I notice his fingers are a mess. Every single nail has been chewed to the quick. Hangnails have been ripped clear down to the knuckle.

I stand utterly still. "You kept him down here all this time."

Dobbs has taken on the symptoms of hypothermia. Even as his teeth chatter he gets out his feeble excuses. Listening to him lie is like listening to someone chew ice. "I tried to save him. I did what I could, but he was already way past it. You saw how he was." He clasps his hands around his forearms, drops his head. "Last thing I wanted was for him to—"

As if dying was Charlie's choice, as if it had nothing to do with what Dobbs did or failed to do. "You could've taken him back!"

He leans toward me. He looks like he's got his arms around a tree and is trying to yank it out of the ground. "I couldn't take him back, you know that." His voice is high-pitched with effort. "Our entire plan would have been in jeopardy. The police, the media—they'd have questioned him, and something would've come out that would've led them to this place, and then what? All this would have been for nothing."

And so it comes back to the Plan. Always the Plan. *Our* plan, he has the gall to say.

Whatever he registers in my face makes him start to plead. "I tried to save him, Blythe. I know what this must look like to you, but it wasn't like that. I sat with him, for hours. Wait, I'll show you. I kept notes—they're somewhere in this stack—" Dobbs starts shuffling through piles of papers because he has run out of lies.

"You didn't try to save him. You're lying. Just like you've been lying about taking us out of here!"

"You're not listening to me; I am trying to tell you—"

"What about the baby? Did you keep her down here, too?"

Dobbs is shaking his head. He keeps rummaging through papers, knocking entire columns of notebooks to the floor. "No, look, you've gotten the wrong idea about all of this. I told you I buried her. If I can just find—"

He stops when I ask, "Where did you put Charlie?"

Dobbs won't answer. Instead, he starts to snivel. I realize that there can be only one place. The silo. Adam must have broken in and gone down that shaft to get his notebooks and found Charlie's remains instead. And all at once, I know that Adam is in grave danger—not from his injury but of winding up like Charlie.

In all the many years I have spent hating this man, I cannot deny the times I have felt sorry for him—isn't this precisely how the devil gets away with murder? But what I feel for him now is nothing akin to hate. You could fire up hell's furnaces with what I feel for this man. You could drill down to the earth's cauldron and find nothing near as fiery.

We are in the kitchen. Dobbs is trying to get me to listen. I am trying to still the hundred voices screaming in my head, not least of which is Charlie's.

Dobbs is not crying anymore; he's gone on the offense. "I get it; I'm the beast. Is that what you want? You want me to be the bad guy, fine. I'll be the bad guy.

"You should thank me, instead of looking at me that way. The lengths I went to to keep you happy—getting the child, then trying to keep him alive for you, even though you near done him in yourself. Unfit is what you were back then. Don't you remember that?"

It's welcome, the sting of his words. It's acid eating through maggoty flesh.

Dobbs sits at the table, more sure of himself now that he doesn't have to bear both his weight and the weight of his lies. Doing us all a favor is what he's going on about, and I can't see straight for the picture of Charlie.

Turning my back to him, I battle for breath. The silence is screeching now. I go to turn the kettle off, but there is no kettle. The screeching is coming from someplace else. It is so loud I have to force myself not to press my hands over my ears. And then I notice the bottle of chloroform has not been put away. I pick up the washrag. I pretend to wipe the counter.

Dobbs is still talking when I quietly open the bottle and empty it into the rag. I turn around. He is still talking when I rush at him and knock back his chair. With every bit of strength I clamp that rag against his nose.

He bucks. I latch on even tighter. Adam is not going to end up like Charlie.

Dobbs wheels onto his side. My grip slips. I go for his face again. He claws me, gets ahold of my shirt and pulls. In the process of wrestling, I strike him in the head. It's the first time I've ever hit him good and proper, and it's as if I've reached in a fire and picked up burning coals. It feels that good. Dobbs strikes me back, and something in my mouth gives way, which feels even better. This is what I should have done years ago, instead of all the arguments and the raging silent protests, the hunger strikes and bargaining, the whoring and hoping. I spit out the tooth and make another go for his jaw, this time knuckles first. My swing is knocked off its trajectory by his hand. Somehow, I still manage to get a handful of hair. His neck is seamed by the knotty, purple vein. I bite it, hard as I can. He grabs my hair, rips my head back. His other hand lashes out and catches me in the windpipe. I keel over.

Dobbs rights me, then twists my arm behind my back and knees me forward, past the doorway and down the stairs. "You want me to show you what I did? I'll show you!"

He aims to lock me up. The silo!

We get to the utility tunnel. I jut my leg against the doorjamb and propel myself backward. He lunges against me with his shoulder, as though I'm a gate he is determined to bust through. I stumble forward and quickly do an about-turn. I grab his shin and sink my teeth into it. As Dobbs screams, I scramble out of the tunnel and fly up the stairs. I make it all the way to the living room before he tackles me from behind. He cinches his arms around my narrow waist and tries jostling me upright. My hands clamor for something to hold on to—a table leg, a chair. The only thing within my reach is my crochet work.

Somehow, Dobbs manages to sling me over his shoulder. He stumbles toward the exit.

I can see where Dobbs is balding, see the scabs between his hair follicles. He has a wet-dog smell. He grunts as he tries to get me through the doorway.

I free the crochet needle from its stitching. I raise my hand. Before he steps across the threshold, I slam it into his neck as hard as I can.

The hook plunges in with little resistance, kind of like driving a screwdriver into a bag of seed corn. It's the sound that's off-putting— the emptying of a pail of slop. I drive it in even farther. His grip around my thighs tightens. I wonder if I am going to have to pull the darn thing out and stab him again. But his arms loosen and then become slack, and next, we are making a graceful arc toward the floor.

DOBBS LIES WHERE he fell, on his chest, his knees folded up beneath him, his arms beside him, palms up. He hasn't moved. Around his head is a bloody halo. His eyes are fixed on some distant horizon. I intend to rob him of it. No gazing into a soft-bellied twilight. The truth at hand is what he must face: blood, guts, death.

After checking on Adam, I unlatch the keys from Dobbs's belt. They jingle when I shake them. The sound seems to distress Dobbs. It is less of a groan, more of a gurgle as he tries to speak. I bend down. His fingers beckon me closer. I put my ear right up next to his mouth.

"Don't," he manages.

"Don't what?"

The darkness is edging in, the walls are stooping forward, the ceiling is lowering itself. Something of the hell I've lived with comes for him now.

A shudder runs through him. "Don't . . . leave me."

Ah, yes.

I make sure he sees me put the keys in my pocket before taking his head in my hands. His eyes close slowly, mistaking the gesture for a caress perhaps, then flick open when I pivot his head to the other side. He now has nothing to obstruct the view of me walking about, able for the first time in years to do as I please. I step over him and follow the stairs down. Not something I please, but something I must. As much as I want to grab Adam and dash outside, I cannot leave Charlie at the bottom of the pit.

At the entrance to the utility tunnel, I take a deep breath. I unlatch the flashlight from its mount on the wall and take determined steps to the silo door. The padlock and chain are lying on the floor.

Penetrating the rank darkness of the silo takes every bit as much will as stabbing Dobbs. There are no lights in here. A beam not much wider than my index finger is all the flashlight can muster against the immensity of the darkness. Dobbs used to frighten Adam about this place with tales of demons, just as he did with Scalpers Above. "The ladder goes all the way down to hell," he'd say. I believe it. I tell myself it is the air finding release, but the sounds coming up from the depths are like the dead calling out a warning.

A narrow platform of rusty metal grates runs alongside the perimeter of the outer wall. Separating me from the yawning void is nothing but a puny rail. I aim the flashlight above. Somewhere up there are two massive doors that used to open for a rocket. I have to take Dobbs's word for it because it seems nothing like being in the earth. Deep space is what it feels like. I shift to the right. Huge metal contraptions are attached to the wall. What I see bears no resemblance to those old blueprints. To me, this looks like the decaying innards of a beast.

With the flashlight trained to the platform and my steps ringing out across the hollowness, I concentrate on not falling. Some of the platform's grates wobble like loose rocks. In several places, the going is slow, especially near the rickety landing of the freight elevator, which seems in danger of coming unbolted from the wall.

I know from Dobbs that the shaft is 174 feet deep. This information is of no use. I take out the glow sticks, snap them, and throw them over the rails. I count to time their descent. They make no sound when they land. Might as well be no bottom.

I come to the creaky, spiral staircase. Armed with the sliver of light, I take a deep breath, tighten the straps of Charlie's backpack, and test my foot on the first rung.

The wall beside me is pitted and pocked and stained with brown streaks, as though the place has been weeping for all time. Best put aside such thoughts. I lower myself to the next rung and then the next. With my left hand, I grip the rail. I count the rungs as I go.

If this is a skyscraper, I am scaling it with a fraying rope.

It's just a building, I keep telling myself. Yes, but what building is large enough to create its own weather? The air was dry where I started; now I am descending into something dewy. I can smell it too—coppery. Like thunderstorms.

I can hear my breath running too fast and too shallow. I am beginning to feel light-headed. I am very grateful for the handrails and the rungs. Until all of a sudden there isn't a rung. My foot dangles in the air. I wave the beam of light until it catches the place where the ladder picks up again. To continue going, I have to breach a gap almost the length of me.

It is a tricky feat, maneuvering the dead space. My arms ache and my hands are sore from gripping, but I make it. The rungs, if not entirely stable, are again evenly spaced. My breath becomes more regular, and with the repetitiveness of putting down one foot after the next, my mind begins to drift. I wonder if I haven't gone to sleep, haven't entered the dream of landing on the moon, when my foot finally finds solid ground. I put a second foot down and even then do not trust what I am standing on.

Turning from the ladder, I sweep the light in front of me. In the green fog is a reeking heap. Burst garbage bags, a tangle of hoses, aluminum tiles, old consoles, an upholstered chair with the springs poking out. Most of the stuff appears to be fixtures from when the place was operational, but there is a lot of Dobbs's trash, too. In an old toolbox is a bolt cutter. I put it in the backpack. I come upon a couple of Adam's notebooks. They go in the backpack, too.

I scramble among the rubble until I find the tiny clothes—a blue shirt, a gray pair of pants. I scoop up the bundle and wrap it in my sweater. Even if I live to be a hundred, there will never be enough ways to atone. "I'm taking you home, Charlie."

According to Dobbs's watch, I have been gone thirty-three minutes. How is it there is still a trickle of life left in him?

"See this?"

Dobbs parts his eyes slowly. A gargle comes from his throat.

"No, don't say anything. I want you just to look." I show him Charlie. More gurgles.

"When you're burning in hell, I don't want you to think about me. I want you to see this child. I want you to picture Adam, too. Picture them in a meadow. Picture them free."

His mouth moves into a "What?" shape, and then a "Why?" shape, and finally it is the shape of a dark, deep well. From it seeps the last that's left inside him, spit and blood. If there are regrets in his last breath, they're lost on me.

Groggy, Adam moans and holds his side. I help him sit up and give him half a painkiller and a cup of water. He scratches the rash around his mouth and nose.

"It's from the chloroform. It'll go away soon," I tell him.

His face looks blotchy, his lips are cracked, and his shirt is damp from sweat. He folds a corner of the bandage to look at the wound.

"Does it hurt real bad?"

He shrugs. "It's okay." He notices the suitcase. I've packed what we can carry: a change of clothes; the knitted stuffed toys I made him; the family of orphaned sock monkeys; Grandpa's watch; the notebooks. "Maybe we can get someone to come back for the rest of your stuff."

"We're leaving?" He struggles to his feet and notices the body in the doorway. "Is he . . . ?"

"Yes."

There comes no how or why or when. Just that same wounded look of someone who's been lied to his whole life. "We weren't here because of the Disaster," Adam says.

"No."

"Because there was no disaster."

"That's right."

Adam starts shaking his head. "I don't understand. Why are we here?"

"He stole me when I was a girl, two years before you were born."

"And Charlie?"

"He stole him, too."

"And that was him down in the silo?"

"Yes. I have him now. We're going to give him back to his family."

"Did Mister . . . ?"

"Yes, he did." And I played my part in that tragedy, too.

"He was never going to let us go, was he?"

"No, he wasn't."

I pick up the suitcase. "I'm going to do my best to answer all your questions." I lay my hand on his arm. "But first, we must get you to a doctor."

I look around the place one last time. It seems different. Not the blood or the smell of death—like sorghum. Everything is exactly as it's always been. And yet, it's all changed. You can't see change; you can only feel it.

I bend down and pull the notepad from Dobbs's top pocket. We step over his body and pass through the entrapment vestibule. I give Adam the notepad. He flips it open to the codes. He punches in the numbers. We look at each other, listening to the locks slide. Adam seems to pay no mind to the pain. Both of us are fixed on one thing, and one thing only—the door at the top of the stairs. Over the years, my mind turned it into the size of a ceiling, and here it is, no bigger than a closet door.

When we get to it, Adam turns around with his eyebrows raised, expecting me to say something.

What is there to say?

My keeper is dead. All that's left of him is the secret. And what a pitiful little secret I have turned out to be. A secret, even a long-held one, can turn out to be such a liar. My son is about to know the extent of this. If only there was one thing I could say, one thing that could explain everything. And if not to explain it, then perhaps to prime the pump for the forgiveness that is his to withhold. And if not to explain it, or have it forgiven, then to prepare him before the lies come at him like starved wolves.

"There are others," I finally manage. "They are not all like him. There are so many who are good, who will be kind to you. Let them."

"Okay."

As for the whole truth—it can't be told; it can only be shown.

I nod. "Go on, then."

He turns the handle and gives it a shove. I can barely utter the words. "We're free."

Part Two

ABOVE

V

T IS NIGHTTIME, not Lights Out. It is Above. It is earth. Kansas. Home. The terrible ordeal is over. I want to tell Adam this, but I have to put my hands on my knees and wait first for the dizziness to pass. It's so loud out here. A pulsing drone is spliced with sudden rustling and retreating whispers. In three-four time, something trills. A chirp close enough to tap me on the shoulder rings out, then takes off. Around us swirls an endless shushing.

My skin crawls. I dust my arms and check to see whether I've stepped in an ant nest. Nothing other than goose bumps. Nothing other than thrill. I straighten up, take another couple of steps, and stumble again. Easy, easy, I tell myself. No need to run. I cover my ears to see if it will improve my balance. Even with black-and-white spots popping in my eyes, I can tell there is something wrong with this darkness. It isn't the impermeable darkness of Below. This is a tricky entity, a space that differentiates itself into varying degrees of densities. It is a space that needs navigating. I no longer trust a darkness I can see through.

I reach for Adam as a blind person might. He takes my arm and we both stand teetering as though on tippy-toes at the edge of a cliff.

"What is that?" Adam buries his nose and mouth in the crook of his arm.

The smell is overpowering, alarming, like a gas leak. Vegetation. The smell of growing things. "Plants," I tell him. "It's okay."

His reply is muffled and I catch only one word: *stings*.

I can't argue. Every inhalation is an assault. Each breath sears the inside of my nose. A memory from light-years ago: Gerhard pushing me into a swimming pool, getting water up my nose. That's what it's like to breathe fresh air. Reflexively, I open my mouth, and just as quickly, find the air has a taste to it. Soapy. "Let's just take it slow."

Two wobbly steps forward, and Adam drops to the ground. I crouch beside him. Is he faint? I feel sick to my stomach, but what I've got is more like stage fright. What Adam has is a knife wound that may have caused damage to his insides. God help me if he succumbs now. Somehow, I have to hurry this process along. In response to my offer to help him to his feet, he makes a sound I have never heard before. A guttural sound, something a dog might make if pelted with a stone. "Adam! What is it?"

He shakes free of my embrace. He lifts up something with both hands. It falls through his fingers. "Earth," he cries. "It's earth!" The stinging air, my ears popping as though from a sudden change in altitude, and still, I can barely believe it. I, too, kneel. It is an act of worship.

Adam runs his hands over the ground. He scratches it, rubs it, scoops it up. Because he insists, I draw my initials in the dirt, too. Soon, the wind will blow it away and there will be nothing of me in this place.

"Why do they call it dirt? It's beautiful."

I tell Adam it's time to go, but he trickles dirt on his legs, then shakes it off, then repeats the process. It looks like he might roll in it. I have to insist.

I hold out my hand to him as he struggles to his feet. "We have to hurry, son. There will be time for all of this later." I pull my shirt up over my nose, hoping to blunt the shock of fresh air.

He slips a handful of dirt into his trouser pocket and faces the night, his head tipped back all the way. I look up, too. Above us is no ceiling, only a startling brilliance, an aperture in the expanse. A peephole, like a giant eyeball is about to roll in front of it, like just maybe there is someone up there looking out for us.

"The moon!" Adam reaches for it, like he can pluck it from sky and pocket it. "It's so close."

He twirls slowly, still looking up. "The sky, Mom!" He names the world for me. He names it as though I've never known it. And perhaps I haven't ever known it, not really. It certainly feels utterly foreign.

"Yes."

"Why isn't it black?"

The sky is layered with orange, purple, and gray streaks. Around the moon is silvery-blue. A blinking light appears in front of him.

"A falling star!"

"It's a firefly," I tell him. Adam has his finger out to see if the light will land on it. "Where'd it go?" He sees another blinking light and stumbles after it, stepping out beyond the triangle of light from the door. I hear the air go out of him. I look to see what has caused him to stop dead in his tracks, and it happens to me, too.

There is no wall. There is no beyond. Here goes on for miles. So overwhelming is this fact that we might as well be faced with a gap too wide to breach.

Adam takes a step backward. His voice has a quaver to it. "Whose is it?"

"Whose is what?"

"This. Outside."

Some invisible border parcels off that which belongs to Dobbs, but I'm sure this isn't what my son is after. I turn to him. He has retreated even farther from the dark mass. In my most reassuring voice, I say, "It belongs to everybody."

He looks at me dubiously. "Us, too?"

I nod.

"Me?"

"Yes. You, especially."

He seems a little more reassured.

"It's probably going to be better if you stay focused on the things that are close," I add, and realize how ridiculous this is. As though the expanse is going to wait for our permission before it advances, a black hole asking politely of the star if it may swallow it. Terrible to think of it this way. The air has given me a headache. No more deep breaths; too much oxygen. I am on the brink of hallucinating.

Adam draws my attention to the fact that there are weeds all around us by pulling one out of the ground and smelling it. "So this is mine?"

"If you want it, yes." Try not to cower at the dark immensity nosing up against us.

He puts it in his pocket and picks up a rock. "This?"

"Yes." Where is Dobbs's car?

Adam goes about stuffing his pockets with stones and leaves and weeds, while I turn my face to the sudden breeze. It's abrasive, like someone has taken sandpaper to my cheeks. It smells wrong, too.

The darkness hisses and whirrs, approaching and retreating. Something is not quite right about the night. Where there should be some sense of triumph, there is in me a growing sense of dread. It should be wonderful—the moon, the fireflies, a young man filling his lungs with fresh air and his pockets with dirt. It is his wound I am worried about, I tell myself. It is the contents of the backpack over my shoulder. It is the need to hurry. It is the hundred things that can go wrong between now and when I find the hospital.

Although it can't possibly be the case, all manner of gnashing, screeching, panting creatures seems to be stalking us. I can't shake the feeling that we are prey. Or specifically, that Adam, injured, bloodied, is prey. For a crazy moment, I feel the urge to turn around and make a dash back to the door. The meek shall inherit the earth was what Reverend Caldwell always used to say. I'm not so sure. The earth doesn't seem to be waiting for anyone to inherit it, least of all someone as meek as my son. What if the world has turned into a hungry beast? What if Adam is nothing but a morsel?

Adam has found a boulder. I tell him no way. I tell him it's time to leave. One last thing: I return to the door. Dobbs can't chase after us, but I slam it shut anyway. He is now the one locked up.

Instead of parked in front of us, Dobbs's car is thirty feet away. It's

Adam who points it out. I'd mistaken it for a tangle of bushes. We approach it cautiously, as though every step could trigger a booby trap. Compared to our confined quarters, the vehicle seems enormous. I pull off the camouflaged netting and hesitate.

Were it not for the urgency of the situation, I'd sooner walk a hundred miles barefoot on a trail of thorns than get in the Oldsmobile again. A century could go by and I would have no less of an urge to smash its windshield, rip the doors off their hinges, slash those leather seats. A car that drives a girl to a hole in the ground has no business carrying any more passengers, least of all my son, who is opening the door on the driver's side. Wincing only a little, he scrambles in. "A car, Mom!" There he sits, manhandling the wheel.

My ears are playing tricks on me. Either that, or the darkness is growling. "Move over." I slam the door, then lock it. A little relief. The night still keeps its unblinking eye on us.

"Jackpot!" Adam is lifting a pair of Dobbs's galoshes. Among Adam's possessions now packed in the suitcase are clothes suitable only for a seventy-four-degree controlled climate. Because he has never needed them, he has no shoes. "Can I have them?" He is peeling off his socks.

I nod.

"Can you drive?" Adam stamps his feet, pleased with his find.

"Sure," I reply, putting the key in the ignition. Truth is, I'd probably do better if this were a tractor. Daddy had given me only a few lessons in a car before Dobbs took me. I ask Adam to hold the flashlight so I can scrutinize the pedals and the gearshift. The dashboard has more dials and buttons than seems possible for one person alone to operate.

"You have to put it in reverse," he says, yanking the lever to R. Adam has always been fascinated by cars and has read everything he can on the subject. A few years back, Dobbs brought him the Oldsmobile owner's manual, and it didn't take him long before he'd committed every detail to memory. From its diagrams and using his own ingenuity, he recently constructed a chassis from salvaged junk that Dobbs brought.

I bat Adam's hand away. "Fasten your seat belt."

Adam leans forward and splays his fingers against the invisible barrier separating us from the outside. He raps on it. "You never see any pictures of windows in books, only what's on the other side of them." He turns to the window next to him and shows it the same reverence. He pushes his nose against it, then his lips, and then gives it a big lick. The world is turning him into a boy again.

I turn the ignition, and the car shudders. Startled by the roar, Adam presses his hands against his ears, then fixes his gaze at the door of the silo. Beneath the full moon about only a dozen yards or so away, it appears to go nowhere. It looks, in fact, like an invitation. If I'd wandered across the prairie and come to a door such as this, I would have wanted to see what was on the other side of it. I'd have gone down those stairs to see if it led to another world. From this angle, there is no trace of my existence for the last seventeen years. Nothing of Adam's childhood. Nothing of the horrors. A door can be such a terrible thing. If I ever live in a house, it will have only windows.

I back the car out from its surrounding nest of bushes before it stalls. I try again, and this time the car hops. I shift the gear into drive, and get a little too eager on the gas pedal turning the car around. It moves in fits and starts down the gravel path while Adam gives me instructions as though he's the expert and I'm the novice. Perhaps he is, and perhaps I am, for this landscape is nothing like the one I remember.

Adam doesn't turn around to see what we are leaving behind, but I keep looking at the door in the rearview mirror. Soon, it is nothing more than a matchbox, and then it isn't anything but a dot. By the time Adam has figured out how to turn on the headlights, there isn't anything to look at, just a place where light leaks from a hole in the sky.

"This is incredible!" Adam has rolled his window down all the way. A chill blows in. He sticks out his head. I grab his shirt to anchor him, even though I'm only going ten miles an hour. I keep my eyes trained for familiar landmarks. This is not a dream, I keep telling myself. This is really happening.

There is nothing to tell what year we're in. It could be a thousand years in either direction. It's almost as disorienting as living underground where there is no day, week, year, no history. Below there are no seasons, and for the life of me I can't seem to figure out what season it is out here. Dobbs mentioned recently it being January, but he must have had it wrong. There's not a scrap of evidence of a Kansas winter. No snow, no frost, no ice on the road. All there is is that dank smell and the chill.

Finally, the country road. It doesn't matter what year, or what season; it only matters that the road leads us home.

Over the years, I've had all kinds of fantasies. Each one has begun with a road or ended with a road or had a road going right through the middle of it. Usually, it would be a smooth two-laner with a lot of traffic. Sometimes, it would be an unpaved road, its surface like polished steel, so hot you have to walk where the weeds grow on the shoulder. This road I barely remember.

"Have you forgotten which way?" Adam asks.

I've forgotten how to decide, is the problem.

I turn right.

One headlamp is out, but there is more than enough moonlight to see the overgrowth. I stick to the center line to avoid driving over ground cover. There are so many more trees than before. A hedge runs rampant alongside us. Adam is still calling out everything he sees in a breathy, unfamiliar voice. I want to roll down my window, too, and shout, "Hello, trees! Hello, prairie! Hello, world!" There must always have been this much of it and I just never noticed.

Not too far up ahead should be the intersection. You live one place your whole life there isn't a road you don't know, but now I have the sneaking suspicion that we are one wrong turn from being utterly lost. I consult my memory for directions, but it keeps insisting it is seventeen years ago, only with more trees.

"The moon's following us!" Adam's blond hair is sticking up straight from being wind-whipped. He is short of breath, his voice pitched high with excitement. "Go faster! Let's see if we can outrun it."

I smile and ease down on the accelerator. The speedometer needle bounces up to fifteen and then twenty miles an hour. It's fun for about five seconds until we hit a ribbed section of road and the tires make popping sounds and the car bounces us up and down. I start to feel queasy. Too much for someone accustomed to being stationary. Adam also seems to have a bout of motion sickness because he rolls up his window and doesn't protest when I go a little slower.

The bitter air has gotten to me, too. How they say venom affects a person is what the cold is doing to me. First, it was stinging, but now it's numbing. I wonder if soon my entire body won't give way to paralysis. I have to force myself to concentrate on the road.

"Is that"—he pauses, runs his fingertips against the knobs—"a radio?"

"Go ahead, turn it on."

Adam pushes a button. The sound of static startles him, and he flinches as though he's been given an electric shock.

"It's okay, here, let me show you." I fiddle with the tuner. Nothing but dead air.

Just as I am about to push the AM button, a monster rises up in front of us and blocks our path. I jam on the brakes and swerve sharply.

Adam is thrown against the dashboard, and knocks his head.

I look behind me. It lingers just at the edge of the brake lights' red glow.

"Stay here."

As soon as I get out, there's that smell again. Those same noises are still in pursuit of us. I much prefer being in the car than out in the open. Forcing myself onward, I walk ten yards before I see it. I still don't understand. Sticking right up through the tarmac in the middle of the road is a tree.

"What is it, Mom?"

"Get back in the car, Adam."

"What's wrong?" he asks, as though it is perfectly natural for a tree to be growing on a broken yellow line.

I usher him back into the car. This time he doesn't argue with me when I tell him to put his seat belt on.

Not too long down the road, we pass a sign I've never seen before: a blue triangle with an emblem that looks like a whirligig. There's another tree in the street, and behind it three others. Slowing down, I steer the car around them. Vines are snaked across the street so thick I can't see the asphalt. And then there is no going forward. Nothing short of an encroaching army of timber barricades our way.

Through the windshield, I watch the scraggly tops of these giants shake their heads at us. Instead of growing straight, their trunks are bent at impossible angles, their twisted branches reaching toward us. Adam is out before I can tell him no. He approaches the front line cautiously, as you would a herd of elephants. By the time I get to him, he is stroking the base of one of the trees. He looks at his fingertips, as if he expects the bark to have stuck to them. He puts his arms around it. "They are wonderful!"

No, not wonderful. I pace from one end of the road to the other. In either direction, the line of trees seems to stretch indefinitely.

When I turn around, Adam is gone.

"Adam?" I wave the flashlight frantically. The beam is scattered against the dense foliage.

"Adam!" I yell. I can feel the earth spinning on its axis. Either that or the road is bucking me. I have a hard time staying upright. "Adam, where are you?"

I rush between two trees, and find myself in a forest so dense I immediately lose my bearings. Did I come from this direction? Or that? "Adam!"

"I'm right here."

I swing the flashlight to the left. He is sitting on a branch that is bent all the way to the ground.

"Don't you ever—" I notice him holding his side. He is laboring.

"I just wanted to climb a tree."

I am trembling so hard when I get him back in the car that it is an effort to turn the ignition. "You cannot just wander off like that! Do you hear me? Ever!"

Theo once wandered away from Mama and me at the grocery store. It didn't take but a minute to find him in the candy aisle filling his pockets, but Mama took him by the shoulders and shook him and yelled loud enough for everyone to hear how he could have been lost forever. On top of everything, there is this new fear. How easy it is going to be for the big, wide world to wedge itself between Adam and me.

"It's okay, Mom."

I nod in agreement, suppressing tears. Neither one of us is terribly composed. Adam starts chewing on his thumbnail, something he hasn't done in years. I try to steady my hands by taking a firm grip on the steering wheel.

"What do we do now?" Adam asks.

Without answering, I turn the Oldsmobile around. We go back the way we've just come, back down this godforsaken road just like all those years ago when Dobbs Hordin was in the driver's seat and I was the teenager who didn't think anything bad could happen to a person.

TO ADAM, ANY direction is as good as another, but I don't know how to get to Lawrence going this way. At least we are going. Going. There has to be a signpost up ahead.

It's silly to think the backwoods has fallen into rank behind us and is advancing on us, but I drive a little faster and keep checking the rearview mirror anyway. Picking up on my cue, Adam looks over his shoulder out the back window, too. I turn on the overhead light. Who'd have thought electrical lighting would be such a comfort?

Gone from Adam's face is the wonder from earlier; it is now bleached with fear. Chewing on his lip and his arms crossed at his chest, he squints into the darkness as though things are about to fly at us out of it. Adam knows nothing at all about anticipating, because in a controlled environment he's never had to anticipate. He can't possibly know to protect himself. This now terrifies me. More terrifying is how terrible I have become at anticipating. How, then, am I to protect him?

It has become stuffy in the car. I roll the window down just an inch. Adam cringes at the cold, pulls his collar up around his ears, and draws his hands into his sleeves. He appears to be shrinking in his clothes. I locate the switch for the heater, but nothing other than cold air blasts through the vents.

I can't decide what exactly the weather is doing. It feels like a storm, but mostly the sky is clear. I used to spend hours describing weather to

Adam—gully washers, hail, you name it. I was so good at describing sticky, hot summers that we'd strip down to our skivvies and shoot each other with water guns made from straws. This here, there's no good description for it.

Where is that intersection?

Adam groans when we go over another bump, which I now realize must be tree roots rumpling the pavement. We pass the turnoff to Dobbs's property. Not only is there no gate, the ten-foot barbed-wire fence that used to front the property is gone, too. All that remains is the same NO TRESPASSING sign.

The car rumbles along. Something in the air catches in my throat. Adam looks over at me.

"It's just a tickle," I tell him, but the cough revs up. Soon it is bad enough that I have to pull over to the side of the road, except there is a thicket where the shoulder ought to be, so I stop the car in the lane and hope a truck doesn't come blaring down on us. Or maybe that would be just fine. I could get out and say, "I am the taken girl. I am Blythe Hallowell," and that would be the end of it.

"Something's in the air. Do you smell that?"

Adam nods.

Not just vegetation. Chemicals, perhaps. Chlorine?

No car is in sight. There are no lights anywhere, not even in the distance where a freeway ought to be. "Lock your door," I tell Adam between coughing spasms. This is all we need now, me to cough myself loopy.

"Here you go." Adam hands me a canteen of water from the backseat.

"What else does he have back there? Any chance of a chain saw?"

It's meant as a joke, but Adam gives me a sober look. "You can't expect it to be how you remember it."

I can't think of anything to say. In fact, I've completely drawn a blank on how to treat him. A few minutes ago, he had the enthusiasm of a young boy, not an iota of caution; now, he is this almost-grown-up telling me not to take my memory so seriously.

When the cough subsides, I put the car back into gear and drive. "People are going to be asking me a lot of questions. You, too."

"Okay." Future tense. His eyes glaze over.

"They're going to ask about what happened to Mister." I don't dare take my eyes off the road. "I might have to go someplace and straighten everything out."

"It's not a crime what you did."

"No, it isn't." Even to my own ears, this has the muffled tone of uncertainty. I don't know any more what a crime is or isn't. It's hard to think of crime the way it is written in books when I've lived so many years with rules instead of laws.

"I won't let them lock you up. I'll tell them I did it."

I shake my head. "Nobody's going to get locked up."

Up ahead is a sign. I stop twenty yards in front of it. Through the vines, I make out, TONGANOXIE, 15 MI. To get to Lawrence, we should be going in the opposite direction. Who knows, perhaps Tonganoxie is no longer the one-horse town it used to be. Maybe it is now the hub of Douglas County, with a state-of-the-art emergency room.

After a while, the jarring and bumping of the uneven road gives way to a smooth, almost pleasing drone. Adam, though, has drawn his legs up to his chest and knotted his arms around them. Without realizing it, he has started to hum. He has hums for different moods—when he's content or bored or lost in thought. High-pitched hums come when he's wound up. The more worried he is, the lower the pitch tends to be. This one has so much bass it can mean only one thing: he is in a full-blown panic. To distract him from his thoughts, I suggest he look through the glove box. He doesn't know what I'm talking about, so I point to the little lever. He pulls it and springs back in his seat when the compartment drops like a big gaping jaw. I've never seen him this jumpy.

"Got a lot of junk in there, doesn't he?" I comment.

Adam rifles through Dobbs's things, holding up each find for me to see: an odd collection of tokens; registration papers so old they are taped together along the folds; something called a Disposal Zone Pass.

"What else does he have in the box back there?"

Adam brings it to the front seat. It is a soup-to-nuts survival kit, complete with army rations, a folding shovel, and a compass. After examining all the items, he puts them back and conducts a search for other secret compartments in the car. He is thrilled to find a map under the visor. He opens it, holds it up to the overhead light, and announces in a trembling voice that Dobbs has crossed out many of the routes.

"Let me see that." I push the brakes and let the car idle where it stops.

Not only has Dobbs scratched out some of the roads, he has penciled in squiggly trails connecting the missile complex to various locations. None of his notations are legible. For some reason, Lawrence has a big *X* through it.

"What does that mean?"

"Who knows?" I answer. "Put it away; we don't need it." I grip the steering wheel and keep driving.

"He's circled Oskaloosa. Is that a town? Maybe we should go there."

"Put it away, Adam."

"I found where we are." He thrusts the map at me. I jam on the brakes again. We follow Adam's finger until it comes to hash marks. "What do you suppose he means by these?"

I snatch the map and toss it over my shoulder. "Nothing. It's one of his crazy ideas, is all. You checked under the seats yet?"

Adam bends down and runs his hand beneath him. He comes up with a cassette tape. "What's this?"

"Watch." I shove the cassette tape into the machine, and Patsy Cline starts singing. With Dobbs, it's always country music.

"I don't want to think about him." Adam pushes buttons until the tape ejects.

"Just wait till you hear all the different kinds of music. You're going to love classical music. Mozart, Bach—"

He cuts me short. "How could you stand it?"

I want to talk about things from before my captivity, and Adam wants a reconfiguration of everything that happened after it. It doesn't matter how far back in time we go; we are both dragging the dead-weight of the past into our fresh new start.

"How could you stand what he did to you? Why didn't you try to escape?"

"Oh, Adam. I tried to get away. I drove myself crazy trying to get out. And then when you came along, I was so scared he'd take you away from me if I tried anything." I tell him about the baby and living without Charlie and the ventilation shaft where I used to scream for help and busting my foot against the door. Instead of a beginning, middle, and end, the story comes out haphazard and makes about as much sense as a riddle told backward.

"Why didn't anyone come for us?" Adam's tone has turned accusatory.

"I'm sure they tried. I'm sure they looked just about everywhere they could think to look."

"Maybe they're all dead."

It's my turn to get short. "Don't you say things like that. If you want to blame someone, blame Mister. Blame me. But you are not to blame them."

"Why didn't you tell me sooner?" he asks after a while. He knows of my deceit, but he still cannot grasp the why of it.

Because I was thinking like a mother—not a narrator. A mother has to find the kinder story. "I'm sorry, son." I am always going to be sorry. Even something as big as being free can't change that.

He gives me that inscrutable look and then stares ahead into the night. "I'd have killed him a long time ago."

We approach another sign too overgrown with vines to be of any use, but I feel my spirits lift. An intersection will be up ahead. If I read the map right, I can make a right and go a few miles till we hit County Road 1057 and then double back toward Lawrence.

"Do you think there are people living in space by now?"

"I don't know."

"Because there sure aren't any people around here."

"There will be. Another few miles and there'll be so many people you won't know what to do with yourself."

No sooner do I make this proclamation than I notice what's wrong with this end of the road: utility poles lying on the ground. None of them have any wires attached to them.

"Do I look like them?" Adam continues.

"Of course you look like them." But if the utility poles aren't up, there can't be any electricity in this area.

"What if your parents don't like me?"

"Adam, don't talk like that." I begin tallying all his many wonderful features because I'd just as soon as not point out the growing list of things wrong with this route.

And then there is no way around it.

I slow down in plenty of time; even lit up by one headlight, it makes no sense. Stranded at the railway crossing is a freight train. Dobbs's hash marks.

"Wow," Adam whispers.

It's immediately apparent the train has been parked here a long time. The containers are rusty and in some places missing their sides altogether. One of the containers has toppled over.

"Can we go look?"

"Stay where you are, Adam."

"It's so huge. Please, Mom, can we just—"

I scream as someone raps on the passenger window. A bearded, dirty face scowls at us and raves some incoherent protest.

Adam lurches toward me as the man bangs against the window so hard it's a wonder it doesn't shatter.

"What does he want?" Adam asks.

I throw the car into gear and hit the gas. "We're not going to find out." I steer the Oldsmobile sharply to the left onto the gravel utility road running beside the tracks. "Hang on!"

There are other shapes emerging from the containers now, some with torches. One of the ragged figures marches straight into our path and I dare not swerve for the ditch beside us. I don't know how to drive this fast. "Get out of the way!" I pummel the center of the steering wheel and the horn blares loudly, but the man continues to advance until his body careens off the hood, and goes flying into the darkness.

"Oh God, oh God."

The back window cracks, and something solid hits the side of the car hard enough to jostle it.

"They're throwing stuff at us!"

"Get down, Adam!"

We are nearing the front of the train, where a blockade is forming across the access road. Men are pushing barrels and shopping carts into a big pile, and they are chanting.

"Mom, what's going on?"

"It's okay, my boy. Everything's going to be okay. Just stay down."

I tighten my grip on the wheel and then jam the accelerator all the way to the floorboard. The tires churn up stones which pelt the undercarriage like machine-gun fire. The barricade is no match for the Oldsmobile. Boxes and carts go flying every which way, and I can't be sure whether the burlap-covered objects we hit are sandbags or bodies.

We go a good ten miles farther before I slow down and check on Adam. He gets back onto the seat, and leans away from the window.

The tightness in my chest returns and between coughing jags, I ask, "Are you okay?"

Adam is bent at the waist, but he gives me a winning smile, which can only mean he's faking.

"Is that what people are like?" His chin is trembling.

Checking the rearview mirror, I tell him it's a homeless camp because that's what my mind would have it be. Never mind this is Douglas County, Kansas, land of miles and miles of nothing. I don't tell him that I am in a lot of trouble now. Folks may let the Dobbs thing go, but a hit-and-run?

No turning back now. We carry along the dirt road until we must be well on our way to Kansas City. Somewhere along the line we are bound to hit a major thoroughfare, a gas station, or a farmhouse.

"Are all roads this long?"

"Oh, son, they're much, much longer than this."

"But where do they end?" He says it like all roads should meet at a wall or a ledge or a dead end. He's been aboveground less than an hour, and already I am forgetting that for him the world fits neatly on textbook-size pages, that countries are confined to diagrams.

"Take a look at that map again. See if you can make head or tail of it."

The smell of fumes sticks to my tongue, thick enough almost to chew. Light-headed, I feel my confidence tapering. Adam won't be fooled by my brave face.

He is poring over the map. His hands are still shaking. "I see the train tracks. He's got a line here with arrows. That's got to be good, right?"

"I'll take another sip of that water, if you don't mind."

Adam hands me the bottle. It is slippery. I turn on the overhead light. Blood on the bottle and his hand.

"I'm okay, Mom," he insists, but the spreading stain on his shirt contradicts him. The stitches must have ruptured. "It'll quit bleeding in a minute; it's just because I twisted funny." He presses his hand to his side and folds over.

Now. I look through the windshield at the moon. Now would be a real good time to help us out a little.

Of its own doing, the car begins to slow. I press the accelerator pedal as far as it will go and then pump it, but the Oldsmobile keeps slowing down and gradually sputters to a complete stop. Several red lights come up on the dashboard. I have no idea what any of them mean. A gust of wind bangs against the car on its way into the pitch of night. I turn over the ignition and pump the gas. Nothing happens.

Adam leans over to look at the control panel. "We're out of gas," he announces matter-of-factly.

FOR YEARS I have dreamed of open spaces, but reality is more terrifying than being confined. If only the expanse could parcel itself to us a little bit at a time. Instead, it is a tide that keeps rising. There is no adjusting to the outside; there is only doggy-paddling through the night, trying to keep the terror from dragging me under.

The light of the moon is now like foggy breath on steel. Adam is not used to dampness and shivers right through the blanket, but he has set a rather demanding pace. The hours he has spent walking up and down stairs and running along the silo's corridors are paying off in every way except one. When we first started out on foot, he marveled at how well shoes work, but now he has started to limp on account of the blisters they've caused. I've had to rip holes in my old pair to make room for my crooked toes. At first, Adam wanted to stop every few yards to pick up something, a stick or a stone. He'd compare weights. Now, he trudges along without even looking down. Although he won't admit it, he's in a lot of pain from the wound. Hunching forward, he refuses to hand me the suitcase, and scans the countryside with the flashlight. I consider telling him to turn it off so we can prolong the battery life, but who's to say we wouldn't walk right by a farmhouse, what with all these trees. They're monstrous, growing outward at queer angles. Each and every one has gnarled, crooked limbs.

I don't know how long we've been walking or how far. I keep trying to place our location. The compass, unable to settle its spinning needle, is of no use. If I didn't know better, I'd swear we were in some other state. We have yet to come to an open field. The land should tell us what season we're in. It's not spring, or there'd be the smell of freshly turned soil, and it's not summer, because there is not a single corn row. Just acres and acres of deformed trees and an unending tangle of greenbrier.

We've got to come across a house. "Anytime now," I say.

In my head, I try to rehearse my story. Do I start with the killing or end with it? Do I save Adam for later, or do I put him out front, the one good thing I have to show for myself? Or do I just give them my name and the date I was kidnapped?

Adam keeps his own counsel, and I've become so accustomed to his silence that he startles me when he says, "Mom, look."

I follow the beam of light, and sure enough, between a clearing of trees is a structure. Instead of hurrying toward it, I put my hand across the front of the flashlight till he turns it off.

"Stay here," I tell him.

"I'm coming with you."

"No. I'll call to you once I know it's safe." The figures from the train are still fresh in my mind. "I'll be right back. Go hide in those hedges till I tell you."

I ball up my handkerchief and press it against my mouth to stifle the cough and proceed.

Something claws my leg and snags my skirt. I rip free of the thorny bush that has overtaken much the driveway.

"Is that a tree house?" whispers Adam from behind me.

"I told you to wait!"

"I don't think anyone lives there."

Without a roof, the house at the end of the drive looks scalped. Growing right up out of it is one of those unsightly trees. Mangled branches are coiling out of the windows. The gutters have fallen down, and the front of the house is completely taken over by ivy. There is no point knocking on the front door. "Let's go."

Not too much further along, the road turns spongy and damp. Adam hasn't said anything for a while. Instead of leading the way as before, he now lags behind. I stop and wait for him to catch up. I feel his forehead—he is burning up. I check the wound. It is red and puffy and beginning to seep pus.

"Let's stop for a while and rest."

He shakes his head. He motions for me to move on.

We keep going even when our feet are soaked and frozen.

I've been trying hard not to jump the gun, but I keep picturing my reunion with Mama. My biggest worry is what she'll make of Adam. I want her to see what a sensitive, curious person he is, how focused he can be on certain things, what a lovely companion he is. I want her to love him. I don't know what I'll do if she doesn't.

Suddenly, there is no going forward. One minute, a road, such as it is; the next, a wash. From the smell alone, it's obvious the water's been sitting a good long time. I grab the flashlight. No wading to the other side—the waterway is fortified with trees. Instead of having burred, bent trunks like the others, these have massive, barrel-shaped bases and thick, tentacle roots that bulge out of the water. I know them only from pictures—mangrove trees. Impossibly, we are in a swamp.

What a Florida mangrove is doing in the middle of Kansas is not nearly the pressing conundrum that Adam's failing condition is. I try leading him in a meandering route around the edge of the swamp until I realize there is no circumventing it. We proceed in another direction, traipsing through bushes and brambles so thick wild animals might as well be mauling us. Desperate, I begin hollering for help.

At first, I think it is Adam who is panting from all the exertion. I stop. While he catches his breath, I hear it again—panting, and then a grunt.

"Do you hear that?" Adam whispers.

I press my hand against his mouth. I cock my head to the left and wait.

This time the sound comes from behind us.

If we were in a field, we might outrun it, but in brush as dense as this, we stand no chance. Quietly, I reach for the backpack and pull out the shovel. I hold it like a spear, and beckon for Adam to get behind me. I wait for the threat to give away its location.

The grunting becomes more insistent. It's getting closer. For a second, everything goes real quiet. And then there is an almighty roar. Branches snap, the ground vibrates. The unmistakable racket of a charging beast.

"Turn on the light!"

The beam finds its mark—a razorback. I am still trying to fathom why such a docile animal, known for being shy and therefore impossible to hunt, would be going against its nature to mount an attack on humans when, seconds later, the impact lifts me clear off my feet. The boar has run smack-dab into the shovel. It squeals and staggers off into the night.

"Mom!" Adam drops next to me.

I'm not gored to death. I get up and dust off my tail end. "I'm fine."

"We have to get away from this place!" He looks behind him.

"It's okay. It won't be back."

"What was it?" Adam can barely get the words out he's shaking so much.

I position the shovel so he can't see how bloodied it is. "A boar, is all." What I don't tell him is that boars never charge people.

My arms ache from the impact. My chest is so tight that my breathing has become a thin whistle. Every little noise startles me. Readying the shovel in the event of another onslaught, I tell Adam to follow me.

"I want to go back to the car." Adam's voice is shrill.

"We have to keep going."

He turns on his heel and hurries the other way. "I don't like it here." I grab his arm, but he pulls away. "We've got to go back to the car and wait until someone finds us. That's what Mister's survival guide said to do."

"Adam, we'll never find our way back to the car!"

Five seconds is all it takes for him to disappear completely. Between us there might as well be an entire forest.

"Wait!" I chase him with a snippet of light.

After a footslog through mud and bushes, we finally emerge from the quagmire. The ground seems to have a little bit of an incline. The dense vegetation falls back, but walking again in the open only makes me feel more vulnerable. I offer Adam a handful of dry noodles, but he shakes his head. When I ask if he wants to rest, he mutters something incoherent.

The gentle rise turns into a serious incline. Adam's convinced we came this way before. I only agree so we can keep going to the top of the rise where we will surely be able to see lights and set our course.

Unlike the ground level, there is not one bush or tree growing on the hill, only a carpet of moss that squeaks as we walk on it. Near the crest, Adam stumbles and falls. He won't let me attend to the bloody gash on his shin. I look for the offending item. It's all wrong—the roads, the derelict train, the strange signposts, the trees I do not recognize, the mangrove swamp—but nothing convinces me the world is up to no good quite as much as this: a half-buried Singer sewing machine. A few paces farther, at the top of the hill, the wind has blown the topsoil away. A host of other items poke up through the ground: a piano, a refrigerator, the base of a floor lamp jutting out like a leg, part of a wrought iron headboard thrusting through the dirt like a flower-bed fence. Loads and loads of pots and pans. No matter where I shine the light, household items are trying to break free of their grave. Whatever the reason for this burial mound of stuff, we shouldn't be on it. We have to get far away from this place.

Adam moans and slumps to the ground as soon as I tell him this. I try encouraging him, but he responds with nonsense murmurings. "I want to go home," he says. Shivers wrack his body. I'd carry him on my back if I could, but these rubber legs now can barely hold me up.

We've come to the end of the line.

I haven't cried for so long I've forgotten what it feels like to have something shake a body so. I sob so quickly and so hard tears haven't a chance to form. A dry, bone-rattling cry that is absolutely silent—this is how I cry. Looking out at the vast, beastly landscape below us, one without a single lamppost or porch light, I can't believe how stupid I've been. To believe the world was waiting for me, ready to welcome my son with open arms, to make right all the wrong that has been done.

Another coughing spasm seizes me. This one will not let go. I double over, gasping for air as a deafening boom goes off beside me. A white flash streaks above us like a comet. I swivel around. Adam is reloading the flare gun. He fires again, and the sky is pelted with another burst of light, and then another. He is using up all the flares. "Get back," he rages at the night. "Get back!" Adam has mistaken the heavens for some kind of assailant. With clouds shifting quickly across the sky, the moon appears to be blinking its disbelief.

Coughing, I scoot over to him and try to still the hallucination. He slumps into my lap.

The world seems to have drawn itself away. Hope of getting to Mama's house has become, again, an impossible dream.

"ADAM? YOU AWAKE?" I shuffle out from under my blanket of carpet scraps and ignore the stiffness in my back to hurry to his side.

Curling up even tighter on the recliner, my boy pulls the torn green drape up over his head and mumbles for me to let him sleep. Where the drape would have been hanging is a veil of morning light. Its hem just touches the floor, rousing the dust mites. Corner by corner, the night dries up, leaving rings of murk on the walls.

When we stumbled upon the house in the middle of the night, we were grateful for its easy access, neither of us having the physical where- withal to break down a door or bust a window. Because the place smelled of smoke, I assumed a fire had at some point driven the occu- pants away. The flashlight's batteries had run down so there was no way to know otherwise. It is now clear that something else has caused the house to be abandoned.

Plaster has fallen from the ceiling and formed a chalky carpet on the buckled linoleum, the blue paint on the walls is in some places blistering and in others peeled all the way through to the framework, and yet, dusty personal effects are scattered throughout the room: a small silver tray of bobby pins and a comb next to it; reading glasses on a glass side table; a cordless telephone. I hurry to pick it up, not really surprised to find the line dead. The ceramic planter is empty, but a rubber tree has reached in through a broken windowpane and appears to be throttling the floor lamp. Two rusty chrome chairs are missing their seats; the chandelier hanging above where a table might have been is missing its lightbulbs. In the adjoining kitchen, heirloom china is still on a draining board, a yellow teapot on the stove, a faded dish towel folded neatly on the oven handle. Someone has left his pipe on the counter. A set of keys hangs from a wire rack next to the back door. Whatever it was that prompted the occupants to leave also insisted they hurry.

If there was any doubt before about the ordeals the house has suffered, there is none now—in the hallway, vandals have spray-painted the walls with illegible words, and on the open door a skull and crossbones. I step past the warning to greet the outdoors.

Instead of waiting for me on the porch, morning has raced up from the hills behind us, spread over the house, and is barreling toward the horizon. It has the clouds on the run, too, parting them like a foamy red sea. For more years than I care to count, morning has been the picture accompanying the April page of the calendar. Static is how I've come to think of morning, and here it is, chasing what's left of the night, nipping at its heels. Everything comes to life because of morning. The trees shiver at the excitement, leaves scatter, even the old house creaks and groans, as though it is trying to pull itself up from its foundations to get a better view of the action. Morning has animated something in me, too, some dormant thing that for years has known only how to sit and wait. Get a move on, it says. Don't let the day get away.

And yet it is hard to do anything but stand and stare. Just because you can see something doesn't mean you can trust it to be real. The other senses are easily tricked, too. Breathing in the scent of lilacs or having your skin react to the damp breeze with gooseflesh is not enough. Someone else needs to confirm the experience. Adam needs to get up.

I walk back inside and give a startled cry at the vagrant behind the door. It's an odd thing to mistake yourself for a stranger, an unfriendly one at that. I wipe the mirror for a better look. There are twigs and leaves in my dirty braids, scratches on my face and neck. My dress, chosen long ago by Dobbs for its modesty, now has a huge slit running up the side showing a lean, bruised leg, and my cardigan has lost all but its top button. The shoes are a disgrace, what with my toes sticking out through the front. Top to bottom, it is a ghastly sight. I go back to the room where Adam is still sleeping and take from the suitcase my spare dress. With the comb and the bobby pins, I return to the mirror to establish some semblance of decency. On closer inspection, I notice that my skin is already responding to moisture; my face seems less parched. Lips are full once more, and without the tinge of blue. *Preserved,* is the word that comes to mind when I note how few wrinkles I have, and I wonder if I won't wake up tomorrow with my due allotment and then some. When I am done, I look like someone to whom I am distantly related. I try out a smile. Not exactly a pretty picture, but not someone who will send children running and screaming either.

"Adam, wake up, son."

He groans again, but this time I shake him until he sits up. He squeezes his eyes shut, then fastens his arm across his brow. "Agh. Turn it off. It's too bright!"

"It's sunlight, son. I can't turn it off."

"I can't take it. Do something, Mom!"

Adam sits cross-legged, covers his head with both arms and begins making high-pitched feedback sounds. I race to the kitchen and get a plastic bowl from under the sink and then yank the lace curtain from the window. It is a struggle to get Adam to cooperate but eventually I have the bowl secured to his head with the lace, which, pulled down in the front like a veil, will hopefully provide some protection against the glare.

"Okay?"

Grudgingly, he gets to his feet, wrapping the green drape around him.

He refuses to let me check his wound but does accept the last of the dried noodles. He doesn't seem to have a fever, and although a little unsteady, he's in better shape than last night. After adjusting the bowl on this head so the veil hangs down to his chest, he presses an arm against his side and limps across the room. In the kitchen, he picks up a chipped enamel mug, a slotted spoon, a saucepan hanging from a rack above the stove. He carries them to the arched doorway. "What's through there?"

I tell him it's time to get a move-on, but he responds by walking into the hall. "Watch your step," I warn him, just as a floorboard gives way under his foot. Adam rights himself, then continues past the tumble-down staircase into another front room.

Something scurries into the hole in a sooty wall where the paneling has been removed. Adam shuffles across the floor after it, sending shred-ded pieces of wallpaper into the air. I, though, approach the cause of the smoky smell: a bathtub in the middle of the room. In it are the charred remains of a bonfire and beside it a couple of balusters from the stair-case. The house has not been vandalized. It's being cannibalized. Some-one is feeding the house, board by board, chair by chair, to the fire that happens in here. I notice the blackened pot. Small bones and some kind of paste are in the bottom of it. This was someone's recent meal.

Not wanting to cause Adam any more alarm, I use a calm voice to tell him that we are leaving. I gather our belongings and meet him in the entry hall.

Adam looks like a tinker. He has fastened the pot, several more mugs, and utensils around his waist with his belt, all of which make a terrible din when he moves. He has also found a ball of twine, a jar of safety pins, and a dusty black umbrella. "What is it?"

"We have to go, Adam."

He empties the pins into his pocket, hands me the twine, then pushes the little stainless-steel button on the umbrella's shaft. The can-vas pops open. Startled, Adam drops it, staggers backward, and loses his balance.

"It's okay, Adam." I help him up. Another clanging, banging ruckus. "It's for when it rains. So you won't get wet."

He picks up the umbrella, examines its sharp tip, gives the air a few lancing blows, and then tests the mechanism that makes it open and close until he gets his fingers pinched for his troubles. "Do you think they're going to come back for it?"

I shake my head. "Nobody's coming back." So much for promising never to lie to him again.

"Can I keep it?"

"We've already got too much to carry." He gives me that look, so I shrug.

As soon as I turn the doorknob, he says, "I don't want to go back out there."

We both stare above us when something creaks. Probably just the wind. I look at Adam again. "It can't be more than a fifteen-minute walk to the road. There'll be cars going by right now. I know you're exhausted, but we've got to go just a little bit farther."

I offer him my hand. Instead of taking it, he turns the umbrella upside down on the floor and twirls it. "You can go."

"Adam, we have to get you help."

"You get help. I'll stay here and wait."

There have been so few occasions in which Adam has ever felt threatened that it takes me this long to cotton on to the fact that he's terrified.

"Everyone's scared of being outside when it's dark, but it's different in the daylight. It won't be like it was last night, I promise. It's wonderful, son. A thousand times better than your mural." At the mention of this, he raises the umbrella so that it blocks his face. "I know this is hard for you. Just a little bit longer, that's all I'm asking."

"Everything hurts." I can hear in his voice that he is close to tears.

It's not just the wound, he tells me, it's his feet, his legs, his back. His nose hurts from the cold air, and he's got a sore throat, but worst of all is the headache that comes and goes depending on how much light there is. Out on that front porch, he says, is enough to split it in two.

Above us is another creak. I hold my hand out to silence him. A shutter banging in the draft, perhaps? But then, another creak, the kind that comes from bearing weight. Adam and I both stare at the ceiling. *Creak-creak-creak.* Not the scuffling of some feral creature, but footsteps. Definitely footsteps. With sudden clarity, I realize that the house is not abandoned, that those personal belongings set about the house still belong to someone.

Adam doesn't need to be convinced. He pulls open the door and we are off the porch and down the stairs in a flash, pots and pans jangling.

Something large enough to cover us in a shadow blows overhead. Adam, leaning into the stiff breeze and limping quickly across the front yard to the meadow, puts up the umbrella only to have it snapped inside out. I look back, but the shadow has disappeared behind the house. What I do see stops me cold. Standing at a streaky window on the second floor is an apparition. Grandma, who was born with the caul, claimed spirits came in all shapes and sizes, just as the living did. Only difference was that light passed right through them. Whatever stands in the window is not what Grandma described, but it is no earthly being, either. The figure is charred as though from the furnaces of hell. It slowly raises its hand. It could be a wave or a signal to stop or it might be clearing the window for a better look at us. I don't wait to find out. I tell Adam if he has it in him, now might be a good time to run.

With a clatter, Adam drops to his knees, panting. I would like to put more distance between us and the house. It's impossible to calculate distances anymore. A mile, maybe two or three, is how far we've come from the house, not far enough to explain why the terrain has changed so dramatically. Instead of trees and shrubbery, we have stumbled onto what looks like a vast dry lake bed. The ground has the texture of sandpaper and is cracked in geometrical patterns like giant lizard skin. To our left is another imposing power-line tower. Following them means we are bound to stumble upon civilization sooner or later, even though it means dealing with Adam's fear that they'll tumble over and squash us to death.

"I can't go any farther, Mom. I just can't."

"Oh, son." I kneel beside him and push the umbrella aside so I can get a look at him. "Is it your wound? Has it started bleeding again?"

"Look what the air did to my umbrella." Adam, clinging to its handle, seems to be in a tug-of-war with the wind. I help him position the canvas so the gust pops it back to its regular position, forming a bit of a break. He fingers its little broken rib. "What if we get separated? What if the air blows me one way and you the other?"

Kansas winds are known for stripping the land down to the bone, for tossing entire towns into the air. They can pick up and carry off rooftops, pluck telephone poles out of the ground and use them as javelins. There is nothing to be done if this turns into one of those winds. Nevertheless, I get out the ball of twine. I unravel it, and attach one end around his waist and the other around mine. "There."

Instead of rolling his eyes at me, Adam checks the knots. He says, "There's too much sky." He pulls the umbrella over him and changes into a large black beetle. We sit like this for a long time, long enough for several plastic bags to stack up against us.

We are not any faster when we head out once more, but our progress is steady, thanks to the portable kiosk I constructed. Draped over the umbrella and secured with safety pins is the green curtain, parted just enough in the front to give Adam a sliver of a view. He is much more sure-footed now that he feels sheltered from the expanse above. I keep an ear tuned for traffic sounds, but what fills the air is the percussion of Adam's souvenirs and the drone from a haze of gnats brazen enough to keep settling on us.

The breeze at our backs finally peters out, as though it no longer has the heart to run us off any faster than what we are already going. It's fanciful to personify everything. The darkness last night; the wind now. Perhaps it's having been deprived of living things for so long that I now can find no inanimate object. A stone trips; clouds cast judgment; a tumbleweed snickers at us as it rolls by. *Tut-tut-tut* goes the hard sand as we walk. And the odd shadow continues to stalk us, gaining ground.

It is not a road we come to. If it were a mirage, I'd feel better, because that would make Adam and me two wayward pilgrims succumbing to heat exhaustion, conjuring water to compensate for the lack of the real thing. When it is, in fact, the real thing. A body of water large enough to have its own beach and sand dunes.

Adam pitches his kiosk and asks if we are in the desert.

"No, son."

A mustard-colored fog rolls in from across the water and turns the air soupy. Adam steps out from under his cover. Without the static electricity from Below, his hair now falls like a mop over his eyes. He takes a handful of sand and watches with fascination as it trickles through his fingers. He throws the next handful up into the air, and an impish gust slaps it back in his face.

Rubbing his eyes, he asks, "Is that the ocean?"

I ought to set him straight on this point. I ought to name bodies of water—lake, reservoir, dam, pond. I ought to say something. It's just the gears in my brain seem to have become jammed. Same with the machinery that operates my mouth, my limbs.

"What's wrong, Mom? Don't you feel well?"

When I don't answer, he rakes the hair out of his face and squints again at the scene before us, finding that which holds my attention. A hundred yards beyond the high-water mark, in the middle of what might well be an ocean, is a street sign. 55 MPH, it reads.

"Is that our street?"

The shadow swoops over us again. This time, it doesn't pass. I don't bother looking up. I know what it is. Doubt.

"Mom? Are you okay?"

The shadow lowers itself. It is exceedingly heavy, impossible to bear standing.

"Mom?"

Adam is yanking on the yarn, and I would really like to tell him what I've been telling him since I killed Dobbs, what I've been telling him since he was a little boy, actually: it's okay. But it is not okay. It has never been okay. Now that we are free, it is less okay than ever. The shadow is this irrefutable truth: something is wrong with Above.

"Talk to me, Mom."

I look at my boy. He is so pure, so beautiful. You'd expect a child like this to be marred, damaged. Unfit for the world. And yet it is the world that is unfit for him. Because he doesn't know any better, he accepts the facts as they present themselves—trees growing up in the middle of a road, one abandoned house after another, street signs in the middle of the sea. What he cannot accept is his mother, defeated.

"Why are you crying? We'll find our way. There'll be another road. Come on, Mom, get up."

I gesture at the water, the massive dunes beside us, the expanse of sand—itself a sea with little meringue tufts. It's not supposed to look like this.

Adam hands me a brown tarry energy bar from Dobbs's survival pack and insists I eat it. "It's a flood, like you said last night. We'll find someone to help us. Don't worry. Now, come on, get up."

"You're right." I ask him to give me a minute. Only because it seems to reassure him, do I take little bite. While I eat, Adam writes his name in the sand again. He does it every time we stop. Putting his stamp on the world, I suppose. He takes off Dobbs's shoes and rolls up his pant legs. He looks at me hopefully, and I nod. He undoes the knot around his waist, hands me his end of the leash, and approaches the water's edge cautiously. When the water surges to greet him, he scurries back. When it retreats, Adam advances. He calls to me that the lake is playing copycat. After many back-and-forths, Adam finally braves the water on tiptoes.

He gasps, then looks over his shoulder at me. "It's cold!" He waves me over.

"You go on."

I was twelve when Daddy took us on vacation to the seaside. Lost to me now is the name of the California town that was a full three days' drive from home, but I can still smell the sea. It was fresh-smelling, not like this, something on the verge of spoiling. Gerhard went bounding into the surf. Daddy followed suit, diving under a wave and coming up a boy again. My sister did the do-si-do with the wind, trying to keep her sarong from flapping every which way, while Mama and I stood together at the water's edge. She slipped one hand into mine and the other settled on her pregnant belly. "You gotta wonder if those scientists are right about us coming from the sea the way it draws us back."

Water has the same pull on Adam. He is fascinated with the current, the way it edges up his legs and then recedes. "Look, I have no feet!"

Adam draws up his feet and then stomps. Spray goes everywhere. He scoops up a handful of water, but it dribbles away before he reaches me. "You've got to come feel it, Mom."

I follow him back to the water. This time, he strolls out till it comes to his knees. He bends down and runs his hands across the surface of the water. He turns, mischief written all over his face. I scoot back, but he still manages to splash me. He laughs, dumps a handful of water on his head, then scoops another handful and holds it up to his mouth.

"Don't drink that!" I rush toward him.

He makes a face, and spits. "Bitter."

I insist he come out of the water and that's when we notice that his feet and ankles are covered in slimy black leeches.

"Agh! What are they?" Adam swats furiously at them. "They're stuck!"

"Hold still. You have to pull them off." We pluck and pluck, and when all the leeches are off, Adam's feet look as though they've been pricked dozens of times with pins. He hurries back to his umbrella and crawls under it.

"What if he was right?" he calls.

I cock my head. Engines?

Whatever the sound, it fades quickly. I begin scanning the meadow behind us, the low hills off to the side. "Right about what?"

"What if the world did come to an end?"

Instead of answering him, I ask him to come out from beneath his umbrella because I need a more reliable set of eyes. Stuck like a blue pushpin on the hill about two miles away appears to be a water tower.

"What's that supposed to mean?"

"A town," I answer. People. Civilization.

MY HANDS ARE blistered from carrying the suitcase, my shoulders are chafed raw from the straps of the backpack, and hunger has made itself known as hot coals in my belly. All of this makes me not the least bit patient when Adam calls for us stop for the hundredth time to examine some natural wonder. A few minutes ago it was a spiny seedpod. I don't bother looking at what it might be this time. "Yes, that's wonderful. Now, come on."

"But we can't leave it; we have to take care of it."

With a sigh, I turn.

Adam is crouching over a nest. We are in a field of short grass, a ways from the nearest tree. Gently, he lifts out a speckled brown egg. It is much too large to be a duck egg. I can't think what kind of bird lays an egg that large. He strokes it with the tip of his finger, then holds it up against his cheek. "Isn't it wonderful? Is it alive? It must be alive, right?" Putting the egg gently on the ground, he twists it like a top, and it spins and wobbles. He spreads out flat on his stomach and stands the egg on its broad end. He forms a little arch with his arm and rolls the egg under it. I don't think I have ever seen Adam play with something the way he does with this. He taps his nail against the shell. "Hello in there." He puts his ear against it, then taps it some more. "You want to be my friend?" He listens and looks up at me with sparkly eyes. "I think that was a yes."

Despite the layer of fog, the sun still scorches. My skin prickles in protest. Parched, I lift the canteen of water only to discover it empty.

"It's okay, little guy, I'll keep you safe."

I tell Adam to leave the egg where it is, but he ignores me, taking the lace curtain he was using as a veil and wrapping it around the egg. He fashions a little sling and carries the egg on his chest. "There, now you'll be warm. You think he's going to hatch soon, Mom?"

I hand him his umbrella. He and the egg retreat into the kiosk, where he resumes his one-sided but very animated conversation.

Adam is too busy with his egg to notice the spicy smell of the woods beside us on our way to the town. He doesn't notice the sky, how the bruise-colored clouds part every so often for a glimpse of blue. And he doesn't notice, as I do, how little progress we make for so great an effort. Everything is oversize, or else I have forgotten how puny people are against such a backdrop.

He sticks his head out from his umbrella when we come to a stop.

"Want a blackberry?" I offer him one the size of a baby's fist and take a bite of mine to show him how it's done.

He smacks his lips together. "Sour." He examines his stained fingers, presses them on his egg. It now looks like something you might find in an Easter basket.

"I've never seen them this size. Aren't they delicious?" They say it's smell that takes you back in time. Not so. Nothing of the outdoors smells right, but one bite of these blackberries is all it takes for me to be in Grandma's kitchen. If she wasn't knitting or canning or tanning your hide for being sassy, Grandma was baking pies. Rolling out the dough for her was almost as much fun as pretending my berry-stained fingers were bleeding and having Grandpa fall for the gag, which he did every time.

Gorging myself, I look to where Adam is pointing. On the other side of the bramble is a four-lane highway. A perfectly good road. No signs of flooding and not one tree. We climb through a thinning in the bush and are treated to an unhindered sight of the hill and the water tower and the town that must surely be around the bend. Up ahead, a couple of grain silos stick out above the thickening of trees. The sun temporarily peeks out from a cloud, and lanky shadows from the telephone poles turn the road into a ladder.

I look both ways for traffic, then step out onto the tarmac. There are no street signs, but painted along the pavement, one after another, are arrows. Hurry, they suggest. This way.

No sooner has Adam joined me on the road when he gasps. I spin around in alarm. The kiosk is lying in a heap and Adam, crouching, is fingering the place where his shoe and his shadow meet. He gets on all fours. Ever so lightly, he runs his fingertips over his shadow and then pats it firmly, as though he can't trust it before frisking it. He stands, marking how his shadow goes from a squat shape into a tall, skinny one. He picks up his foot, watches as his two-dimensional companion does the same. He takes a step, and then another, lifting his feet as though he's stepped in gum. Adam turns his back on the shadow and pivots his head quickly to look over his shoulder. His shadow is still there. He walks, watching himself being tailed. He picks up the egg. Facing his shadow again, he extends the egg toward it, as though by way of introduction. Wonderment is written all over his face. Eager as I am to get to the town, I cannot draw myself away from the sight of my child being a child. Thanks to him, I do a little jig with my own shadow.

Adam doesn't want to put up his mobile tent when he realizes there are certain places his inky friend can't go, so he proceeds under a scorching sun, allotting equal amounts of attention to his two new companions, the egg and his shadow. None of his focus is directed to what may lie ahead, which is why I have to point out the miracle to him. A ways before we get to the bend is a line of cars. "Adam, look!"

He joins in cheering. "See that, little egg? No, you don't need to be afraid. My mom says people are nice. They aren't going to hurt us; they're just going to ask a lot of questions."

We hurry toward them.

"Hey! Hello!" I untie the twine-leash and race ahead, waving my hands, screaming on top of my lungs. "Over here!" I keep running and running, and the closer I get the more cars I see. They are not moving. As luck would have it, they're in some kind of traffic jam.

"Hello! Hey! Behind you!"

Adam is shouting, too.

"Come on, son." I look behind me and wave to encourage him. In the bright sun, his hair now looks like sparks.

We are eighty yards from the first car, close enough to tell that both lanes of traffic are stopped all the way past the next bend. A pileup. Or maybe a roadblock.

I keep shouting and running and waving my hands. Until the futility of this socks me right in the windpipe.

I check on Adam, who is hobbling as fast he can, in one hand his umbrella-tent and in the other the egg. I turn back to the disturbing scene. Out of breath, or hyperventilating—I don't know what my breathing is doing. Hiccup sounds come out of me. Find an explanation before he gets here. Find something to say when he asks. Because he will ask. "Where are all the people?" he's going to say.

I stumble to the last car in the lineup, run my hand across its weathered trunk, its streaky windows. Empty. Even the seats are missing. I move to the car in front of it, a blotchy red Ford pickup with no tires. Nobody. Each car I pass is the same way. Doors unlocked, insides gutted, blocks where wheels ought to be. Some of the vehicles have their hoods propped open. Rusty car parts and cracked hoses are strewn along the side of the road like entrails.

When Adam catches up to me, he doesn't ask. He gives the horizon the hard look I know is meant for me. The clouds draw together and Adam marks the disappearance of his shadow in silence. Then he opens the door of an old Buick, one that still has its backseat, gets in with his egg, and closes the door.

"Adam—"

Before I can lift the handle, he pushes down the lock. He averts my gaze. He lowers himself on the seat and cradles the egg in his lap.

"Adam, open up."

Eventually, I give up pleading with him. I get in the car behind his and close the door and sit on the console. I watch the back of my son's head. Eventually, his face appears in the back window. I wave sadly. After a long time, he waves back.

If I have learned anything from being around Dobbs, it's not to succumb to the unruly voices in your head. A certain interior discipline is necessary if logic, not lunacy, is to prevail. Scientists used to harp about how global warming would change weather patterns—this would certainly explain the strange trees and altered landscape, might even account for this abandoned line of cars. Maybe these cars weren't evacuating. Maybe the fuel ran out, like they said it would. Whatever the cause, this is no time to give in. Though I am being forced once again to bear circumstances that are unbearable, to face facts more frightful than nightmares, I must put to good use everything I learned about survival from Dobbs and get Adam to safety.

I rap on Adam's window again. He pokes his head out from under the curtain, first to check on his egg and then to look at me.

"Adam, we have to find water." There's bound to be something up ahead, at the very least a faucet.

He shakes his head at me.

"Come on, son. We can't just sit here. We've got to keep moving."

Already the sun has dipped below the hill. I'm not sure how much daylight we have left. I insist he open the door.

He refuses. He strokes the egg.

"Adam!"

"I'm not going!" he shouts at me. "You go!"

I pace back and forth beside the car. Worst-case scenario, I'll have to go back and gather blackberries. Best case, I find something up ahead in the form of a house or a store. *How about a pot of gold?* That Dobbs's sneering face is now as clear to me as my own hand is all the argument I need for taking off.

"I won't be long, okay?" I'll go as far as the next bend.

Adam has taken off his belt and is arranging the pots and mugs and spoons throughout the car the way a newlywed might decorate her cottage.

"You stay right here. Keep the doors locked. Are you listening to me, Adam?"

I am given the barest of nods.

"I'll be right back."

It is much quicker going it alone, even though I keep stopping to look back at Adam's junker, now a bead in a rosary of cars.

A massive bleached tree with shattered limbs lies beside the road. I pass a boat half-buried beneath a pile of river rocks. A little farther along is another boat. One of its sides has burned away, leaving old coals in a makeshift hearth beside it.

There is no town, not even a row of abandoned houses. The only indications that people ever occupied this desolate patch of land are a couple dozen slab foundations, an orchard of apple trees, and a cemetery. In a weedy pasture partially fenced with crooked iron railings are hundreds of lichen-covered crosses. Most are constructed from timber scraps and tree branches, but a few are fashioned from car bumpers. One is marked with a steering wheel. Someone has used pebbles to identify one grave. BABY, it states. It would be too wild a coincidence, but it makes me think of my baby Freedom. Somewhere out in this godforsaken territory Dobbs buried her. I ought to stop and pay my respects. Someone ought to mourn loss on so large a scale. Instead, I hurry through the graveyard and gather apples from a nearby tree. Every task, even the toil of putting one foot in front of the other, is an act of determination. Outdoors, I feel every bit as trapped as I did down below. Shelter is my impulse now, not freedom. Fighting it, I do what I must to keep Adam safe.

A rusty gas station is up ahead, but the line of cars veers sharply off the highway, as though in some kind of detour. Many of the vehicles in the meadow are half-buried. Beyond them, on the hillside, is an arrangement of rocks—a message now illegible. What doesn't need deciphering is the frayed flag on the homemade mast beside it. It is flying upside down.

I hurry on to the gas station, which is surrounded by a formation of vehicles. Cars, RVs, even a horse trailer, are parked like circled wagons.

This encampment must be what the line of cars was trying to avoid, although not everyone kept the distance—some of the vehicles are riddled with bullet holes. The drivers and passengers seem to have set up some kind of camp beneath the massive canopy, with lean-tos made from display counters, Coca-Cola machines, and scrap metal. Two Texaco pumps stand like hostages in the midst of the disarray. A gas shortage, then.

I wander inside the store. Nothing is left, not even water pipes. As I wander back outside, I hear that sound again. The buzzing of a lawn mower. A motorbike, perhaps. I rush over the hood of a car and race back to the street. I look in all directions, but the sound peters out some distance beyond the water tower.

I hurry back to Adam, who is sitting beside his shadow on top of the Buick, with his umbrella, tracking my return.

"Did you hear that noise?"

"There was a really screechy black bird with long legs. It landed in the field over there. I think it was looking for my little buddy here." The egg is nestled safely in his lap.

"Didn't you hear engines?"

Adam gives me a blank look, so I do my best imitation of a dentist's drill, but he wants to talk more about the bird. "It was as big as me, Mom, and when it took off, its wings were as long as this car. It wasn't like the birds they talk about in books. If that bird landed on this car, I would've been crushed. And it didn't sing. It just screeched and screeched like it was real mad. I don't like birds. Except for Buddy, here, and when he hatches, I am going to teach him to be nice. Did you find us anything to eat?"

I offer Adam an apple. He accepts it eagerly but then is at a loss. I can count on one hand the number of times he's eaten fresh fruit, never an apple. "Just take a bite, like this." The skin is so tough my teeth can't pierce it. Eventually, I have to use a rock to smash it open. It is mostly core.

"I think it's time to bury Charlie," I tell him, pulling off my shoes to inspect my blisters. Large red craters have formed on the sides of my feet. The pain from the stinging air is nothing compared to the ache that has settled in my hips and knees. My shins are too tender even to touch.

"But you said we were going to give him back to his family."

I look at him. If only it were a matter of walking into a police station and handing them Charlie's remains, of having them notify the next of kin. "When we come to a town and find the people in charge, we'll tell them where Charlie rests," I say. What we cannot do is carry so heavy a responsibility when all the attention must be focused on taking care of ourselves. Between us passes the understanding that our plight is now desperate.

Adam fetches the first-aid kit and helps me patch my feet with the last of the Band-Aids. The overcast has turned a sickly olive-green color. Spilling through a rupture at its center are coppery clouds. It's not so much a setting sun as it is a festering one.

Adam's first encounter with people Above are the dead and buried. Nevertheless, he pays attention to each tombstone as though he were being formally introduced.

"Here's another one named Rip."

"Rest in Peace," I correct. "It's what people say when they bury someone."

He examines one of the old headstones. "They should build a big house for people when they die, not just leave them outside like this."

I find an empty spot and get out the folding shovel.

Adam insists on digging. The ground is soft and yields easily. Before long, he has dug a hole, not quite four feet around, more suitable for planting a tree than burying a body. "Did I dig it deep enough?"

"It's just right, Adam. Thank you." With care, I remove the bundle from my backpack and lower it into the earth. If you don't look at the queue of abandoned cars, it's not an altogether disagreeable landscape. Prairie grass, a gentle hill with more shades of green than what you thought existed, a view unhindered by telephone wires or electric cables. Certainly, it is a resting place one thousand times better than the silo floor. Yet, I have to ask Charlie once again to forgive me—this time, for leaving him in no-man's-land.

Adam has collected a posy of wildflowers. He hands it to me. I gently lay them on top of the bundle.

"Aren't you going to say something?"

Quietly, so quietly even the spirits won't hear, I say, "You rest here, Charlie, but you will always live in my heart."

Adam digs in his pocket and pulls out a key. It's from Dobbs's ring. He places it gently on top of the bundle. "Everyone ought to have their own key." He recites both the Our Father and the Pledge of Allegiance. And then there isn't anything left to do but fill the hole.

I shovel the dirt and pat down the sod. We gather stones to circle the grave. Adam stakes a car antenna in the middle of the mound. He bows his head. I'd pray, too, but I know one of two things will happen—either there'll be no words, or I'll start and never get stopped. When I sling the backpack over my shoulder, it feels heavier than it did before. What things need bearing now?

Adam gives the graveyard one last look. "I don't want to be buried in a place like this. When I die, I want to be put on a boat and get pushed out to sea."

By the time we get back to the Buick, Adam is shivering uncontrollably. My joints have seized up. I can't seem to bend my knees. After wrapping the drape tightly around Adam, I check the survival kit. Dobbs has sealed in a Ziploc bag three packs of matches. I crack the window just enough for fresh air, then pat Adam's leg. "I won't be long."

"Where are you going?"

"I'm going to collect some wood so we can build a fire."

Adam begs me to reconsider. "It's not safe out there." He stares out the window. Evening is almost upon us. "I don't want you to leave me alone. What if that horrible bird comes back and breaks in and attacks me?"

"Birds don't attack, son." I don't want to explain how much more the temperature will drop or what it will be like a few hours from now when the cold goes after our organs, so I hand him the egg. "You've got your little buddy to keep you company. And I'll be back in two shakes. You can't see it from here, but just a little ways up the street is a dead tree—"

"Dead?" He looked nowhere near as appalled as when we were in the graveyard.

"It's not just people who die, Adam. You know that."

He is shaking his head as though this is all news to him.

"If you get scared, just honk the horn."

I close the door and hurry up the road again. It is the thought of a warm fire that keeps me from falling down. That and the insects. The road is now teeming with millipedes the length of garden snakes and cockroaches so bold even the threat of a shoe coming down on them is no deterrent. Beside me, the field is awash in strange blue phosphorescence, and the same unsettling noises from last night start to ring out from every direction, as though some otherworldly animal kingdom is starting to stir.

I collect as much wood as will fit in the backpack and what my arms can carry, not nearly enough to keep a fire burning through the night. Perhaps my legs have it in them for one more trip. I hurry back just as a car horn begins blaring.

"I'm coming; I'm coming."

The fire sends sparks into the air and Adam back behind the Buick door. It takes much coaxing for him to get close enough to benefit from the heat. I hold out my palms toward the flames. It pops and cracks and spits out an ember, and Adam gives a cry of alarm. He fetches his umbrella. I tell him it's not a good idea to prop it so close to the fire, so he sits three feet away with his egg instead. After a while, he draws closer. Once he's sure that the flames aren't going to reach out and grab him, he kneels and leans toward the warmth. He smiles, closes his eyes, and tilts his head a little.

In one long sentence come a dozen questions about tomorrow, none of which I can answer. Adam is accustomed to certainty. It has to be terrifying, a mother whose best is, "I don't know."

The flames burn green at their tips and give off a faint whiff of boot polish. The deadwood is quickly reduced to coals that tinkle like Mama's wind chimes. There is a physical ache to thinking about Mama now, a pressure that builds up behind my eyes and turns everything blurry. I've always thought of Mama waiting—maybe not waiting for me in the house on Fall Leaf Road, but waiting in some living room where she knows the exact number of hours I've been gone. That Mama might have moved her waiting to the shores of eternity is too much to bear.

Adam is transfixed by the glowing embers and the short bursts of flame they occasionally throw up. Just as with the body of water earlier today, he becomes brazen. More than once I have to caution him not to touch the white ash. He blackens the end of a stick and then scrapes it against the ground. *Adam,* he writes.

"I'm starving," he says, after a long silence. We've finished off the apples and the blackberries, and there is nothing left in Dobbs's survival kit except a packet of powdered milk.

I fetch the pot from the car. Away from the hearth, the cold is an assault. I can't remember ever being this cold before. It's like being gripped by a burglar and shaken vigorously enough to empty the contents of my pockets.

"But we haven't got anything to cook," Adam remarks.

I sit on my haunches beside him. "I don't want you to get upset now," I begin. "But we have to eat."

He agrees until he sees me looking at his egg. He jerks it away from me. "You can't eat Buddy!"

"Listen to me, Adam. We have to eat. If we don't, we won't have energy tomorrow to do anything. We won't be able to——"

"I don't want to do anything! I want to stay here and take care of Buddy."

The campfire casts a glow on our faces. Adam's is full of indignation and hurt and fear. Mine obviously needs to show more assertiveness. "We're going to eat the egg, and tomorrow we'll see if we can't find you another one."

"I don't want another one!" he screams. The sound echoes across the night.

We don't have time to argue because already the fire is petering out. "Give me the egg, Adam."

He whips away, jumps to his feet, and disappears into the blackness. I know he aims to lock himself in that car again, and the fire is going to burn out, and we are going to be two ashen stick figures by the time the sun rises. I go after Adam. I grab his arm as he reaches for the door handle, and somehow, in the tussle, there is an awful cracking sound.

Adam holds up his hands, yolk dripping from them. He turns a shrieking, crazed face to me. "Look what you've done! *Look what you've done!*"

Collecting another bundle of wood, I berate myself. In a car down the road is my child. Ever since doing Dobbs in, ever since we came Above and found it godforsaken, I have been waiting for the right moment to comfort him. Comfort him for everything, my wrongdoings especially. Now, he won't let me.

I think he is letting me know just how angry he is when I hear the horn start up blaring again, until I realize that there is also the sound from earlier. Engines. I peer into the darkness at two headlights. They are moving very fast. Dropping the firewood, I start to run toward them.

The horn keeps blaring and the lights come to a halt next to the car and my chest feels like it is about to crack open. Coughing and wheezing, I keep running. I try shouting to let Adam know I'm coming, but my lungs erupt with resin instead. The horn stops. Voices are telegraphed across the tarmac by a cable of bright white light. We've been found.

I can hear Adam's voice. He must be telling them where I am. I see three figures move in front of the headlights, Adam's distinct by his stoop.

"Over here! I'm coming!"

I'm only a few cars away. They can see me. And yet one of the figures takes Adam to a vehicle. Shoves him, actually. "Mom!" he cries out. "Mom!"

The engine revs. With a lurch, it bounces across the ditch and into the field, taking Adam with it.

"Adam! *Adam! Adam!*" I dash into the damp grass thick with slithery things. *"Adam!"* And as I watch the red taillight bounce into the night, first a voice and then a hand comes for me. I think I am to get on a vehicle, too, but I suddenly can't breathe and the darkness makes a fist around my chest and squeezes with all its might.

VI

OPEN MY EYES and quickly shut them tight. Above me is a disc so bright it all but burns through my eyelids. Not the sun—it does little to push back the cold and keeps making a frizzing noise. There is a voice. Rather than coming from a single source, it seems to be coming, impossibly, from every direction at once.

It says, "No airway obstruction. Head and neck are otherwise unremarkable. Cardiopulmonary systems seem stable. Pressures normal. Start a large-bore IV. Draw a blood culture, and run a set of chemistries."

I try to get up, see what all the fuss is about, and realize I don't have any legs or arms. All that's left of me is my mind. It should be fixed on a single task, but I can't think what. Seems like I was on my way somewhere—to heaven, maybe.

An angel moves in front of the not-sun. The angel's eyes are very red. The angel hasn't had enough sleep. Without warning, she directs a tine of light into my eye. "Pupils are not obtunded, but she is somewhat photophobic." The beam clicks off, but it's too late; it has scrambled my thoughts.

Something is clamped around my mouth to keep me from talking. I try pulling it off, but the angel stops me. "No, you must leave the mask on until your breathing treatment is over."

Heaven is a very tiring place, so tiring I can't keep from drifting away from the brightness and the jangling sounds to the beautiful darkness.

From far away someone keeps asking the same thing. I wish the soul being addressed would hurry up and do as told, so everything can go back to being quiet again.

"Open your eyes, ma'am." The order is repeated, this time close enough for me to detect the smell of mothballs. "I need you to look at me."

Through a crack in my eyelids, I see a tall white-haired woman in a white jacket. It is to me she is talking. The not-sun is gone. The angels are gone. Heaven is gone, too. To make doubly sure I am not dead, I chance a look at my body. Everything's where it ought to be. I watch my hand raise five fingers, see the shadow forming beneath them.

"Right, keep them open."

I look around me. Indoors, except the spatial dimensions are all wrong. Instead of being smooth and vertical, the walls are ribbed and curved. Reflexively, I bring my arms up over my head. The wall doesn't collapse but arches over me and disappears behind a black plastic curtain across the way.

The woman holds up three fingers, and asks me in a heavy accent to count them. I inspect the tube in my arm. It runs to a bag that is hooked onto a towel rack on the corrugated wall. Also attached to the wall is a long string of bulbs.

"How many fingers?" she persists.

Minnesotan? German? "Three."

"Do you know what day this is?"

I shake my head.

"Do you remember how you got here?"

Again, I let my body answer for me.

"Neither of you were carrying any identification. Can you tell me what you were doing in the Disposal Zone?"

It all rushes back in one quick wave: Dobbs dead in a puddle of blood, Adam and me in the car, then on foot, an ocean where streets used to be, Charlie in a poorly marked grave, a motorbike making off with my child. "Adam!" I try sitting up, but there's a block of lead on my chest.

"Easy." The woman puts her hand on my shoulder. "You had an asthma attack. It is best not to try getting up right now."

"My son!" My voice is raspy and sore from screaming—vaguely, I recall hooded figures and motorbikes.

"He's right here." The woman parts the black curtain. Adam is in the bed next to mine, being tended to by figures in green outfits.

"Adam! Are you all right?"

He looks at me, the whites of his eyes showing, his teeth clenched as though on a piece of wood. In his fist is a mess of twine, our leash.

"We made it, my boy. We're safe." Found, rescued, restored—all the words I was beginning to believe would never apply to us I say to him now. But there is this stupid mask over my face and what I say sounds ghastly. No wonder he looks even more alarmed. I give him a thumbs-up, and just as he is about to return the gesture, one of the figures draws back the sheet covering his naked torso. He reacts by curling into a ball. Instead of reassuring him, she tries to straighten his legs. Adam yelps, and scoots up to the head of the bed. "No, no, no, no."

"Go easy with him. He is not used to strangers," I instruct, pulling the mask away from my mouth. To Adam, I say, "Son, you don't have to worry; these are nice people." These are the good guys is what I mean, because we've both heard Dobbs talk so much about Scalpers. "We've been outside for two days without much to drink or eat," I explain to the woman beside me.

"I see." She introduces herself as Harriet Fletcher, the attending physician. Clearly, I am expected to give more details.

"He's never been outside before. Could you please dim the lights? I think he'd do better if it wasn't so bright."

Adam has regained control over the covers again. Burying himself under them, he begins humming and rocking. The attendants have fallen back and seem to be awaiting further instructions from the doctor.

"He's never been outside before?"

Shielding my eyes with one hand, I take my first look in seventeen years at another person. Her skin is a funny color, like she's been over-cooked. Either she spends a lot of time looking directly into the sun or frowning because her forehead is scored with lines. Her lips are flat-tened into a broad line. It does not look quite like a smile. There is no hint of makeup, but she has obviously spent a great deal of time teasing her short hair in such a way as to cover the bald spots. Curious how I have lost the ability to gauge a person's age. She cannot possibly be a hundred and twenty.

"We were—" *Hostages* doesn't seem like the right word. *Captives* nei-ther. "I was taken. A long time ago. We've been kept." Surely she can see how relieved and grateful I am.

But Harriet Fletcher seems to be distracted by a spot on the cuff of her coat. "I see." In the middle of explaining about Dobbs, she asks me my name.

"His name is Adam, and mine's Blythe," I tell her. "Blythe Hallo-well."

"Well, Mrs. Hallowell, once we get the wound tended to, we'll have him up and about in no time." She replaces the mask over my mouth.

I couldn't have hoped for greater news, but I need to correct her on one point. "Miss," I say. "My mother is Mrs. Hallowell—Irene. Hank Hallowell is my father, from Eudora." I lift the mask slightly so she can hear me better. I tell her my phone number.

"You are very lucky we found you in time," she says, not, "I'll bring you the telephone."

"There is also a cut on his leg from a rusty piece of metal." When I get no response to this other than a curt nod, I have to add, "He's never been vaccinated."

"We will continue to keep a close watch."

"Shouldn't he get a tetanus shot, just to be on the safe side?"

She cocks her head to one side. "You're not from the Renu Project, are you?"

I frown. "Where?"

She fastens her hands on her hips. "If he's one of Renu's people, you need to tell me right now, and we can make arrangements to have you transferred."

I don't understand. Have we done something wrong? "Where are we?" Because, come to think of it, this is like no hospital I've ever seen. An army barracks, more like it.

"The infirmary at Sunflower."

"Sunflower Ordnance Works?" "The scab of the county" was what Grandpa used to call it, telling us how Eudora's folks resisted the building of a munitions plant in the Second World War. Not that they had anything against bombs or war for that matter. What they didn't want were empty stores, abandoned trailers, and unused Quonset huts when the war was over.

"We don't call it that anymore, but yes."

The confirmation brings me close to tears. Six miles, that's how far we are from Eudora. Only six miles!

"Are we at war?" I ask. That would explain the blackout, the exodus of cars, the graves. Hadn't I smelled gunpowder in the air?

Perhaps I have asked this with a little too much eagerness because the lines on Harriet Fletcher's forehead have bunched together. "You said you'd been 'taken.' How long ago exactly?"

"Seventeen years." She doesn't seem nearly as interested in the other details—who took me and why—as she is in the date.

"And you said your son has never been outside?"

"That's right. As I said, we were locked away in a missile silo. It's off County Road—"

"And you can confirm this by what means?"

"Confirm?"

She excuses herself without answering my question and walks over to Adam.

Beside him is a portable table with instruments and jars. She speaks to Adam in a soothing tone, asking him the very questions for which I have just given her answers. In response, Adam draws the sheet over his head and remains silent.

"Okay, we will save the questions for later." She picks up a syringe and instructs the nurse to pull back the sheet. Adam's arms are doubled over his head. "Now, we're just going to take a little blood from your arm. Okay?"

I lift the mask. "He's not going to let you do that." Adam is terrified, and the mention of blood does not help. I fight to get the covers off me so I can get out of bed.

Harriet Fletcher touches Adam's arm, and he knocks the needle straight out of her hand. He bolts off the bed, landing hard on his bad knee. He yanks out his IV and scuttles under the bed.

"It's okay, young man. A little prick, that's all." Harriet Fletcher's knees creak something terrible when she crouches next to the bed. She reaches her hand toward Adam. Her voice becomes high. "Come on, I'm not going to hurt you."

Adam is making growling sounds. I can't seem to get myself untangled from the tubes. "Adam, she's a doctor; it's okay."

"I have something for you, if you come out." Seeing Adam is not about to take the bait, the woman rises to her feet with some effort and gives her instruction in a tone that means business. "Two milligrams Lorazepam. We're not going to get anywhere without sedation."

Freed of mask and tubes and covers, I swing my legs over the side of the bed. As soon as I try standing, the ground begins to list. I try to catch my breath and realize there isn't enough air to go around. Air is being drained from the room somehow. The floor begins to tilt to such an extent I lean back to avoid being splattered against the corrugated wall. There is nothing to grasp on to for balance, and the floor rises up and smacks me upside the head.

I look over at Adam. "I'm okay."

He's even more panicked now.

I try crawling to him. "These people are nice, Adam. You've got to let them—"

Something goes wrong with his face. His expression closes in on itself, and he slumps over. Hands latch onto his legs. They drag him out from under the bed and swing him back onto the bed as if he's a sack.

"What have you done to him? Don't pull him like that! You're going to hurt him!"

I try rushing to him, but an arm fences me in and drags me back to my bed. I insist on my release and when that doesn't work, I kick and pull and finally sink my teeth into the arm.

"Jesus, Mary, and Joseph!"

And then something very stinging happens to my thigh. The lights start to flicker and dim, and the voices run together in a dull drone. The baby I named Freedom, Charlie, Adam, Mama—they're all calling me. I walk toward them and step into a very deep hole.

THE BLACK PLASTIC curtains have been rolled up and fastened to hooks on the ceiling. The Quonset hut is the size of a warehouse, about a hundred feet long. Two rows of beds are separated by a wide center aisle. I could have sworn there were other people in here with us earlier, but now the beds are empty and the hut is silent except for the sound of snapping sheets. Across the way, a woman is making up a bed. She keeps looking over at Adam, who is still sleeping. The woman can't take her eyes off him. There's something peculiar about her expression, as though she can't quite believe what she is seeing. Fixated, even though he is doing nothing more remarkable than snoring lightly in that puppy-dog way of his.

The woman is afflicted by the same unfortunate color as Harriet Fletcher and also has very little hair, a fact she is trying to conceal with an ill-fitting headscarf. She wears a single item of clothing—a cross between a raincoat and a choir robe. Not once does she look at me, not even when I call out a greeting.

I look around. Near the door is a rack of wooden crutches. Underneath the beds are old-fashioned chamber pots. No telephone, no television, no familiar face. Shouldn't there be a policeman by now?

"Do you know if they've managed to make contact with my parents?"

The woman does not turn around, but a wisp of a voice flits by the window above me. Is someone spying on us?

"Hello?"

I strain the silenced air for other fragments, but there is nothing except the brightness. I can't think straight with it being so bright. Even when you close your eyes, there's no way around it—it bleeds straight through your eyelids. The brightness has a smell, too; sharp enough to make your nose sting. Unless you want it to stick to your gums, it's best to keep your mouth closed. If only there were one giant lightbulb, I could smash it into a thousand pieces and be done with it; I could think. Instead, there is row after row of bulbs.

"Hello? Excuse me?"

It occurs to me when I start banging my hand on the bedside table that the woman is not ignoring me; she is unable to hear me.

Adam wakes up disoriented. "What are you doing?"

From his suitcase, I fish out his notebook and a pen. "Just a minute, son." The woman turns when she catches me waving. I hold the sheet so she can read its emphatic demand: *Please fetch Dr. Fletcher.*

She hurries from the room and returns moments later with a carbon copy of herself. They bring us trays of food.

I wave the piece of paper again, but all I get is polite nodding.

"We need to speak to the doctor right away. It's very important."

Blank stare.

I mouth, "Im-por-tant."

On the other side of the paper, I scribble my name, my parents' names and telephone number, and in big beseeching letters, I add, *Please call.* One of them takes the paper. I start thanking her profusely until I see her fold it into an impossibly small square and stick it in her pocket as though she intends to forget it.

"Why are they looking at me like that?" Adam is peering at them over the top of his sheet. Each time the one with the tray tries to hand him his food, he yelps in protest and raises the sheet again.

"He doesn't like it if you get too close." I flag them, then gesture. Somehow, the message gets across. They leave his tray on the bedside table and keep to the other side of the aisle, where they watch him with unabashed fascination.

I tear out another page from Adam's notebook. This time I begin writing a list of people from Eudora, starting with Mercy Gaines. This close to town, one of the names is bound to ring a bell.

"What's wrong with them, Mom?"

"They're deaf, Adam." From the flapping of hands, they appear to be having a very animated conversation. As though choreographed, they lift imaginary spoons to their mouths, indicating for Adam to do likewise.

Adam glances at his tray. "What is it?"

He used to beg me for food stories when we were Below. I'd tell him about pies, and he'd savor my words as though they were loaded on the end of a fork. Now, you'd swear he was being served roadkill.

"I don't know, but you should probably get something in your stomach." Only the carrots are recognizable. So that Adam will follow my example, I take a bite. The meat is gamy and tough.

Adam accepts his tray this time and acknowledges the women with an ever-so-slight nod. "It's good," he mumbles, after a spoonful. He looks directly at them and is rewarded for this effort with applause. He gives them a thumbs-up, which they both find terribly amusing. My son is having his first conversation with deaf people.

The women are elated with Adam's progress until he pushes aside his tray, leaps out of bed, and retches violently on the floor.

I shove another piece of paper at one of the women. *Dr. Fletcher. Right now!*

In a clean hospital gown and settled back in bed, Adam is still apologizing when the doctor finally comes. Ignoring me, she marches straight over to Adam's bed. To her credit, she leaves a little room between herself and Adam and makes an effort to speak softly. "How is our patient doing today? I hear lunch didn't agree with you."

Adam starts winding the twine into a ball. Even from here, I can see his hands trembling.

"Don't worry, young man. No more needles." She apologizes for last night and tells him that it was necessary to sedate him to clean his wound and do the necessary blood work. She addresses me next, saying, "Fortunately, the laceration is superficial. Much of the redness and swelling has subsided, so I don't think we are dealing with an infection."

"Thank you for helping us."

She acknowledges this with the slightest of nods. "You want to tell me what happened?"

Adam has that wide-eyed look again. It's about all he can do to shake his head, so I repeat the details—the date I was taken, a physical description of Dobbs, my parents' address and telephone number. I give her a rough sketch of the last seventeen years, leaving out details Adam doesn't need to hear, as well as the small matter of killing Dobbs.

"You've been through quite a lot, haven't you, Adam?" She's good with him, almost maternal. "You don't need to worry; nobody here is going to hurt you."

As reassuring as this clearly is to Adam, it awakens in me a possessiveness. Exactly how I felt whenever Dobbs took Adam into his private quarters is how I feel with her. I tell myself Adam is my son, not my property. I am going to have to share him.

"We would like to do some additional testing on Adam."

Out the corner of my eye I can see Adam shaking his head.

"It shouldn't take long, and he'll just be a few doors down," she continues. "We'll have him back by dinnertime."

Alarmed that they might have picked up something in those blood tests, I ask, "He's not sick, is he?" *Leukemia* is all I can think.

"No, nothing like that." She turns to Adam, who looks like he might be a flight risk, and lowers her voice. I catch just a few words—something about him and her having a private talk. I realize suddenly what this is about. They want to question Adam without me being present, the way they do children who are abused by their parents. They think I hurt him.

"The man who kept us did that to Adam. They were fighting. It all happened very quickly. I didn't even know Adam had a weapon." Why do I sound so guilty?

"I see."

Surging inside me is a new fear. It is worse than being in the swamp in the dead of night or being charged by a wild boar or fleeing the phantom in the window. It is the fear of not being believed. "I would never do anything to hurt my son. Never." Adam looks as horrified as I feel. "My whole life, I've tried to protect—"

"My mother was only defending herself when she killed Mister!" Adam blurts.

Harriet Fletcher flicker-blinks. "I'm sorry—did you just say she killed someone?"

Realizing his words have made things worse, Adam now clams up and winds twine for all he's worth.

I draw my legs to my chest. "Is someone coming for us?" I ask. Someone who can vouch for me. "I have a list of people's names, if you can't get ahold of my parents. Sheriff Rumboldt—I don't know if he's still in charge at the station—he'll tell you." The deaf women are peering at me through narrowed eyes.

"The authorities have been notified," Harriet Fletcher replies, her attention fixed on Adam. "It will take them a while yet to reach us, and in the meantime, we will continue with our tests." She assures Adam that it is okay to come out from under the covers, that he isn't in any trouble. When asked what his favorite thing to eat is, he murmurs through the sheets that he likes ramen and jerky.

"Well, let's see what we can do." She signs to the women, and one of them scurries off. "Do you like technology, Adam? When my son was your age he was always into the latest gadgets." She takes a walkie-talkie out of her pocket and turns the knob until a hiss of static fills the air.

Adam can't resist. He lowers the covers, brushes the hair out of his eyes.

"It's called a two-way." After giving instructions about how to operate it, she hands it to him. She retrieves a second device from the deaf woman and proceeds to transmit a message to him. "We're glad you're here, Adam."

He stares at the device in his hand, seems incredulous that her voice can come out from its tiny holes. He pushes the button. "Hello."

She praises him for his effort. "I'm going to leave my two-way with you, so if you ever want to call me or talk to me, you just push that button."

The bribe works. Adam allows her to apply a clean dressing to his wound. Instead of looking at his injury, he stares intently at her, as though committing every blemish and wrinkle to memory.

"Feel like stretching your legs now?" she asks.

Getting out of bed, Adam has me hold the end of the twine. Spooling it out from the ball, he allows Harriet Fletcher to lead him down the center aisle for a stroll. If the doctor thinks this is peculiar, she does not remark on it. The two deaf women are observing the goings-on with the same enthused looks on their faces.

"They seem quite taken with my son," I mention as Harriet Fletcher passes by my bed.

She can't quite decide whether to put her hand on Adam's arm, so it lingers in the space above it. "He is a remarkable find."

Adam is not altogether displeased with her pronouncement. I, on the other hand, feel this is an odd choice of words. Find? Like he's some artifact from an archeological dig?

"It's rather careless what you did," she continues, steering him past the deaf women.

"What I did?"

"Taking him out there without any means of protection." She can barely conceal her disapproval.

"We were escaping!" I try not to sound hysterical when I tell her once again that I was kidnapped, that we were held underground for years, and that I would like very much to speak to someone who can help me find my family. Raising my voice sets off another round of coughing.

Handing Adam off to a deaf woman, she comes to my side and tries to get me to put the mask on.

I push it away.

"If you refuse your breathing treatments, your lungs will not get better." Her expression means to convey just how much I am trying her patience, and I look back at her in such a way that she will know that I don't care if my lungs harden, I don't care if I turn into cement and crack in two the next time I cough, I'm not taking anything that keeps me from thinking straight.

"I'm fine," I insist, but she already has the blood pressure cuff attached to my upper arm.

She goes from buckram to downright chummy. "Do you mind if I ask whether you have had any other live births?"

I am still deciding how best to answer when Adam pipes up, "Tell her about Charlie."

Harriet Fletcher's head swings from me to Adam and back to me. She already thinks I am capable of hurting Adam—what will she make of the dead child who doesn't belong to me? What will she make of the baby I didn't raise, whose whereabouts are unknown to me? My explanation—rambling and rife with omission—ends with where we buried Charlie.

None of this seems to make any impression. "How about any live births since Adam?" She peers at me as though she's trying to thread a needle and finding difficulty with the focal point. "What I mean is, Mrs. Hallowell, are you capable of bearing children?"

If my life depended on it, I couldn't say when last I had my period. And I can't think why she still needs to be corrected on the issue of marital status. Only in Dobbs's mind were we ever married, and now that mind is no more. "It's 'Miss,'" I snap. "And no."

"I see." Whatever piqued her curiosity is now gone. Her attention shifts again to Adam, who, having gone as far as the twine will allow, is reeling himself back to his bed. "As I said, the testing won't take long. A couple of hours, at the most. What do you say, Adam? Are you ready to come with me?"

You'd have to be blind to mistake Adam's frozen posture as the go-ahead. So that Harriet Fletcher will drop the matter, I say, "No more tests."

She approaches me as though having to penetrate an unbearable stench. "I understand your hesitation about being separated from your son. I know you think you are protecting him, and I am not saying you haven't done an admirable job of it in the past."

Admirable job. Protecting my son. I've lied to my son, is what I've done. I've prepared him not at all for the ways people can deceive and manipulate.

"But if you can put aside your own needs and wishes for a moment and think about what is best for Adam——"

I leap out of bed. "You know what? I think Adam and I will find our own way from here." Adam's jaw drops when I tell him to change into his clothes. I pack the bottled water that came on our lunch trays into the suitcase. Six miles is the distance from here to Eudora. If Adam and I put our backs into it, we can be there in a couple of hours.

Harriet Fletcher is pinching the bridge of her nose and looking up at the ceiling when I grab the extra bandages from the bedside table drawer. It is to Adam she speaks. "Your mother intends to leave our compound. Is that what you want, Adam?"

Adam's head flicks from me to her to me again.

"I don't know what she has led you to believe about the world, Adam, but it can be a very dangerous place. She intends to take you out there without a gun, without any ammunition, without any knowledge of the safe passages. And to what end? Except for a few old people and a herd of buffalo, Eudora isn't anything but a ghost town. Is that where you want to go, Adam?"

What she says frightens me as much as it does Adam. Nevertheless, I throw the backpack over my shoulder. Better out there than in here, where people don't seem to respect free will. First free, I tell myself. Now, will. "Adam wants to go where I want to go."

"You, my dear, want to go home, and it is my fault for not having been straight with you sooner. What I am trying to say is that your home is not how you left it."

She is choosing her words, being careful with the truth. Still, I don't care for her use of one word—*left*—as though my absence was somehow my own choosing. Who would choose to be hidden? To be kept underground for all these years? I have denied the question for two days, but now it comes begging: Has Dobbs, who did my choosing for me, saved us from a terrible trial?

Adam is thinking along the same lines. "So there was some kind of disaster."

She pulls out what looks to be a handmade booklet from her pocket and gives it to Adam. "I brought this for you to read. It is certainly a more complete account than what I could give. I suggest you read it before making any hasty decisions."

"I'll take that." Adam hands me the book as four people stomp into the infirmary. Recoiling in fright, Adam jumps into bed, throws the covers over his head, and cinches the edges. The ball of twine falls to the floor and unravels as fast as Adam pulls on the string.

From under his sheets comes a static voice. "Adam, are you there? Over." Harriet Fletcher has her walkie-talkie pressed against her mouth and is signaling the four men to be still. The room is hollow-quiet.

When the last of the twine is gathered under the sheet, Adam's tiny whisper is amplified on Harriet's transmitter. "Yes, I'm here."

Smiling, Harriet pushes the button and tells Adam some very important people have come to see him. Has he ever met a scientist before? No, is Adam's tentative answer. Well, wouldn't he like to meet one? Adam doesn't answer, but he does lower the sheet. He assesses the men as if they were specters, not men of science. And they certainly are peculiar-looking. Their skin seems raw and has a sheen to it. They stoop like stacks of boxes piled too high and have the same odor about them, too, like they are in need of a good airing.

"I have asked a few colleagues to join me today, Adam. They have traveled a considerable distance to be here. They are very excited to meet you."

Adam shields his eyes with one hand, clenches the walkie-talkie with the other.

"Hello, young man." A man steps forward and extends his hand, a gesture Adam mistakes as being required to give back his walkie-talkie.

He tucks it under his arm.

"Nobody's going to hurt you, Adam. This is just an evaluation. Okay?"

It has taken as little as a gadget for Adam to let Harriet Fletcher treat him like something under a microscope. He looks my way. Everything's going to be all right, isn't it?

I muster a smile. Everything's fine.

All the same, I keep the backpack on my shoulder and the suitcase in my hand and wait for Harriet Fletcher to finish talking about the knife wound and presenting symptoms of dehydration and anemia. She asks Adam to pull his garment down a little in the front. It's my fault, the way he does her bidding. Haven't I taught him that sometimes the best resistance is to give way?

"A mild case of rickets, the beginning of a rachitic rosary." She points to Adam's chest, which has recently sprouted soft blond chest hair, an asset of which he is extremely proud. "Deficiencies in vitamin D, calcium, and iron would suggest a limited diet and limited exposure to light, which would correspond with his pigmentation. A somewhat abnormal response to touch. It's possible he has some kind of autistic disorder, Kanner's syndrome perhaps, judging by the poor social and communication skills, the high sensitivity to bright lights and noises."

Adam does not have poor communication skills. There are times he'll talk your ear off. If he's quiet, it means he's working on something in his head. Lord only knows what he's trying to work out now.

One from the crowd raises his pen. "You said he'd been confined?"

"According to the mother, since birth." Harriet Fletcher looks over at me and lowers her voice so I cannot hear what she says next, but all heads turn to me, faces without expression.

"There seems to be some unwillingness to cooperate fully."

Cooperate fully? I've given that woman fact after fact, and what I've received in return is an offer to separate me and Adam.

One of the scientists asks me about Adam's upbringing. Did I keep a journal of his development? What illnesses has he had? How often does he get sick? How long does it take for him to recover from an illness? At what age did he start puberty?

"Has he ever had intercourse?"

"Excuse me?" What kind of question is that of a kid who has been confined his entire life? And then the lightbulb goes on. They're insinuating I've slept with him.

There is but the tiniest pause before Harriet Fletcher resumes her rundown. "No goiter, normal thyroid functioning, no cutaneous ulcerations or necrosis. In summary, no visible signs of exposure."

"How old are you, son?" one of them asks.

"Seventy-eight," Adam answers. Going by birthdays, he's right, but they misread him and crack up. One has a laugh that sounds exactly like the squeaky door between the lower level and the silo tunnel.

"Intact sense of humor." Harriet Fletcher smiles proudly. "At first, we put him around twelve or thirteen because of his muscle tone; however, genital development is definitely that of a postpubertal male."

"I told you, he's fifteen!" All this time I've waited for them, and this is what we end up with: stupid people. How can they look and look at my boy, at me, and not see? They scribble on their notebooks what they can't see, and then they come back again to make sure their looking hasn't changed into something else. If there was any doubt before, I know now with certainty that they are not, as Dobbs used to categorized a very small portion of the people he encountered, Friendlies. There is something about this place that is not entirely on the up-and-up. Their scrutiny of Adam, for one. It is Dobbs's voice in my head, clear as a bell: *Get him out of here.*

"And the bioassays?" one asks.

Harriet Fletcher can't resist touching Adam. She gives his arm a little pat. "Labs came back clean as a whistle."

As one, the group folds toward Adam in a bow. It's not evaluation. It's veneration.

Get him out of here.

HARRIET FLETCHER DOESN'T come right out and say we're being held against our will, just as she doesn't say when exactly the police are arriving, only that they are on their way. She suggests we bathe before they arrive, and because it is critical we make a good impression, I agree. When we follow her outside, the sky is a menacing stew of grays, the air balmy and the mist a soft, sheer curtain. Something in me breaks open. No matter what the weather is doing—giant balls of ice could be falling, for all I care—the simple act of stepping outside is exalting. I tug on the string so Adam will look at me, but he, too, is stunned, though apparently for different reasons. Lowering the umbrella, he cocks his head to the side. Can we can hear it, he wants to know.

"Hear what, Adam?" Harriet Fletcher asks.

I can hear it—a groaning sound, or humming, perhaps. Adam holds his walkie-talkie in front of him and pushes the button.

"Oh, that's just the generators. Come along."

On either side of us is a row of Quonset huts. Each is fronted with an overhang, a number, and a porch light. There isn't a soul in sight, and yet I have the distinct feeling we are being watched.

"Are other people here?" I ask.

Harriet Fletcher makes a flicking motion with her head that could be construed either way. As she leads us past the huts, the fine mist turns to a drizzle. Instantly, the ground turns to slop. Adam stops. Instead of opening his umbrella, Adam lifts his palm and watches tiny droplets land on it. He lifts his face to the heavens, shutters his eyes against the drops, and sticks out his tongue. He has fallen under the spell of rain.

Harriet Fletcher lifts her coat over her head and insists Adam take cover under the umbrella. She tries to hurry him, but he scuffs his feet against the ground. "I get it, Mom. I get it!" He's remembering the time I mixed up a batch of flour and water and chocolate powder, and ordered him to unwrap his feet and stick his toes in the gooey mixture. "Mud," I told him, insisting he make footprints all over my clean floor. He was quite unsure of me that day. Now, he stoops to get his hands dirty, and I can't bring myself to tell him no. I open my arms. Maybe if the rain soaks in, something in me will be renewed.

Harriet Fletcher shoos us to a hut with a sign of a shower painted on its door. "The bathhouse," she announces. Inside, the building is draped with black plastic sheets except for a window covered with burlap. Instead of the cold glare from our quarters, the lamps strung at each end of the hut give off a warm yellow haze. It's humid inside and smells faintly of chemicals. An enormous plastic pool, the kind people put up in their backyards, takes up almost half the space. It's filled with liquid so green it is almost neon. The other side of the Quonset hut is trussed with pipes. At evenly spaced intervals about two feet above the floor are a faucet, a hose with a showerhead, and a step stool. The black rubber floor is dappled with puddles, and the water in the giant tub is still eddying from recent use.

Harriet points to a wooden cubicle near the entrance and explains that I am to wait in it until it is my turn to bathe. Adam, she says, will go first. Adam unties the string from his waist and hands it to me. Gathering up the twine, I take a seat on the bench, but as soon as she aims to close the door, I stand up. "I'm not good with confined spaces."

"If you don't mind, Mrs. Hallowell, a man needs his privacy," she insists, all but putting her hand against my chest.

Adam hardly qualifies as a man, I do not say, deciding to keep my quarrel for what counts. "It's 'Miss,'" I mumble through the slats, as she closes the door on my protest.

I listen to her giving Adam instructions, listen to her helping him out of his clothes. And then comes the sound of Adam entering the water, and the sharp intake of breath that accompanies it. I have not heard her steps retreat, so I imagine she is doing what she has deprived me of: seeing Adam take his first bath.

"It's warm," he says, before giving a satisfied moan.

"You take as long as you like."

There is some splashing and then much sloshing about, as though Adam is doing laps.

Of all the things I liked to tell Adam about, water was my favorite subject. It was a watery globe, I taught him. Even when you stood on dry ground, water was running under your feet. Dig down deep enough and it would go spurting into the air. Below, water came in a big tank and with a warning from Dobbs about using too much. You could lick the floor and have a drink of water and not taste the difference. Above, water came from heaven, I told him. The cleverest thing anybody had ever done was find a way to put it into pipes so people could turn a faucet on and have it run all day if they wanted.

Heaven's what gave me the idea to baptize him. When I emptied the water over him, I pictured him in a river, floating across county lines, emptying first into the great Pottawamie, and then into the kingdom of found souls. I knew I'd secured for him some kind of salvation with that water.

Now here he is, submerged. Free. But not quite.

After a while, I hear Adam get out of the pool. Harriet Fletcher invites him to move over to the wall with the pipes so he can shower off. When she offers to help him do what he is perfectly capable of doing himself, I can take no more. I barge out of the wooden shed. Adam is seated on the footstool, his head tipped forward, a small towel draped over his lap. Harriet Fletcher is holding the showerhead so water can cascade over his shoulders and down his back. The deaf women and their staring, the visiting doctors and their valuating, and now Harriet Fletcher tending my son as though an unearthed treasure, like she is laying a claim to him—it no longer makes me uneasy. It makes me afraid.

"Get your hands off my son!" I shout.

We return to the Quonset hut, and still the police have not arrived. We eat lunch, and they have not arrived. We wait for three hours more, until Harriet Fletcher makes an unconvincing speech about how she can't imagine what has held them up, but that they will surely arrive in the morning. And then when the day is drawing to a close, I say, "They aren't coming, are they?"

Choosing not to answer my question, she bids us good night and leaves the Quonset hut. Adam comes over to my bed. Through gritted teeth, he says, "Mom! You are going to get us into a lot of trouble."

I don't tell him we are in a lot of trouble. Instead, I tell him to get ready. The moment the rain lets up, we're leaving.

"We're not going back out there."

"Yes, we are. I'm taking you home."

"There is no home; didn't you hear what she said?"

"Our home is with each other."

He looks at his walkie-talkie, as though he might just need to consult the woman on this issue.

I snatch it from him. "We do not belong here. With these people. They aim to separate us. Probably tonight, when we fall asleep."

"These are nice people. You said so." He grabs the walkie-talkie from me, scowling.

I try a different tack. "We're free now, Adam. We get to do what we want."

"What I want is to stay here."

"We're leaving, and that's the end of it."

I pack the leftover dinner in the backpack. Which is another thing that bugs me—they've been through our belongings. I am glad we buried Charlie; who knows what they would've held against us if they found a bundle of bones. They're a bunch of thieves, too—the bolt cutter is missing. It's only fair, then, that I take the inhaler.

I am pacing in front of the windows, glaring at those rain clouds, willing them to part, when the door opens. The others are a heavy-handed bunch, but this one takes my hand gently and shakes it.

"Marcus Hill, at your service." His toe catches the edge of the suitcase. "You planning on heading out?"

I don't say anything, but he responds as if I do.

"I don't blame you none." And I can weep for the way he says it, full of tenderness. I try to size him up—he's larger than the others, and darker. His head is shiny, and his lips are the size of thumbs. Only one of his black eyes looks at me; the other settles off to the side.

Adam is mesmerized. "Are you a policeman?"

He laughs and says, "No, son, that I ain't. I'm a sitter. That means whatever you want, for the next twelve hours, you just ask me." He speaks as though he has hot butter beans in his mouth.

I fold my arms in response. A sitter? Someone to keep us from running off, more like.

Adam, who has up to this point retreated from strangers, now volunteers his name and shows him the walkie-talkie. He is delighted when the sitter pulls out his own transmitter. The sitter tells him that unless he wants to transmit to every Tom, Dick, and Harry, he better change the channel. Thirteen is what they decide on, but this sounds very unlucky to me.

"Adam won't be transmitting anything," I clarify.

Not at all put off by my tone, the sitter asks again my name.

I do my deaf-nurse impression.

Adam makes his eyes go wide at me, then apologizes. "My mother's not in a talking mood right now."

"That's okay. I respect that. I know some people who flap their gums all day. You want my opinion, it's fools who talk the most."

An awful lot of words for one breath of air, is what I think, but Adam grins. If he had a tail, it would be wagging. Three days ago, confronting Dobbs with a knife, and here he is, as eager to please as a young boy. All that time worrying about how I would deal with his fears about the world, the disappointment that was sure to come from having been raised on fantasies, and I haven't made any preparations for how to deal with his blind faith. How do I keep him from falling for every smile, every slick word? How a man holds himself, what he does with his hands, can tell a straighter story. If living with Dobbs should have taught Adam anything, it should be at least this much.

"I've got a buddy like your mama here." The sitter takes a seat next to Adam. "He ain't much of a talker, either. He has his reasons, as I'm sure she does. Tunnels of Cu Chi—you ever heard about those?"

Adam draws a blank.

"'Nam, brother. 1974. Dyno was a tunnel rat. It was his job to crawl down those holes to find Charlie."

Adam swings around to look at me.

"Different Charlie," I say.

"Dyno never knew if he was about to step into a booby trap, if some trapdoor of nails was going to slam down on top of him." The sitter smashes his fist in the palm of his other hand. Adam flinches. "The guy's one tough sonofabitch, I'll tell you that. Nothing fazes him. Not much of a talker, but one very wily cat. Got out of 'Nam with all ten fingers and ten toes, unlike most. Started his own dealership back in the day. How d'you like that? A car salesman who don't talk! Damned if he didn't make himself a ton of money, too. One year he even got some fancy award for having the best dealership in the state of Ohio. People went to his place, see, they didn't need no sales pitch. Dyno was an honest-to-god war hero, and folks found a way to show their appreciation. Some said it was a shame he ended up on the street so soon after, but the way I figure, he got those tunnels inside him."

"My mother killed the man who kept us locked up. Are they going to put her in jail? Is that why they won't let us leave?"

"Adam!"

The sitter holds up his hands, and goes, "Whoa, whoa, whoa."

"She was going to tell the police as soon as she got me to the hospital. We couldn't drive there because of the trees."

The sitter leans past Adam to look at me. "You have a car that runs?"

"It ran out of gas," Adam replies, shrugging off my glare.

The man's face drops. "Scavengers have got to it by now."

Adam snaps his fingers. "We saw them! They live in a train. I think my mom ran over one of them."

"Okay, that's enough, Adam!" I stride toward him and situate myself between him and the sitter.

"She didn't mean it, though." He knows I'd like to throttle him.

And in this way we put on a nice little show for the man with one good eye until he offers to turn out the lights so we might sleep.

Darkness feels like a respite. As long as the lights aren't on, I don't have to pretend. Between me and the sitter are only a few feet, but in the dark it might as well be miles. Lit up, this place gives the wrong impression, that with people around we are found. Truth is, the more there are of them, the more isolated I feel. Cut off is what the darkness shows. On our own. Silo-alone.

"We lived underground where they used to put rockets," Adam whispers.

"You mean, like a missile silo?"

"Yup."

"Son, you bullshitting me? Because I've heard some stories in my day."

"No. It's true."

The sitter mumbles about children having being squirreled away in all sorts of places, but never a missile silo.

"He wasn't protecting us." Adam explains a truth that for him has only barely set. "He kept us locked up. That's why my mom doesn't like it here—she doesn't want to be a prisoner. We're not prisoners, right?"

The sitter is silent for a moment, as though he's forgotten it is a per-

son next to him and not a story. "How long you been living in that missile silo, Adam?"

"My whole life."

"Your whole life." He says it real slow. "And your mama's been down
there that whole time, too?"

"She's been there longer. Since before I was born."

"Since before you were born."

The sitter repeats everything Adam says—about getting the door
open; about never having seen the moon or stars till a few days ago;
about never having been outside. It's as if he can believe the words only
if they come from his own mouth.

Adam is out of bed, rummaging in his trousers. He asks the sitter to
hold out his hand. "That's some of the gravel I've collected. There are so
many different kinds of earth. But rain's my favorite thing so far; it turns
this stuff to mush."

Just when I've decided to hate this man, he pipes up, "There's lots of
different kinds of rain, too." For a minute, we listen to it *thunk* down on
the corrugated siding. "You afraid of getting wet?"

The sitter and Adam stand in the doorway where the rain makes a
beaded curtain against the porch light. Adam sticks his hand in it, pulls
it back, and then rubs his head. Watching Adam is like watching an as-
tronaut on a new planet. You see him experiencing the world, it's like
you're experiencing it for the first time, too.

The sitter steps into the porch-lit rain and holds out his hand. Adam
takes it. I lean forward on my elbows and watch two boys dance under a
cloudburst and kick up puddles.

We are back Below, having to listen to what's wrong with the world.

"No!" I shout, sitting up. Not in my cot in the silo, but in the Quonset hut. The storyteller is a hunched shape beside my son's bed—not
Dobbs, but that sitter, Marcus.

"Can you turn on the lights, please?"

We all squint at each other when he does.

"What's going on here?"

Adam hesitates, like he doesn't want to be the one to break the news. "It *was* Diablo, Mom. Just like Mister said. The solar flares, the electromagnetic storms shutting down the grid, the nuclear reactors melting down—it all happened."

Dobbs sometimes referred to what was happening on the surface as AD, meaning After Diablo. Diablo Canyon was supposedly a nuclear reactor in California that was the first to melt down.

"Ninety reactors around the world, all told," Marcus chimes in.

"There's no more Korea," Adam adds. He looks as though he might weep. "Or Russia. Almost everyone in Europe died."

No, no, no. It's supposed to be a fossil-fuel crisis. It's supposed to have affected only parts of Kansas, not the entire country. Not the world. Hollowed out is how I feel.

"We took the biggest hit, even bigger than the Asians," Marcus continues.

"Not everyone died, surely," I manage. Twelve people here, the four visitors, the people living in the abandoned train, the charred soul in the old farmhouse. Mightn't there be a chance that my kin survived? That in some tucked-away place Mama is still waiting for me?

"No, not everyone." But the way he says it—apologetic, cautionary—means I shouldn't go asking for specifics. I ask anyway.

He explains that in the first month, the population of the country saw a 20 percent drop. Six months later, fewer than 20 percent were still alive. By the time a year rolled by, there was nobody around to keep track of the numbers. Estimates still swing widely, he says. Being an optimist, he puts the number somewhere between seventy-five and two hundred thousand. "That's just North America. Nobody can hazard a guess as for the other continents."

He runs his hand across his brow. "Hard to believe that this coming May will make it fifteen years since Diablo. Seems a lot longer. Many a day I wake up and wonder how come I'm not six feet under yet."

I think back. Adam would have been three months old. Dobbs moved down with us around that time. I remember because Adam had started teething and I was worried because it was too early for a baby to start teething, and his crying made Dobbs even more testy than usual. I told Dobbs to sleep in his own house if it bothered him so, but he jumped down my throat: when would I get it into my thick skull that he didn't have a home anymore, is how he put it. I thought this meant he'd lost his job and the bank had taken his house. For eight months straight he stayed down there, not once going up for supplies. Then there's the time he rushed Below and went for his shotgun, before dragging me up to the exit door and telling me the Scalpers were after us. I thought perhaps the police had come for me. I kept waiting for the door to bust open. When Dobbs did eventually make a foray back outside, I was bitterly disappointed. It meant that he wasn't on anyone's radar. No one was coming for us. All that talk of the Last Days during those months— I mistook it for craziness. He'd come back with few supplies but plenty of biblical references. The Parable of the Sower was a popular one. He spoke of refugees on their way to Mexico, likened them to seeds falling by the wayside. Where they fell, they were literally eaten by crows. The seed left to wither on stony ground were the survivors who supposedly stayed put and tried to tough it out, only to starve later. The criminal element that rose up was the weedy patch. Dobbs would talk Bible stories, and then look over at Adam as though one boy wasn't going to do the trick. I thought all of it was to get me to stop begging him.

"Is there any way to know who survived?"

To my surprise, he mentions a group in Utah. "Cockroaches, yeah, but Mormons? Who'd have thought, right?" The Saints, he says, spend their days baptizing posthumously the millions who have died using something called the Ancestral Index, a handwritten database of the deceased. Updates are made to it frequently, although he doubts a request for information on surviving relatives has been submitted to them in the last few years. Everyone pretty much knows by now who made it and who didn't. "Tricky part is communicating with them. That much distance with the CB radio has gotta involve a lot of Skippers, and once you involve more than two or three of them—well, it's often a case of the Telephone Game."

"What are Skippers?" Adam asks.

"You know about skipping stones on a lake? Well, it's kinda like that with broadcasting a message across the country. You gotta bounce it from one CB operator to another. Get some rookie mixed up in the process, and a request for information on Uncle Joe could end up getting you a report on radiation levels in Uganda."

Radiation levels in Uganda seem to Adam to be a topic worthy of conversation, but I ask them both to be quiet for a moment.

Silence doesn't help. I ask Marcus if I might get some air.

It is my turn to stand in the rain.

Could it be that they are all gone? Could it be that they suffered something I can't even comprehend? Something far worse than what I have had to endure? Could it be that Dobbs, my assailant, my jailor, the man against whom my will was sharpened, then dulled, and then sharpened once more has, in fact, saved me, saved my son? And having surely saved my son from suffering and death, is he not owed a debt, a debt for which I can never repay him? Am I not now beholden to him in a way I wasn't before? Will I now never be free of him? There has been but one constant over the last seventeen years: the moral certainty that comes from distinguishing right from wrong—Dobbs was wrong; I was right. Once such a sure platform, that moral certainty now seems no more dependable than a trapdoor on the gallows. Was he wrong to take me? Was he right to keep us down there?

Behind me, I hear Adam tell about the strange blue street signs. Marcus explains about evacuation routes. Did Mama and Daddy live long enough to be evacuated? Adam mentions the mound with all the buried things, and Marcus explains the massive cleanup of anything that might have been contaminated by fallout. Dobbs used to say the very young and the very old were most susceptible to radiation, that Adam had to be sheltered as long as possible. What chance is there that my brothers and sister have survived?

Adam mentions the mangrove swamp. Marcus explains, "We got species of trees from South America I don't even know the names of, but that's what happens when birds don't know which way to migrate."

"My mom thinks the trees are ugly."

"Some of them are, the ones from the early years. The newer ones are doing better. People the same way. Won't be no more Defectives in a hundred years, some say."

I cringe at the word.

"What's a Defective?" Adam asks.

"The ones who don't come out right. The exact opposite of you."

Marcus is in the chair with his elbows on his thighs and his hands clasped. "Doctors and scientists have been working for years to come up with someone pure, who ain't going to pass on radioactive cells, and then you guys show up outta nowhere. Man, they must think they've hit the jackpot with you, pal."

So that explains their fascination with Adam.

"My mom thought they were making bombs here. She doesn't like weapons."

"Bombs? Ain't no point in making bombs. But they're cooking up stuff, that's for sure."

"Hill!" Nobody has heard Harriet Fletcher come in. She marches over to us and plants herself between the sitter and me. "What exactly are you doing?"

Marcus winks at Adam, as if to counter her crossness.

"You are not here to fraternize with the patients." She checks the small container next to Adam's bed.

"He's not giving any more urine samples," I announce.

"I see." She narrows her eyes at Marcus as though this is somehow his doing. Her tone softens when she speaks to my son. "Adam, you do need to give us a specimen. We really are trying to help. Despite what your mother thinks."

Harriet Fletcher pulls Marcus to one side. Something about getting restraints from Quadrant D should the need arise. Before leaving, she takes an armload of files off the shelf and dumps it into his arms and says, "Since you've got so much free time on your hands."

I approach Marcus. "These tests they want to do on my son—"

He cuts me off by flicking a chart. "This patient's got failed kidneys."

He pulls out the folding chair, sits down, and leafs through another chart. "This one's got no iron in her blood, and this poor kid's got lymph nodes the size of oranges. We get a lot of sick people come through these doors. I've been doing this job for two years, and it never ceases to amaze me, the things they do. Cut open a man's throat, take his thyroid out and sew it up again, good as new. Tumors the same way. Fifteen years ago, you couldn't get treatment, good or otherwise. This place, they got the aces working here."

"You said they hit the jackpot with Adam. What do you mean?"

Marcus points up at a little black speaker and says unnecessarily loud, "What you got here is a five-star facility. That's right, uh-huh." Judging from the look on Marcus's face, this fact is not something about which we should feel thrilled. He pulls us close and whispers for Adam to bring over his notepad. He draws on the page, and hands it to me.

A squiggle. I frown and shrug.

He outlines his drawing again, and this time it looks like a tadpole, until he draws a big circle next to it.

I mouth the word. *Sperm?*

Marcus nods and then erases his sketch. I snatch the pad from him and fill the page with a giant question mark.

Marcus spends several minutes designing a comic strip. The first square is jam-packed with stick figures, the second square has half as many, and in the third square the remaining stick figures fall on top of one another. Next is a diagram of a big syringe with bubbles inside, and a fried egg. I draw a complete blank. Adam, on the other hand, is spurring Marcus on with vigorous nodding.

Marcus hands us the notepad when he's done. Something about sick people, and beans on a conveyer belt, and beans being packaged in a bag, and the bagged beans going for a ride on a cart into a forest.

I would still be wondering what beans have to do with this place if Adam hadn't whispered, "Mom, they're making babies here."

So there can be no doubt, Marcus nods deliberately.

"And they intend to use Adam in their operation?"

Marcus shrug-nods.

ADAM HAS SPENT the better part of the morning watching the wall clock. He has tested each bed for springiness, fiddled with every latch and knob and wire, turned on and off the faucet at the sink a thousand times. He has exhausted every activity and is now waiting for when the deaf woman pretending not to guard the door will leave and Marcus will return. Until I have some idea from Marcus where Adam and I could go, we're not about to leave, but each attempt to communicate this to the woman results in more food trays.

According to the booklet Harriet Fletcher gave us, when geomagnetic storms knocked out the transformers and shut down the grid fifteen years ago, emergency generators were used to pump coolant so the nuclear rods at power stations wouldn't melt down. Some plants didn't have more than a few days' worth of diesel to keep the generators running. Trucks carrying diesel got waylaid in massive traffic jams and then hijacked. The government called for the pumping of more diesel, but you can't pump it out of the ground by hand. Just as you cannot pump by hand water to houses or sewage from them. Without power, ATMs and credit card machines were useless. Good-bye, NYSE; hello, mattress money. Refugee camps sprang up hundreds of miles from cities where rioting, looting, and murder became the order of the day. Most camps dried up quickly for lack of supplies, but a few became cities themselves, with local municipalities run like co-ops. Apparently, there are no more states, no central government. There are prefectures, provinces, something called the North American Confederacy. America is now a no-name-brand country. A hand-drawn diagram on the back page shows only two borders—the Atlantic and the Pacific.

"What if his clock and this clock are different?" Adam asks.

"Time is time; it's the same for everybody."

"But who decides what time it is?"

I don't know anymore. Is there still Greenwich mean time?

"There's something wrong with this clock," Adam says two minutes later. "It was going much faster last night, and now it keeps stopping."

I look at the clock; the long hand snaps to the next marker. I suggest Adam open his notebook and work on some of his designs.

"Why does time go slower in the day than it does at night?"

"It only seems that way because you are waiting."

"Last night was ten hours and thirty minutes long," Adam announces. "That means today will last thirteen hours and thirty minutes. Is that normal? Shouldn't it be equal?"

I don't know any more what's normal. I still can't tell from the weather what season it is. "It means it's probably late spring, or else early fall. Nothing to worry about."

But Adam does look worried. He keeps his attention fixed on the clock. "Do you think he's going to come back?"

Don't get your hopes up about people, I want to tell him. Don't get your hopes up about anything.

I should keep reading, but every page I turn, I see more of Dobbs's disaster play out. The world is not my home. Instead of returning to the scene of my youth, I am set down among the artifacts of Dobbs's invention. Between every line, lines he could have written himself, his face appears, taunting. *How you going to protect him now?* I hear him wheeze in my ear. *What are you going to do without me?* I don't know what to say to him.

Marcus returns a little before noon. Besides the deaf woman, he is the only other face we've seen all day.

"I come bearing gifts," he proclaims, dropping a flat brown slab on my lap. "Hershey's counts as food, don't it?"

I finger the shiny foil paper.

"Brought something for you, too, Sunshine."

Adam perches on the end of my bed and eagerly accepts the small yellow pillow in a plastic wrapper. He's elated. "What's it for?"

"Eating, kid! That right there is the genuine article. I have a friend who's a trader; says they've got another factory running again. On the black market, Twinkies used to fetch an arm and a leg. Now, you can trade as little as a sack of flour for one."

Marcus has something else tucked behind his back. "Got you another present, but you have to guess first."

I catch the look on Adam's face: oh no, not another birthday— something bad's about to happen.

Something bad has happened.

"Hey, don't look so worried." He hands Adam a silver bar not much bigger than the Twinkie.

"Thanks." Adam inspects it one way, then another, and holds it up for me. "Isn't it great?" He has no idea what it is.

"What'sa matter? Never taken a bite out of a tin sandwich before?" Because Adam still looks foggy, Marcus shows him. The instrument disappears in his palm. He cups his hand around his mouth, and the room fills with honky-tonk. After a few bars of "Oh! Susanna," he rubs the harmonica on his trousers and gives it back to Adam.

Nothing has ever fit Adam properly, not the clothes Dobbs occasionally brought for him or the sweaters I knit; not the belt to hold up his pants or his newly acquired pair of shoes. But this harmonica seems custom-made for him. Who knew the first thing to fit my son so perfectly would be music?

Adam runs the instrument back and forth across his lips, puffing out one chord after another. He beams at Marcus.

"You're welcome, Sunshine."

Adam takes off to the far side of the hut looking like a drum major in front of a marching band. For him, the world is emerging one note at a time, one new face at a time; my world, however, continues its retreat. Beloved faces turn out like lights, one after another. Like cardboard cutouts, Mama's house, Grandpa's farm, the old redbrick schoolhouse fall flat. The longed-for is now a parched idea existing only in my faulty memory. I wanted so much to give Adam a tour. I wanted the forgotten things to pull me from the tomb. I am not resurrected; I am merely aboveground.

Marcus takes a seat, folds his arms across his chest, and seems perfectly content to watch Adam. Adam told me earlier that Marcus is his friend, told me to be nice to him. He said the way I talked about Mercy, the way we'd become instant friends, how we'd just looked at each other and knew right away we could tell each other things we'd never tell anybody else, that's how it is with him and Marcus.

With Adam out of earshot, I ask Marcus if things are as bad now as the brochure makes them out to be. Marcus keeps his seeing eye on Adam. In his voice is nothing but patience. "Folks don't talk anymore about what's bad, what's good. Bad and good all got mixed together. Still mixed together. Nobody can say for sure which is gonna come out ahead."

Marcus smiles at the string of flat notes. "I had a boy. About the same age as Adam when he died. He and his mother lived in Wilmington, eighteen miles from the Salem plant. The government had to send people door-to-door with orders to evacuate, the communications satellites being fried and all. Turns out, they get to the poor neighborhoods last."

"I'm sorry."

"Sometimes, I wonder if it wouldn't have been better for a bomb to drop, ended it right there in one fell swoop instead of being hit with wave after wave of radiation. Folks starving. Cities on fire. Armed militias gunning people down for stealing bread. You can be glad he missed all that."

Marcus clearly divulged more than he ought to last night, but I'm not sure he won't rat on us if I ask him straight-out about the closest community and how we might get there. I feel him out by asking him about tent cities. "People are pack animals," he says. "All those preppers from before Diablo—the one thing they failed to prepare for was our need to congregate."

"Are any of these places near Eudora?"

He shakes his head. "Except for a few, these are mobile villages. The most they spend in any one place is a couple of months. A certain caravan might pass by here every four or five years, depending on how big their loop is. Some folks, their whole entire lives are spent on one migration." Marcus explains how each nomadic group establishes its own migratory pattern, some tied to seasonal availability of wild crops, others to trade exchanges. "Chances of survival went up once people started to move. You settle down somewhere and you have to defend yourself against looters, wildlife, squatters. If the fires come through, there go all your provisions."

I tell him Harriet Fletcher mentioned a few old people in Eudora.

"Some of us ain't cut out for a life on the road, the old-timers, especially. Some of them get road-weary, and some are still perfectly capable of keeping up with their group, but they opt to move back to their hometowns anyway. Homesick is what it is."

"What about kids?" Adam has stopped playing. The images that sicken me, tales of a land gone to seed, seem to have no effect on him. And why should they? This is the boy who has been immunized against disaster, who has been told his entire life that the day would come for him to fulfill his destiny in a postapocalyptic world. Why shouldn't he look as if he's poised to do exactly that?

Marcus pegs his nose with his fingers, as if he's equalizing pressure in his ears. "You don't see many kids out there."

"Where do you live?" Adam asks.

"Where I live ain't no picnic." Marcus studies my face, sizes up my intentions. "Look, folks would be lining up to get into a place like this. Round-the-clock security, health care, three squares a day. You gone and won the lotto, they'd say."

From outside comes the sudden sound of marching. Adam goes to the window to check.

"Yes, but what do *you* say?"

"I don't tell you this to scare you," Marcus says quietly, leaning toward me, "but out there, you could cross paths with traffickers, and if they get their hands on him, there's no telling where he'd end up. In the early years, you'd hear the occasional story of a family popping up from their storm shelter or crawling out of a cave, and you couldn't help but feel sorry for them. You knew they were going to die from exposure or starvation or because they hadn't become part of a pack, like the rest of us. But we haven't heard of survivors for years, and now I'd say the premium for an untainted boy, one with clean genes, is sky-high."

When two men wearing hoods and army fatigues come in, Adam races back to us and takes shelter behind Marcus.

"We're here to escort Adam Hallowell to the conservatory."

I begin protesting, but the cadet pulls out a piece of paper. "Dr. Fletcher signed an order for tests."

I ask Adam for the walkie-talkie. "I'll straighten this out."

While I am scrambling among the sheets looking for the darn thing, one of the cadets has whipped some kind of canvas sack over Adam's head, transforming him into a beekeeper.

"Mom," he mutters through the mesh.

I throw myself at the cadet, but it is like trying to move a tank. They hustle Adam out the door despite my thrashing. "There is some mistake! Let go of him!" The fight spills out onto the path where I am almost knocked off my feet by the noonday brightness. Light can be a violent thing, a thing that screeches and howls so loud you have to force yourself not to turn and run the other way. It is a pushy thing, greedy. Daylight lathers my face and spreads down my neck. I can't help but gasp as it forces its way down my throat. Searing, scalding, like acid. Still, I keep screaming for them to unhand Adam.

"It's okay, Mom. I'm okay." Adam's had to grow up with Dobbs clanging on about how unreasonable survivors are—fear-riddled, squabbling rumormongers who'd sooner slit a man's throat than shake his hand. If anything, Adam is at risk of believing people aren't nearly as bad as they've been made out to be.

"Do something!" I yell at Marcus, who just stands there, running his hand back and forth across his head.

The cadet makes the mistake of assuming phrases like "just a few doors down," "back by dinnertime," and "painless procedure" are going to change my mind. I lunge for Adam and get shoved hard enough that I lose my balance and land on all fours. I look up. Already Adam is ten yards away. It's like watching a maple leaf on the surface of a rushing river. A picture flashes into my head of Mama standing at the back door. In her face is the tepid morning sunlight. She blows me a kiss, then waves as I rush to meet the bus. I don't want to blow my son a kiss because this is not a good-bye. This is a rescue.

I stumble to my feet, rub the dust out of my eyes, and start to run after Adam just as the sky turns grainy. Oddly, the grains shift and swoop into a dense shadow eclipsing the sun. A sudden wind stirs up more dust, and I hear the whining of a two-stroke engine. I realize the sound is the massive shadow plummeting toward me. For some reason my legs will not move. I am in that dream where I've gone lame. Run. Run! Somebody is screaming at me.

An arm scoops me up and yanks me back inside. The door slams. It sounds as if an army has opened fire on it. I cover my face, but it doesn't help. Flapping, creeping, biting things are all about my head, tangled in my hair. I flog my legs, but three-inch bugs with wings are glued to them.

"Get them off!"

"Locusts." Marcus is picking them off me. "They come out here from the east, looking for food." Some fly about the room, dive-bombing me and taking off again for the windows. Before Marcus has clobbered them all, I run to the window. The day looks benign, sunny once again. Picnic weather. Adam is gone.

There is only one place to start my story. With him, my story begins. Without him, it might as well end, too.

I SLING MY backpack over my shoulder, grab the suitcase, and check through a crack in the door for foot traffic. No sign of Marcus. He said he'd be right back. I am to wait for him to return. I am to trust him to help us escape. Trust the man who did nothing but watch Adam get carted off against his will. Trust the man who is on Harriet Fletcher's payroll. It's been five minutes. If he went to get a trash can to hide me in as he said, he'd be back by now. What's to say he isn't part of a plan to move Adam out of the complex entirely? What's to say this wasn't Harriet Fletcher's doing, that it is the work of those traffickers he was so eager to tell me about? What's to say he isn't one of them?

I pick up the walkie-talkie, check to make sure it's on channel thirteen, and then transmit. "Marcus, are you there?"

Nothing.

I try a second time. "Marcus?"

Again, nothing but static.

I've already wasted too much time. I dash outside and dart down the side path. No use consulting my instincts—they are entirely useless to me here. Other than a desperate need to hurry, I have no sense of where to go next. I am right-side up after all these years, and everything feels upside down. I have become hopeless at anticipating. If I guess left, trouble is likely to come from the right. I follow the row of sheds. Each screened window I pass is thick with odor. I am about to cross an intersection when I hear what sounds like a squadron approaching from the

side street. I dash into the nearest shed and close the door. Quite mirac-
ulously, the footsteps race by without stopping. Relief is so overwhelming I have to keep myself from collapsing to the floor.

I spin around, aware that I am not alone. Sitting on a small wooden
pallet are a middle-aged man and a boy so hunched he could be ten years
old or a hundred. Both of them have thick, white padding bound to their
necks, with plastic tubing leading from the dressing to bottles beside
them. Each is naked from the waist up. On their chests are several circular white stickers, each with a metal nipple. The man has a thick black
mustache, but no eyebrows and no hair. The boy's head is too large for
his body. He looks like a cartoon character, only one with no laughs in
him.

Neither seems surprised by my intrusion.

I say very quietly, "I'm looking for my son." I lift my hand a couple of
inches above my head. "About this tall, blond hair."

The man clears his throat, gargles, "Operating room." He points to
the way I've just come.

"No, he's not having surgery. The conservatory?"

I want to get him by the shoulders and shake him so he will spit out
the words he seems to have such difficulty forming.

"Is he. A candidate?"

I have no idea what this means. I nod vigorously.

This time he points in the other direction. "Big. building."

"Thank you."

The man shrugs. The boy never looks up from the dark stain on the
floor beside the bed.

At the end of the row is a warehouse-looking structure with a sign on it
that reads, AUTHORIZED PERSONNEL ONLY. I try peering in the side
windows, but the dark tint makes it impossible to see anything. Through
the air vents come strains of classical music and the faint smell of lilacs.
The door around the back is unlocked. The handle turns without making a sound. I slip in.

Women. About a dozen of them. Some of them are resting on their beds, some are seated in chairs next to their beds, their feet propped on stools. One woman is picking out a book from a tall shelf. The walls are painted a cheery yellow, lace curtains frame each window, and the floor is carpeted. All the women are barefoot. Without exception, all of them have swollen bellies, all of them too old for having babies.

I turn around to leave, but the one nearest me calls, "You can have Linda's spot." A tall woman with graying hair in a loose bun ambles over. She points out an available bed. Everyone turns to stare. "We ain't going to bite you." She stares at my shape, as though trying to assess how far along I might be. "Bashful one, Bernice," she says over her shoulder to the woman with the book.

"Sorry, I think I have the wrong place." I try to retreat, but the tall woman blocks the door.

"Bit late for second thoughts, don't you think?"

"Leave her be." The one called Bernice steps forward. She might have been pretty once, if it weren't for the dark blemish that covers one whole side of her face, the discolored teeth, heavy hips that come from bearing many children. "It's all right; we're all just girls here." There is something about her voice, something about her soothing tone. "Name's Bernice." She sticks out her hand. "I'm the Supervising Birther. Why don't you put your things down and introduce yourself."

I don't want to raise the alarm, so I ask her as casually as possible if she would direct me to the conservatory.

Her head falls to the side, and her eyes soften. "Oh, honey."

Some alarm goes off inside me. I stare at the woman, Bernice, but there is nothing familiar about her face. It's that word—honey—and the way she uses it on me, as though she's sorry for all the things I have yet to learn. Bernice. Bernice. A tendril of a memory, a voice from long ago.

"Lord help us, Bernice, but I think they sent us another soft-boiled one again."

"Bernice," I say, tentatively, because I'm not sure I ought to risk it. "From Eudora?"

Her widening eyes and smile confirm she is. "Do I know you, honey? Have we met before? Here, sit down; you're looking a little peaked." She tells the tall one to fetch some lemonade. Patting my arm, she says, "This can't be your first time, can it?"

All those years ago on the phone, Daddy's lady-friend told me to go looking for rainbows. It's a wonder cracked lips can form words, a throat this parched can issue sound. "I'm Blythe."

She starts to say what you'd expect from someone with good manners—what a nice name—but stops. She draws in her lips, frowns. I let her search my face. Her chin begins to quiver. So she will not have to ask, I tell her my last name.

The instant Bernice starts to cry, the women rise up. They close in and form an outer circle of murmuring. "Didn't like the looks of her the moment she walked through that door," I hear someone say; meanwhile, Bernice might as well be watching the dead being raised.

"What happened to my family, Bernice? Did any of them survive?"

She covers her mouth. "It can't be." Her hand reaches out to touch my arm, then stroke my face. As though to alleviate a sharp pain, she clasps her side as I tell her I just now got free, that I want to go home, if she could just tell me if anyone's there. "Oh, honey, they never stopped looking for you. Not even after Diablo. Every time those posters faded, I'd see your ma out there putting up new ones, sick as she was." She takes my hand and starts rubbing the back of it. "She took it hard, real hard. We all did. Your friend, Mercy, she was about the only one your ma could stand to talk to. Remember that boy you were with that night? What was his name?"

"Arlo."

She snaps her fingers. "Arlo Meier, that's right. You being gone tore him up something awful, too. He joined the force because of you. Swore up one side and down the other he was going to find you. Folks figured you had to have been taken by one of those rings—that you were probably in Mexico or someplace overseas."

I tell her about the silo, about Dobbs Hordin keeping me there. Describing him in objective terms is near impossible. "He was a survivalist.

He predicted all of this. That's why he took me. I have a son, Bernice. They've taken him somewhere. He's never been around people before. He'll be scared. Please, you must help me!" Bernice looks terribly confused. I don't know if it's because of what I've said or what the woman whispering in her ear is saying.

"He's not a trader, by any chance?" Bernice rattles off Dobbs's weight, height, and hair color, all the details I should've been able to provide.

"Yes, that's him." A trader? Dobbs coming back to the silo with tinned food, that ridiculous prom dress, one time a full set of dishes— did he get our supplies here? And if so, in exchange for what? It occurs to me just how much stuff is left Below. Not only food provisions, but the books, the guns, Krugerrands, all those historical documents. Aren't they going to be even more valuable now? And if he came here to trade, can I? Will these women help me find Adam if I promise them Dobbs's nest egg?

"The Hoarder's what we call him," the tall one bellows. "Always suspected he was feeding an army, the amount of contributions he makes. He certainly never acts like he's doing it for the enjoyment."

"Contributions?" Besides those stupid tracts, I can't imagine what Dobbs might have taken from the silo to trade. Unless. The thought stops the blood dead in its tracks. "Did he bring you a child?" Was Dobbs one of those human traffickers that Marcus was telling me about?

A snicker breaks the silence. The tall one gives herself away with a hee-haw. "A child? Can't say the poor bastard didn't try!" The group erupts into raucous laughter. Bernice's deadpan splits into a wide grin, which she quickly covers with her fingers. Other women are not so similarly restrained. They hold their bellies and slap their thighs.

"You don't know what he was up to?" Bernice asks me, putting her hand on my knee.

I shake my head. Something's off about these women. I'm not at all sure I should bring up the idea of trading with them.

"He came here to trade his seed for supplies." For a second, I think she's talking about tomato seeds, his precious repository, and then she says, "We do it the old-fashioned way here, not like test tubes or anything. I think the only reason management kept him on as a contributor was because there are so few men who aren't contaminated."

The smell of lilac perfume, him not looking me in the eye when he put the duffel bag on the table, scrubbing his hands till they were almost raw. These were the women he was having sex with?

"Bernice, I need you to help me find my son."

To signal that the time for discussing Dobbs is over, that we really must be about finding Adam, I stand. Bernice, though, is flagging over a tiny middle-aged woman with buck ears, a receding chin, and the beginning stages of a baby bump. "Fiona was the one most often assigned to him. This may or may not be his doing."

The tall one snorts. "We'll know if it's born with horns and a forked tail."

"He's dead," I say impatiently, because we must hurry now.

For a moment, the women fall silent. And then a couple of elbows are jammed into Fiona's side, and she heaves a sigh, and the tall one makes a snorting sound. "Can't say it's a loss."

"Where do they keep the kids?" I grab Bernice's arm.

Gently but with a warning attached it, Bernice removes my hand and says the birthers are kept separate from the offspring.

"She's not in enlisted in the program, is she?" asks the tall one. There is suddenly a straightening of maternity gowns, the shuffling of feet, clucking of tongues. What was camaraderie only a minute ago is now out-and-out hostility.

Bernice is directing everyone back to their respective beds, and I have begun to insist in a crazy banshee kind of way that someone take me to my son. "I'll pay you!" I shout. "I've got money!" And all at once, I realize how ridiculous it is to offer money. Money is surely worthless now. But what do I have that would be of value to these people? I try to fight the panic, try to push it way down so I can think straight, but it only causes havoc with my innards. Everything's coming loose. Bernice is ushering me to the back door, suggesting that I should probably leave, when it flies open. Marcus, sweating and breathing heavily, is on the other side of it. He has a plastic garbage container with him.

"All the trouble I went to find you a ride as nice as this, and you split."

"That's him!" I yell, pointing the walkie-talkie at him. "He's one of them who took my son!"

Bernice and Marcus try to conduct a conversation while I pound on his chest.

He catches my wrists, but before he can drag me outside, my protests are interrupted by a pulsing, earsplitting ring. All heads swings in one direction. Near the front door is the tall woman. Her fingers are pressed against the red button.

Bernice and Marcus push me outside. He lifts the lid.

"I'm not getting in there!"

Bernice drops my backpack and suitcase on the ground, wishes me good luck, and hurries back inside, slamming the door.

Marcus grips me around the waist. I did not kill Dobbs for this. I did not live through that hell so someone could pull me into another one. I ram my hand up against his jaw and wriggle free. "Adam!" I call, taking off. I scream for him again, this time into the walkie-talkie. How far can he be that he cannot answer?

Marcus tackles me from behind. He clamps his hand around my mouth and tells me for the love of God to quit yelling. "I'm getting you outta here. Like I told you."

I mumble against his hand and somehow he understands what I mean.

"We gonna go get your son. But you keep hollering, and it's going to be next to impossible." A big guy like this, you'd expect strong-arm tactics, especially with a siren going off, but he's got his eyebrows raised, waiting for permission, and his eyes are wet with either apology or guilt. He pulls his hand away from my mouth just a fraction.

"How do I know you're not going to turn me in?"

"You don't. You trust me or you wait here for management, it's that simple."

There is no acclimating to a thing like trust. It presents itself, and there are but seconds to accept or reject it. A blink is all it takes for Marcus to lift me clear off my feet and deposit me into the trash can.

"Fight like a cornered cat and weigh just as much." The lid slams shut, and Marcus starts wheeling me away. "Hold on tight now. It's gonna be a bumpy ride." We both know a bumpy ride is the least of our worries.

THE LID FLIES open. Marcus hauls me into a cinder-block building. Its huge windows are open, but there is no breeze to dispel either the soapy smell or sticky air. Mounted along the sides of the interior are tub-size concrete basins with faucets. At each washing station is a freestanding vat with a handle, a canvas laundry basket, and a shelf stacked with boxes of Borax. Trestle tables are piled high with folded sheets and blankets. The middle of the room is taken up with a drying rack the size of scaffolding. From its steel arms hang dozens of uniforms in assorted colors.

Marcus snatches a green one-piece and holds it up against me. "That'll do."

I hurry into it, zipping up the front. When I turn around, Marcus has changed from his outfit into a green uniform, too. We put on matching screened helmets. He grabs sheets from the table and towels from the rack, tosses them into a laundry cart, and then wheels it to me. He does likewise with a second cart. Pushing it, he heads for the door.

"Act normal, and follow me. You're on housekeeping duty now."

The siren is still wailing, in the nearness or distance, it's hard to tell which with this thing over my head. "Aren't they going to recognize us?"

"Nobody sees the laundry people. Come on, we're close. It's only four blocks."

We wheel our laundry carts outside just as someone approaches from the direction we aim to go. I am about to make a U-turn and retreat into the laundry room when I hear Marcus murmur, "Keep going."

I can't quite muster the strength to move, even though Marcus keeps urging me. The person is wearing a lab coat and carrying a tool tray of what look like milk bottles. He is seconds away, and still I cannot get my arms to push the laundry basket. My muscles have turned to dough.

Marcus spins around and drops to the ground beside me. "That wheel giving you trouble again?"

I hope my head is nodding. Through the mesh, I watch the person, wait for him to stop and jerk Marcus to his feet.

"How you doing?" Marcus says, tipping an imaginary hat.

Instead of answering, the man hurries around us without so much as a glance.

We roll the carts around the bend and into a great commotion. We are in some kind of courtyard, and the noise is not turkeys gobbling but a crush of young men, a few stooped and bald, some of them younger than Adam. I scan the group, quickly noting that Adam is not among them. They elbow and jostle one another to get closer to a concession stand from which food is being distributed. Those who are handed bowls eat standing up, tipping food straight into their mouths. Many of them are missing limbs. Marcus begins to steer us through the havoc when I notice a uniformed woman barking orders at the server. It's Harriet Fletcher. The stand is in danger of being toppled by the boys. To avoid this, she grabs a bucket from the table and tosses its contents out into the crowd.

Sweat is pouring down my sides. I am sure Harriet Fletcher is going to notice us. A rush of blood fills my mouth when she flags us over. I must have bitten my cheek.

"Steady, now," Marcus commands. He pushes the cart toward her. I swallow blood.

"Savages!" Harriet Fletcher complains. She leans into my cart to grab a towel. She wipes her hands, watching the mass of misery slither at her feet. She flings the towel into my cart and turns to me. "A little late for housekeeping, isn't it?"

I freeze.

"Fecal emergency," Marcus says in an altered voice.

"Is that what the fuss is all about? Every little thing, they sound the alarm." She asks if we have a two-way so she might radio for someone to shut the darn alarm off, but Marcus shakes his head.

Dismissed with a wave, we pass by the crowd, turn right at the next intersection, and come to a huge glass building. Through the mesh, I read the sign out front, CONSERVATORY—AUTHORIZED PERSONNEL ONLY. Beside it are half a dozen Airstream trailers. Marcus has us stop at the first one. A face peers from behind a curtain when he raps against the door. "Laundry services." He steps inside and a minute later throws me towels. I look in my basket and hand him a couple of replacements. "Thank you," he says, closing the door. We move to the next trailer as two cadets jog by. Only one of them looks our way.

A brief glimpse of an arm is all it takes to convince me that Adam is the one behind the open door. I barge up the steps and into the trailer. Wearing what looks like a Mylar poncho, Adam is sitting stiffly on the edge of the bed. I fly into his arms, but he recoils from me. "Son," I say. "Adam, it's me." Even then, he seems unconvinced. I lift the edge of my hood.

"I'm sorry, Mom," he says, embracing me. "I'm so sorry."

"Don't be silly; you haven't done anything wrong."

I hug my son. He smells of antiseptic.

Adam wants to explain something, but Marcus shushes us both.

"Do as he says," I tell Adam when Marcus starts wrapping him in a sheet.

Thirty seconds later, Marcus is carrying a very heavy bundle of laundry out of the trailer and into the laundry basket. And then we are off, pushing our carts as casually as possible through the late-afternoon sun.

VII

T SEEMS UNLIKELY that Marcus would have gone to such trouble to get us away from Sunflower if he didn't intend to come back and help us further, and yet with each minute that goes by I can't help but wonder if Adam and I are on our own. Each minute I wait to hear the whine of engines, wait to see ATVs tearing across the prairie toward us. Under a sheet of corrugated metal at the foot of a windmill now seems the most obvious space to hide. I'm getting antsy. I don't know how much longer I can sit here and do nothing. It's not only arthritis that's stiffening my joints, it's also the dread of being found and dragged back to that place. If only killing Dobbs would be the end of him, but he's taken up residence in my head, and in my head he grouses about my lack of skills, how I should have paid better attention to those lessons on survival. He grades our chances as slim, very slim. There is another soft voice, my own, that is inclined to agree with him.

Running all the way from the hole in the fence at Sunflower to this place, I thought I'd cough up my lungs. They are still sputtering. I fish around in the backpack for the pump and take two more quick puffs and peer out. The temperature has dropped suddenly, and the wind has picked up. Evening is approaching. I wonder if we shouldn't take our chances, leave our hiding spot, and make a run for the forest.

We wait, and wait, until Adam announces he can't hold it anymore. I stick my head out to check whether the coast is clear. From this distance, the camp is barely visible. It looks nothing like the rampart I took it to be. Nearby is a dense patch of ragweed. I tell Adam to crawl to it and find a spot behind it to relieve himself. He does as instructed. Even being separated by a distance of ten feet makes my heart pound. I call out to him, and the ragweed rustles back in reply. I keep a watchful eye until Adam calls for me to look at the sky.

"Get down."

He ignores me, keeps his face turned to the west. In the last light, he is like a filament, bright gold.

"Get back in here."

"Nobody's coming," he says. "Come out; you've got to see this."

I wriggle out and stand up. I arch my back and shake off my stiff legs.

"Isn't it beautiful?" he exclaims.

I catch my breath. Sundown on the prairie. Either this has become more spectacular in my seventeen-year absence, or I must have walked around half-asleep before. The sun looks like a single piece of confetti against a scarlet sky. Streaks of orange and gold are unrolled across it like streamers. If you'd never seen a sunset before, it would be easy to imagine this a once-in-a-lifetime event.

I tug on Adam's sleeve. "We should get back under that cover. It'll do this again tomorrow."

He is a very old shaman, some holy man on a mountaintop, when he says, "But, it is happening now," so we stay where we are. A perfect sky is mirrored in the nearby lake. On its dark surface, the lacy clouds look like doilies. There is a ravaged field beside the lake, but everywhere else the land is a thick green pelt. A bellow from the thicket startles a flock of birds into a waving flag. Cawing, trilling, tweeting—all of nature is engaged in some call-and-response, some primal litany. Adam watches the spectacle, and I watch him.

"They wanted me to be some lady's boyfriend," he says after a while. He says it as though he'd been asked to eat worms. "They said I was to love her. I didn't have to love her for very long, they said. I think they wanted me to, you know . . ."

One night when Adam was about three or four, he woke up from a bad dream, crawled over to my cot for comfort, and found Dobbs, rigid, on top of me. He tugged Dobbs's arm, insisting he get off. "You're hurting my mommy!" Instead of pushing Dobbs aside and taking Adam in my arms, I told him to do as Mister said and go back to bed. I can't imagine Adam having anything but the same disgust for sex that I do. I hope that'll change for him one day.

"Don't think about it anymore, Adam. We're not going back there."

We watch the confetti-sun make landfall. A squawking flock of birds drops out of the sky and settles on the remains of an old barbed-wire fence. They peck at one another, jostling for more room. One voices its displeasure when it is knocked off its perch; a devious cackle rings out among the others. Adam finds this funny, too.

"What kind of birds are they?"

"Seagulls," I answer, as if it's the most natural thing in the world for seabirds to be nesting in the middle of Kansas.

Adam spots Marcus before I do. Hurrying toward us with a shopping cart, he is panting. Droplets of sweat roll off his forehead. He lifts a bundle out of the front seat. "She's hungry."

Amid the jumble of rags is a tiny face. A pert nose and a broad forehead and two dark, tear-filled eyes form the very picture of vexation. She opens her tiny mouth and belts out a full-throated yell.

"You're going to have to wait a bit longer, little lady," he tells the crying infant, while Adam and I both stand, stunned.

The cardboard box in the back contains a second bundle of rags, which I confirm is another baby.

"Careful not to wake that one; I only just got her to sleep." Marcus holds out his little finger to the baby in his arms, and the tiny mouth latches on to it. "This trick won't last long."

Adam has not moved. He's staring at the baby. Spellbound.

"What? You want to hold her?"

Marcus extends his arms to Adam. I am sure my son is going to shake his head. Adam's eyes flick from the bundle to Marcus's face. A look of uncertainty grows into a small smile, and he accepts the package.

"You mind she don't boss you around now."

"She's so light." Adam speaks softly, as though any louder, his words might injure her.

Adam touches her tiny fingers. He studies her fingernails. He runs the tip of his finger across her arm. He glances at me to see if I, too, am witnessing this miracle. "Her head is so soft." She startles him by squirming a little, and he clutches her close like he's afraid of dropping her. "Why is she so small? Is there something wrong with her?"

All Adam knows of children is Charlie's bones. "You were this small once."

Adam presses the tip of his finger into the baby's palm, and her fingers close around it. They search each other's eyes and seem to make one another's acquaintance on some other plane.

"Whose babies are these?"

Marcus sidesteps my question and instructs me to gather our belongings. We must hurry, he says. He straps the second child to his back with a towel. It is obviously not the first time he's done this. He pushes the cart into the greenbrier. "With a bit of luck, we can get to Ginny's in time for grub." I take this to be code for, "We must try to outrun them." He offers to take the little girl from Adam, but Adam won't give her up, so Marcus hustles toward the nearby copse, beckoning for us to follow.

I bring up the rear, all the time watching my son and his cargo. Moments ago, he'd been quick to dismiss the idea of love, and here he is, smitten. Without having to be told, he supports the baby's head in the crook of his elbow and keeps her against his chest. As soon as her lips start to quiver, he offers her his little finger. Adam beams when she sucks it. He keeps a beady eye on the path, but every so often bends to her with an encouraging word. "Hold on, baby girl." "We're going to get you some food real soon." "Who's a clever girl?"

"She likes you."

"You think so?" he asks, clearly pleased.

We continue weaving our way quickly through the scrappy, juvenile trees until we reach a jungle with nooses for vines and ground cover spiny enough to be barbed wire. Adam is careful to step over every tree root and around every rock. I trip enough times that Marcus offers to assist me.

"They'll know you helped us escape."

Marcus doesn't understand that this is my apology for landing him in deep trouble, too. Instead, he assures me Sunflower doesn't know where he lives or what paths he takes. We are headed to a safe house, he adds, and he's taking us the long way because they won't be able to drive the ATVs through woods this dense. They'll have to pursue us on foot. No use in stating the obvious, that we won't be able to outrun them if they come this way. Instead, I change the subject. "They wanted Adam for breeding purposes."

"Everyone's trying to forget Diablo, but they keep getting reminded all over again when them babies don't come out right. Soon as the Confederacy can show folks a perfect baby, the sooner we can put the past behind us, is what they think. You have no idea what people are willing to put up with for the possibility of a perfect kid."

"The booklet didn't say what the Confederacy is."

Marcus explains about an alliance between separate, loosely governed bands of people. First formed to keep disputes between neighboring camps and villages from mushrooming into wars and later to form a united front against the free-range bandits, it now mostly exists to promote trade. Overseeing the Confederacy is the Grand Council, its members former politicians from Canada, the United States, and Mexico. Fidel Castro's second cousin sits in the big chair, Marcus says. The funding of places like Sunflower is his brainchild.

I look over my shoulder. Adam is singing the baby a lullaby. Lyrics about rolling rivers, mandolin players, and men home from the war. Singing so tenderly you'd think he has firsthand experience of such things. The last of the sunlight falls between the leaves, wafting down on him like Communion wafers. A Baltimore oriole chants. In the air is the faint smell of skunk. For just a moment, it is not the scary woods, but the Garden of Eden.

"These babies are, what, a month old?"

"Three weeks," Marcus tells me. "Most of them that make it to term die the first week."

It makes no sense what he says—unviable fetuses, late-term abortions on those that test positive for defects, infanticide in those cases where defects go undetected until birth. Very few are spared, he remarks.

"And these two?"

Marcus explains the arrangement he has with Sunflower. Rather than euthanizing all the defective newborns, they have agreed to let Marcus take those with the highest chance of survival. It's not policy but rather a case of officials turning a blind eye.

Fortunately, Adam doesn't hear any of this. "They don't look defective to me," I insist. I am about to ask Marcus where he takes the babies, but he silences me with his hand and comes to an abrupt halt. He motions for Adam to be quiet, for us not to move. He cocks his head. I can't hear anything but the ringing of cicadas, the rapid clicks of crickets, the harsh singsong tone of katydids—it's the sound of the daytime and nighttime critters changing guard.

"Is it them?"

"Ssh."

After a while, he bids us move. We walk no more than ten paces farther when he stops us again.

Very quietly, he announces, "We're being followed."

I swing around and can't be sure if several heads have just darted behind the spindly eucalyptus trees or if it is the trickery of fading light and shimmering leaves.

Marcus crouches. Adam and I do the same. Marcus makes some flicking motion with two fingers. I don't know if he intends for us to head to the nearest tree for protection or to run like hell.

Adam creeps up next to me. "What is it, Mom?" He looks terrified, not just for himself now, but for his ward, too.

"Deer, probably," I tell him, because this is better than saying, "Them." I show him the same signal Marcus flashed me.

Instead of running, Adam stands up and points at what Marcus has chased out from behind a bush. "Is that a hog?"

It is a dog without any fur.

Marcus throws a stone at it, and the mutt scampers away. "Got separated from its pack most likely. It'll get picked off by a bear or a mountain lion soon enough."

There isn't a mountain for a thousand miles. I pick up the suitcase and take off after Marcus again. "Mountain lions? In Douglas County?"

"A lot of game in these parts." Marcus gives a rundown of what a diminished human population has done for wildlife.

I look behind me to see what Adam makes of all of this, and he is lagging behind. At first glance, it appears as though he's taking a breather, but then I notice he has one hand extended. A few yards behind him is the cowering dog trying to settle an age-old dilemma of whether to risk its neck for the sake of a morsel.

"Adam! Get away from that animal!"

A stone goes whizzing by my head and finds its intended target. The dog yelps and falls back.

"What'd you do that for?" Adam straightens up with the baby and glares at Marcus.

"You give it something to eat, and it's going to be a menace the rest of the trip."

"It's probably got rabies," I add.

I know exactly what Adam is thinking. He is remembering an old conversation and now aims to cash in on the promise he'd extracted at the end of it.

"No," I insist.

"You said."

I clarify what I meant—a pet, not a cross between a pit bull and a coyote. Besides, what kind of dog doesn't have hair?

"You said I could choose, and I choose this one."

We argue back and forth until Marcus insists we get a move on.

"I'm not going."

"Adam . . ."

"You can't make me."

"Son, your mother's right. You don't know where this stray comes from. Trust me, there are hundreds of dogs running around. You'll have so many to pick from, it'll make your head spin."

While we are trying to talk some sense into him, he claps his hand against his thigh and the stupid mutt advances another two feet.

"He's limping!" Adam notes.

Oh, dear God. "Injured animals bite, Adam. Just leave him be."

The standoff lasts until Marcus strikes a bargain. "Let's just keep walking. Don't feed him. If he wants you for a friend, he's going to have to walk on that foot a good way yet."

Adam brightens.

Marcus leans over to me and whispers, "Trust me, the dog will tire of this in a few minutes."

Having settled in the recesses of the forest, nightfall now edges toward us. We try to outpace it. Only once do I need to stop and use the inhaler. The rest of the time, I keep up with Marcus and try to ignore the fact that Adam has already named the dog Oracle and is giving it all sorts of commands, not least of which is, "Come."

My eyes have adjusted to the dark, but my nerves have not. When Marcus leads us out of the woods, there is just enough light to make out the contours of the land, land that could easily be traversed by vehicles. I scan the hill, waiting for the beam of a headlight to skim it.

"Mom!"

I swing around, thinking Adam has dropped the baby or been bitten by the dog, but he is staring up at the sky. Swirls of bright green flick across the heavens, rolling into a curlicue, then falling like a curtain. The lights move so fast I get dizzy and reach out for Marcus's arm to steady myself.

"Aurora borealis," Marcus replies when Adam asks if they are angels. "Don't see this nearly as much as we used to."

We fall into single file on a narrow path that leads across another meadow and up a slight rise. Adam and I duck each time the lights swoop down, one time a vast skin that looked as though it would encase us. Both babies are asleep. Adam refuses to trade me a baby for the suitcase. He is ever more sure-footed; the dog, too, which trots on three legs beside him with the same kind of confidence.

That fishy smell I detected when we first drove away from the silo is strongest here. I now see the source. Mushrooms. They are strewn across the path and have claimed every inch of available ground in the clearing to our right. The smaller ones are the size of volleyballs, the bigger ones boulders. Adam kicks one and the dog chases after it. He brings it back to Adam and lays it on his shoe.

"What's the deal with all these mushrooms?" I ask Marcus.

"This is nothing. Some colonies are the size of counties. Especially where the blood rains fall."

"Blood rains?" Adam asks.

"Some say it's dust from up north where the deserts are, and some say it's iron oxide. With everything rusting, the powder gets blown up into the clouds and comes back down red. Most folks are superstitious now; they'll tell you it's the blood of all them people who died. Don't worry; we don't get much of it here anymore."

My head starts filling up with pictures of corroding cities and deserts where Canada ought to be until a high-pitched howl is broadcast from the ridge above us.

"Come on," Marcus urges. "Not much farther."

When another howl rings out in reply from the edge of forest in reply, we break into a light trot.

NO MATTER WHAT we do, the babies will not be pacified. Marcus has moved the sling from his back to his front where he can pat his baby. In his other hand is a switchblade. Adam hands me the baby he's been carrying, but she only cries louder, so he snatches her back. Darkness has a way of amplifying the sound. If the people from Sunflower are anywhere in the vicinity, they will be able to draw a bead on us without any trouble, and the same goes for the pack of wolves that have us pegged as easy prey. The only thing more frightening than their excitable yips and howls is when they fall silent. Several times, the mongrel dog stops to growl at the bushes beside us.

"See if she won't take your finger again."

I know I have taken a testy tone with Adam when he snaps back that it's not her fault we're out here in the middle of nowhere. He sets the baby against his shoulder and tells her what Marcus has been telling us for miles: not much longer now.

Through a stand of buckled trees, I see a pair of lights approach from the opposite direction. The ATVs have found us. No point in stifling the babies' cries now. I can't decide if it's better to run into the woods and take our chances with the wolves or surrender. The lights slow down just ahead of us and turn off the street. I notice it is a car, not an ATV. We are only a few yards from a road.

Marcus nudges me. "You gonna just stand there?"

"That's not them?" I whisper.

"No."

"How can you be sure?"

"Hear that sound? That's a bad axle. Can't tell you how often I've worked on that old Ford. I know it like it's my own flesh and blood."

Marcus leads us across the street to where it turned.

Thanks to a rising moon, there's enough light to see the mailbox, the flagstone paving, the appearance of normal. At the end of the drive-way is a house. Each of its windows is lit by an orange glow. We can smell the smoke coming from the chimney. Family is what this scene spells, and the longing hits me hard.

Sunflower will keep up the search for a day or two, Marcus explains as he leads us through the front yard. After that, they'll count Adam and me dead, or good as. We are to stay here until then, and afterward Marcus will either escort us to Eudora or help us with arrangements to ren-dezvous with a caravan.

But for the old pine standing guard at the front porch, every tree around the house has been cleared. Nothing is left of those pests except for a woodpile almost as high as the roof. Parked beside it are two trail motorbikes and the car, which can't possibly be roadworthy. We take two steps up onto the broad wooden porch. Four rocking chairs are swaying, recently vacated. Inside, voices quiet down as soon as Marcus raps on the door. There is a braided doormat at our feet, and someone has gone to the trouble of making and hanging a pine-cone wreath.

"The Bowerses are good people. You don't have to worry. They'll hide you if anyone comes."

A woman on the downswing of middle age opens the door. She is stocky, a feature she makes no attempt to hide with a man's chambray shirt and grubby jeans. Her white hair is cropped close. Everything else about her is feminine—the way she holds herself; her soft, gray eyes; her fuzzy pink house slippers. She smiles broadly when she sees Marcus and keeps her smile in place despite seeing two complete strangers, a couple of squalling babies, and an injured, hairless dog. She reaches up to accept Marcus's one-armed embrace.

"Any room at the inn?" he asks.

She replies with that same wide smile and waves us in.

"The dog will have to stay outside, Adam," I say.

"You said we could feed him if he came all the way."

I look at Marcus, who turns to the woman. She lifts an index finger and hurries into the house. A man joins us in the foyer. He is stoop-shouldered in the way very tall men are and has a face the color of eggplant. Where his nose ought to be are two slit-shaped holes, and because he has no lips, he appears to be grimacing. With a bloated, scarred hand, he shakes Marcus's hand, then mine, and finally Adam's. "Bill Bowers, pleased to make your acquaintance."

Bill Bowers and Adam are equally dumbstruck at the sight of each other. I am about to make an excuse for Adam, about his being shy around strangers so the man won't assume Adam thinks him a monster, when Adam says breathily, "Are you a cowboy?" Adam, who has always dreamed of meeting a cowboy, is riveted by the man's large silver belt buckle and pointy boots.

You'd swear this was the funniest thing Bill Bowers ever heard.

"Outlaw's more like it," Marcus says.

Nodding in agreement, the returning woman puts down two bowls, one with water, one with pellets. Bill places one hand protectively around her shoulders, and says, "This lovely lady is my wife, Ginny." Because of his disfigurement, he makes lots of hissing sounds. He and his wife commence staring at Adam. And then they stare at me, too.

They must notice my embarrassment because the woman makes hand signals that her husband is quick to translate. "She says you've got such beautiful skin. Like a porcelain doll."

I can't think what my response ought to be.

Adam is the one to speak. He gives our names. "And this is Angel. Say hi, Angel."

The baby responds with a full-throttled shriek.

"She's a cutie, isn't she, Gin?" Bill responds.

Ginny smiles. Adam is flustered now on account of his ill-tempered companion, but Ginny does not race to remedy the situation by taking the child. Instead, she takes the other baby and motions for Adam to accompany her down the hallway. He gives the dog the command to stay and follows the woman into the warm house.

Bill offers to take the backpack and suitcase, but I hold them tightly. Marcus and I follow him into the living room, where half a dozen people are gathered. There is enough light from various oil lamps to notice that they are all disfigured. Most of them look burned, although not as badly as our host, and I can't tell if it's my imagination or if they really do smell of smoke. Names and how-dos are exchanged. The shriveled woman in the wheelchair who wheels herself up to me gives me an unabashed once-over. Why, she wants to know, am I not burned or disfigured? Who has that much hair anymore? How is it a boy can be fifteen and not be confined to a bed? Marcus does my explaining for me. Only because he promises that Adam will soon be in to meet her does she not make a mad dash down the hall to find him.

A bearded man goes around covering the windows with horse blankets, while I take quick stock of the room. Walls covered with paintings, potted plants in hanging macramé baskets, cushions, clocks that run. In one corner is a small stand with electronic equipment. Marcus asks that the CB radio be turned on in case anyone's broadcasting.

"What kind of nonsense is this?" huffs an elderly man. "We don't want to get mixed up in your skullduggery, Hill. Sunflower's not going to take kindly to those caught aidin' and abettin' fugitives. Remember what happened to the Pattersons—"

"Oh, hush up, Sheldon," the woman in the wheelchair hisses. "Can't you see the poor woman's scared half to death?"

Bill clarifies that Adam and I are not fugitives but guests. Indicating that we are to be treated as such, he hands me a glass.

The bearded man who was talking when we first entered now resumes his speech. As he begins to tell of a study done on soybeans, I take a sip and wheeze.

Marcus whispers in my ear, "Bill makes a mean rosé. Best go easy."

The storyteller is standing beside the fireplace with his elbow on the mantel. The others seem to find his story fascinating, but I am easily distracted. Facial expressions, how loud things are said, how they lean forward to listen, draw back to ponder, glance at one another. From some shuttered part of my mind come memories of youth meetings at church, of being part of a group that behaved like this. I was once part of a community. Belonging—it's what I envy these people. I take another sip and am waylaid again, this time by how sharp everything tastes.

"The seeds were taken from the Inola Exclusion Zone fifteen years ago, about four months after Diablo," the storyteller continues. "They were planted in uncontaminated soil, and now they are no longer producing mutant strains; they are becoming more genetically stable."

"Which means?" Bill asks.

"Which means the plants have made adaptations at the cellular level to radiation. What's true for plants may be true for humans."

The elderly man puffs out his chest. "Sunflower just came out with their findings on barn swallows. They put it just the opposite."

"Is it not in their interest to display the odd mutant specimen? And bear in mind, they don't let any independent researchers verify their findings. We don't know what their methodology is. For all we know, their research is based on one corrupted nest. Let me ask you this, Sheldon: What do you think would happen to Sunflower's funding if their findings were to corroborate those of our researchers?"

"They should shut the place down!" says the woman in the wheelchair. It's a wonder a figure so frail can fuel so much fire.

Sheldon shoots her a look, but she raises her chin defiantly.

"Not going to happen, Maude. Not after the council got so many different parties vested in the project." The storyteller checks off his fingers. "You've got the administrators of these programs who have pretty much been granted tribal chief status; you've got the medical suppliers, the merchants who are running the candidate shipping lanes from Alaska, and let's not forget our dear Castro who keeps trumping up promises of an untainted generation born during his tenure."

Everyone takes a sip of their drinks, so I do, too.

"Some might argue that the candidates and their families, the surrogates and support staff have a source of livelihood," Bill adds.

Maude smarts. "You're not suggesting the surrogates are contributing to the problem? Because as I see it, they're little more than slaves."

Sheldon, who has been muttering to himself, now chimes in. "It's the defectives we should be worried about!"

Maude looks fit to be tied. "Pay him no never mind," she says to the three on the couch who thus far have contributed to the discussion only with nods. Turning an icy stare on the old man, she says, "We are all defective, Sheldon."

Sheldon shakes his cane at the storyteller. "Won't matter none if the soybeans done come out right when them defectives start breedin'. Before you know it, they'll be runnin' the place!"

The rest of the group shifts uncomfortably.

"You're just repeating what you hear on Republic Radio. If you actually gave some thought—"

The old lady's accusation only makes Sheldon more excitable. "Haverty's laying out what others are too dern cowardly to say," he insists. "We should've had the whole lot sterilized when we had the chance! Mandatory, 'stead of giving people a choice. Haverty's right, and you lot know it!"

"About as right as two left turns!" Maude replies.

People find other places to look. Togetherness seems to be wearing thin in places.

"Anyone care for more wine?" Bill's flask provides the interruption the storyteller needs to steer the conversation back on track.

"Even if public opinion turned and you had more people calling for these kinds of places to shut down, does anyone for one minute think the Confederacy is going to let that happen?"

I only notice the child-size man in the shadows when he addresses the storyteller. "You said it all along, Ned. You said we'd be in trouble if we made this a political issue."

There is some discussion along the lines of who predicted what until Maude raises her hand and proceeds with her question as if she'd been called on. "What I'd like to know is if humans are more like soybeans or barn swallows?"

"As long as there are still mutagens in the environment, we are going to see some incidence of maladaptation. It is going to be several generations yet until we know for sure—"

"There you have it, straight from the horse's mouth!"

"Oh, put a spoon in it, Sheldon, and let the man finish!"

The storyteller holds up his hand. "It is going to be a while before we know for sure, but in my opinion, yes, we will continue to see a decrease in radiation-induced mutations in humans. Nature finds a way."

"I'll drink to that," says Bill.

Everyone drains their glasses. I do, too.

The conversation takes a turn to the life expectancy rate, and I pick up my bags and hurry down the hallway to see what's taking Adam so long. At the farthest end is a brightly lit room. I can't hear the babies crying or Adam chattering away. It is too quiet. How stupid of me to let Adam out of my sight. What if the woman has led him out of the house and down the path and into the night? What do I know of these people? They all sound like lunatics.

I rush toward the room, which turns out to be a kitchen, a kitchen where my son is sitting in a rocking chair beside a woodstove, giving the baby a bottle. Ginny, holding the other child on her hip, is putting a burp cloth over Adam's shoulder. She offers me the baby.

"No, that's okay," I tell her.

Ginny insists by nodding at the stove where three large pots are simmering. She wants to attend to dinner.

"Oh, okay." I take my backpack off my shoulder, put the suitcase down, and set my empty glass on the table.

I take the baby and the bottle. Feeling a little light-headed, I sit at the table. The baby draws hard on the bottle teat, her eyes fixed on me. "Better now?" I've forgotten how easily babies are satisfied, how trusting they are. There is about them an otherworldliness. I look at this baby the way I used to look at Adam—with delight, but also with the vaguely unsettling feeling she knows more about the universe than I do.

While she nurses, I take stock of my surroundings. Stationed in the corners of the kitchen are high chairs. There is a diaper pail next to the back door, and hanging from the light fixture is a mobile. The window-sill is lined with baby bottles. Marcus brings the children from the compound here, I immediately realize.

"Boy, was she hungry!" Adam exclaims, putting the empty bottle on the table.

Ginny demonstrates how to pat the baby's back. As soon as the baby burps, Adam says, "Whoa!" He strokes her head and stops, suddenly alarmed. The tip of his finger is resting on the top of her head. You can see the whites of his eyes. "There's something wrong!"

Ginny and I both get up. He has her feel where his finger is touching. "It's a hole!"

Ginny waves at him not to worry, and I explain about a baby's soft spot. "The bones haven't closed all the way yet, but they will."

Not at all assured, he strokes her head very gently and says, "Shouldn't she wear a helmet until then?"

I can't get over how good he is with this baby. How quick he is to give his heart. Even before we got out of the silo, when Dobbs first started promising to take us out, I worried whether Adam would adapt. I wondered how long it would take him not to be frightened by everything he saw. Now I wonder whether I am ever going to adapt. Will I ever stop being frightened? Dead, Dobbs is every bit as dismissive as he was in the flesh. *Above for less than a week and already you have him relying on strangers.*

Ginny puts a bowl on the table and signals Adam to eat. He hands over the baby reluctantly and wolfs down his food.

"Thank you," I offer, on Adam's behalf.

He looks up, startled. "Oh, yes, thank you so much."

If he finds it odd that Ginny does not talk, he gives no indication. I, on the other hand, react to this fact in all the wrong ways. I tell her how kind she is to take us in without any advance notice and what a lovely home she has, and Adam stops chewing and says, "Mom, she's not deaf." My next effort at communication is part lip-synch, part sign language. This, too, is frowned upon by my son.

With the baby on her hip, Ginny dishes up stew and sets down a bowl for me. Adam follows her silent directions to take the baby from me to give me a chance to eat. Everyone seems comfortable with the quiet except me. Without meaning to, I volunteer details about our ordeal. I tell Ginny how the people at the compound separated Adam and me despite my wishes, and when she shakes her head and looks at me with such empathy, I feel compelled to tell her about Dobbs and the silo and being kept underground for all these years. Partway through the telling she steps beside me and rubs my back. "I was sixteen when he took me. I went mad for a while. I lost a child." Facts fall out of my mouth, one after another.

Adam hears about Charlie, who I have not been able to talk about in detail until now, now that I am in a warm kitchen, a real kitchen, having my shoulder patted by a smiling woman and my story extracted by her big, accommodating silence. "Do you have any more wine?"

She pours me a glass.

I take a big sip. "We buried him in a cemetery nobody visits. A place you wouldn't even want to bury a criminal. I have to go back. I have to put flowers on his grave so he knows he's missed." I speak of all the many other things I want to do and how none of it might be possible. Eventually, I run out of words. "I'm sorry; you didn't need to hear all that."

Ginny waves away my apology and screws up her face.

"She says not to worry," Adam explains. And then he makes his own face. Uh . . . uhm . . ."

From the way he holds the baby away from his body, Ginny and I get the picture. Exchanging glances, I laugh and she makes a wheezy hiccup sound. She takes us into an adjoining room, a sunroom with lots of windows and cribs. She puts Angel into a crib, grabs a diaper, and pats the changing table. As soon as Adam lays the baby down, he makes as though to leave, but Ginny latches onto his shirtsleeve, and I voice my agreement. "Oh no you don't. You want to take care of a baby, then you've got to know how to do this."

"Eew," he says, but only once. After that, he is riveted.

The swaddling is unwrapped, revealing the child's calico skin. The brown patches look like giant scabs. The red patches look scaly, like burns starting to heal. The baby gives no indication that she is in pain. Adam is wrapped up in her toes. He measures the length of her foot against the palm of his hand. She responds to his tickling by kicking her legs. Adam laughs and tickles her some more.

Ginny changes her, tucks her into a onesie, and then swaddles her in a yellow blanket. She lifts the baby off the table and hands her to Adam, who understands he is being told to put her in a crib.

"Shouldn't we give her a name?" he asks.

Ginny's flattened hand makes a loop: you name her.

"Molly, how about that?"

Ginny gives the A-OK sign.

"Good night, Molly," he says, planting a kiss on top of her head. I make a mental note of another first: the first time he's kissed an Outsider.

He fetches Angel, and with the same care, separates her from her rags and soiled diaper. She is perfect but for the paddle where her right foot ought to be. She fusses a little when he uses the damp cloth to wipe her clean and pumps her tiny legs. Instead of remarking on her peculiarity, he folds the diaper perfectly around her little buttocks and hands Ginny the pin. "I'm afraid I'm going to stick her."

Marcus joins us just as Angel is laid down in her bed. "Shouldn't have trouble placing these two, right, Gin?"

"You leave the babies here?" Adam asks. His little friend has gone to sleep with her fist curled around his finger.

Marcus nods. "Don't you worry none. Ginny and Bill will take good care of these girls until the right parents come along."

Ginny makes some gesture I do not understand.

He translates for Adam and me. "She's got someone specific in mind for one of them."

"Which one?" Adam wants to know.

Ginny signals again by rubbing her arm: the child with the mottled skin, Molly.

"What about Angel?"

She raises her eyebrows at Adam and bobs her head slightly. I'm learning to understand her: we'll have to wait and see.

"There are people who are willing to adopt"—I struggle for the right words—"children like this?"

"Sure. Right after Diablo, the surgeon general called for a ban on baby making, and scores of survivors who were being treated at field clinics opted to get fixed as well. Nobody wanted to pass on the effects of radiation. Well, some of those folks managed to survive, and now they want to raise a family. There are others who just want to do their bit to help out those less fortunate. Sheldon back there will tell you it's survivor's guilt. I don't think so. Caring for a child can give a person hope."

"Did you work with children before Diablo?" Someone who speaks this way must have been a teacher, a coach, a social worker, perhaps.

Marcus runs his hand over his bald head, sets his glance to a place under the table.

Ginny looks at Adam and cups her hands on her head. Dog.

"We found him in the forest," Adam answers. "His name is Oracle. He's got a sore paw."

She fetches a first-aid kit from the cupboard and motions that she and Adam should tend to it.

"You lost your job helping me and my son," I say as soon as we have the kitchen to ourselves.

"I ain't no hero, if that's what you're thinking."

Breaking us out of Sunflower, guiding us through hostile terrain, fending off wolves to bring us to safety—if that isn't valor, I don't know what is. I start to thank him, but he cuts me off.

"I told you about my boy who died." He clears his throat. It doesn't help. Gravelly is how he sounds when he goes on. "Truth is, I hadn't seen him for years before he passed, not since he was a little kid. Never did marry his mama, like I promised. Never went to one of his Little League games or his school plays." Marcus looks as though he has something unpleasant in his mouth, a spoonful of rancid meat with no water to wash it down. "You'd think with the kinda dough I was pulling in off the street, I'd have set him and his mama up someplace decent. The last

Christmas before Diablo, I showed up with a Happy Meal, and his mama pushed my sorry ass off the porch, told me never to come back. I coulda gone back, made it right, but I used her as an excuse. The morning of the first explosion, I was hustling business through a fence at a middle school playground. Did I work with kids? I did a pretty good job messing them up, is what I did."

He turns his milky eye to me before bowing his head. "Yeah. Some hero, right?" Marcus looks at me. "You doing all right?"

I stand up. "Thish ish . . ." I stop, horrified. My tongue's not working.

Marcus takes the wineglass, which, oddly, has been in my hand this whole time. "Looks like someone's had enough for one night."

Maybe it's the wine, but maybe it is being in a home that looks nothing like the silo or the clinic at Sunflower; maybe it's the smell of beef stew, the slumber of rescued babies, my son administering care to another living thing for the first time—maybe all of this makes me take the man's hand. It is not for me to pardon. It is for me to hold the hand of a sinner, so that mine, too, may be held. Because the weight of the world can be held for only so long, I lift his hand and perform a pirouette beneath it.

"Well . . ." he says.

"Well," I declare.

I AM AWOKEN by cawing birds and screeching insects. Adam is digging around in the backpack. He fishes out Dobbs's key ring and shoves
it in his trouser pocket before throwing on his shoes.

"Your hood."

He grabs it and takes off. I hear the screen door squeak open, then
bang shut before I am fully upright.

I look in the mirror on the vanity just to make sure there isn't a huge
crack running down the middle of my head, because that's very much
what it feels like, and am surprised to find a hint of color in my cheeks.
My freckles have faded, but for as old as I feel, I have very few wrinkles.
Only the thick streak of silver hair hints at any disturbance in the aging
process. I undo my braid, rake my fingers through my hair. I screw up
my eyes, try to imagine what of me would Mama see, or Mercy, someone from my past? Anything of the girl I once was? What would a man
see? All those years ago on the bleachers at the Horse Thieves Picnic
Arlo had called me pretty. If he saw me now, would he want to kiss me?
I pucker my lips at my image and then smile. Not likely.

I have a vague recollection of the room but not of how I got into bed.
I use the jug of silty water on the washstand to bathe and brush my
teeth, then change into the embroidered linen shirt and gathered skirt
that have a note with my name on them. I follow the voices to a dining
room, where Bill Bowers and three of the guests from last night are
seated around a wooden table. Missing is the elderly couple. They all

call out a greeting. Too loud. They want to know where Adam is, if he might be persuaded to sit and talk with them. I tell them I'll find out and head for the kitchen. Marcus is pouring juice from a jug. He hands me the glass and takes in the flowing skirt. "You look . . . "

I cock an eyebrow.

"Real nice."

Like a woman, maybe, and not some stark-raving-mad fugitive. "Where's Adam?"

He turns to the open window. A warm, wisteria-scented breeze blows in. On a screened patio, Adam is holding a piece of a biscuit in front of the dog. Smeared on his face is some kind of yellow paste.

"Ginny's sunblock," Marcus explains. "Don't ask me what's in it. All I know is it works."

"Look, Mom, I've taught Oracle how to shake." To demonstrate, the dog lifts up its bound paw and extends it to Adam. "He's supersmart. Ginny thinks he could be trained to do just about anything."

Our host is sitting nearby on a rocking chair with a baby in her lap. In a bassinet beside her is the other child.

"I'm going to take him for a walk, okay? We won't go far; I'll stay where you can see me."

Beyond the patio is an expansive lawn. Like the front yard, it is devoid of trees. Off to the right is a red barn, and forming a boundary to the left is the first row of what look like grapevines. Exactly the kind of scene that would have you believe there are no dangers. "I don't think so, Adam. What about locusts?"

Ginny shakes her head and taps her wrist.

"She says it's too early for swarms. C'mon, Mom, it's beautiful out."

"He'll be okay," Marcus says, handing me a slice of buttered bread. I join Ginny outside so I can keep an eye on Adam. "Thank you for the clothes. I haven't worn a skirt in ages."

She smiles.

I watch Adam break out into a run with the dog at his side. The scene could be taken straight from the catalog of fantasies I kept Below. What is new for him might as well be new for me, because I, too, am stunned by the countless shades of green, by goose bumps and sunburn and the many other ways skin reacts to open air. Still, I don't trust what I see. New clothes, loose hair, guard still very much up. "I don't know how I'm going to take care of him out here. I worry that I might only be any good at my job in a controlled environment. This"—I sweep my hand across the expanse—"this terrifies me. How do people do it, let their children make their own decisions?" How do I make my own decisions? Are we to take up the life of gypsies or become homesteaders? Should Adam be allowed to interact freely with others or should I shelter him, hide him, even? Without Dobbs deciding for me, I can't seem to get my bearings. I must have assumed someone would do all the deciding for us.

A look of understanding crosses her face.

Adam is attempting a cartwheel, and the dog is barking excitedly at him. He doesn't have enough muscle tone, so he goes butt over applecart and lands flat on his back. The dog is licking his face. Germs! I almost shriek.

"I don't know why I thought everything was still going to be the same. He kept telling me it was different, but I never believed him, not a single word. Now, I'm the crazy one." Crazy for thinking it would be exactly how I left it. Crazy for thinking my family and friends would all fall into one long receiving line. Crazy for thinking that my son would need me more, not less.

Ginny lays the baby tummy-down on the mat and nods. It is some kind of rare talent, this ability of hers to turn an otherwise private person into a magpie.

"You know what the strangest thing about being back is?" Besides the hostile takeover of trees, the sinister enterprise at Sunflower, the frequency with which the hairs on the back of my neck are raised— what Grandma would attribute to a haunting. "Not having any children around."

By way of protest, Ginny rests her hand on the baby's head.

"But I mean, regular children." As soon as the words leave my lips, I regret them. Quickly, I backtrack, but Ginny turns her head to watch Adam as if to say, Regular children, indeed.

There wells up between us a polite silence until Marcus and Bill bail us out with steaming coffee and banter.

"Electricity's on," Bill says, handing his wife a mug and kissing the top of her head. He sees his wife look at her watch and says, "That's right, an hour earlier than yesterday." Bill explains the reason he and Ginny, along with many others, moved here from other parts of the country was because Douglas County had one of the few geothermal power stations still operable. He points out the power lines hooked to the roof. "Labor's the issue. If we can get enough volunteers to run the operation, we can go back to having electricity twenty-four/seven. God, can you imagine the possibilities?"

"Commercial television," Marcus pipes up.

"Kill me now."

"What'd you give me for a PlayStation, still in the box?"

"How about a five-thousand-watt generator?" Bill takes a peek at each baby. "But never mind the virtual world when we have the heavenly host for company."

There's what I should have said.

The Bowerses retreat to the kitchen, and Marcus takes Ginny's seat. He smiles at the babies. I tell him about my remark, and he assures me Ginny's not one to keep grudges, that she used to be quick to shoot off her mouth back in the day before her vocal cords got damaged from the operation.

He watches Adam, who now appears to be inspecting grass. The dog finds it equally fascinating. "I think that hound is here to stay."

After the longest time, he says, "It ain't all bad. What you saw back there at Sunflower, that's the worst of it. There are enough of us trying to do right. It'll add up. Maybe not to the point where we'll have all the luxuries like before, but it'll be one of God's sweet mercies if we don't get back no cable television.

"You'll see." He pats my knee. "You'll see."

All this, and I didn't even have to ask, What hope is there for us?

Bill is giving Adam and me a tour of his workshop. The barn smells of sawdust and green wood and furniture polish. Timber is stacked in neat piles and there is a heap of shavings off to one side. Adam runs his fingers through it, asks if he might keep a handful. He says he didn't realize how every solitary thing would have its own special feel. Texture, dimensions, how no two voices sound the same, how no two things weigh the same. It seems every time I look at Adam, he has something in each hand, acting the part of a scale. I weigh stuff, too: my grief against Adam's delight; the insufferable predictability of our lives in the silo against the fear of an unknowable future; the hospitality of strangers against the instinct for flight.

Showing us furniture in various stages of completion, Bill explains that he became a carpenter only after he and Ginny moved out here eight years ago. Acacia, he tells us, is his favorite wood to work with, that hickory can be a bitch, and that milling alder is like trying to throttle a snake. He holds up his hand so we can see where two fingers end at the middle knuckle. The cradle and the set of dining room chairs are to be sold later in the month at the swap meet. Swap meets, we learn, are the new shopping plazas. Everyone from doctors to barbers sets up business at swap meets. Cash is in circulation again, he says, but people are leery of it. Trading goods and services is still the choice of most settlers. A dining table can fetch enough homemade baby formula to feed six infants for two months, a liter of wine will fetch a tooth filling. Nothing is more valuable than gasoline. Bill tells us the biggest pitfall to skillful trading is nostalgia. He shows us his office where shelves are crammed with memorabilia.

Adam studies each item—a corkscrew, a coffeemaker, the SIM card Bill says holds a thousand photographs. Adam screws up his eyes to make sure tiny images are not printed on the piece of plastic, then looks at Bill and nods slowly like all adults really are dippy. Bill hands him a tin box and gestures for Adam to turn the lever. He does as he's told, humoring our host. Just as he's about to put it back on the shelf, the top flies off and a scruffy clown launches at him. Adam recoils, loses his balance, and lands flat on his backside. Bill is very apologetic. Adam turns bright red. He dusts himself off. Instead of returning it to its place, he picks up the tin box again and repeats the process. The next time the clown pops up, Adam is almost as startled as the first time. He is positively shiny with delight.

"I get scolded every time I bring stuff like this home, but I have no restraint." Bill powers up a row of lava lamps. "Now, you tell me that's not American ingenuity at its finest."

"Wow." Adam exhales. For someone who's grown up with a father like Dobbs, you'd think Adam would shy away from men, but already he is forming strong alliances, first with Marcus, now Bill. That they treat him nothing like an artifact to be preserved might have something to do with it. To them, he is but an ordinary boy who must graze his knee and face his fears and let go of his mother's apron strings if he hopes to become a man.

Adam examines a pair of binoculars, looks through the large exit lenses. "You're so small, Mom."

I have him turn it around, then point him toward the open door. Adam gasps, takes a step back, and quickly lowers the binoculars. He looks through them again. "Who are those guys?"

I snatch the binoculars from Adam. Securing the vineyard are half a dozen scarecrows. I heave a sigh of relief. No need to run, I tell Bill, who, now armed with a blowtorch, has taken up a defensive position.

Adam thinks there ought to be better ways of scaring off birds other than wasting a perfectly good set of clothes on a bunch of straw. "Why don't you just chase them away yourself?" As if people have nothing better to do all day than to watch for birds. He puts the binoculars back on the shelf, but Bill tells him to keep them. Adam insists it be a trade and hands Bill the only thing of value he has, another one of Dobbs's keys. Having hung the binoculars around his neck, he returns his attention to the shelf. He thumbs a small metal ring of spikes that whirrs as it spins.

"Spurs," explains Bill.

When Adam hears how cowboys used to attach them to their boots, his eyes light up. He asks if he might go with Bill to a swap meet sometime.

"You have something to trade?"

"I've got stuff."

I see straightaway where Adam is going with this. "No, you don't."

"It's ours now," he argues. "Mister's got no use for it." That he speaks of Dobbs in nothing but a passing manner concerns me. The man's voice has to be in Adam's head just as it is in mine, his moods and theories and explanations exerting the same kind of push and pull. If we'd talk about him, we could decide together what to make of the man. Instead of waging our own personal battles, we could figure out the new battle lines, because somehow, being Above still feels like a fight to be free. But whenever I bring up Dobbs, Adam clams up.

"We're not going back there, and that's final."

"You have supplies?" Bill asks.

Though I wish he'd drop it, I nod.

Adam is eager to fill him in. "We've got tons of supplies. Food, diesel, tools."

Bill interrupts him and says to me, "Have you told anyone this?"

I shake my head at Bill.

"Good. How secure is the place?"

Adam tells him the locks to the main doors can only be opened with codes and that a bunch of the supplies inside are kept under lock and key.

Bill pulls out the key Adam gave him.

"That one opens the filing cabinet where the microfiche is kept. Mom says Abraham Lincoln's speech is probably the finest thing ever written, but I like the diagrams of Benjamin Franklin's inventions best."

This gets Bill's attention. "You have documents? Historical documents?"

"The Declaration of Independence and the Bill of Rights and one page with a bunch of signatures. We've got tons of stuff in those cabinets."

Bill's mouth opens, closes, and opens again. "No one thought to safeguard our nation's archives, or at least anyone that we've come across until now. The founding documents went the way of everything else combustible in museums and libraries. You going to preserve a book or are you going to build a fire to keep warm? And all those digital copies are lost in the ether, never to be retrieved. So, we're left with this." Bill Bowers taps his temple. "Less than one percent of the US population survived, and now we're down to fifty thousand, maybe a little more—how many of them do you think were scholars and teachers of history? Not enough, is how many. We've all just assumed that when the last of us died off, there wouldn't be anything of an oral history, either. Legends and fables are what the future generations were going to inherit, but this"—Bill holds up Adam's key—"this changes everything. This is the key to who we once were, and to what greatness we are capable of." Bill turns his gaze of wonderment to me. "You, my dear, have the keys to a gold mine. Have you considered how this resource might be utilized?"

Gold mine? Below has been nothing but a dungeon. Returning, even if it is to collect the commodities that will help me and Adam and be of some use to the survivors, fills me with dread.

"Perhaps we can have this discussion another time."

Bill hands Adam the key. "Son, you hang on to this, and when you and your mother are ready to share those documents, you let me know." And because he is a kind man, he changes the subject. "You mentioned diagrams of inventions. Do you like to make things?"

Adam nods.

"Tell him about that car you made, Adam."

"Mom, it was a toy."

I tell Bill about how Adam constructed a vehicle out of this and that.

Bill looks at Adam intently. "Very few folks can earn or trade enough for a car, son, so if you can build even a go-kart, you can do very nicely indeed."

Bill is teaching Adam how to attach a piece of wood to a spindle on a lathe. He suggests I might want to visit with Ginny. I take the hint.

She is in the kitchen, filling up two baby bottles. She seems pleased to see me. She offers me a bottle and gives me the choice of which baby to feed. I lift Molly out of the bassinet and situate her in the crook of my arm. She is eager for her meal and seems to hold no grudge against me for my earlier remarks. Babies are a forgiving lot.

"Adam's taken quite a liking to Bill."

Ginny presses her throat, and a husky whisper comes out. "Lava . . . lamps."

I laugh. "Yes. I expect I'm not going to hear the end of it until Adam gets himself one.

"Do you find families for all the children who come here?"

She shakes her head. Her smile slips ever so slightly.

"What happens to them?"

"I take 'em." Marcus enters the kitchen with a bouquet of wildflowers. He fills an enamel pitcher with water and puts the flowers in it. He peers at each baby face. "How my girls doing? Can you say hi to Uncle Marcus? No? Too busy eating, I guess."

"Take them where?"

Marcus doesn't answer me but asks Ginny if she has any idea who they might recruit to rescue babies from Sunflower now that he's no longer working there. She brings him a big leather book and leafs through the pages until she comes to a name. She copies the details onto a slip of paper while Marcus explains that the book lists all the people who've adopted children. "Any number of these folks will step forward. It's just a matter of asking."

He hands me the book. There are dozens of entries. In the box designated for address, many people have written "East Prefecture," or "Maynard Caravan," or "NPA." No permanent abode, Marcus says. Only in two spaces have people written "Eudora." One is written in a hand too illegible to make out the name. The other, printed in tiny capitals, is a name I recognize. I bend down close to make sure it is not the fault of weak eyes. Mercy Coleman. She has given her address as 41 Terrace Street, Eudora. Out near the river. I scoot the journal over to Ginny and tap on the entry dated only months ago. It must surely be an error. In the name, in the date. "Do you remember this person?"

Ginny examines the book and, without hesitation, nods. She rubs her fingers over her arm, the same sign she uses to refer to baby Molly.

"An albino, yes!"

Ginny and Marcus are both taken aback. "You know this person?" asks Marcus.

I can't possibly know her. It's been seventeen years since I last saw her. The person I know who shares the same name surely exists only in my head. And yet I say, "Know her? She's my best friend!"

We are all standing and cheering and hugging and saying things like what a small world it is, when three people hurry into the kitchen—the owner of the car from last night and the oddest pair of prospective parents I have ever clapped eyes on. They are both bald and dressed in long, tunic-type garments cinched with cord belts. It is impossible to tell whether we have a father and a mother, or two fathers, or two mothers, whether they are eighteen years old or eighty. Their faces are wrinkled and marred with warts the size of grapes, yet their postures are upright and their eyes undimmed.

The driver, Anton, is in some sort of huff and beckons to speak to Marcus privately. When Marcus swings his head my direction, I don't have to be told that I am the subject of their fevered discussion. My gut tightens, a belt with no more notches. Ginny quickly leads the couple to Molly's crib, and I approach Marcus. "They know where we are, don't they?"

"Get Adam."

I run out to the barn. By the time we return, Ginny is stuffing provisions in a bag, the couple with their new baby are already headed for the car, and Marcus has retrieved our belongings from upstairs. It occurs to me that for this man we've just become a burden.

"Where are we going?"

"To my place. Lawrence."

Bill is shaking his head. "Let me guess: Sheldon."

Marcus nods. "Called in to Republic Radio this morning to announce that if the Grand Council had any sense at all, they'd be supplying their breeding programs with untainted stock like the kid here instead of candidates who were practically defectives themselves."

The sound Bill makes is the same as a teakettle about to boil. "I don't know why I didn't send them home when you arrived."

Adam has picked up Angel and seems to be ignoring all this. He adjusts her knitted cap, then takes her tiny hand in his and gives it a shake.

Ginny comes up beside him, but he does not pass her the baby. In fact, he holds her even closer.

Ginny makes some gesture to Bill.

He answers her. "It's not Sunflower I'm worried about. If anything, they're going to deny it and save themselves the embarrassment of having let Adam slip through their fingers."

Ginny's face darkens.

"Why do we need to run, then?" I ask.

Nobody wants to look at me. They prefer to watch Adam and the baby, who have locked eyes. The baby pumps her little legs.

"Tell me!"

"It's open season," Marcus says. "For the next few days, every trader, bounty hunter, and crackpot out there is going to be trying to make a score with Adam."

Adam presses his lips against Angel's forehead, then hands the baby to Ginny as if he might change his mind. He picks up his suitcase. It's the resigned way he walks to the front door that breaks my heart.

When it comes to saying good-bye, Adam and I are both at a loss. Bill slips Adam a baseball card. "Shoeless Joe Jackson. That's gold at the swap meet." He also gives Adam the spurs. Ginny hands Marcus the bag of provisions, which gives the impression we're about to hit the Appalachian Trail, not drive twelve miles to Lawrence. She gives me a hug, hands me the tube of sunscreen, and tucks an envelope in my shirt pocket.

We race to the car where the dog is already sitting in the passenger seat. Adam and I are once again on the run. Tumbleweed people in a land where the wind has its way. I unfold the note when I'm in the car. It's a packet of peony seeds with a note that reads, *Flowers for Charlie's grave.* It seems to confirm my fear. Only the dead put down roots.

HAVING TRAVELED MOST of the way via firebreaks, the car now turns onto what is left of Haskell Road. The ravages of a recent fire can be seen long before we get to the sign that reads, WELCOME TO LAWRENCE. We've been given to understand that there are no longer seasons like winter and spring. With weather patterns having changed, there is now only rainy season and fire season. The meadow to our left is nothing but cinders. The breeze blows across it, forming dirt devils of ash. On my side of the car, the world is a monochromatic canvas. Scorched tree trunks are snapped in two, as though from a failed effort of retrieving their splintered limbs. Adam, squashed on the other side of the monks and Molly, with the dog on his lap, is looking out at a different scene altogether. So much color it can make your eyes water.

Anybody who went to public school in Kansas was taught that seismic activity millions of years ago caused much of the state to sag. Water seeped into the great basin, forming wetlands. On field trips to this area, teachers would have us look out at the federally protected land and ask us to imagine what it might have been like in eons past, when thousands of species of birds feasted at a banquet of bugs and larvae. What we'd see was a bunch of grass, maybe a duck or two. We'd all yawn and scratch, and someone would raise his hand and ask if there was someplace to go potty. Well, it seems as though Eons Past has returned, taken up where it left off, and then some. The bright pink smear along the water's edge is a flock of flamingos. Scores of blue heron have claimed much of the marsh. Every reed is gussied up with the iridescence of a kingfisher. A flock of goldfinches takes off from the bushes, and all at once the sky is strewn with sequins.

The driver has asked us to keep the windows closed because we've already had to drive through one locust swarm, but you can still hear it, the sound of bursting seams. I look across the charred landscape and can hear it on this side, too. The earth can't contain itself. Should we drive down this very road tomorrow, I wouldn't be at all surprised if it turned as green as a golf course.

There is something comforting about my side of the road. It is the side of loss. It is the side of mourning, of things past. The remains of a tree, the remains of the fence rail, the implied remains of the man who pegged that fence in place. Nature is making a spectacle of herself on Adam's side, but the landscape sketched in charcoal on my side speaks to how I feel. What remains of me?

Once the main thoroughfare, Haskell Road is cracked and marred by potholes big enough to swallow a vehicle. The driver steers the car around trees growing up through the tarmac until there is no going forward. The rest of the way is going to have to be traveled by foot. We thank our driver for the ride and bid a hasty farewell to Molly and her parents, who are to meet a caravan near Baldwin City, ten miles farther. We pull on our canvas helmets and jackets, grab our belongings, and wave at the retreating car.

To the east, the sky is beginning to darken. Instead of being dazzled by sunlight, we are now being stalked by a sobering gray.

We are ten or so blocks from downtown, and a good walk farther, we are told, to our final destination. Adam and I both assure Marcus we are up to the task. I haven't coughed all day, and it might just be wishful thinking, but Adam's legs don't look nearly as bowed as they used to be. It's our vision that's the issue. Never having needed our eyes for long ranges, we are both nearsighted. Adam overcompensates by using the binoculars. I rely on memory.

————

The Victorian two- and three-story brick houses along the road are abandoned. Some have their roofs caved in and others their windows blown out, but many are not as far gone as you might expect. Prop up the leaning porch rails, clear away the hammock-size spiderwebs, and slap on a fresh coat of paint, and you might have something habitable.

"Was this the biggest city in America?" Adam asks.

"Kid, Lawrence had a population of eighty thousand. New York had close to eight million."

Adam smarts, like he's just run smack-dab into a force field. He grows more pensive the farther we walk, the more homes we pass. "Doesn't anybody live here?" His disappointment goes echoing down the street ahead of us, as though it would like to rustle up, at the very least, a few ghosts.

Marcus explains that Lawrence has gone the way of most towns. Survivors migrated for all kinds of reasons—to volunteer in the rebuilding efforts, to look for work, to move their kids closer to treatment centers. To forget, is what he doesn't say. Who would want to be reminded of such loss? Who could stand to look at the empty tire swing or the driveway into which that certain car will never pull? Who could look across the backyard fence when the much-loved or even much-despised neighbor is not there to look back? Who would want to listen to those church bells just hang there, plugging up your ears with silence?

We turn onto Eleventh Street. Trees encroach from both sides, turning what used to be a two-lane street into a narrow path. The trail is a bright green carpet of moss. The dog, which has been five paces ahead of us with his nose to the ground, stops and barks. Marcus bends down to see what caught his interest. Crossing the path and headed into a forest that used to be Hobbs Park's baseball field are tire tracks. The mud is still wet.

"Don't worry. If they come back this way, we'll hear them in plenty of time to hide," he says.

The dog resumes his loping stride. Adam picks up a gnarled stick. I take the shovel out of my backpack.

At the corner of Eleventh and Rhode Island Streets is a field of nettles and bull thistle, what used to be a parking lot. Taking a shortcut across it, Marcus points out the giant nests on the second-floor window-sills of a building. "Bald eagles. A menace," he remarks. Adam looks through his binoculars. He scans the surrounding area and points out a row of goalposts.

"You don't want to tarry in a place like this." Marcus urges us to move quickly. I do as I'm told. Adam, on the other hand, walks over to one of the goalposts. The dog looks reluctant to join him and tucks his tail between his legs. For the first time, Adam yells at him to come. The change in Adam frightens me. His enthusiasm has gone. In its place is this fretfulness. I reach Adam and see what has disturbed him so. Instead of a net, the basketball hoop is threaded with a noose. A sign welded to it reads, SOCRATES CHOICE.

"Executions?" I whisper to Marcus.

He shakes his head. "Assisted suicides."

Adam has moved to a sign on the door of the building. "What is Young Men's Christian Association?"

I shrug. "They used to do a lot of stuff with kids."

That's all it takes for Adam to throw open the door and dart inside.

"Adam, come back!"

The foyer has brown water marks on the ceiling. Every wall is streaked with rust stains. In places, plaster has fallen away like giant scabs, exposing the rotting substructure. In the corners, rubble is stacked like snowdrifts. The floor is ankle-deep in debris. I worry the ceiling is about to cave in on us but forge ahead after Adam. We pass an old classroom where desks are covered with a thick layer of gray chalk but are still in mostly neat rows, facing front. Where a blackboard should be is a gaping hole. Were students to take their seats they would stare straight into the lavatory, where porcelain basins lie on the floor along with broken wall tiles. At the hall, we step over the metal doors. Nothing is left of the gymnasium except a couple of risers and a pile of rubber that was once basketballs. The wooden floor is a carpet of splinters too treacherous to walk on.

"So, children were kept in places like this?" Adam asks.

The way he says "kept" is the way I say "kept" when referring to what Dobbs did with me. I try to explain day care and working parents, how kids liked hanging out in places like this. He lowers his chin and looks at me as though over the rim of a pair of glasses. Sure.

Next door is a two-level, white-tiled hole in the ground, the deep end of which is full of shattered glass. Blotches of green mold bloom on the pool tiles, the metal lockers, and the ceiling. It blooms where only moments before was a bare wall. Lest we break out in lichen, I insist we leave, hurrying through the broken window onto Massachusetts Street.

Downtown Lawrence used to pride itself on its historic buildings. Now without caretakers, the landmarks of Massachusetts Street have been left to fend for themselves. In the war against the elements, they are taking a beating. Mangled elm and twisted sycamore trees have the court-house in a chokehold. The clock in the tower puts the time of death at two fifteen. The red stone building that used to be the county museum has it-self become a relic. Liberty Hall has only three letters on its marquee: SOS. The storefronts—those that are visible through the broomstick trees—are dilapidated. All that remains of Restaurant Row are wire spokes where awnings used to be and old menus taped to windows. Adam pauses to read one of them. "Did people spend all their time eating?"

On the corner of Massachusetts and Ninth is Weaver's, the city's first department store. Mannequins lie in a heap in the display window, and behind them are scores of empty clothes racks. Adam says a hard-ware store with three floors he can understand, but not one this big just for clothes. "Why would anyone need more than two outfits?"

Across the street is Farmers Bank, another multistory structure. Adam asks how much gold a building this big could have held, and I ex-plain that banks in a small town like this didn't keep gold or much money, for that matter. "They mostly kept track of numbers."

Adam wants to look inside, but we all stop dead in our tracks when Oracle starts barking madly.

Marcus looks down the street, and says, "Oh hell."

Roaring toward us from the south end of town is a three-wheeler. Marcus doesn't have to tell us to run. We charge down Ninth Street. I wonder if it's possible the biker hasn't seen us, until I hear the bike slow down just enough to bank the corner. Marcus has found the entrance to Weaver's basement, but Adam and I both shake our heads. Anything but going down below. We dart into the back alley. A pile of bricks makes the access too narrow for the three-wheeler. It skids to a halt. For a brief moment, we stare at the driver. He's wearing a wet suit, a vest with a tangle of hoses, and the kind of mask that scuba divers wear. Oracle stands in front of Adam, looking rabid.

As soon as the biker backs out into the street, we take off in the opposite direction. He is going around the block to cut us off at the pass. Marcus has anticipated this and is trying each back door we pass. For a ghost town with broken windows, it makes no sense that these doors should all be locked. He tries putting his shoulder against one of them; it budges not one inch. The three-wheeler gains access to the alley two blocks down. Left to us is only one way out: the fire escape.

We bolt up the stairs. It sways and scrapes against the bricks as we scramble to the top. It is a wonder the whole thing doesn't collapse with the weight of us all. I reach behind me to give Adam a hand over the parapet, only to find he is not there.

"Adam!"

Marcus and I run in opposite directions, each of us peering over the edge to see where he might be. Despite the revving of the three-wheeler's engine and its squealing tires, I hear Adam call for me. Marcus and I rush to the side of the roof that fronts the main drag just in time to see Adam dart into the hair salon next door. The three-wheeler pauses and then makes another loop. When Adam pops back out into the alley, the driver has already blocked one side of the alley with a sheet of corrugated iron. At the other end, he dismounts his bike and stalks Adam.

"Leave him alone!" I scream. The wind gobbles up my words.

Marcus is already backing down the staircase. He's not going to reach Adam in time.

The biker is directly below me. He is negotiating with Adam. He doesn't want a fight, he wants Adam to surrender; take the easy way, kid, I hear him say. If the self-preservation instinct played a role in getting me through all those years of being a captive, there is not one tiny vestige of it left. My only concern is to launch myself in such a way that I land on the biker. I step up on the parapet. I shuffle a few paces to the left. The biker is only about ten or twelve feet from Adam. Every joint becomes spring-loaded.

The biker hesitates.

The moment presents.

Just as I am about to jump, a streak of fury flashes out from the side ally. Adam's dog sails across the air and hits its target squarely on the chest. The biker goes down. Shrieking turns to wailing. Adam is frozen in place. We all watch the dog go for the man's throat. It doesn't take long for flailing legs to still, for arms to slacken. By the time Marcus reaches the scene, the bloodied dog has loosened its grip and returned to Adam's side to have his head petted.

Marcus stubs the figure with his foot. By the time I reach the bottom of the ladder, he has both boy and dog packed up on the back of the ATV. "Hop on," he says. "There's bound to be another headhunter on the way."

I have the backpack but not Adam's suitcase. "Our stuff."

Oracle's ears prick, and he yaps a short warning bark. We all think the same thing—they are coming.

That's when we hear another engine.

"There's no time." Marcus cranks the kick-starter with his foot, but the engine sputters, whines, and quits. "You can do better than that." He tries again. Still nothing. He has us get off, and then jumps down on the lever several times.

A voice comes over a bullhorn. "Surrender, nobody gets hurt."

"Hurry! Hurry!" I tell Marcus. We can't see them, but the noise is getting louder. They have to be seconds away.

Marcus strokes the gas tank. "Come on, baby, show me some love." He twists the throttle and thrusts down on the lever again. This time, the bike jerks to life. I scoop up Oracle and we all pile on. The ATV swerves out of the alley and shoots down Vermont Street. Behind us, the voice on a bullhorn is calling for us to stop.

THE BIKE SKIDS to a stop in front of a wire fence. We have driven a wide loop, only to end up four blocks north of downtown, a stone's throw from the bridge, or what's left of it. The Kaw River may be high or dried up; there's no telling for all the bracken. Down a little ways is an abandoned construction site with a jackknifed tower crane.

Marcus shuts off the three-wheeler and slides off the seat. He offers me his arm. "You don't look too peachy."

"I'm okay." I lock my knees, just in case.

The air has turned bitter. The cold makes my ears ache. Large, dark clouds have pulled together, and the wind carries in it menace. A wind like this—the latches on storm cellars should be ringing clear as church bells. Instead, there is an eerie quiet.

Marcus is sweating a great deal and doing a very poor imitation of keeping calm. He doesn't need to tell us twice to hurry.

The ground is rocky. Marcus lifts a flap on the chain-link fence and puts his hand on Adam's head as he crouches through the gap. On the other side, we scuttle down the sandy embankment and come to a smooth concrete pathway. It leads to two round entrances, like gaping mouths. I am both eager to find shelter and afraid to take another step. Above the entrance is a painting that looks like stained glass of a robed creature with long hair and outstretched arms. Trailing from her hands are stars.

"Our guardian angel," Marcus explains.

Each tunnel entrance is draped with mesh that is weighted at the bottom with fishing sinkers. Marcus lifts it up and we scoot under, but not before hearing what sounds like laughter, children's laughter, coming from the other tunnel.

"What's in there?" Adam has heard it, too.

"We'll get to that later."

The curtain falls back into place. Marcus tells us we can now relax, leaving me to wonder how so flimsy a net is supposed to deter bad guys. He reaches into his pocket and pulls out a small flashlight. A familiar dread rises up in me. I tell myself this hole in the ground will be different. There is no door, for one. I have my son with me, and a friend. I have a dog that knows how to rip out a man's throat.

We proceed deeper into the tunnel. The beam of light instills the same confidence that caulking on a crack in a dam wall would.

"Bet you never imagined you and me would have anything in common. See, I've lived underground for years, too." Marcus leans toward Adam. "You aren't afraid of spiders, are you? Get them as big as your hand in here." Marcus uses the flashlight to scan the ceiling and the walls, and what pops out are colorful pictures painted in the same style as the angel at the entrance. Adam stops to examine the naked-lady picture.

"Nikon mostly practices in this tunnel. His best work is in the other one. To me, they're pretty pictures, but he says everything means something."

I startle when the thunder booms. "Isn't this a storm drain?"

Marcus has us keep walking. "I know what you're thinking—soon as those clouds start dumping water, we best have snorkels. Fifteen years ago, you'd have been right. When we first started living down here, we'd get washed out every other week. Now, we got those gutters at street level plugged up tight, let me tell you. It rains, and a river as big as the Missouri runs down Mass Street, but we stay bone-dry."

The air is moist, almost thick enough to swill and spit out. Beyond the light is nothing but the cloying void, at least that's what I think until the dog breaks rank and growls. His ears are flattened against his head, and the sole tuft of hair on his neck is raised in a spiky ridge. Another dog, one that looks like it's been stitched together from patchwork squares, stares at us from the scrap of light.

Marcus calls out, "How you doing, Lexie?"

The two dogs circle each other, exchange smells. The patchwork dog approaches Marcus, sniffs his shoes and pants, and sits up on its back paws.

"What makes you think I have something to eat?" He pets the dog's grotesque head and tells us Lexie's a friend, then rustles around in his pack and comes out with a wedge of cheese. He hands the dog a piece and then turns around and gives some to Oracle, too.

"She don't bite," Marcus says, when the mongrel begs off Adam.

Adam digs out the Twinkie and gets a slobbered hand for his troubles.

"Now, stay close," Marcus whispers. "Lexie's owner can be a spooky sonofabitch, but he keeps out the riff-raff. No headhunter's going to come down here with Blade around. He tries talking to you, you just keep your head down. Let me do the talking."

We've not gone a dozen paces farther when a jagged voice rips the darkness. The sound is distorted, as though it has traveled through a stretched-out coil. "Abandon all hope!" Coming off the phantom is a foul smell. "Through me you enter into the city of woes!"

I reach for Adam's hand.

"Blade's got a thing for Dante," Marcus whispers, putting a protective arm around me. Obviously got a thing for vinegar, too. The odor burns my nose. Marcus keeps the beam of light focused ahead and not to the side where the voice is hissing more warnings.

"Abandon all hope, ye who enter here!"

"Hey there, Blade. How you doing? We're making our way to camp; be outta your hair in just a minute." Because Marcus takes to humming an overly cheerful tune, I worry even more.

"The city of woes!"

"Just passin' through, Blade; just passin' through."

"Abandon all hope!" He's standing close enough that I can smell his vile breath. I don't turn my head, not even when a rawboned hand grazes my shoulder.

"Mom!" Adam whispers, trying to wriggle free of my grasp. I realize I have dug my nails into his palm.

After walking through a maze of tunnels, Marcus steers us through a tight gulch that opens to an antechamber about the size of a bowling alley. A string of bulbs light only part of the space. Groups of people are gathered around fiery drums. One group is singing. Lit by the orange glow, the figures don't resemble castaway people, vagrants like those at the train, but more like bronze statues come to life.

But for a loincloth, the man in front of us is naked. Stringy white hair hangs in long strands from the sides of his head and chin. Whiskers spring from his nose, and his eyebrows are so overgrown, he has to squint to keep from being poked in the eye. Where his cheeks are supposed to be are deep crevices, and instead of a row of teeth, there is a single incisor sharpened to a point.

"I was wondering when you were going to show up. We got word on the CB. These are your fellow bandits, I take it."

Adam can't stop staring at the man. He has grown up being told that people Above don't live to be old, that they are taken out by radiation or disease or wild animals, but here is one surely as ancient as God.

"Adam, Blythe, I'd like you to meet Pops."

The old man shakes my hand and peers at Adam. "Adam, huh? So you're the one causing all the fuss?"

I wink at Adam, but he looks at his feet.

Marcus comments on the singing, which is now even louder and not exactly on key, and Pops explains that we have arrived during rehearsals and that it is going to be a madhouse until opening night of the musical. *The Wizard of Oz*, we are told. To me and Adam he gives this warning: "Unless you want to be put in a ridiculous outfit, I suggest you tell the director in unequivocal terms when he comes and pesters you to audition that you are not interested in a part."

No sooner are we warned when someone with a long red cloak waves frantically at us from one of the drums to come on over.

Pops makes shooing gestures. "Stark-raving mad, the lot of them, and he's the ringleader." To Marcus, he asks, "Are we to assume your guests will be staying awhile?"

As Marcus pulls Pops into a tight huddle off to the side, I nudge Adam. "You okay?"

"I didn't mean to cause 'a fuss.'"

"The man was teasing, Adam." How to explain teasing?

"Above is not how I thought it would be."

If he'd let me, I'd take him in my arms and hug him.

When you've lived your whole life with elaborate fantasies, how can reality stand a chance? You think if only you can see with your own two eyes, taste with your own lips, you will know the truth. You think if you can kiss the soil and breathe the fresh air, you'll be free. Freedom has always been a matter of getting out, of being Above. And here we are, discovering what a flash in the pan it can be.

"If it weren't for me," Adam continues, "you wouldn't be in all this trouble."

I take a breath. I hold him by the shoulders so he knows that what's coming is big. "If I could go back in time to that moment when Dobbs stopped the car where I was walking, do you know what I would do? Do you? I'd get in. I'd go through it all over again just so I could have you."

I make him say okay before I let him go.

"Marcus is going to help build a new city someplace south of here. I want us to go with him."

"What?"

"I don't want to go to Eudora. I want to go where the people are."

It would have been better if my son punched me in the gut. I am the people, I want to scream. If I could breathe.

"Your mom and dad aren't there. Nobody's there, Mom."

"You don't know that."

"Mom, the odds are—"

"You know nothing about odds, Adam. Nothing!"

Having concluded their discussion, presumably about us, Pops interjects, "Why don't we let these good folk sit down and have something to eat? The lady over here looks like she's about ready to pass out." From out of thin air, the old man conjures a bench.

I sit down hard.

Marcus announces that he is going to sort out a place for us to sleep. Not until he walks toward the far wall do I notice a long row of tents and lean-tos.

"Marcus has shared a little of your and Adam's remarkable history. The world must appear very different from what you imagined; disappointing, I daresay."

Adam bends to pet his dog. I suspect it is to keep from showing just how disappointed he is.

"You must know the allegory of Plato's cave?" Pops asks.

I shake my head.

He looks like a hobo, but he talks like someone with an education, like he might have been somebody important before. He tells the story of people chained since infancy by their hands and necks in a cave. Rather than facing the light from the entrance, they have been forced to spend their lives watching shadows on the dark wall in front of them, unaware that the images are cast by puppeteers behind them. A prisoner who is released from the cave ventures outside only to find he has great trouble believing the objects he finds there are more real than the illusions they cast on the cave wall.

"According to Plato, the released captive will at first see only the shadows best, then the reflections of objects in the water, and then, as he adjusts, the objects themselves. Eventually, he will see himself as he truly is and will discover his proper place in the world." He gestures to our surroundings. "If we rely only on our senses, what we see can imprison us. To Plato, in order to be free, one must journey above to the realm of knowledge, where we must strain our eyes for what is last to appear."

"What is last to appear?" Adam asks as two plates hover toward us.

Pops is obviously pleased to be asked. "The idea of good. When we behold the idea of good, Plato teaches, then all that is right and beautiful is possible."

Adam looks up to see his plate being offered by a girl, a girl with huge brown eyes, a wide smile and wheat-colored hair woven into many long braids. Talk about right and beautiful, is his expression.

"Chili?" she says. "It's really good."

He's seen pictures. Dobbs once brought down a magazine of women without clothes, and men, too, with their whatsits out. I could have scalped him when I found it in Adam's room. Here now is a real girl—a young woman, actually. Nothing at all like a shadow or a picture. Yet, she is every bit as pretty as make-believe.

Adam takes the plate and watches the girl with the same kind of blinkered concentration usually set aside for mechanical devices as she walks to a row of tables and pours water from a pitcher. When she brings him the glass, you'd think she was showing him how to split atoms.

"My name's Bea—not in the buzz-buzz kind, but short for Beatrice. But nobody calls me Beatrice." There's a musical lilt to the way she speaks.

Adam has yet to take a bite of food.

She upends a bucket and sits next to him, fluffing out a skirt that seems to be made out of neckties. Her shirt appears to be woven out of shoelaces. "Pete's a really good cook; you should try it." She points to Adam's plate and lifts an invisible spoon to her mouth.

Adam takes a mouthful.

Bea nods and smiles. "Your dog friendly?" She bends to pet Oracle's head. I have the urge to tell her not to get too close, that the dog has a thing for throats. It's Adam I'm mad at, but she's to blame, too. She and all the other Outsiders who are exerting their collective pull on my son, people who are not my people.

"I like dogs. Birds, too. I had a crow for a while. It could sing. We like to sing around here. Are those real binoculars?" Adam takes them off and lets her look through them. She points them straight at him and giggles, and I wonder if the girl is not a bit loopy. After giving them back, she flits over to a basket and comes back with two sticks crossed together at the middle. She weaves yarn around them. "You're not one for talking, are you? It's okay. Ask anyone here and they'll tell you I talk enough for everyone put together. Except for Pops, maybe." For a brief moment, we all look at the old man, who holds up his hands as if to say, Guilty as charged.

"It's just that there's so much to talk about," Bea continues. "You put words to your life and tell it like a story, and, *ta-da!* you're a main character. Now, people say there are things that shouldn't be spoken of— bad things. But I think those ought to be spoken of first. Get them out of the way. Make room for all the good things, don't you think?"

Does she have an OFF button?

Her handiwork produces an intricate pattern of greens, reds, and yellows. She tells him it's called a God's eye.

"My mom likes crafts," Adam finally manages.

Yes, she's especially good with a crochet needle.

The girl looks over at me as though I just materialized. "Oh, hello."

"Hello."

Returning, Marcus claps Adam on the shoulder. "You and your mom can have my tent. I'm going to room with my buddy, Dyno. Remember, I told you about him? He's still got a Buick from his dealership days, near-mint condition, too. Maybe tomorrow we'll go take a look at it."

"Can I talk to you for a minute?" I pull Marcus out of earshot. "You need to make it clear to Adam that we are not to come with you to wherever it is you're planning on going."

"Osage Indian Reservation, Oklahoma. In a few years, there's going to be a city out there."

"We're going to Eudora. First there, and then we'll see."

"I hear you."

I look over at Adam and the girl, at the old man who speaks of shadows and ideas. "How long do we have to stay here?"

"Pops pretty much stays glued to the CB. As soon as we know interest has petered out, we'll get you home. Couple, three days is all. Any longer than that, a headhunter's going to think you've been snapped up by someone else or else, joined a caravan or . . . you know . . ."

We watch the two youngsters. The girl is showing Adam how to wind yarn around the sticks.

"Nothing wrong with his eyes." Marcus grins.

"Who is she?"

"Bea can be a bit—you know . . . " He makes a quacking gesture with his hand. "But she's a good girl. Heart of gold."

"She looks—"

"Normal. Yup. Just like your boy, she's uncontaminated." Marcus winks, as though I am being let in on a big secret. "Folks keep waiting for science to come up with a solution, but I've been saying all along, it's going to happen the good old-fashioned way: boy meets girl."

Before I can protest this line of thinking, he dashes off to the food table.

I return to my seat only to find the girl has performed a very neat trick in the few moments I've been gone. She has made off with Adam's heart.

SHOULD SOMEONE ASK, I'll say I'm trying to figure out how they run electricity down here. Or maybe I'll come right out and say it: I have a hard time letting Adam out of my sight for very long. Bea said she was taking Adam on a tour, and they ended up here, at what looks like a shantytown. I watched the girl enter the tent and then come back out with a lamp. She practically dragged Adam inside.

Most of the dwellings are tents, but some are constructed from cardboard, corrugated iron, and bricks. Up close, it's clear how much care has gone into each home. Some even have tiny porches with rails and shingled overhangs. Bea's tent is shaped like a wigwam and is made from animal skins. It is decorated with colorful scarves and hundreds of ribbons. At the opening of the tent is a mat that reads, WIPE YOUR PAWS, and next to it, in a pot of real dirt, a silk geranium. Coming from the tent is the pungent smell of incense and the sound of her giggling.

I take another step closer. She's saying something about cinnamon. She's having him touch something.

Then she asks, "Are you guys in trouble?"

"I don't know. Maybe," comes Adam's reply.

"You didn't rob a bank, or anything, did you?" She laughs again. "It's okay, you don't have to tell me; I'm just being a busybody."

There's a brief pause, and she says, "It's toenail polish, silly."

Instead of going in and asking that they return to the common area, I hold back. Being drawn to this pretty girl has come naturally to Adam.

He is behaving like any teenage boy would, not like someone who has lived his entire life in isolation. Why should I now interrupt something that I feared would never happen to Adam? Why should I let my own fears ruin a perfectly good experience for him?

I sneak around the other side. As luck would have it, there is a tiny mesh window on the other side of the tent. I peek through. Candles in little colored jars and an oil lamp light the space surprisingly well. It's like looking into a kaleidoscope. Carpet scraps cover the floor. Pinned to the inside walls are pictures of birds and flowers and a sun with sleepy eyes, and dangling by threads from the center post are paper doves and butterflies and lollipops. A narrow cot is piled with pink and red blankets, a fluffy purple pillow, and a herd of stuffed toy animals. Instead of chairs, yellow cushions are scattered on the floor. Adam is seated on one of them next to a white Buddha statue. Bea, cross-legged opposite him, is showing him a scrapbook.

"How long have you lived here?" he asks, flustered when she catches him staring at her freckled chest.

She shrugs and flicks several braided strands off her shoulder. "I don't know. I really don't keep track of time. I know I probably should and all, but clocks are just so mechanical. I don't care for them at all."

Instead of telling her he loves mechanical things, that if he had his way, he'd make things that tick and turn all day long, he announces that he doesn't care much for clocks, either.

She grins, then springs up. She hurries over to a plastic tub and comes back with a box of cookies. "Dessert!"

Adam's got the look of craving written all over his face, except not for food.

She takes a cookie apart and licks the center. Adam about chokes on his.

"Why do you live here and not outside?"

"I like it here," she answers. "It's peaceful. Nobody bothers you."

"It's dark."

"You can be in the dark and still have light in your life." The girl makes her point by flicking her braids. The effect has Adam bewitched.

"It's not all it's cracked up to be, living out there. You'd be surprised what people are capable of doing in broad daylight. Sometimes, I think all that sunshine blinds them."

Adam takes a bite of his cookie.

"I'm not saying all of them are like that." She pauses. "You're not like that."

"I'm not from out there."

She stops chewing. "You're not? Where are you from?"

The question has him stumped. "Nowhere," he finally answers.

"No one's from nowhere. Where are your people from?"

Why doesn't she drop it?

I have to strain to hear Adam's answer. "I don't have any people, except for my mom."

Yes, and what a disappointment she has turned out to be. The freed captive will eventually see herself as she really is—isn't that what Pops said about the allegory? I am Adam's mother, but I am also the puppeteer who has given him shadows to name.

The girl says, "Marcus is one of your people."

Adam half nods, half shrugs.

"I'll be one of your people."

Adam goes from looking like someone who doesn't have much to show for himself to a kid who has suddenly struck it rich. As he takes in his good fortune, Bea leans across the space between them and just as quickly flits back again. Adam appears dazed, like he can't believe what just happened. Kissed, right on the lips.

OUR SECOND DAY in the tunnel and we are off to day care—Marcus, Adam, Pops, Bea, and me. A crowd. I'm not sure I'm ever going to get used to one. In some sense, the more people around, the more isolated I feel. No one knows me—the me from before—and no one asks after her. She might as well never have existed. To Mama she mattered, to Daddy, to little Theo, to Grandpa and Grandma. Any one of them would've helped me find my way back to her. And I was so hoping to find her. The more Outsiders I meet, the more a stranger I am to myself.

Marcus went outside at dawn to retrieve our suitcase from the alley and came back restless. He has spent much of the day talking to Dyno about heading south to the Indian reservation. Dyno did a lot of nodding and uh-huhing, but gave the impression he'd just as soon have a hole swallow him up than go riding off into the sunset on one of Marcus's big ideas.

Adam and Bea skip ahead. Since meeting, they have become inseparable. One minute they'll be sitting next to us, the next they'll have snuck off. They've attended a rehearsal, gone to see the murals, and helped prepare and serve lunch. And now, they've consented to let the adults go with them to day care. They remind me a little of Arlo and me, except with the roles reversed. Bea is the one brimming with confidence, the one doing the leading, and Adam looks like you could measure him in volts.

This second tunnel echoes with the sounds of a playground. Its sides are painted with colorful scenes, the floor is lined with Astroturf, and artwork is pinned to a zigzagging clothesline. We go through a gate in a white picket fence and enter into a large, brightly lit antechamber. Children flock toward us. Some of them hobble, some of them crawl, their limbs too twisted to stand. A barrel-chested boy carries a shrunken boy with an enormous head. There must be twenty of them, thirty perhaps, none without deformity. It's like looking at a different species. Adam, not used to being handled, laughs nervously as a kid latches on to him. It's me who takes a step back.

At various stations in the room are several other children, each with an adult. A little boy spinning in circles is settled into the lap of a large-bosomed woman. Pops, waving to her, tells us she is the day-care director. "A saint at school and a devil in bed," he says, matter-of-factly. I give Marcus my big-eyes look, and he shakes his head just enough as though to say, Don't do anything that might encourage him.

We head for an area of the room that is lined with deck chairs. On one of them is a sickly little girl.

Pops greets her with a bow. "Your Highness. May I present Sir Marcus and Lady Blythe?"

Marcus kisses her forehead. "A little bird told me it is your birthday today."

It's hard to tell her age. She is exquisite even without hair, even with the large tumor on the side of her neck.

She smiles. I have to listen real close to hear her. "I'm turning ten."

"Can't be! It was just yesterday when you were a baby, this big." He cups his hand.

"Toadstool," she manages to say.

"That's right. I found you curled up on a toadstool. Lucky the fairies didn't find you first."

"Kidder."

"Now, would I kid when it comes to fairies?"

She smiles, all the way this time.

He hands her a necklace of wooden birds, something from Bill Bowers's workshop, if I'm not mistaken, while Pops chats to a child half her age who is lying on his side because a massive tumor prevents him from lying on his back. What Pops says must be very funny because the boy about falls off his cot laughing.

"Isn't there anyone who can treat them?" I ask as we pass a play area with wooden toys, homemade plush toys, buckets of building materials. Bea is playing dress-up with a group of children, and Adam is helping three boys assemble a pile of rocks into a tower.

"Laura's got her brains outside her skull and Thomas has his kidneys in that pouch on his back. We make the long journey to a clinic and they gon' tell us no-can-do. Even the can-dos are no-cans. Can't justify the expense is what they'll say. Then they'll talk life expectancy, and who needs to hear that?"

Pops chimes in. "None of us are to be spared suffering. The better question is, are we being defined by our afflictions? Are we to live with them or live above them?"

We come to a smaller room where children are rolling around on mats, honking and squeaking. It's worse than a barnyard. Marcus explains that they are unable to sit or stand or walk, but lying in a crib all day is not good for them. If I pay close attention, he says, I will notice that they have a language all their own. It's hard to watch—if ever there was an argument for sterilization, this is it—but after a few minutes, it becomes clear that these children are playing. They gently bump their foreheads together and then spin around and bump their feet together, reminding me, in a way, of water ballet.

We return to the main portion of the antechamber, where Bea is braiding the hair of a little girl who looks as old as a wizard. Adam is giving a piggyback ride to a humpbacked boy.

"These are the children you brought from Sunflower?"

Marcus nods.

"But not Bea."

"No. Her father brought her here when she was still a baby," Marcus explains. "He was dying and couldn't take care of her and figured the best place to hide her was with the children everyone wants to forget about."

"Why hide her?"

"For the same reason you didn't want doctors messing with your boy."

Pops wanders off to talk to the director, while Marcus and I stand at the gate and watch the kids.

"If Diablo had been a war, this would be written about in the history books," he says. "If we'd won—or if we'd lost—there would be pictures of these kids. People would've built a monument. NEVER FORGET THEM would've been engraved on it. Instead, folks saw these children and felt like their noses were getting rubbed in it. They got angry. They felt like Diablo was going to keep happening to them, over and over. Not too many years back, a vigilante group went around to group homes where orphans were being cared for and gassed everyone, even some of the kids who were fine. That's when we got the idea to start bringing them here and hiding them."

He goes on. "Like Pops says, though, you can't let the past keep on dictating. Got to give the future a say-so, too. One day there won't be no need for a place like this. Every kid's going to find hisself a home. They'll shut down Sunflower and others like it and just let us mixed-bag race sort ourselves out, one way or the other."

A woman comes rushing to us from the other end of the tunnel. She's sweating. "Got a call coming through on channel twelve from E22. They bought it."

Marcus gives me a look as if I'm supposed to know what this means. "I had a friend of mine put out word that they'd found you and Adam dead from exposure on the northbound trade route." He grins. "People believe everything they hear on the CB."

"Does this mean . . . " I'm almost too afraid to ask, too afraid to jinx it with the words.

"That's right. You're going home."

Long ago, when I was first taken Below, I would wake up in the middle of the night terrified that the darkness had swallowed me whole. Not anymore. I am the one who has swallowed the darkness. Small enough to pass through membranes, to be carried around in my bloodstream, small enough to circulate through my heart and settle in my cells, the darkness has been grafted to me. We are one. That's why when the last of the lanterns goes out, I feel relief. I wish it weren't so. I wish daylight had the effect on me that darkness does. But maybe Pops and Plato are right. Maybe after a while, the light will dazzle me less. Perhaps my eyes will adjust. Perhaps tomorrow when we go to Eudora, Adam and I will begin to name the things that are real. Maybe a few we might even call Good.

Lying on Marcus's cot, I turn my back against the wave of smells— smoke, boiled meat, urine—and listen to people acclimating to their own darkness. Beside me is the lengthening of Adam's breath, the gentle snore that comes so quickly, and in some recess not too far away someone's urgent toil for gratification. There are creaking knees, a cough like a car engine turning over, mutterings, recited prayers, and an endless shifting of bodies that cannot get comfortable. I pull the covers over my head.

Hours must have passed because there is absolute silence when someone pulls them off again. At first, I think it is Adam who rouses me, until a claw clamps around my mouth and the sharp odor of vinegar stings my nose. I leap out of bed. Fully upright, I strain the pitch darkness for any sound of Adam. The only thing I hear is the faint whistle of air being expunged from rancid lungs. Clenching even harder, talons dig into my cheek. In case there is any mistaking the intruder's intentions, something equally sharp is shoved against the small of my back. I am to move out of the tent. Shuffling forward, I confirm Adam is no longer on the floor. I step over his blankets. Outside the tent, I take big sweeping steps forward, hoping my foot will knock something over and alert Marcus, who is sleeping a few doors down. Where is the dog? My insides lurch. Dread dams my arteries. I feel my heart as soon as it stops beating. *Whump.*

Death for everyone, I now realize, comes right in the middle of things. When you most want to stay alive, even if it's just long enough to see your boy one more time, it ferrets you away.

Turning from the hollowness of the cavern, the apparition forces me into a tunnel that requires crouching. Something puts its wet nose against my leg. Not Adam's dog, but the mangy hound that greeted us when we first arrived. The apparition is Blade, then. I yank his bony hand away from my face—cannot be sure that the fleshless contraption hasn't fallen to pieces—and get out only a partial protest. What he says keeps me from yelling another syllable.

"I have the boy."

We come to a hole in the wall. I know this by the rush of dank air that smells of tobacco. By wedging a screwdriver finger between my shoulder blades, the specter indicates that I am to climb up into it. Without being able to see where to put my feet or hands, I scramble in. I try straightening up, and ram my head against the ceiling. I have to keep to all fours. Unlike the other tunnels, this one is cobbled with river rocks. I crawl forward. In my head, I go over his exact words. *I have the boy.* Aren't there other ways he might have phrased it if Adam were not still alive?

"What did you do with my son?"

His answer is indecipherable, something you might hear the devil say. Pig latin, perhaps. He prods me sharply again.

The cobblestone artery empties into another antechamber. I know immediately that Adam is in the space, even before the devil lights the lamp. That mix of sweat and sweet hay smell. I call to him in a panic.

"I'm okay, Mom."

I rush toward his voice, my hands outstretched, and a small flame from a paraffin lamp grants my wish. Adam is rising from a throne in the center of the room, his dog at his side.

"Adam!"

"I'm okay," he repeats, and though his face is a perfect study in composure, his voice is hollow, like he's had the marrow scared out of him.

Whatever it is now closes off my airways, flips my insides upside down, and causes a great and terrible hallucination. The specter lights another lamp, giving more depth to the room's ghastly dimensions. Adam and I are in a crypt lined with bones. They are not cobblestones beneath my feet but skulls. Human skulls. Above us, the domed ceiling is a warp and woof of bones. Columns of femurs rise up to support arches of hip bones. I squint at a wall. Stacked like firewood are arm bones and thigh bones. Gauging from the alcoves, the walls are at least two feet deep with bones.

"He said he's not going to hurt us," Adam murmurs when I grasp his hand. He sounds not at all assured. I look around for something with which to defend ourselves and notice that the throne, too, is an elaborately stacked pile of bones. And that is when I have the feeling I am being watched from above. I slowly turn my gaze upward. Suspended from the ceiling is a chandelier of bones connected to each corner of the room by a garland of skulls.

"What do you want?" I ask the devil who materializes from the shadows as a tangle of bandages and rags. Tucked in his bindings are chisels and hammers and brushes, and in his hand a bone large enough to be a club.

Rather than answer, he lights a third lamp. Beside him are pelvises shaped into a bell, its clapper a femur. He puts the lamp on an ornate pedestal of ribs and approaches us. He raises the bone like a baseball bat, as if he intends to swing at us. I pull Adam with me to the floor and fold over him. The man grunts for us to get up. He has to prod us with his foot and grunt several more times before I do as I'm told. He points first to a coat of arms fashioned from small bones, then to a series of Roman numerals above the doorway, and finally to the formation of an anchor in the floor. A chapel of death is what I see. History written with jawbones, locked up with vertebrae shaped like padlocks.

"Mom, I want to go," Adam whispers.

Before I can state our case, Blade shows us a jumble of bones near a recess. They are not chalky white like the others. Instead, they are caked with grime. Beside them is a stool, a bucket, and a scouring pad. He has us come to a small wooden table where hip bones have been wired together like petals in a corolla. He marks our reactions closely and is irked when Adam repeats that he would like to leave. It's how he assesses Adam that terrifies me, like the man is making a mental note of every rib, and somehow I realize that we have been brought here to admire his handiwork.

"You did all this?" I manage.

He looks as if he has in mind the perfect place for my skull, and yet he nods.

"It must have taken you a long time." Many are the dead. Too many for graves. In this ghastly place, the extent of Diablo's destruction sets in. Also, the extent of Dobbs's efforts in keeping Adam and me from it. Should there be space in my hating him for thanks? For forgiveness? And if I let slip through a crack one cubit of gratitude, won't then come a rush of pardon, and if pardoned, won't the gates of hell open for Dobbs, a free man?

The custodian of the bones begins a recitation. "The Lord set me down in the valley which was full of bones. And behold, there were very many in the open valley, and lo, they were very dry. And he said unto me, 'Behold I will lay sinew upon them and will bring flesh upon them and cover them with skin, and put breath in them and they shall live.' And there was a noise, a shaking, and the bones came together, bone upon bone. And he commanded the wind breathe into them, and they stood up upon their feet, and lived."

Adam and I do not reply. We stand while the dead gaze at us without favor, without finding fault, either.

The third time Adam asks to leave, Blade waves his permission.

"Ezekiel thirty-seven," he mutters.

"Hurry, son." Adam, the dog, and I are crawling back into the tunnel as his haggard voice follows us.

"I will open your graves and cause you to come up out of your graves, and I will put my spirit in you and place you in your own land, and ye shall live!"

"I don't want to end up like these people, Mom. I don't want to die."

"You're not going to die, Adam. You're going to live."

We scramble over the stony heads of the long gone.

A CROWD ESCORTS us down the tunnel with the choir singing "Over the Rainbow." Adam points out where he has painted his name on the side of the tunnel. A few of the children from day care meet us at the tunnel entrance with homemade cards.

I feel as though my legs are about to take off with or without me. Adam, on the other hand, has grown lead feet. He and Bea are facing each other. For the first time since we've arrived, she is not talking.

"I'll come back."

She makes only the barest indication that she's heard him.

"I'll call you on the radio."

I don't have the heart to hurry him, not when it comes to good-byes.

He grabs her hand. "Come with us."

She shakes her head.

He opens the suitcase, sorts through his stuff, and brings out his favorite sock monkey.

She holds it against her heart.

Adam is calling it a trade. What he asks of her I don't know because the transaction is done with cupped hands and whispers. And then he hands her one of Dobbs's keys.

"What does this unlock?"

Blushing, he makes the tiniest of gestures. He aims his thumb at himself.

She makes a little *oh* shape with her mouth.

I thank Pops for his hospitality and wave to the others over his shoulder. Most of them have put on goggles made from plastic cups and raised homemade umbrellas to combat the glare.

"Dwell not too much on the former things, my dear. Consider that what is yet ahead might be right and beautiful."

Marcus is standing at the top of the embankment beside a car in near-mint condition. In a soft voice, I tell Adam it is time to get a move-on and lead the way up the gravelly path. I lift the flap in the fence for Adam and Oracle to climb through. Adam avoids my eyes and then swings around when he hears his name being called.

Bea has stepped out of the tunnel. She is a vision in the daylight. "You're going to dazzle them!" She waves a bright pink scarf.

"I'll come back!" he replies.

And then everyone is waving and making a commotion, and Marcus is in the driver's seat, opening the passenger door for me just as Dobbs once did. For just a second, I hesitate. Sitting in that seat is the closest I can come to trusting a person. I ease down onto the cracked leather seat and find the seat belt.

I am going home.

VIII

HAVE TO SHADE my eyes when I get out of the car. Still the same old achy legs and the same buckled feet, but this time with the overwhelming urge to run ahead. This is how you greet the long-lost world, isn't it? At full speed and with open arms?

The breeze is swift, as if it aims to blow the dust out of me. It's too bright to look up, so the sun reaches down. It's a warmth you can't get from a blanket. It soaks into my body, into my bones. If I ever find myself underground again, I'll be carrying the sunlight in me.

I've asked Marcus to park on Church Street so I can walk the rest of the way. Tree roots are still pushing up the bricks on the sidewalk, and I find myself tripping just like I did when I was a girl. In the window of a yellow house, a face appears behind lace curtains. It startles me. Marcus explains that there may be as many as thirty or forty people who have moved back to Eudora. Along the side of the house is a clothesline with britches and cotton vests pinned to it, and in the front yard is a well-tended vegetable garden. The fruit trees have been pruned into dwarf versions and are bowed with fruit. Marcus says much of Eudora's produce, along with that from a neighboring camp, is donated to the tunnels. Handmade toys, crocheted afghans, knitted cardigans are the same way.

Adam's spurs, now attached to his shoes, sound like coins falling, as though our every step were a jackpot. We pass another yard where an old man calls out a greeting. I want so badly to recognize him and wave as if I do. He goes back to tending his washing line, which is full of skinned rabbits. I remember when Dobbs first brought a rabbit Below. I almost hugged him because I mistook it as a pet for Adam. But then I saw it was limp and bloodied around the puncture. Dobbs said for me to quit crying, to skin it and throw it in the freezer, that it was no wonder the boy was so soft. Adam came over to see what caused the fuss. He stroked the dead animal, then begged us to let him play with it. He dragged that bunny around with him till it started to smell because I didn't have the heart to take it from him. That was the last time Dobbs left skinning to me.

Someone is playing a piano in the house. The bright notes glance off windowpanes and drift away with the breeze. It's silly, but I have the urge to knock on the door to see if it isn't Mrs. Littleton at her upright.

We turn the corner onto Main Street and find ourselves at the start of the old parade route. It's not hard to imagine the crowds, even with all the blooming crabapple trees in the way. I hold Adam's hand. I feared it would be ruins, but it is all still here. I point out the redbrick two-story that used to belong to the International Order of Odd Fellows. Mama was once the angel in their float. She had to stretch out her arms and hold her angel wings open for the entire parade, and her back hurt something awful for the next few days. The parade is a memory, but the building hasn't fared too bad. Nor has the drugstore beside it. We cut a path to the front window. I could've sworn Doc Hubacher and Mr. Minta were toasting us from their places at the dusty counter, but now all I see are our reflections. I turn, feeling scarcely more substantial than my reflection. I feel like I could pass through solid objects—the rusty mailbox outside the post office, the town's only stop sign, the lampposts that now serve as potting sticks for fragrant vines. I am the one doing the haunting.

My hometown. How shrunken it seems, how aged. Wasn't it a good long walk from the soda fountain to the grocery store? Didn't the buildings stand taller, more proud? Wasn't the church steeple high enough to put a crick in your neck looking up at its cross? The street seems hardly wide enough for two cars to pass and yet memory insists it was once a showcase for hot rods cruising Main after Friday's football game. Memory summons the people, too. Becky Willoby talking loudly on her cell phone outside her salon; the varsity team on a run to the water tower and back; Virgilian Witt doing his rounds, garnering donations from business owners for the historical society. People I haven't thought about in years rise up like the dead on Judgment Day. How I long to see them now in the flesh, alongside Mama, Daddy, little Theo pummeling the pedals of his Radio Flyer. Something rips off the callus of my heart. Raw is the only way to put it. To be utterly sad is not to cry, but to make unreasonable pledges, the kind of promises that weigh like prison sentences. If I do nothing else with my life, I will write about my people—on these walls, if I have to—so they will exist somewhere other than my memory. I will tell of them even if Adam grows so tired of the stories that I have to whisper them to him when he's asleep. I will teach ravens how to say their names.

I stop at the statue of Chief Paschal Fish and Eudora. The last time I saw it, I mostly paid attention to the girl. Now, as a parent, it's Paschal Fish I mind. He looks like a man who knows a good-bye's coming, that even though his little girl clings to him now with both arms, approaching is the time when she will let go. She'll go about her way, the way all children eventually do. The man has braced himself for this eventuality with an oar. Rivers to paddle yet.

We continue along Main Street. For me, it is a homecoming. For Adam, it might as well be any other street. He looks down this street as though he'd just as soon take off, probably straight back to Lawrence. For Adam, when it comes to roads, they go only in one direction: to the future. I look at these streets and see them stretching all the way back to yesteryear.

The sun bounces on every surface—on the store windows; on the polished surface of the black-and-white parked out front of the police station; on the dewdrops still clinging to tufts of grass. Everywhere brilliant beams are cast, joyous sounds chime along. Jingles, tweets, chirps, squawks, squeaks, whistles. I don't know the names for all the sounds. I am a deaf person having my hearing restored.

"Perfect spring day, just like old times," Marcus muses aloud. "Day like this can break your heart."

He's wrong. A day like this can mend a heart, heal a person, make her back a little straighter. A day to make wrongs right, make straight the path.

And here we are at the police station. On the roof are antennae the size of light posts. The flag, frayed only a little, flaps at full mast.

The door opens before I reach for the handle.

The uniform is a little too tight around the middle, the collar is frayed, and the shirt has been washed so many times there's no color to it but in the seams. It's freshly ironed, though; the creases on the sleeves and the trousers as precise as a straightedge. Brass buckle is shiny, and I can see my reflection in those worn black boots. There's no gun, no set of handcuffs, nothing but a weathered face that's seen it all and then some.

"Blythe."

He says it like he knows me, not just expecting me.

I don't know how much Marcus told him about me on the CB radio, more than he ought to by the looks of things. Tracing my kin is what this meeting's supposed to be about, so I say, "Hallowell," to keep things on track.

"Blythe," he says again.

I don't know what I'm looking at. Handsome might be the word for it. Worn-out would do probably just as well. Scar around his neck, hair too long for a small-town man, cataract on one eye, which is a shame given how blue the other is. With hands that look almost rubbery from burns, he clasps his forearms. I can't imagine why he sizes me up so, but he has to get a good look, even from the side. I put my hand up to cover the birthmark on my neck. He keeps standing there, looking at me with his arms crossed, hugging himself, like I am ten kinds of wonderful.

I'm not sure what I'm supposed to do, but all of a sudden I wish I'd done a better job fixing my hair.

"Rand McNally."

And just like that, I see it: the bend in his jaw where the acne has left scars, the mischief in his cocked eyebrow, the lips that kissed mine a million years ago. Arlo Meier. This childhood friend; this boy from my backyard; this prince of the bleachers. He lives! The end of times is not an apocalypse; it is a reception. It is seeing the face you recognize—that recognizes you—and feasting on it. The table is set with a thousand empty spaces but here is one. One!

I am the first to break the silence. "I waited for you."

Seventeen years, and it still has the ring of an accusation. If he'd have come back to me on those stands, I would never have walked home, would never have climbed into Dobbs Hordin's car. Maybe we would have been sweethearts, made plans to marry. There have been times I blamed Arlo almost as much as I blamed Dobbs. But it's not blame I intend now—it's so he will know that I was a girl who was once willing to give her heart away.

"I'm so sorry we never found you." Arlo looks like a man who's beat up so bad he can barely see straight and yet wants to stand up to take one more round of punches.

He shakes his head. "We looked everywhere, chased every lead, brought in dogs, psychics, you name it. And then Diablo happened. I guess we gave up after that, gave up on near everything. I'm so sorry, Blythe."

It comes very near to being breached, that levee in me.

What keeps me upright is the realization brought home by the tunnel people, by the man standing in front of me: I am not the only one to have been robbed. We've all been left behind. Seems to me none of us are entirely up to the task of being the remnant.

"It's okay, Arlo." I touch his arm. Because he finds such hope in that gesture, I pull Adam up beside me. "This is my son, Adam." You want hope, here it is.

Arlo pumps Adam's hand. "Son, you're the spittin' image of your granddaddy." Which is about the kindest thing anyone could say in my hearing.

"Well, come on in, don't just stand there," he tells the three of us.

You'd think there were a dozen people in the room, but the voices come from a single item in the middle of his desk. A scanner, Arlo calls it. Turning down the volume, he explains it's supposed to be used only for emergencies, but it's become the main source of communication for survivors. "Organizing a buffalo hunt is what's going on right now." He has us all sit and seems not to mind that a mutt makes itself at home on the rug.

Concerning Mama and Daddy's whereabouts, the news isn't promising. Arlo waits for me to steady myself with a good number of breaths before he uses several ledgers to make his point. Some of the names I recognize, although most without faces to go along with them. In the early years, he explains, information on people's whereabouts was routinely broadcast; now, months can go by before he gets a tip about someone listing Eudora as their hometown. Usually, it is a deceased notice. He flips to another ledger. A long list of names, columns for name, date of birth, place and cause of death. At this point, he comes around the desk to where I'm sitting. He puts his arm on my shoulder.

I tell him to go ahead, I know what's coming.

He shows me the listings for 'Hallowell.' It's done no good preparing myself.

Theodore T.; Twelfth Prefecture, Ill.; cause of death, radiation
    sickness.
Suzie F.; Twelfth Prefecture, Ill.; cause of death, radiation sickness.
Gerhard P.; Sonora, Mexico; cause of death, unknown.

I look at Adam, now without an aunt and two uncles.

Mama and Daddy aren't listed. I don't have to ask. Arlo says, "I've put out a lot of calls. People all over the country are going through the ledgers."

Here I am, smack-dab in the middle of Eudora, and suddenly I feel a long, long way from home. You'd think there wouldn't be any place lonelier than the bottom of a missile silo. And then over and over again you find a place more desolate than the last. A roomful of expecting mothers, a tunnel of children too damaged for heaven. This time, it is the space in Arlo's ledger where Mama's and Daddy's names are not re-corded.

"It's not out of the question, you know," says Arlo. "Kin show up all the time. You just never know."

Before he closes the ledger, I flip through another page of *H*'s and pick up the pen on his table. "I'd like to add a name."

Adam and I exchange weary glances.

Besides giving birth, there surely cannot be anything more powerful than writing the name of your warden in the Book of Life. All those years ago when I was forced to write that letter about having run away, I could not tell the truth. Now, I can spell out his name. I will press down hard enough to leave a mark on the next three pages, so there can't be any doubt, so I will never have to write his name again. Capital letters and underlined.

I run my hand down the lines to the first available space and stop short. An entry for Hordin already exists.

Freedom.

So there can be no mistaking it, the baby's birth date is listed.

Perhaps because of some sound I made, some gesture, Adam scruti-nizes the page, too.

"Mom, is that . . . ?"

"Who wrote this?" I ask Arlo.

He tells about a trader who passed through Eudora and stopped at the station. "Strange fellow. Claimed he was curious about who was running the place now. Ran off the names of sheriffs all the way back to Rumboldt and then said it was a wonder that none of them had hauled his ass back here. I figured him for one of those who don't have all their oars in the water, especially when he wanted to add this here name to the ledger. 'Freedom,' I said. 'That's quite a name.' He just gave me a real queer look and said the mama named her, that she might come looking some day and that's why he wanted to add it. So she'd know he kept his word."

Adam and Arlo seem to be having a conversation, but I have trouble hearing them. Cotton seems to have plugged up my ears.

"It was Dobbs Hordin," I finally manage. "Don't you remember him from the school library?"

Arlo shrugs apologetically. "Radiation eats great big holes in your long-term memory. One day you wake up and discover you can't remember anything about your wife except a yellow dress and the smell of hair spray." Arlo closes the ledger gently, as if a slam will expel those resting in it, and sets it on his desk where he keeps faded pictures of what must be his family from before. He then comes back and pats my knee with his burned hand and tells me again how sorry he is.

I stand up. I think I'd like to go outside in the sunshine again.

"You okay, Mom?"

Just as I turn to tell Adam to give me a few moments to myself, I hear the main door open and a voice cry out from the foyer, "Where she at?"

The spirit so ready to fly out beyond the hills and out to the wide yonder in search of those who cannot be found in ledgers is now seized by a voice calling for me.

"Hello? Anyone home?"

No one in Arlo's office replies. I listen to the hurried footsteps come closer. I shake my head. I have to press both hands against my chest to keep it from bursting clear open.

Should I believe it?

"Blythe Hallowell, you there?"

If there was any doubt, there is none now. Suddenly, it is not a doorway. It is the portal through which the past returns. It is the face and shape of one who loved me, loves me still.

"Blythe," her voice goes from booming to quivery when she sees me. "It's me." There's a clicking, a series of steady ticks, a metronome cuing some forgotten melody. "Me, Mercy."

The air is not dead. It is not empty. It is the sum of all things. It is a cloud full of sighs, stifled cries, snickers leaked between fingers. Were whispered prayers and secrets shared to have weight, we wouldn't need gravity. The air would pin us down.

She is crying. *Click, click, tap, tap* are the sounds of teardrops hitting the floor.

"Mercy."

That's all it takes for the great rift between the past and the present to form a seam. Mercy gathers me in her arms.

She and I commence to repeating each other's names. She's crying sometimes when she says my name, and sometimes she's laughing, and sometimes she's saying it in that singsong way of hers like we're back to being girls playing ring-around-the-rosy. I just say her name one way, the way you'd say *Jesus Christ* on that first Easter Sunday.

"You came back! You came back!" Her happiness is a faucet open all the way. Mercy handles me the way a blind person would. She runs her hands across my head and my face, rubs my hands. She touches my birthmark and smiles, like she can't believe it's all still there, every blemish, every fingernail. "You made it, Blythe!"

I do my own assessing. She's a good fifty pounds heavier and has an enormous Afro instead of braids, but she is still my best friend, just the way I remembered. Same round-cheeked face caught in a moonbeam. No burn marks, no scars, no goiter or tumors. "You made it, too, Mercy. You made it, too." And I figure we will grow old together the way friends are supposed to.

"I didn't believe Arlo when he told me. And then Ginny Bowers sent someone over to tell me and I knew it had to be true. Blythe Hallowell!"

"Mercy Coleman."

"You made it!"

Behind her, in a neat row of descending height, stand four children, the last still in diapers. Not one of them resembles Mercy, and each has disfigurement. I was mistaken in thinking Mercy had come through Diablo intact—missing from the bunch is the girl from the picture Dobbs brought me all those years ago.

"Come here, kids," Mercy says. "This here's your aunt Blythe." She shoves the oldest toward me, a boy about twelve years old who is unable to hold his head completely straight. He offers to shake my hand, but

Mercy pokes him in the ribs, so he reconsiders and gives me the lame-armed hug of an awkward adolescent. The next boy has his mama's Afro and her pluck. He barrels into my embrace and latches the stumps he has for arms around me. The other two crowd in.

And then Mercy goes stiff in front of Adam.

One of these days someone's going to come out and say something along the lines of what an awful thing it must be to have Adam be Dobbs's son, but I just don't want that day to be today or that someone to be Mercy. I know the look on her face, though. I know she's got that bitter taste of Dobbs Hordin in her mouth. I love her all over again like she's my twin, but I will disown her if she so much as draws her tongue over her teeth.

Mercy reaches into her bosom and pulls out a handkerchief. She balls it against each eye, then tucks it away. "Come here you," she says to Adam. "Come here so your aunt Mercy can love on you."

Mercy has her arms around Adam, like he needn't ever have to hold himself up again if he doesn't want to, that she'll be happy to do it for him. How brave Adam is to let someone do this. I look at the others. They are being brave, too—the children holding one another's hands. Arlo and Marcus not saying anything at all, their silence is a kind of bravery, too. I can feel it, not just in this room, but beyond it, too—people bravely bearing each other up. The world is being held together with hands on elbows, tissues and tears, with soft words and sighs. When Mercy looks at me, I see the bearing up is meant for me, too.

Somehow, we are back on Main Street, Mercy and me arm in arm, a bevy of children behind us. What she says about me being back home and how she always knew this day would come she says loud. Even what she says about Arlo still being easy on the eyes and don't I agree, wink-wink, is done at full volume. It's when she gazes over at Marcus and leans in to whisper in my ear that I know she's planning trouble. I know her, oh, how I still know her.

"Who's Captain America?"

HOME HAS A smell. Strong, sweet, pungent as the redbuds that used to bloom along the ditch in front of our house. Home smells of wild plums and meadows thick with lavender, of violets and rose verbena. It's the smell of stiff, winter-weary prairies bending into color.

I shiver and open my eyes. No matter how many times I wake up to the smell of home, I am always surprised that it's Grandpa's farm that surrounds me and not a concrete cylinder. It doesn't get old, the simple act of opening my eyes. It doesn't matter that looters have taken everything of value from the house. Under the debris and dust, it is still a home, a home full of memories. I suppose with Adam living here, it's a home full of promise, too. Marcus believes it would make a great place as a babies' safe house, but that's a decision for down the road.

I get up on one elbow and admire the house from the porch. It is already getting that lived-in look. Mercy's the decorator, turning feed sacks into drapes and vines into door wreaths. She's tireless. I suspect she's hoping all her efforts will entice me to sleep indoors. I haven't the heart to tell her paper doilies and old newspaper comics for wallpaper aren't going to do the trick, not when there's this—a panorama.

I get up from my bedroll on the porch. On newborn colt legs, I greet the day. The earth has kept its promise. Splendor knows no bounds. Over my right shoulder, the sky is a ridge of gray clouds, an old washboard. To my left is a clearing so blue whales could breach from it. Out yonder is a field of little bluestem and switchgrass swaying to and fro, their conductor the gentle spring breeze. The fields run all the way to the line of sycamore trees. Beyond them are the buffalo.

It takes several moments to decide what the yellow flecks twirling above the garden are. Is it my eyes, still spotty from too much light, or is it really confetti? One of the pieces drifts over to me. A butterfly. Grandpa always made sure to leave milkweed in the soybean rows so the monarchs would lay their eggs on them. And here they are, paying him tribute. A public service announcement that the earth is recovering. Some said the *Mona Lisa* was the most beautiful thing in the world, but I bet it's only because those folk never went to Kansas in May when the newly hatched butterflies shimmy their wings and lift off out of the field. Reverend Caldwell used to talk an awful lot about the Second Coming of Christ, how two people would be in a field and one would be taken and the other left behind. He'd say it in such a way that we all knew it was the worst thing to be left in the field. Not me. Not on a day like today.

I fold up the blankets and stack them on the porch swing. Oracle is pawing at the screen door. I let him out and stick my head into the dark house. It still smells of smoke. Last night, Adam collected wood and built in the hearth a fire big enough to melt rocks. It was warm and toasty, and we were some family out of a Norman Rockwell picture—for about five minutes. And then smoke filled the air so thick we had to open all the windows and doors and pull up our sweaters over our noses so we didn't choke to death.

There are no sounds of Adam stirring. I won't wake him. Instead, I sit on the top step of the porch. The dog takes up his post beside me and noses me until I rub his head. We listen to the robin trill its morning salutation. You can almost hear the land sigh, not quite ready for the day. It lets out its breath, and the mist rolls across the range. I wait, and soon enough Grandma and Grandpa come out. As ghosts, they are still early risers.

Grandma is wearing one of her flower-print dresses, the pocket bulging with tissues. Having just taken off her hairnet, there is a thin, red ring around her forehead, as though the top of her head has a hinge, like you could pop it open and take a look inside. No telling what you'd see, but I suspect it wouldn't be all pie recipes and Bible verses. Grandpa comes behind her, bringing the kitchen stool. On an ordinary day, Grandpa will wear the blue collared shirt and britches held up with suspenders, but today is a special day, so he has on his mustard-yellow cowboy shirt with the mother-of-pearl snaps. He sits on the stool, wraps an old towel around his shoulders, and ceremoniously hands Grandma a sharpened pair of scissors. "Not too much off the front this time, Mabel," he says. "Don't want to go to the service looking like a shorn sheep."

"Oh, hush up. You going to let me do this or not?"

Here we are on a crisp morning, the pinch-pink sky reflecting in Grandma's bifocals, the first of the day's rays glinting off the edge of the scissors. Grandpa has his head tilted to the side, doing as he's told, getting his "big ol' ears out the way." At his feet is the scruffy gray cat, rubbing its head against who-knows-what smell on Grandpa's boot. Everyday missing is for the easy things, but a day like today brings back the forgotten things: a cat they call No Good, Grandpa's front curl and the way he fusses over it, Grandma dusting her hands against her apron because she's not one to gush and hug like grandmothers in storybooks. Missing can make a day take forever to end; remembering, though, can make it fly.

Dawn is rising out of the fields as though the lid of a simmering pot's just been lifted. I head over to Grandpa's shed, collecting dew on the hem of my nightgown as I go. Oracle trots ahead. I've come to rely on the dog's companionship during my early-morning rounds. Several times, he has to stop and mark his territory. What's a dog to do when there are all these trees?

"Come on, you."

We pass the small vegetable garden that I've started with some of the seeds from Dobbs's repository. When Adam was still little, I got the urge to teach him about planting and growing and harvesting. I convinced Dobbs to bring down bags of topsoil and some wooden planks, and I set up a sandbox of sorts. The seeds weren't fooled for very long by the lamp. Straggly stalks tottered from their dank bed and, finding their surroundings more bleak than they could bear, collapsed before putting out so much as a leaf, so I planted other things—the head of a spoon, passages clipped from the Bible, a lock of hair, an old key that fit none of the locks. It was a garden, and I tended the hope buried in it. Now, hope takes the shape of tomatoes.

A hoe and a rake and various other gardening tools cluster in one corner of the shed. Bags of cement are stacked in another. In the middle of the hut is a workbench with a hacksaw, a table saw, and a mess of other rusting tools. A sawhorse holds warped pieces of lumber. Along one wall are shelves stacked with extension cords and gallon drums of paint, electrical wires, and countless jars of nails and screws. Anything of real use, the tractor and all the other farming implements, are long gone. But there are plenty of provisions. Arlo's deliveries from the silo are stacked up on wooden pallets—toilet supplies; untold toys still in their boxes, which Dobbs kept hidden; enough seed for dozens of harvests. Dobbs is providing for us still. I'm sure he rolls in his grave every time Arlo goes Below, especially when the historical records and Krugerrands get hauled off to the police station, the new Fort Knox.

Last night's delivery from the silo is a cardboard box. Arlo didn't ask questions—he never asks questions. He simply set this box aside and said, "You might want to look at this." I lift the lid, and almost close it just as quickly. To think I lived with this smell for seventeen years. I take out an empty IV bag. I've never seen it before. There are two empty bottles of children's cough syrup, a third still sealed. A child's nebulizer, a dropper, and a palm-size notebook. The page I turn to has several entries, all of them dated more than fifteen years ago. "Charlie shows no improvement. He took in very little fluids. Will increase dosage." In another entry, Dobbs writes of my deteriorating mental state, that I still have not asked about Charlie's whereabouts, and how I sleep almost constantly. "Once she is stable, she might be able to assist in his care. Despite being weak, he fights treatment. Administered Albuterol three times today."

I drop the book. I fold my arms around my waist and squeeze to make the ache go away. I want to hate Dobbs. I want him to be in the wrong, about everything. How much easier it would be for me always to be the one harmed. He did try to keep little Charlie alive. What am I to do with that except forgive him a little? He took baby Freedom Above, as he said. Forgive a little there, too, I suppose. Maybe forgiving him a little at a time is the only way I'm ever going to be truly free of him.

When Oracle and I get back to the house, the sun has gotten itself caught in the lowest branches of the sycamore trees. Adam is sitting on the porch steps, peeling an orange. He hands me a glass of water.

"Did you open the box?"

"Yes." I tell him about its contents, and although he tries not to give himself away, I can see how relieved he is. It'll do him good to feel something for his father other than scorn.

We wander over to Adam's workstation. The picnic table is filled with various bicycle and lawn mower parts. This prototype—a rather dubious-looking mode of transportation, if you ask me—is intended for himself, but the next one is to be traded at the swap meet for enough gasoline to travel to and from Lawrence a hundred times. My son, going a-courtin'.

"Is Arlo coming by today?" he asks.

I take a big slug of water. "I don't know."

Each time Arlo comes, it's with a reason. He'll make a delivery at the shed, then swing by the house to see what Adam is building. Or he'll come by to fix the roof and end up spending half the day talking with Adam. He misses his own kids something terrible, I can tell. Sometimes, he'll take Adam down to the station for a few hours, and sometimes they'll go on patrol together. Every once in a while, I can be persuaded to ride along, too.

We don't go too far on those drives because gasoline's hard to come by, even for a sheriff. Only once did we swing by the house on Fall Leaf Road, what's left of it, that is. Without Mama and Daddy, without Suzie, Gerhard, and Theo, it's too painful to get any closer than the curb. And only once did we go to Oaksview Cemetery. Grandpa got his wish and is buried under the old oak tree on his own property, but Grandma has a boilerplate headstone along with hundreds of other graves, many of which share the same year of death. I'd hoped to find the baby's grave, but Dobbs wouldn't have buried her there. She's some-place close, of that I have no doubt. I scan roadsides, and sometimes I'll have Arlo stop the car so we can walk in a wide-open field and look for a grave marker. Someday, I'll find her.

On those drives, we stick to the city limits mostly and make up sto-ries about the people who used to live in the houses we drive by. It's not unusual to be flagged down by someone tending his garden. People want to talk about the past, but they want to talk about the future, too. They'll talk about the little signs that give them hope. They'll point to Adam and say, "Young man like that, now there's what I call hope." Good wins out in the end, is what they say, even though they've had to bury their kin, even though they have cancer crawling up around in them.

Adam loves to spend time with Arlo, but it's with Mercy where I find my company. She lives now in Miss Winter's old place down by the creek. She'll send the kids down to the water with their fishing poles and then fry up a feast for us when they come back with their baskets full. Only once has she mentioned her firstborn, the little girl from the photograph, and it was a long while before we could take up shelling the peas again. When everyone's asleep, her children in their beds and Adam on the couch, she'll take me into her bedroom. She'll lift up her shirt and have me measure that big dark blemish on her back. Every day, it's bigger. I've seen the scars from where she's cut out the other moles. "This one's different," she says of the one on her back. "I cut it out, but it came back. This one means business."

Looking at that growing stain on Mercy's white skin is like standing on the rickety platform of the silo and looking down. Losses are going to keep piling up. Mercy says this is one way to look at it, but it won't be telling the whole story. Got to see the others piling up, too, she says, the blessings. And then she'll have me crawl under the covers with her and we'll talk long into the night, sometimes laughing just like the girls we once were. No matter how late, though, I always want to be home before the sun rises.

"I'm going out to Grandpa's grave," I tell Adam now. "Want to come?"

Adam nods. He dashes inside and returns with Grandpa's old fob watch. "He should have it, don't you think?"

Both hands are missing and all that's left of the inscription is the last line: *Not a stone tell where I lie*. I fetch my own gift for the grave.

Oracle, Adam, and I form a solemn procession. The saints and all the company of heaven fall in behind us. We march past the pond where the walleye are the size of barrels, past the weather-whipped hay baler, past the sunflowers that stand exactly like schoolgirls—hips out, heads cocked to one side. I find the massive oak tree. The grasses stop tittering, the boughs of the trees cease their gossiping, the sky draws in its breath as we gather around his grave.

Beside the cross, Adam makes a hole in the ground. In it, he puts the watch and another one of Dobbs's keys. Putting to rest some of the past is what we are doing. I pick up the trowel and dig a furrow around the grave. I sprinkle some of Ginny's seeds in it, careful to leave enough for when we go back to visit Charlie's grave, and cover them over with soil. Not a stone, Grandpa, but peonies.

When the ritual is over, I tell Adam to go on back, I'm going to sit awhile. I lean against the oak tree, watch the man-boy throw a stick for his dog, then gaze at the mound of soil. I suspect the dead find me better company than the living.

If I am ever to be granted the luxury of a tombstone, I would have it say simply: MOTHER. Somewhere along the line, I stopped being the abducted girl. Forget Blythe Hallowell. Remember me only as a mother to three of the finest. If ever there is to be an obituary for me, I hope it will say more about my children than me. The child named Freedom, whose whereabouts I will do my best to find. There is the boy I mothered for only a short while. Much of that mothering was madness, I admit, but over the years, I have loved him wholly, with wishing-prayers and worry, just as surely as any mother does for any child. And then there is Adam, child sprung from the dirt, whose every breath has given this old clay shell a reason for being. Because of Adam, I face each new day with high hopes.

In my pocket are a pencil and a piece of paper. I write poems all the time now, just as I once did. I leave them all over the place—pinned to the laundry line, squished between porch rails, folded up under the leg of a wobbly chair. Adam treats my poetry endeavors as he would an Easter egg hunt. He keeps telling me not to leave them lying about, but he takes such delight in finding them. I write another one for him. This time I am going to leave it here, under a rock at the foot of this tree where the shade falls like a shroud. One day he will bury me here, and the poem will be waiting.

> We were fish once;
> Before: a glimmer in God's eye,
> And for a while, amphibians
> and later, crocodiles.
> One day we gave up water altogether
> and found the nearest tree,
> where we danced among its branches
> till Death gave us reprieve.
> Next time, born were you a boy,
> me your nursing mam
> and happier was I never,
> keeping time at bay.
> We may yet have another round,
> and who knows what'll be—
> perhaps you an emperor king
> and me your gran' fairy.
> Or perhaps to our Creator we'll go
> and the earth will hold us not;
> to us angels might bow
> The triumph of things forgot.

I open my eyes. I didn't intend to fall asleep. The shade has chilled me. I try locating that which disturbed my sleep. A storm rumbling in from the west, one of those showers that wipes the earth clean. I get up, step out from beneath the tree, and shade my eyes. The sky is clear. The ghost train, perhaps. It comes often, though mostly at night. I'll feel its wheels running along buried tracks, sending vibrations across the fields and all the way up my legs. Mama's voice will be its whistle. The rhythm of those wheels will begin to match the beating of my heart, stronger, faster, and there'll be nothing to do but brace for the impact or wait for it to stop and pick me up.

But it is not a train. There is a cloud gathering dust along the road. Three hundred yards, it's hard to gauge distances anymore. I make my way to the house. I am almost to the porch before Arlo's car skids to a stop.

Arlo gets out. At first, I think he has come for Adam, but instead of heading to the pond where Adam is fishing, he stands beside his car, his arm resting on the top of the door. A gust blows my hair across my face. When I brush it back, he is still just looking at me. We are like two passengers standing at a train depot, waiting for the train that never comes, each with battered luggage and expired tickets. Nowhere to go but here is how Arlo and I stand and watch each other.

I glance out at the fields, at the wild beyond them. This is not the world to which I wanted to return. It does not yield. Then again, it does not drive me away, either. I look back at Arlo, who is not the person to whom I wanted to return. To his credit, he has never rushed to comfort, nor has he asked me to name the things that cannot be named. He's always like this, allowing for the silence. Waiting for an invitation, it now occurs to me. He is waiting with the same kind of acceptance with which this land would let me pick up my bags and find some other ground to call home. It's as if both land and man know that it is only with a loose grip that I can be held. Anything tighter would be a tether.

Freedom. It's not something big, like being rid of Dobbs. It's something small, something that might slip between atoms. Its other name is Choosing. Deciding for yourself what to eat is part of it, and when to turn out the light. It is tending tomato plants all day, if you want, or walking the boundaries. Deciding not to make a fortress of pain. Being free has more to do with living outside my own walls than living within Dobbs's. It means loving Mercy all the way, even though the mark on her back is going to take her sooner rather than later. It means letting my boy drive his contraption back to the girl who can't possibly live up to his imagination. Not just protecting, but risking. Some small part also has to do with this man—standing there as if he doesn't mind if it takes all day.

A voice inside me gives directions, and the path holds steady. Still, it is hard to move.

In the bright morning sun, Arlo might be mistaken for a younger man, and my fears might be mistaken for being as slight as shadows. Yet, it is into this light that I wave and smile. And then I take a step forward.

Acknowledgments

A debt of gratitude is owed to my agent, Emma Sweeney, for her wise counsel, steadfast support and advocacy over the years.

Thank you to Karen Kosztolnyik whose extraordinary commitment to this book made the collaborative phase such a pleasure. I could not have hoped for a more wonderful editor. Also deserving of credit at Gallery Books are Alex Lewis, Erica Ferguson, John Paul Jones, Lisa Litwack, Jen Robinson, Liz Psaltis, Jen Bergstrom and Louise Burke.

I am much obliged to Lisa Highton and the team at Two Roads for championing my books in the U.K.

To Noah Ballard, Benee Knauer, and Todd Siegel for their insights, I offer my thanks. I am especially grateful for the support of Irene Parker, Barbara Baker and Carol Saggese.

Invaluable is the help in all its many forms I receive from my husband, Bob, and inexpressible is my appreciation. Only this—everything I write is a tribute to him and our sweet girl, Emily, whose big-heartedness inspires me. My cup overflows.